All the
QUEEN'S
SPIES

ALSO BY OLIVER CLEMENTS

The Queen's Men
The Eyes of the Queen

All *the* QUEEN'S SPIES

An Agents of the Crown Novel

OLIVER CLEMENTS

LEOPOLDO & CO

ATRIA

NEW YORK   LONDON   TORONTO   SYDNEY   NEW DELHI

**LEOPOLDO
& CO**

ATRIA

An Imprint of Simon & Schuster, Inc.
1230 Avenue of the Americas
New York, NY 10020

First Leopoldo & Co/Atria Books hardcover edition March 2023

LEOPOLDO & CO/ATRIA BOOKS and colophon
are trademarks of Simon & Schuster, Inc.

For information about special discounts for bulk purchases, please contact Simon & Schuster Special Sales at 1-866-506-1949 or business@simonandschuster.com.

The Simon & Schuster Speakers Bureau can bring authors to your live event. For more information or to book an event, contact the Simon & Schuster Speakers Bureau at 1-866-248-3049 or visit our website at www.simonspeakers.com.

Interior design by Kyoko Watanabe

Manufactured in the United States of America

1 3 5 7 9 10 8 6 4 2

Library of Congress Cataloging-in-Publication Data

Names: Clements, Oliver, 1972– author.
Title: All the queen's spies : a novel / by Oliver Clements.
Description: First Leopoldo & Co/Atria Books trade paperback edition. |
New York : Leopoldo & Co/Atria, 2023. | Series: Agents of the crown ; 3
Identifiers: LCCN 2022043407 (print) | LCCN 2022043408 (ebook) |
ISBN 9781982197469 (hardcover) | ISBN 9781668022146
(paperback) | ISBN 9781982197476 (ebook)
Subjects: LCGFT: Novels.
Classification: LCC PR6103.L448 A45 2023 (print) |
LCC PR6103.L448 (ebook) | DDC 823/.92—dc23/eng/20220912
LC record available at https://lccn.loc.gov/2022043407
LC ebook record available at https://lccn.loc.gov/2022043408

ISBN 978-1-9821-9746-9
ISBN 978-1-9821-9747-6 (ebook)

For the magical Gigi Pritzker, *the seer and architect of so many dreams: Ic þe þancas do*

PART | ONE

CHAPTER ONE

North Sea, last week of September 1583

When John Dee thinks about it later, when he is crouched covered in blood in the stern of a fluyt and watching the coast of Kent disappear forever into the sea mist, he wonders again why he had ever supposed, even for a solitary instant, that this could or would have ever ended otherwise.

Had the heavens not sent a sign? Had the skies over Mortlake that night not turned blood red? Had the clouds not burned bright with an unearthly glow, as if they were set aflame?

They had, hadn't they?

And yet.

✛

CHAPTER TWO

Mortlake, three weeks previously,
first week of September 1583

And yet when John Dee is woken by someone knocking on
his gate, he himself descends to answer it, for the knocking has a furtive quality he half recognizes, and he is unsurprised by
what he finds: a rough-looking beggar in a coat that looks to have
been buried in a field for a year or two, with lank hair over his ears,
who says in a strange, soft accent, "I am Edward Kelley. Master
Clerkson says you have need of a scryer?"

Which is true: Dee does need a scryer to read his magic show
stone; to summon the Angelic Spirits from above to appear in its
glossy surface, for he lacks the gift. He cannot scry, much to his
shame, and so Master Clerkson oftentimes sends him such men
who can do so. Ordinarily they are quickly revealed as chancers
or charlatans and are sent on their way with little or no harm
done—once Roger Cooke, Dee's assistant, has shaken them down
to retrieve what has been stolen—and this Kelley, in his filthy,

high-collared cloak and unwashed state, appears no different from those others. But it is soon obvious that he knows whereof he speaks, and he steals nothing, so Dee gives him a chance and sets him up in the library with a show stone that he bought—though is yet to pay for—from a man who promised it answerable only to good spirits.

"Summon for me if you will," Dee tells Kelley, "Anachor or Anilos."

Both are considered good spirits.

Kelley nods and settles at the stone and begins the Action with a murmured prayer that Dee recognizes from Trithemius's work on the art of drawing spirits into crystals. When Kelley has finished, he sits in silence, staring into the stone. Nothing seems to be happening, and the change is so slow that at first Dee does not register it, but then he does: the temperature in the library drops, as if a mist has entered the room, and Kelley's face has become waxy. And now Dee's heart slows, and slows, and then slows some more, and the room grows colder yet, and then the walls and floor and ceiling seem to thrum to the beats of his heart and the air becomes dense in his ears, thick and ripe, and then suddenly Kelley stirs and addresses the show stone.

"In the name of the holy and undefiled Spirit, the Father, the Begotten Son, and Holy Ghost, what is your true name?"

Nothing. Dee can hear nothing. But Kelley can, and hearing an answer that Dee cannot, he asks a next question: "Will you swear by the blood and righteousness of our Lord Jesus Christ that you are truly Uriel?"

The hair on Dee's scalp rises as Kelley listens in silence a moment, and then he confirms he has sight of the angel Uriel.

Uriel! It is *Uriel*!

Dee restrains himself, just—for anyone can just *say* that, can't they?—but because every fiber of his being yearns to believe what he hears, he comes to kneel next to Kelley. Though he sees nothing in the glossy facet of the stone, through Kelley he asks some questions that, while not precisely trick, require care in the answering.

"Are there any other angelic spirits that might be reached through the stone?"

Kelley tells him that Michael and Raphael are there, but Michael is "first in our works." This last phrase is telling, Dee thinks, for it is complicated and ambiguous and exactly how the angelic spirits might speak.

He rises and closes the door so that what happens next will not be overheard, even by Roger Cooke, who is at work in the laboratory, and then he returns to kneeling to ask Kelley to ask if Uriel thinks the *Book of Soyga* to be any excellency. Only a true adept will know the answer to that.

"The good angels of God revealed the *Book of Soyga* to Adam in Paradise," Kelley tells him, "but only Michael can interpret it."

Hmmm, Dee thinks. Neither wrong nor right, that one.

"I was told that if ever I managed to read it," Dee then asks, "I should only live for a further two and a half years?"

That is true. Someone did tell him that, though he cannot recall who. Or why.

"You shall live to be a hundred-odd years," Uriel tells Kelley to tell him.

And Dee is pleased, not only for the tidings of a further lease of life, but because such an answer sounds authoritative.

"Is there anything else I should know?" he then asks, which is wonderfully vague and will test Kelley if he is making this up, and then Dee becomes astonished as for the next half hour, Uriel describes—through Kelley—a triangular seal that they are to engrave with gold and wear around their necks which will serve as a defense against harm "at every time, place, and occasion."

Hearing this, Dee is persuaded to allow Kelley lunch—soup, which he bolts as if he has not eaten in a week—and to send Roger Cooke from the house, so that they might have it to themselves, for Dee knows these are dark and dangerous waters in which to sail. And yet the prospect of communing with the angelic spirits, after so many years trying, is irresistible and exhilarating.

And so after a pause for more prayer, they set to again, with even more success this time, and Dee writes down all Kelley tells him. Together they learn that the angel Michael can be invoked by the reciting of certain psalms of David and by certain other prayers, and that it is the will of God that Dee and Kelley shall gain knowledge of God's angels *together*, and that together they must write a book, to be called the *Book of Loagaeth*. It will be a new Book of Revelation and will be dictated in the Adamic language, by divine spirits, and it will allow an understanding of the secret levers that underpin all God's marvelous works, even unto the cherubim and seraphim. In addition, there is housekeeping: in the future, they must place the show stone on a wooden altar two cubits cubed, on the sides of which are to be painted symbols and words in yellow oil; and it is to be placed on four seals and then on a square of red silk.

So the afternoon wears by, and Dee must make himself new ink, and find new paper, for there is so much information to be recorded, and it is just at that moment when Dee is beginning to wonder if this is all too much, and that Kelley must surely be telling him only that which he knows Dee wants to hear, that Kelley suddenly becomes concerned and then fearful. Dee stops his writing.

"What is it?"

"An evil spirit," Kelley breathes. "An evil spirit abroad. It is named Lundrumguffa. It intends harm. Intends harm to your wife, and to your son, too."

Both wife and child are staying a few days with Jane's brother, Nicholas Frommond, upriver in Cheam, which explains why Kelley was ever let in to the house in the first place.

"What manner of harm?" Dee demands. "What can be done?"

But now Kelley throws up his hands, exhausted, defeated, and the Action is ended and there is nothing more that may be done that night, at least on the astral plane. Dee sends word with Roger Cooke to Jane to tell her that on no account must she stray from her brother's house until Dee comes for her, and then he feeds Kelley more soup, fresh ale, beef, and then good wine for strength. He gives Kelley the best room in the house, above the kitchen where Dee's mother used to sleep, and finds him fresh linens, and even some soap.

⊕

The next day Dee is up before dawn, praying to God to keep Jane and his son safe, praying to divert the evil spirit's intent. Kelley rises late. Bacon for breakfast, oysters, and ale—though not too much—and then he prays for an hour or more, alone in Dee's oratory, while Dee paces outside. When that is done, they start the Action again, back in the library, the same as yesterday, and Kelley soon has sight of Michael.

"Ask him about Lundrumguffa," Dee demands. "Ask him about my wife."

And Kelley does, but the archangel will only talk of a new seal of colorless wax that promises divine power over all creatures save the archangels, the details of which are so enthrallingly complex that before Dee knows it, it is dusk. It is only then that one of the many angelic spirits to appear assures Dee that Lundrumguffa had been banished, and Dee feels a wash of shamed relief that nearly knocks him from his feet; that relief lasts only a few moments, however, until this new angelic spirit tells them that they are being watched.

The hair on Dee's head stands on end again.

"And even now," the archangel goes on, "there is someone at your gate."

They hurriedly end the Action, and with Kelley slumped on the ground, too drained to move, Dee thrusts all the trappings and paraphernalia away, in a rush, unsure if this is necessary, or insane, or what. He has just stuffed all his notes into a pouch and hidden the velvet-wrapped show stone behind some books when there is a thunderous knock on the gate. Both men start and look at each other in terror.

"You must answer it," Kelley says.

Dee's heart is booming. Whom can he expect? A demon? Satan himself?

"Who is it?" he calls over the wall.

"Open the gate, Dee," comes a voice he knows, "before I have it smashed down."

Jesu! It is Sir Francis Walsingham.

Almost as bad as Satan!

A cold sweat washes Dee's face. Conjuring for treasure or evil spirits carries the death penalty.

"What do you want, Walsingham?"

"To speak to you, for my sins."

Dee opens the gate to find Walsingham warmly wrapped in black, wearing long riding boots and accompanied by a troop of the Queen's horsemen. It must have been six of the clock, the dog star already showing, but no moon yet, and Walsingham studies Dee closely, his dark eyes seeing things they have no right to see.

He knows! He knows!

"What are you up to in there, Dee?"

"I was enjoying my evening, Walsingham, until you came along. And what about you? Been out torturing Jesuits?"

Walsingham feigns a thin smile and takes off his hat. His hair is cut very short, sleek as a mole. By now they are already in Dee's hallway, where Walsingham's shrewd gaze probes the dark spots Dee wishes noticed least.

"A drink perhaps?" he asks.

"Nothing in the house," Dee lies, and he stands blocking the doorway to his library, but Walsingham has an insidious way of moving so that within the moment, there they are, standing in the middle of the library, on Dee's best Turkey carpet, where just a moment before, he had taken part in an Action to summon spirits. Kelley is vanished, and there remains no clue that anything illicit has occurred, save a good altar candle burning, but every fiber of the room vibrates with the need to confess. Walsingham stares at Dee again, with eyes that seem to bore into Dee's core.

"Oh, Christ, Walsingham, stop it," Dee tells him. "You know your pretense of genius doesn't work on me. What is that you actually want?"

Walsingham laughs. They have never had the easiest of relationships, for various reasons, but both recognize the other as an equal—well, almost—and they both understand each other's value.

"I actually want to pick your brains," Walsingham admits.

Dee feels a great wash of relief. Walsingham is not here to find him scrying! But he knows he must not show this. He must play his part as the tetchy philosopher. He throws up his hands.

"Oh, Jesu," he says. "This is how it always starts, doesn't it? A squirt of molten treacle and then within a day or two I'll be being shot at in a rising tide or caught in some conspiracy that will see me hanged, drawn, and quartered. Whatever it is, Walsingham, I won't do it."

"Calm yourself, Dee," Walsingham reassures him, still looking around the library, still searching for something that he seems to know is there and shouldn't be, or isn't there but should be. "I want only to know if you know anything of Olbrecht Łaski? The Polish count?"

"Oh, he's not that bad, surely?" Dee laughs, for of course he knows of Olbrecht Łaski—the Palatine of Sieradz, to give him his full title—who has, since his exile from Poland after supporting the wrong candidate in a coup, wandered Christendom posing as a soldier, a poet, a lover. But Dee knows Łaski first and foremost to be a man with a keen interest in matters close to John Dee's heart: in philosophy, mathematics, and even alchemy, yes, but most especially in the ways of communication between man and angelic spirits.

Walsingham ignores him.

"Her Majesty, and Lord Burghley," he says, "believe he may be of use."

"How?"

"He is said to have the ear of the Holy Roman Emperor, Rudolf."

Yes. Dee had heard something of this: that Count Łaski had found favor with Emperor Rudolf, who was well-known for his interest in the same field as Dee and Łaski, and even in the kabbalah. The two men were supposed to have spent months, even years, closeted together in the emperor's private library when the emperor's court was based in Vienna, much to the vociferous envy of the Empire's many other occultists, and the empress, too.

"So?"

Walsingham paces the room and lets out a theatrical sigh.

"So since the emperor left Vienna and established his court in

Prague, we have lost our placement and are living on mere rumor as to his intentions."

"You don't have a man in Prague? No one *at all*?"

Dee is astonished. Walsingham looks at him beadily.

"These things don't just *happen*, Dee. They take planning. Time. Money. And putting someone in Rudolf's court is especially hard—almost impossible—since he is become a recluse. Kings wait weeks for an audience; princes, months. So I cannot send just anyone."

"Which is why you are after Łaski?"

Walsingham pulls a face.

"Merely as a . . . presence."

Dee scoffs.

"But you do know he's here in England?" he checks.

"Of course," Walsingham tells him. "He is petitioning for money to fund his challenge for the Polish throne."

"From Bess?"

Walsingham gives him one of those looks.

"From Her Majesty, yes."

Dee smiles. Good luck with that, he thinks.

"Her Majesty is very taken with him," Walsingham says.

Both men are silent a moment.

"He'd be ideal in Prague," Dee supposes. He does not like the idea of another philosopher mathematician, however inferior, catching Her Majesty's eye. Walsingham laughs. He knows what Dee is thinking.

"And have you met him at all?"

Dee shakes his head.

"We've exchanged formal notes to express an as yet unconsummated desire to meet. I can show you them if you like. You would find no sniff of a cipher."

Dee supposes Walsingham has probably already seen them, but the Queen's principal private secretary frowns.

"Yet Łaski claims that apart from wishing to raise money for his campaign, one of the reasons he is here is to meet you," he says. "He tells me your reputation as a scholar runs very high throughout the courts of Europe. In Prague, especially."

"In Prague especially, eh?"

Dee is beginning to like the sound of the man, more and more, but why is Walsingham telling him all this?

"What is it you want, Walsingham? What scheme are you cooking up in that sleek little head of yours? You want me to persuade Łaski to leave England and go to Prague to act as your spy in the court of the Holy Roman Emperor? Seriously?"

"Just meet him. Get to know him. Get into his company. His mind. Ingratiate yourself. He's interested in your line of work, isn't he? Show him your . . . your quadrant, is it? Or your *radius astronomicus*. Or your show stone, perhaps?"

Walsingham says this with added meaning, and his stare glisters with that telling, dark intensity. *He knows! He knows!*

"You know I lost my show stone in the river," Dee reminds him. "While saving Her Majesty's life."

And still no recompense, of course, though Dee does not tell Walsingham that he has since found a new stone—hidden now behind some books—and a new scryer to read it, too, likewise hiding, though where he has got to, Dee has no clue. Behind an arras?

Walsingham sighs.

"Well, I don't know, do I, Dee?" he says. "Her Majesty has lent Łaski Winchester House, in Southwark, just down the river, so just do what you . . . you *wizards* do with one another."

Dee thinks for a moment, then asks why he should.

"I always end up doing these awful things for you, Walsingham, and never a penny or a word in recompense. So I ask again, what's in it for me?"

Walsingham feigns surprise.

"Why, Doctor Dee! What's in it for you? Why, the chance to serve your country, of course. To serve Her Majesty!"

Dee has heard all this before. Besides: "What do you think I've been doing these last months?"

Walsingham smiles and tells Dee exactly what he has been doing these last few months: he has written a paper to prove that since the birth of Christ the old calendar—the so-called Julian calendar—has gained exactly eleven days and fifty-three minutes on the sun, and that this being the case, a new calendar is needed— which Dee has also drawn up and christened Queen Elizabeth's Perpetual Calendar—to align the civil year with heaven's year without plunging day into night, and night into day.

"And?" Dee asks. "What are you going to do about it?"

"About the calendar? Nothing," Walsingham tells him with another smile. "It sits on my desk, where it will remain until I divine a way to scotch it."

Which is exactly what Dee feared: Walsingham will squash it because he knows that following its recommendation will set England apart from her Reformed allies in Holland and Germany and, for complex and unfortunate reasons, make it appear as if England were still subject to the papal bulla.

"And likewise on my desk is your *Geographical or Hydrographical Description of the Northern Hemisphere*," Walsingham goes on, referring to the extremely comprehensive evidence Dee has submitted in support of his application for a Grant of Discovery to the north of Atlantis on behalf of his newly formed Fellowship for New Navigations Atlantical and Septentrional, which—if granted—would allow him to attract investors and so fund an expedition to find the Northwest Passage, again on behalf of Her Majesty, but—and it is a crucial but—also to make a profit from any discoveries made and pay no duties on anything that might be brought back, which might, of course, include what everyone is after: gold.

"And you will sit on that, too, will you?" he asks.

"Might do," Walsingham agrees. "Oh, and there is also that horoscope you cast on Her Majesty's personal behalf, of Philip of Anjou."

Ah. That. That was supposed to be a thing kept secret between himself and Her Majesty, for the casting of such charts is frowned upon these days, when it is widely believed there is a thin line between divining what is already written in the stars and conniving to influence a man's future. Dee once spent months under lock and key in the Tower accused of that very thing, after having cast the chart of Her Majesty's late, unlamented sister Mary, and he had only agreed to cast this one of the man whom Her Majesty is considering—against Walsingham's advice and wishes—marrying after she asked Dee as a special favor, and on the understanding that she would keep it a secret.

"I was very pleased to read your final judgment," Walsingham goes on with a smirk. "Biothanatos, is it? Which I take to mean you believe Anjou is born to die a violent death? Very pleased to read that, I was, but I wonder: Would the gentleman himself be happy to hear it?"

No, Dee supposes. He would probably send an assassin.

"But that is not the point, Walsingham. The point is that I have been busy about Her Majesty's benefit. Which is more than I can say for you and your intelligencer in Prague. Or lack of one. What will she say when she hears that?"

Walsingham pulls a lemon-sucking face, and is about to say

something sharp perhaps, when there comes the sound of someone trying and failing to stifle a cough, as if from a priest hole, and both men hear it, and Dee could have sworn he sees Walsingham's ears actually prick up, and so he gives a possibly even more incriminating cough of his own, and before Walsingham can make anything of it, Dee agrees.

"All right," he says. "All right. Very well, I will meet Łaski."

And he bustles Walsingham out of the library and out into the courtyard, telling him that he will see Łaski and listen to what he has to say, if anything, on the matter of returning to Prague, but upon God's Truth, that is it, and no more.

"Not one single thing."

"Good," Walsingham says. "I hoped you would say that, so I have already taken the precaution of sending word on your behalf, telling Łaski to expect you tomorrow around noon."

⊕

CHAPTER THREE

Mortlake, two weeks previously,
second week in September 1583

The next morning is blustery, unnaturally cold for the time of year, and the river very choppy, and Dee, wrapped in his best—only—cloak, is forced to leave Kelley alone in the house while he is taken downriver in the boatman Jiggins's low-gunwaled wherry to the Southwark steps.

"Bit early for the pits, isn't it, Doctor?" Jiggins asks. "Or are you after pleasures of an altogether saltier nature?"

Dee has always hated the bear pits and has never—knowingly— lain with a Winchester goose, and he feels furious this morning, for this is a waste of time that might be spent scrying for angelic wisdom, but he remains polite and tells Jiggins that he is to see a Polish count.

"Though in fact he is not so bad a fellow."

"Old Łaski, is it?" Jiggins wonders. "A generous fellow, by all accounts. Gave a friend of mine a linnet in a cage, he did, just for taking him across the river. Imagine that!"

Dee thinks: Is that normal? A linnet in a cage? Probably not. But coming to no conclusion, he diverts his thoughts to all that he has learned in the last few days from Kelley, and from Uriel, and all that is yet to be learned, and his blood fizzes with the excitement. He is amazed it cannot be seen through his skin. He will write a book on the matter that will render all others obsolete. Even Trithemius. *On the Mystical Rule of the Seven Planets*, by Doctor John Dee, Astrologer to the Court of Saint James. Ha.

He thinks for a moment about Kelley and finds he minds less what Kelley gets up to in his house, just so long as he stays there, for the visions the man has had since he arrived have been far more powerful than any Dee has ever even heard of before. He has been feeling the connection to the higher planes like a power coursing through his body, as if something were moving within him. It has been astonishing.

Jiggins tuts at Dee's tip—meager in comparison to a linnet in a cage—and refuses to wait for him. By now the rain has turned to hail, and up the steps and along the lane at Winchester House, Dee finds the porter standing huddled under an awning with four of Her Majesty's halberdiers and some idlers who might be Italian, all staring sourly at the hail-pitted puddles that threaten their toecaps.

"Fucking snow in August, mate," a Yeoman mutters. "Don't make no sense."

"The count's having his dinner," the porter tells Dee as he shows him across the yard toward the solar where Łaski takes his meals. "Actually, he's all right, you'll see. Got a huge beard, he has, like this."

And he does. Long enough to tuck into his belt, bushy enough to hide a breastplate, and worn in a knot this morning, to keep it from his soup. When the count stands to greet his guest—his head nearly touching the low ceiling—Dee sees he wears crimson. A brave choice, that, and not merely because Łaski is so fat: crimson is the color of royalty.

"Doctor Dee!" Łaski booms and moves upon Dee with the force of an Atlantic roller, taking him into an irresistible embrace that is soft and dark and smells of sebum, pork fat, good wine, and black Castile soap. After a moment Dee is released and pushed a pace back so that Łaski can grip his shoulders between powerful hands and inspect his face very closely, as might a long-absent father seeking genealogical certainty in the face of a son he has not yet met. After a moment he seems satisfied.

"Yes," he says letting Dee go. "Yes. I have heard much things about you, Doctor. Much things. Please. Sit. A cup of wine?"

He motions to a servant, who pours them wine from a silver jug on a silver tray with silver cups.

"Leave us, Emericus," Łaski then says, and the servant bows and retreats into the shadows. A door opens, closes. Łaski tastes the wine.

"Is not bad," he says. "Is gift from your queen."

They sit on a settle by a damp-logged fire in a brick-built hearth, in front of which sleeps an old and enormous gray dog on dirty rushes, and they drink their wine. Łaski sits upright, legs spread, in old-fashioned shoes of the sort that have not graced the streets of London since Chaucer's day, and he stares at Dee with his hands on his fat knees and a big, expectant smile hidden in his beard but obvious in his eyes. At length he announces in a resonant rumble that he has read all Dee's works.

Dee is pleased.

"Tell me," Łaski goes on. "Let me be first to know. You are working on something new?"

And Dee admits that he is, perhaps, about to start on something new, concerning the Mystical Rule of the Seven Planets, about which he is excited. It will be his best book yet, he confidently avers.

"My most important."

Łaski is delighted and tells him that he would be proud to sponsor it, just as he once sponsored the printing and publication of one of Paracelsus's early books, if Dee would but do him the honor. And Dee tells him that on the contrary: being in such distinguished company would be doing him the honor, and after this they slide happily into a discussion of the relative merits of salamanders and gnomes and undines and sylphs for a good long while until they have finished the first jug of wine and Łaski calls for a second.

"*Sola dosis facit venenum!*" he says with a laugh. It is only the dose that makes it a poison.

But after the wine arrives, he becomes serious.

"So what you make of heaven's current aspect?" he asks, as you might ask after the tidings from France. "You believe Great Conjunction of Saturn and Jupiter in first sign of fiery trigon predicts great cataclysmic event? Like it did Noah's flood?"

Before Dee can remind him that the Cardinal of Cambrai—who first claimed the Great Conjunction in Aries augured Noah's flood—had later conceded the two events were separated by two hundred and seventy-nine years, Łaski leans forward and grips Dee's knee.

"Doctor," he says, very serious now, "you know work of Cyprian Leowitz?"

Dee does. He has long pored over the Bohemian philosopher's paper *On the Great Conjunction*, underlining words and phrases as they leapt out at him: "boisterous winds"; "extraordinary floods"; "sorrow"; "envy"; "hatred"; "contention"; "strife"; "violent oppression"; "extreme poverty and hunger"; "persecution of ecclesiastical persons"; "the ruin of great men"; "shipwrecks"; "burnings and other fiery calamities"; and—which he had underlined twice— "the final dissolution of the world and the second coming of the son of man."

"It is coming," Łaski growls, with a finger in the air. "Oh yes. It is coming. Third age of the angel Gabriel. Next August, it will be, when God punish neglect of his truth."

Dee has traveled widely and knows these sorts of learned men from the eastern margins of Christendom are ever prey to astonishingly detailed and vivid apocalyptic scenarios. On bad days— when it is raining or things are not going his way in his alchemical laboratory—Dee sometimes yields to such impulses himself, and it is only in the last few years, since marrying Jane Frommond and having a son, he must suppose, that these sorts of fatalistic prognostications have lost their appeal.

When Łaski has finished describing the End Times, when the oceans will boil with blood, owls will be seen at midday, and corpses will rise of their own volition, he sits back, apparently exhausted, and is silent a moment, staring at the smouldering logs in the hearth, and he seems, as exiles often do, filled with a tremendous melancholy. He is like a great sad bear, Dee thinks.

After a while Łaski lets out a gusty sigh and watches a spume of steam jet from the end of one of the damp logs.

"This country," he says, "is not like mine."

"No," Dee supposes. "So why did you ever leave? Yours, I mean? Poland?"

Łaski purses his lips and blows out a long sigh.

"Who knows, you know?" he says after a while. "Maybe to come here?"

"To England? Why?"

"Not for weather!" Łaski laughs. "Look! Is shit!"

"That can hardly be blamed on England, though," Dee reminds him, for they both know snowstorms in summer are one sign of the coming of End Times.

"And it must be like this in Prague, also?" Dee supposes.

Łaski dismisses Prague with a soft "pffft," which Dee takes to mean he can forget about Prague.

"You are not enamored with Prague?" he presses. "In no hurry to return?"

Łaski shifts evasively, and Dee recognizes his discomfort as deriving from owing someone—presumably in Prague—an awful lot of money. Or perhaps there is something more?

"You left under a shadow?" he risks pushing.

A quick flashing glance from Łaski. Yes, he left under a shadow all right. But he recognizes in Dee a man who is also used to leaving under shadows.

"It was nothing," Łaski claims weakly. "I brought with me to court a slippery little Dutchman—perhaps you know of him? Cornelius de Lannoy?"

"Oh yes. I know of Cornelius," Dee affirms. De Lannoy is an itinerant alchemist who had made a very handsome living defrauding first Lord Burghley, and then Her Majesty, and then most recently Sir Christopher Hatton out of small, medium, and large fortunes. It was news to Dee that he had moved on to Prague, but then again, why ever would he not? Rudolf's interest in natural philosophy—and other such things—made his court a honeypot for such men.

"Yes. Well. I bring him along, present him to Emperor Rudolf, and they get on famously until—poof!—Cornelius vanishes with ten thousand silver thalers and a carriage made of gold or something, which we hear he then gives to William the Silent, you know? The leader of the Dutch rebels, so Emperor thinks de Lannoy not only a fraudster, but also all along working for Protestants, and who bring him to the court? Yes! Łaski. So Łaski thinks it time he make himself like de Lannoy's product."

"Scarce?"

Łaski laughs delightedly.

"You understand me, Doctor!"

There is a pause, a regathering. Dee wonders if de Lannoy was really ever an intelligencer for the Dutch. It hardly matters, he supposes, so long as Rudolf came to believe it.

"Anyway," Łaski says, all bright and insincere, "I am in England now enjoying favor of your Queen, and now I am meeting the great Doctor Dee. I hoped we might have chance to further our philosophical studies. To share our findings. Your name is held in very high regard all over Christendom, and in Prague, at the court of Emperor Rudolf, most especially. He has copies of your books."

Emperor Rudolf is well-known to be obsessed with the invocation of angelic spirits and other kabbalistic matters, and so he should have copies of Dee's books on those matters—which are surely among the most authoritative ever written—but nevertheless Dee is still flattered to think of it, even if Łaski is careful not to say the emperor has actually read them.

"I heard he has a copy of the third volume of Trithemius's *Steganographia*?" Dee asks. He has long sought that book and would willingly lose a leg to own it.

Łaski nods.

"Indeed! Along with every other title on the *Decretum Glasianum*."

He means the pope's list of banned books.

"The Inquisition must be itching to get their hands on it?"

Łaski scratches his cheeks with both sets of fingers, up and down. Flakes float free and hang in the smoky light filtering through the window. There is a table under the window on which Dee thinks any other man would place a cage, say, with a linnet or a finch in it, to sing in the mornings to cheer him up.

"Is big worry," Łaski agrees. "And as long as Rudolf is more interested in kabbalah than in his kingdom, and so long as his brother Matthias is heir, then they have reason to hope."

Wait! *What?*

"Matthias would permit the Inquisition to operate throughout the Empire?"

"Matthias will do what his uncle tells him."

Matthias's uncle is Philip, King of Spain, Elizabeth of England's most implacable enemy, determined to dethrone her and unleash the Inquisition upon her subjects. Dee knows his own name must be among the first on a list scheduled for a fiery death on the auto-da-fé.

"So when Rudolf dies, Matthias inherits the Empire, and King Philip will be able to count on the Empire's support in all things?"

Łaski nods and pulls an "oh yes" face.

"Even in an attack on England?"

"Of course England! Of course England, why not? You English are strange people, I find. You think you are special and believe it so much that it comes true. It makes you invincible. You start every war losing all battles, but still think you will win in end, so enemy starts to think you know something they don't; they begin to doubt themselves, and they lose courage, and so in the end you *do* win, and then everybody looks back at what has happened and they kick themselves. But it is only England, they say. It is only Englishmen!"

He's obviously given this some thought.

"My father was Welsh," Dee corrects.

"Even worse!"

"Though less successful."

"For being more realistic."

"Exactly."

Both men laugh. It is all nonsense of course.

And then Łaski says, almost casually, as if it hardly mattered: "Anyway, by now is not *Spain's* attack on England that Rudolf will be supporting."

Dee sits up.

"Whose attack *is* he supporting?"

Łaski looks confused, as if Dee were simple, or should have known something.

"De Guise. You know the Duc de Guise?"

"Oh yes," Dee mutters. "I know de Guise."

The Duc de Guise is the leader of the Catholic League in France, brother to the Cardinal of Lorraine, and, crucially, cousin to Mary Queen of Scots. Dee holds him responsible for the death of Isobel Cochet, and hearing his name now is like catching a whiff of plague pits. In fact, Dee feels a strong jolt of alarm, just as if he has found himself walking dizzily among such pits: Walsingham did not warn him of this. He wonders if he even knows?

"Yes," Łaski agrees, correctly interpreting Dee's expression. "Is nasty bit of work."

"But why would Rudolf support de Guise in any invasion of England? I thought he was a man of science? A philosopher? Surely he would not wish the Inquisition imposed upon England?"

Łaski looks sly.

"Is true," he agrees. "Is true. Rudolf *is* man of science, but you know what else he is man of?"

Dee does not.

"What is the word you use in English? Fanny? Pussy? Quim?"

25

"Women?"

"Women! Yes! Women! Rudolf is man of women. A professor of women! But not only women! My God. He likes boys, too. And men. Everything. He likes them. He likes them all. And a lot of them."

Łaski roars with sudden mirthless laughter.

"But that doesn't explain his change of heart," Dee points out.

"Ah, no. But there is a special woman he likes. A woman who is not his wife, or he would have a son of his own now, eh? No. A woman called Kitty de Fleurier. You ever hear of her?"

Dee shakes his head. Łaski, uncharacteristically lively, suddenly more Italian than Pole, pulls a particular face, rolls his eyes, and shakes a hand in the air as if he has just burned his fingers.

"Where she comes from no one knows," he says. "Land of Prester John, in the heart of Africa maybe, for she is color of polished rosewood, and my God! What you would not do for such a woman, if only she would let you—I don't know: lick her wrist—you cannot even imagine. You would refuse her nothing, you understand me? Nothing. And nor does Rudolf. She has him cupped in her palm. Like this."

He makes a gesture, the meaning of which is curiously obvious.

"But who is she, beyond her name?"

"She is member of *L'Escadron Volant*."

Dee has never heard of *L'Escadron Volant*. Łaski slaps a palm to his forehead in disbelief.

"No? Doctor! I can't believe it! Where have you been all these years?"

Dee shrugs.

"Mortlake," he says, though that is not entirely true.

Łaski takes a long pull of his wine, looking at Dee over the cup's rim.

"My God," he says when he's done and has wiped his mouth on his crimson sleeve. "All right. You know Catherine de Medici?"

"I know of her," Dee admits. "The French king's mother. The Jezebel of our times."

Łaski disagrees. He even seems to admire her.

"She is ruthless, yes, but to be power behind the throne of four kings of France! Four!"

And he holds up his fingers in case Dee does not know what four is.

"How you get that?" he asks. "Not by stitching."

He mimes embroidery.

"No. By being *clever*. By doing clever things."

And now he taps his temple.

"Such as?" Dee asks, wearying slightly.

"Such as recruiting what is called in Louvre *L'Escadron Volant*. Yes?"

"The Flying Squadron, yes. But what *is* it?"

"Ahh! Exactly! Now we come to it. *L'Escadron Volant* is a stable—is right word? (probably not, Dee thinks)—of beautiful women. Beautiful women who Catherine de Medici has recruited and trained and can send out to any court in Christendom, to climb into the beds of any man she likes. To seduce him, yes? And lead him by his pizzle wherever she wants!"

It sounds absurd, Dee thinks, and yet . . .

"And each girl is carefully chosen to suit a man's taste, yes?" Łaski goes on, "So Kitty is black skinned, but say you like blond girls? Well, Catherine has blond girls. You like bald girls? She's got them. Ginger? Old? Very young? She's got them, too. A girl from Cathay! Yes! Yes! Why not? And fat girls, too. She even has a giantess with one leg."

"I don't believe you," Dee tells him, for he doesn't. Not just about the one-legged giantess, which can only be nonsense, surely, but about the whole thing. Łaski is affronted.

"No? All right then. An example: Charlotte de Sauve. You heard of her? Yes? She is one of *L'Escadron*'s best. Top woman, yes? Very beautiful. Elegant. Clever. All things, yes? Catherine de Medici first sends her to seduce her son-in-law, Henry of Navarre, to make him stop sleeping with his wife—her own *daughter*—to make sure no Protestant heirs threaten Catherine's Catholic sons' heirs. Boom. Done. Navarre no longer sleeping with Marguerite. But that is not enough. Then Catherine takes Charlotte from Navarre and sends her to seduce *her own son*—Francis—who was a friend to Navarre, to cause them to hate each other, and so not conspire against her older son."

Dee thinks about it for a moment. Yes, it sounds brilliant: a group of beautiful, intelligent young women sent out to the great houses of Christendom to influence events in France's—or, more likely, the Valois family's—favor, but the enterprise raises so many questions to which the answers are bound to be shaming.

Still though, just the thought of it leaves a glint in Łaski's eye, and he leans forward to grip Dee's knee once more to ensure his attention and in a low voice confides, "If Catherine de Medici ever asks what my taste in women is, you tell her I am relaxed: all sorts, so long as they come in multiples of six, and they are built like this?"

He mimes large breasts and then roars with that same joyless laughter again, this time until tears leak into his beard, and after a moment Dee smiles, too, because you don't get on in this world if you don't find that sort of thing funny.

"And so Kitty de Fleurier has seduced Rudolf on behalf of Catherine de Medici?"

Łaski stops laughing.

"Ah," he admits, somewhat sorrowfully. "No. That is twist. Mistress de Fleurier *was* one of *L'Escadron's* most accomplished members, and last year she was sent to seduce the Duc de Guise, but something happened. As we say: de Guise is clever man. Also: very handsome. Personable, yes? Or maybe had something on her, you know? A secret or something?"

This sounds exactly like de Guise. It is what he did to Isobel Cochet. He kidnapped her child and forced her to steal a document from Francis Walsingham.

"Does this Kitty have a child?" he asks.

"A child? I don't know. Does she?"

I bet she does, Dee thinks. Or did.

"Anyway," Łaski goes on, "whatever happened, he turned Mistress de Fleurier to his own purposes and then, knowing something of Rudolf, and his tastes, sent her instead to Prague to seduce him and persuade him to back his attack on your country."

"De Guise? He is powerful in France, but—to mount an attack on England?"

"Not on his own, of course," Łaski admits. "But with help in England? Maybe."

"And does he have this help?"

Dee feels the ground opening up beneath his feet. Does Walsingham know all this? Is this why he sent him?

"Three men," Łaski continues. "Three of your English milords."

Dee feels fresh sweat on his collar.

"*English* milords? Who?"

But at this Łaski just shrugs wearily.

"Oh, your names all same to me: if you are not called John, you are Thomas; if not Thomas, you are William; and when you talk about your milords is impossible to know if you talking about place or person, and milord of This comes not from This, but from That."

Which is true, but still: *Who?*

But Łaski genuinely does not seem to know. Or shows no further inclination to discuss England's future; he wishes instead to discuss alchemy, and in particular whether there is any truth in the rumor that he heard in Milan that Dee had repeated George Ripley's experiment as described in the English alchemist's most famous book, *The Key to the Twelve Gates*, and that he had had some great success in transmuting into pure gold some humble black ore brought from the New World.

Dee hardly listens as Łaski witters on about his own efforts to transmute base metal—all failed, of course, "but not for want to trying!"—and about his lost laboratory in Sieradz with its twelve furnaces, the finest glassware from Holland, and five careful assistants, for Dee's mind is elsewhere grappling with the news of de Guise's swiftly hatching plot. If Łaski is telling the truth, then England is in mortal, deadly danger, and they will need something a little more drastic than a mere recorder-of, and passer-on, of tittle-tattle from Rudolf's court: they will need an assassin.

⊕

By the time Dee manages to leave Łaski's house it is early evening, and despite being increasingly anxious at the thought of having left Edward Kelley the freedom of his house—*and* of his laboratory, *and* of his library—when Dee climbs into the wherry on St. Mary Overy steps, he asks not to be taken upstream and home, but across the river to the Whitehall Palace watergate.

"And as fast as you can."

He needs to see Bess.

"Just seen old Walsingham's barge up there," the boatman—not Jiggins this time, but someone similar—tells Dee as he takes up his oars, and when they reach the Whitehall watergate, pulling against a heavy flow, the halberdiers on duty confirm the principal private secretary is already arrived and is with Lord Burghley.

"Take me to them," Dee says.

"I'll take you to the duty sergeant," the halberdier tells him. "See what he says."

"I need to see Her Majesty now."

"Piss off, Doctor, you know how this works."

Even if Her Majesty is expecting you, the process of actually finding yourself before her is elaborate and lengthy, but if she is not expecting you, then if you do not wish to be diverted into some back room to pass your life away being asked questions by some incurious minor official with all the intelligence of a goose, something special is required.

Across the garden the windows of the Receiving Room are brightly lit, he sees, so as they tread the path that will lead them nowhere, Dee makes a swift calculation: How far can a man run in the length of time it takes to light a fuse and for the flame to reach the powder charge and the bullet to fly from the end of the gun and catch the aforesaid running man between the shoulder blades? There are certainties and there are variables, of course, but really all that matters is that even if you are not in a tearing hurry, and even if your target is not moving fast, and it is not falling dark, then the chances of hitting the side of a barn with the ball of an arquebus from almost any distance greater than five paces are vanishingly small. It'd be better to throw the whole gun at your target.

So with a sudden wrench, Dee tears himself away and makes a break for it across the various shin-high hedges and lawns that separate him from the windows.

"Oy!" a guard cries. "Come back, you fucker!"

But he is across the low hedges of the knot garden and the gravel infills, and after a running leap he is up onto the sill below the broad spread of glass window before any shot is taken, and by then it is too late, surely? No one would shoot at the windows of the palace, would they? Knowing the Queen was likely within?

Would they?

No.

He presses his face to the glass, thick and wavered and divided by strips of lead into a hundred palm-size diamonds. He can see nothing within and doubts those within can see much without. But she is in there, he is sure.

"Bess!" he shouts. "Bess!"

And he hammers on the glass.

The guards are coming fast.

And then there, a little to his right: a casement window, jacked a notch. Almost perfect. He yanks it open and squeezes in, just as the first guards arrive, their thundering footsteps scraping on the gravel below, and he tumbles the five feet to the polished oak floor, only to be dragged back to his feet by men pulling on his cloak— his best, his only—from outside.

He registers the shocked faces of Her Majesty on her throne; Sir Francis Walsingham and Lord Burghley are turned to him, mouths round as coins, Walsingham reaching for his knife. But Dee has no time for any show of obeisance, for he is being hanged by his own cloak. He snatches his eating knife from his belt and slashes the points tying his collar together, freeing the cloak and silently bidding it farewell as it vanishes back through the window accompanied by a cry of frustrated rage from beyond.

Dee still has his cap, which he now removes, and holds against his chest as he makes his formal bow to Her Majesty.

"Your Majesty," he says.

"What in the name of God are you doing, Dee?" Burghley rumbles.

"Testing your security, Lord Burghley. And I have to say—"

"Oh, shut up, John!"

This is from Her Majesty, and delivered with real vim, and Dee's words die in his throat. She is flushed, and her eyes gluey, and she is obviously not well, he thinks. Coming down with something again.

"Guards!" Walsingham calls, and the doors fly open and the room is filled with large men with sharp-edged weapons, all pointed at Dee.

"Wait! Wait!" he shouts. "I have something for you! I've just come from Łaski. Your Pole. He says he is certain Emperor Rudolf will give Duc de Guise the money he needs for ships and troops! And that de Guise is in contact with someone over here. Three lords—he doesn't know who—who'll rally all the recusants when they land."

It all comes out in a blurt. Burghley, the old man, looks at him as if he has shat himself, and Walsingham, too, but Her Majesty—forever better disposed to the man whom she calls her "eyes"—extends one of her beautiful hands to stay the guards.

"Leave him be!" she orders, and the blades of the halberds and the swords cease their advance, even if they remain aimed at Dee's sternum.

"Explain," she commands, and he does. He tells them what Łaski had told him, and while it all sounded so plausible from Łaski, from his mouth it sounds gossamer thin, a deranged fantasy, mere tittle-tattle peddled by a disgruntled exile, and Burghley's look of pained disgust confirms this impression. But seated on her throne under her Cloth of State, Her Majesty is looking increasingly furious.

"*L'Escadron Volant?*" she barks. "*L'Escadron Volant?* Sir Francis, why do we not have an English Flying Squadron?"

Walsingham shifts from foot to foot and defers to Burghley, who is chewing the ends of his mustache and looking anywhere but at the Queen.

"Lord Burghley?" she commands.

"It—ah—seems very un-English, Your Majesty," he admits at last.

"So you have heard of it?"

"Certainly, Your Majesty. Certainly. Charlotte de Sauve, Your Majesty. Yes."

He coughs and clears his throat and there is a long rumble somewhere in his chest that is akin to a growl. The Queen's scowl is very fierce, and her mouth like a button. She says nothing, but her meaning is very clear: Get me a Flying Squadron, now.

"I will see to it in the morning, Your Majesty," Burghley says, though even he can hear how ridiculous this sounds. Her Majesty scoffs, and Burghley flushes red and looks very out of his depth.

"I am not without contacts," he protests, "in the world of . . . of beautiful women. And so on."

The Queen sends him a withering glance and turns on Walsingham, and for the moment, Dee is a delighted spectator. This is how it must be, he thinks, to be a statue in a royal palace.

"And what about you, Sir Francis? You have an espial in every court in Christendom. What do you know of de Guise's harlot?"

Walsingham dabs his mouth with a kerchief to gain time.

"We learned something was afoot with de Guise," he tells her. "The duke held a meeting, in Paris, this last month, with Doctor Allen of Douai and various others, including a military man, Francois de Roncherolles, who has resurrected the notion of landing an army of five thousand arquebusiers at Framlingham in Suffolk."

The Queen clutches her throat.

"With the aim of ousting us, and placing our cousin of Scotland on our throne?"

Walsingham nods, and Burghley tuts, drawing breath to speak, but the Queen holds up a hand to stop him.

"Yes, Lord Burghley," she says, "we are well aware of your thoughts on how we should treat our cousin of Scotland, just as you must surely be aware of our thoughts on the matter. We will not see her executed. We will not set such a precedent. We will not turn every prince in Christendom against us."

Burghley sighs very quietly and bows acquiescence, for the Queen is right: this is an old matter, gone over many times, over many years, and always ending the same way. One day, though, one day they will change her mind and then they will be free to rid England's side of her foremost thorn.

Until then, though, they must do what they can, however grim the prospects.

"Go on," she says, for she knows there is more. There is always more.

"And it was understood from this meeting that should de Guise successfully land his five thousand arquebusiers, then Spain will send twenty thousand *tercios* from the Low Countries to land somewhere in Yorkshire."

"*Yorkshire?*"

"A shorter sea voyage from Flanders, Your Majesty," Walsingham reminds her.

"And nearer your cousin Mary of Scotland," Burghley adds, but his point is lost.

"Could they do that? Invade, I mean?"

"It has been done before."

Her Majesty's grandfather did it, of course, as did her great-grandfather, as did her great-great-great-grandfather. She turns to Dee.

"And Count Łaski gave no names?"

Dee shakes his head.

"He said there were three of them. Three 'milords.' That is the word he used. He said they might have been called Thomas. Or John. Or William. And he complained that all Your Majesty's lords are named after one place, but live elsewhere."

"Well, that's no bloody good," Burghley barks. "Let's get him in here and ask him again. Better still, Sir Francis, call him to the Tower. Get him on the Earl of Exeter's Daughter and he'll soon spill his guts."

"We can't rack a Polish count, Lord Burghley," Walsingham tells him. "Not if we wish him to be of service in the future."

Walsingham still has an eye on sending Łaski to Prague, Dee sees, but surely it is too late for that? Burghley takes Walsingham's point, though, and emits a growl, and Her Majesty turns to Walsingham to ask who among her lords would help an armed landing and Dee thinks, Oh Jesu: he is surely not going to list them, is he? They'll be here all night if that is the case, and he has to be home to ensure that Kelley does not clear off, taking half his valuables with him. He will never be able to replace either of Mercator's globes.

Walsingham tells her the list is lengthy.

"But we must assume that the Earl of Arundel is somehow involved, either by commission or omission, if the landing is proposed for Framlingham. Framlingham was his father's castle, as you know, Your Majesty, before—"

The Queen holds up a palm. She does not wish to hear any mention of the Duke of Norfolk, the Earl of Arundel's father, whom she had executed for treason a little more than ten years earlier and was still much missed, not only by Her Majesty, for they were close, but—it turns out—also his tenants in Suffolk. His son—the Earl of Arundel—holds a special place in the Queen's heart, Dee knows, and she is forever trying to make up for having had his father killed. In fact, Dee has often wondered if the off-spring of parents put to death in the Tower become guildsmen of a particular and peculiar guild? Do they look out for one another? Jealously guard privileges? Look down on outsiders? Would joining be worth the price? It is only then that he supposes that a man whose father has been put to death by a woman whose father put her own mother to death might well be considered an alderman of such a guild and be treated accordingly.

Meanwhile Walsingham has opened his mouth to say something—to *tell* Her Majesty something—but he seems to think better of it, and he closes his mouth with a dry clack. What's he up to? Dee wonders.

"And should the emperor lend de Guise the money," the Queen begins, "how soon will he be in position to launch this monstrous attack?"

Here Walsingham appears on safer ground.

"He will have to raise troops, and hire ships to bring them over, and he will not risk a single day of having them stand idle in Flanders, waiting for good weather, so they will not risk it this year. Sometime next summer is the earliest."

"It will be August," Dee tells them. Walsingham looks startled, as if he had half forgotten Dee was there.

"Why?"

"Because the conjunction of Saturn and Jupiter in first sign of fiery trigon augurs a cataclysmic event such as . . . such as an invasion."

He dares not tell them it augurs the overthrow of princes, the final dissolution of the world, and of the second coming of the son of man, but that is what he means, and that, at least, is what Lord Burghley understands. He looks quite pale.

"Then we have a scant year," Burghley murmurs.

"For what?" Her Majesty snaps.

"To-to-to put our affairs in order . . . ," he trails off lamely.

"You may be thinking of putting your affairs in order, Lord Burghley, but we shall be passing our time in preparation to see off this invasion; to fight like a lion and to send each and every filthy-footed foreign soldier from our isle!"

The effort of her words drains Elizabeth, and she slumps, coughing weakly for a moment. From the shadows Mistress Parry appears with a cloth. The Queen takes it, dabs her lips, returns it, and Mistress Parry reverts very reluctantly to shadow.

"Tell us," Her Majesty says after she is recovered. "Does our cousin of Scotland know of this plot?"

Walsingham is uncertain.

"We have no certain proof, Your Majesty, for she is not so careless as she once was, but she still receives word from her people in France."

"Receives word? How? After all our efforts?"

Dee finds himself smiling. All *our* efforts. It is only Walsingham. It is only ever Walsingham.

"I believe," Walsingham says, enunciating very carefully, "I may have a pinch on the threads that hold the scheme together."

"Really?" Burghley asks. "Anyone we know?"

"It is still too early to say," Walsingham tells them, and the Queen looks ever more anxious, but her eyes are quick, and there is something else: something she's thought of, or is trying to remember, that bothers her.

And then she has it.

"This meeting in Paris. The Duc de Guise's meeting," she says. "That was last month, yes? And yet you greet its implication—that our good Doctor Dee has brought to us—as if it were new?"

At which Walsingham flinches.

"Yes, Your Majesty."

"Why?"

"Because it was believed the scheme to be wishful thinking, since there was no moneyman involved; and no one was there to represent King Philip, or the pope."

"But de Guise needs neither if he is to be funded by Rudolf?"

There is the slightest pause before Walsingham speaks.

"This is a new development," he has to admit.

"And so what is being said about de Guise's whore in Prague?" the Queen asks. "About this Kitty de Fleurier?"

Dee cannot help but smile to see Walsingham flinch at this question, which surely he'd known was coming? Beads of sweat glisten on his tall forehead and he actually pulls on his ruff and tries to look somewhere else, praying for divine intervention perhaps, but the Queen is like a wren with a worm, and she awaits his answer with a beady glare.

After a long moment, Walsingham must speak.

"I confess, Your Majesty, this is the first I have heard of her."

"You have heard *nothing* from Prague?" she snaps. "Nothing of this Kitty de Fleurier and Emperor Rudolf?"

Walsingham looks at the ground. Will it swallow him up? No.

"Nothing, Your Majesty," he must eventually confess.

"Nothing? Not a thing? And who have we placed within Emperor Rudolf's court?"

Again the long pause, and again the slow words.

"No one, Your Majesty," he admits. "Not since the emperor moved his court from Vienna to Prague, just this last year. We have as yet found no reliable source within."

There is a long moment's incredulous silence before the Queen erupts.

"By Christ, Master Walsingham!" she shouts. "Is this what I pay you for?"

She is on her feet now, shouting full-throated. Dee cannot help but smile for he knows she pays Walsingham almost nothing, and that he is deep in debt on her behalf. He prays Walsingham will say something to that effect, for it would see him marched off the premises, but no: whatever else he is, Walsingham is no fool. He keeps mum.

"Why do you not have anyone in Prague?" she continues. "In the Holy bloody Roman Emperor's court? Dear Christ! This cannot be so very hard, can it? We need someone in there! We need to nip this Kitty de Fleurier plot in the bud. Send someone! Now! Today! Someone able or I will find someone more able than you!"

Walsingham hangs his head, and he is, for a moment, like a dog being beaten for the cat's crime.

⊕

CHAPTER FOUR

Mortlake, next day, second week of September 1583

The library is shuttered-dark save for the flame of a single candle, low set, and into its orbit of golden light is thrust the bony face of Edward Kelley, who kneels with his eyes shut, intoning the form of words recommended by Johannes Trithemius in his manual *On the Art of Drawing Spirits into Crystals*.

"In the name of the blessed and Holy Trinity," Kelley says, "I do desire you, good angel Anachor, that if it be the divine will of him who is called Tetragrammaton, the Holy God, the Father, that you take upon yourself some shape as best becomes your celestial nature and that you appear visibly here in this crystal and answer our demands in as far as we shall not transgress the bounds of the divine mercy and goodness by requesting unlawful knowledge, but that you will graciously show us what things are most profitable for us to know and do, to the glory and honor of this divine Majesty, who lives and reigns, world without end. Amen."

Before him Dee's show stone is placed within its usual frame, for they are yet to afford the time or the expense of the altar the angelic spirits have demanded, and there is nothing for a good long while. Dee is just wondering whether they ought to abandon attempts and concentrate on the altar when, instead of Anachor, it is the angel Michael who appears first to accuse them of slackness, before then continuing on to describe what it is that the angelic spirits wish from Dee: he is to prepare a book that will be dictated to him in the language of the angelic spirits, as spoken by Adam in the Garden of Eden and written by Enoch in his book of divine revelation that was lost in Noah's great flood. Hearing this, Dee feels as if the window of his senses and the doors of his imagination have been blown open by a great force, for it is what he has ever wanted: something to lead to a new Book of Revelation and a putting to an end of all the world's religious strifes.

"In forty days must this *Book of Loagaeth* be written, failing which the Lord shall raze your names from the number of the blessed and those who are anointed with his blood."

Dee and Kelley break off and stare at each other.

Is forty days a lot? Or a little? How long will this *Book of Loagaeth* be? Kelley has no idea, and the angels will say no more.

After the Action they eat in the kitchen alone. Kelley sits stooped over his bowl, protecting it with one arm on the table, and he turns away from Dee and scoops the soup into his mouth hurriedly, his eyes ever watchful. Dee supposes he might be the younger child in a large family, say, or have been in service somewhere rough. When Kelley is done, and has torn into the bread and guzzled the ale, he is only marginally more civilized, which Dee believes is only right, for scryers need unformed, malleable minds, unconstrained by convention or order or rationality if they are to be truly receptive to angelic signals, which is why children are often used as scryers. Though he does wonder what Jane will make of him?

Dee is not sure what he himself makes of him, come to that, though. When he got back from seeing Łaski, the house was almost exactly as he had left it that morning, except it wasn't *quite*. Despite his best care, Kelley had disturbed everything that he had touched, and it turned out that he had touched absolutely everything. He had been into every nook, every cranny, far more thoroughly than any customs searcher, or any one of Walsingham's men seeking priest holes.

Nothing now, as far as Dee knows, is missing, but what had Kelley been *after*? What was he looking for? A general if very thorough rummage, or something in particular? And if he had found it, would he have stolen it? Would he still be here if he had? Or gone along the road to wherever it—whatever it was—would benefit him most? If that were the case, then he had not found it. Yet. Or perhaps it did not exist? Or perhaps it existed, but only as a thought within Dee's head?

He knows he will have to watch him carefully, of course, but meanwhile there is the *Book of Loagaeth* to be considered, and so Dee describes to Kelley the practical difficulties he foresees, not the least of which is the cost.

"So—you have no money then?"

Dee tells him not to worry about it, for there are always ways around that, but he can feel the disappointment rising from Kelley like gaol scent.

"Besides," he goes on. "I have already found a sponsor for our book. The same man who saw to the publication of one of Paracelsus's books in Augsburg."

"How can he do that," Kelley asks, "since we have only just learned we are to produce a book?"

It is a good point, and Dee is once again mortified by his intellectual pride.

"I told him I was working on one," he admits. "He said he would be honored to sponsor it. So he will be an ever more enthusiastic sponsor of the *Book of Loagaeth*, won't he?"

"Who is he?" Kelley asks.

"He is the Palatine of Sieradz," Dee tells him. "Count Olbrecht Łaski."

He does not mention his suspicion that despite his grand title and ways, Łaski likewise lacks for funds, for why else would you pay for a river crossing with a linnet in a cage?

"Łaski? The Polish count you went to see yesterday?"

Dee is not certain he ever told Kelley that is where he was going, but he is pleased to note that the smell of disappointment recedes, and that Kelley sits upright, leans in.

"And a man of our way of thinking," Dee confirms.

"Well, that's good then," Kelley says. He even manages a smile, the first Dee has seen from him, but it is very quick, ferrety, and Dee sees he must be embarrassed by his teeth for they are long, yellow, and sharp.

⊕

That afternoon they start another Action in the library, hoping for some material on the *Book of Loagaeth*, the name of which signifies "speech from God," and which is to be written backward with the first page at the back, and they are told—by an angel named Galvah—that they are to start work on Tuesday next, which surprises Dee, for surely they should start as soon as possible to meet the forty-day deadline? Galvah tells them it is as it is, and so Dee asks after Łaski, wondering if he will prosper. He only means insofar as whether he will be able to pay for the publication of the *Book of Loagaeth*, but Galvah describes far grander plans for the count.

"Behold," she says, "when he comes I shall pour water into him and I shall anoint him, as I have determined. Hide, therefore, nothing from him, for you belong to him. I speak this for your understanding."

Dee is startled, and a little frightened. The angel means for them to include Łaski in the Actions. Widening this circle is a terrible risk, for he knows little of Łaski, and though he is certain that together he and Kelley have done nothing in the way of conjuring evil spirits, Dee knows how easily it might be spun otherwise by those—a frighteningly long list—who would see him discredited, and/or even dead.

"You wish the count to attend an Action?" he verifies.

"Those that are of this house are not to be denied the banquets therein."

"But he is not of this house?"

"He will be, tomorrow."

Dee doubts this, but if the angelic spirits can predict the day of the end of the world, then surely the movements of a Pole from Southwark are not beyond their powers? And besides, had not Michael foretold Walsingham's arrival at his gate just two nights earlier?

✠

And sure enough, it becomes so, though in a way Dee could hardly have expected: Łaski arrives from upriver, still in crimson, on the Queen's barge, with the Queen's oarsman, under the Queen's Cloth of State, with her trumpeter blaring, too, which is an extraordinary honor.

"Yes," Łaski agrees when he has descended the gangplank to Dee's water steps. "A wedding in the town of Oxford."

He gestures upriver. With him are Lord Russell, whom Dee

does not know, and Sir Phillip Sidney, whom Dee taught Latin and mathematics, and whose birth chart he once cast on behalf of the boy's father.

"Still alive, Sir Phillip?" he jokes.

"A few years yet, Doctor, and then I shall play it very safe, don't you worry. No swords; no guns."

"Very wise," Dee tells him. "Come and stay with us here in Mortlake all that year, why don't you? We live a very quiet life, as you know, and Jane would love it above all things."

Which is true, for Sir Phillip is a very engaging and handsome young man, as well as a talented poet and soldier, and his chart suggests he will go on to very great things, so long as he can survive his thirty-first year, when he faces mortal danger from sword or gunshot. He is, though, married to Frances Walsingham, Sir Francis's daughter, and duty calls, so he and Lord Russell must climb back aboard the barge and continue on down the river to London, leaving Dee with Count Olbrecht Łaski.

"You don't mind?" Łaski asks.

"It is an honor," Dee tells him, and he sends Roger Cooke in search of Kelley, to have him move out of Dee's mother's room, but Cooke tells him Kelley has gone fishing. Dee wishes Jane were home. There are some curious swirling undercurrents to this affair that alone he cannot pin down to identify. He senses Walsingham's hand in it, but what is he up to? Dee cannot for the moment guess.

He escorts Łaski to his library, where Łaski marvels at the collection.

"My God," he rumbles, "so many."

He runs his hand over their spines. He is looking for the Paracelsus book he helped into publication, but he does not find it, for Dee had to sell it.

"And what is this?"

He indicates the magical mirror that Sir William Pickering had given Dee, but before Dee can demonstrate its qualities, the count seizes upon Mercator's globes, one of the earth and one of the heavens, and Dee has to intervene before he crushes their delicate mechanisms in his clumsy hands.

At last Kelley reappears, carrying a fish, to justify his absence. Łaski does not instantly take to him, but in fact Kelley has tidied himself up: a new coat—or new to him—and though he still wears his hair in that unusual style, clumped about his ears, he has washed it, it seems, as well as his face and his hands, and he is positively obsequious.

"Count Łaski! Your Highness!" he says, putting aside the fish and removing his greasy old hat and bowing deeply. "What an honor."

He is even satisfied to discover he is to be sleeping in the hall with Roger Cooke and Łaski's servant, not the one who brought the wine when Dee saw him in Winchester House, but a man Łaski calls Tanfield.

That night they discuss the possibility of Łaski joining tomorrow's Action.

"You may not wish to?" Dee supposes.

"But of course I do," Łaski booms. "The chance to communicate with the angels? My God."

"And you probably have some questions for them?" Kelley suggests with a simpering laugh that leaves Dee unsettled again.

"Oh yes, certainly. And what is more, I have a show stone."

This is welcome news indeed.

"Does it work?" Dee asks.

Łaski gives his downturned-mouth shrug.

"Not so far," he admits, "but it cost lot of money, you know? So."

"Perhaps it is just the reader?" Kelley wonders. "I will see what I can see."

✠

The next day, the last before Jane returns, it rains again, and Dee and Łaski convene early in the hall this time, to be near the fire, and they wait for Kelley, who has retired to pray in the oratory. Dee has sent Roger Cooke away again—to the market to buy something, anything—and now he finds himself peering down the length of the orchard toward the river, and then returning to check the locks on the gate are fastened and that the windows are shuttered. He keeps pacing, in a heightened state, and he keeps checking the show stones—now including Łaski's magnificent agate show stone—on their altar, and then puts another log on the fire while Łaski sits canted sideways on a settle, both meaty hands clasped over his belly, watching Dee through heavy-lidded eyes. He has not slept well on an uncomfortable bed he is not used to.

"You swear by this fellow, Doctor?"

Dee feels he has no choice, especially as just then Kelley emerges from the oratory and the Action can begin with the by-now-familiar prayer, and beside him Dee can almost hear Łaski craning forward to peer into the stone's polished facet in the hope of catching his first glimpse of an angelic spirit. Dee can sense the man's yearning. And now, for being a witness to what might yet be a gulling, he is filled with doubt. He believes in one part of his mind that this can only be showmanship, mere trickery on Kelley's part, and that just as it ever was, Łaski is only cozened because he *wishes* to be cozened; and yet Dee finds as he watches Kelley's face, who keeps murmuring Trithemius's words, that his own heart is beating faster than it ought and that he, too, is quick of breath.

And then it all changes, as it did in earlier Actions: his heart slows and, despite the fire, the room cools and next to him Łaski looks to have been overbled by some careless physician for his face is become sallow and waxen behind the beard. After a moment, there is release: an angelic spirit, and life and warmth flood the room.

It is not Uriel, Kelley tells them, but Galvah again, who tells Kelley—through Kelley—that he ought to have been in communication the day before, and that he would do better to hunt and fish after verity than God's creatures.

Łaski is impressed.

Kelley apologizes and tells Galvah that Count Olbrecht Łaski is among them and Galvah tells them that Łaski's name is in the Book of Life, which delights Łaski, who feels emboldened to ask a question, one that has obviously been on his mind for some time now.

"What can be said about the life of Stephen Báthory, King of Poland?" he asks, and hearing this, Dee starts. This is not the sort of thing you should ask angelic spirits. This is the sort of thing you ask dark spirits. He cannot stop himself glancing at the door: Is it shut? Yes. But is it locked?

After a moment Kelley speaks.

"Consider it," he says, which is no proper answer, and Łaski narrows his eyes.

"Well, then," he tries, "will Olbrecht Łaski, Palatine of Sieradz, have the kingdom of Moravia?"

Jesu, Dee thinks, that is even worse! He stops writing his notes, for these are not philosophical questions, but touch on matters of state. He understands now that Łaski has not given up the idea of a return to the fray in Poland. What chance now has Walsingham of diverting him back to Prague?

By now the room has become very warm, and very close, and

Dee's ears are thudding with his pulse, and Kelley is speaking in a very different sort of voice, deeper and more authoritative. "Measure yourselves," he parlays. "For what you were and shall be is already appointed. And what he was and is, and shall be, is not of our determination. His purposes are without end, yet to you there be an end. So therefore prepare yourselves, and when you shall be called upon, do that which is commanded. Many witches and devils have risen up against this stranger, but I will grant him his desire. Your names are in one book."

There is much more besides, for Galvah knows that Łaski has many enemies and even names Burghley and Walsingham among them, but Łaski has ears only for the promises he hears: that he shall be king over two kingdoms, protected under a cross, and that he shall overcome the Jews, the Saracens, and the Paynims.

Dee thinks fast.

"How shall Count Łaski fund such a venture? Should he seek the help of the emperor?"

Kelley—Galvah—hardly hesitates.

"He whom God hath armed," he says, "no man may prevail against, and whatsoever he takes in hand shall prosper, and he shall be helped here, there, and elsewhere, miraculously, so let him go, so soon as he conveniently can."

Łaski is delighted. His eyes are alight with pleasure and he is just leaning in to ask another question, or thank the angelic spirit perhaps, when there is a sudden terrible disturbance from elsewhere in the house, a ripping of its fabric and an upending of order that makes Dee leap to his feet. There is a great thundering beyond the door, and a vengeful splintering of wood and the charging stamp of many heavy booted feet on flagstones and Kelley seems to roll back from the dais as if struck faint, while Łaski rises slowly to his feet, all amazed, with his eyes popping in fright.

The moment before the door smashes open, Dee seizes the show stone and tosses it into the flames.

Then the door smashes open and in among the flying shards of wood there is a sudden surge of bulky men with staffs and swords and axes, all in red, to fill all space, and Dee cannot move before two or more of them in thick gloves seize him and fling him across the room where he lands against his shelves. Before he can even fall, he is snatched up again and thrust back against the books and pressed there by more men, their snarling faces inches from his own, their spit in his mouth as they bellow words at him that are too horrible to be understood. Łaski and Kelley are likewise pushed back and held in place by roaring men so that almost nothing can be understood.

And then above it all another voice, like a knife.

"Dee! Where is John Dee? Where are you, Dee?"

And there is still more splintered wood and now the crash of earthenware and Jesu! He recognizes that voice.

Hatton! It is Sir Christopher bloody Hatton. Sir Christopher bloody Hatton who has been itching to avenge himself on Dee, who had a few years previously sold him a ton of worthless ore from the New World, which turned out to be useless.

And now Hatton has at last caught Dee with his show stone and his altar, and he will swear blind that he found Dee conjuring for treasure, the punishment for which is death by burning. And Hatton's eyes are become like dark gemstones and he jigs from foot to foot and the light from his guards' lanterns catches the gold thread in the dark cloth of his doublet, and Dee has never seen a man so triumphant.

"I've got you now." Hatton laughs. "I've got you now, John Dee! Conjuring wicked and damnable spirits, is it? Or seeking buried treasure? You know the penalty for that?"

"I was not conjuring wicked spirits! It was the angel Galvah."

"Shut the fuck up!" the guard with his elbow across Dee's throat bellows in his face. "Shut the fuck up, you fuck!"

And Dee recognizes him as the sergeant at arms from whom he ran at Whitehall Palace earlier. He supposes him demoted, and so here is yet another man who'd like to see Dee brought low, and so for now there is nothing Dee can do save what he is told.

"You're fucked now, you little shitbag, John Dee! And now you and your friends are going to burn!"

⊕

CHAPTER FIVE

*The Beauchamp Tower, Tower of London,
third week of September 1583*

Dawn finds Dee awake, standing on a stool, staring through the bars of his cell onto Tower Green, down at the scaffold where Her Majesty's mother met her end, and he wonders if she had as many regrets on the morning of her death as he does now. Possibly, he supposes, though by all accounts she did not believe it was going to be done even as she mounted the scaffold because she saw her executioner had brought nothing with which a man might chop off a woman's head. So she made a brave, forgiving speech, confident that it would find its way to her husband's ears, and was then blindfolded and knelt to pray. When she was done, she heard a shout from someone on the scaffold and turned to it, stretching her neck, and—that was all she knew. The swordsman had hidden his sword under the straw. A mercy. Dee wonders what has happened to the swordsman since. Is he retired now, and sitting in a tavern, having drinks bought for him by men eager to hear about the Boleyn job?

"You all right, Doctor?" a Yeoman calls through the bars of the cell door.

"A little ale, if you have it?" Dee asks.

The man laughs.

"If it were up to me, Doctor, you'd have a sausage, too, but Sir Christopher Hatton has issued his orders."

Fucking Hatton.

"Any news of my wife?"

"None so far, Doctor."

"What about the others?"

"They've let the Polish fella go. On account of him being a count of Poland or some such. And the other one's down below."

"He's not—being racked?"

"No. He's just— To be honest, Doctor, he seems just a common villain, he is. He should be in the Tun or something."

He means the prison for the lowest sort of criminal, and Dee supposes that every society has its stratifications, so why should prison guards be different? As above, so below. They'd made this clear the night before, as they were brought downriver in one of the Queen's barges, and while Dee—for being a familiar figure among some of the guards—and Łaski—on account of being a count, and also on account of exuding the certainty that someone here was making a very big mistake for which they would be made to pay, and he to receive handsome recompense—were permitted to sit on a thwart, Kelley was pressed under the guards' feet to soak in slopping bilge water. He'd wept as they were brought through the Tower's watergate and he clawed at Dee, begging him to save him.

"Tell them I have a family!"

Which Dee had not known.

Anyway, it had done no good: they were all quickly separated, and Dee was taken to the Beauchamp Tower, where he was greeted with boisterous affection.

"Not going to blow us up again are you, Doctor?"

To much guffawing Dee had shown them he came unarmed. He was grateful, then, that they remembered his last stay in the Tower—when he had been more of a guest, rather than a conjurer of hellhounds. Still, they had to obey Hatton's orders, and so he was marched up to one of the cells and locked within, with only a privy bucket and some foul hay for company.

He sat where he had always sat when locked up in times past, in one corner so that he might keep an eye on the top of the steps, and once the ravens had finished their noisy roostings and the bell for compline had rung, he fell asleep and dreamed of Jane, his wife, whom even now he oftentimes calls Frommond, and his son, Arthur. He sees them in his house in Mortlake and upon the roof are animals that might be monkeys and they carry flaming torches and he shouts in his sleep and wakes himself and finds he sits in the dark, his shirt drenched in sweat and his heart pounding.

After that he dares not sleep again, but stands at the window and is awake to hear the first bell. The ravens noisily rouse themselves and Dee watches the dawn fill the sky, then the castle's ward, but it is not until later in the morning that he sees the sun clip the uppermost battlements of the White Tower just as if it were emerging from within, and it is just then that Walsingham comes.

"Well, Dee, you have done it this time."

"Save it, Walsingham. I'm not interested in anything you have to say."

"No? You don't want me to take a message to Her Majesty?"

"Would you?"

"No."

"Well then."

Walsingham summons the guard.

"Give him some ale, for the love of God, and some bread and soup."

"He's not to be given nothing, sir, on Sir Christopher Hatton's orders."

"Oh, fuck Hatton."

"Right you are, sir. Right away."

"And bring me a stool."

When it comes, Walsingham sits beyond the bars and says nothing, not until the ale arrives and some pottage and bread that Dee, with no pride in such things, eats with gratitude. Any fool can be uncomfortable, unless the food is poisoned.

"So Hatton has you, Doctor, right where he wants you."

Dee nods. That's undeniable.

"Who was it?" he asks.

"Łaski's servant. Edmund Tanfield."

"One of yours?"

Walsingham shakes his head sadly.

"I had thought so," he says, "but he is as thick as Ash Wednesday's turd, so."

Dee pictures this a moment and puts aside his soup.

"We were not conjuring evil spirits," he tells Walsingham. "Nor seeking buried treasure, you know? And we harmed none."

Under Lord Burghley's Act of 1563, only those who conjure harm can expect to be burned.

"Hatton's found someone from Letchworth who's given birth to a child with the feet of an eagle. Says you cursed her."

Dee manages a wheezy laugh.

"Letchworth? Christ."

There is a long silence.

"So, anyway, Walsingham, it was good of you to drop by, but can I just ask why?"

Walsingham doesn't answer for a moment, and suddenly now Dee sees it, sees it all.

"Oh Jesu," he murmurs. "No. I won't do it, Walsingham. I won't whatever it is you want me to do. I'd rather burn."

And Walsingham laughs.

"Oh Christ, stop being so dramatic, Dee. You've no idea what I am suggesting."

But he does.

⊕

Later, and at last, Jane comes, and Dee is off his feet and at the grate in an instant.

"John," she says, "I leave you for a week and you get yourself condemned to death?"

It's a line she's rehearsed on the way down from Mortlake perhaps, but halfway through her chin begins to wobble, and by the time she reaches the word *death* she is choking with grief.

"Jane," Dee says, taking her hands in his through the bars. "Jane. It is not what it seems."

"No?"

She pulls away and wipes her snot with the back of her glove, an extraordinarily un-Frommond-like thing to do.

"We were not— Well. It was— I cannot say," he stammers. "We did nothing wrong; nothing that is against any law, but that is of course—"

"—neither here nor there?"

He nods.

"So who is behind it? Roger says Sir Christopher Hatton led Her Majesty's Yeomen personally. Can he hate you so much?"

Dee is unsure if he ever told Frommond where his money came

from, or how much of it there was. It all went to books, of course, and chemicals, and glassware. And meat and drink, too. It was not as if he was at the Greenwich Armoury having himself fitted up for a suit of tournament armor. Would that he had.

"I think he does, rather," Dee admits.

"But there will be a trial? They cannot just— Can they?"

"A trial, yes. They have to have that. But—"

"—But what about Her Majesty? She loves you! She will not let you die like this. She cannot. I will go to her. She must just not know you are here."

"She does, Jane. She does. But listen. Please. For a moment. Walsingham has been. He came from Bess. From Whitehall. She... he, really, I suppose . . . together they have a— Well, it is not so much a plan as an offer. Bess does not want me burned. Of course she doesn't, but there is only so much she can do to thwart Hatton, who does. And she cannot make an enemy of him. And she cannot be seen to break her own laws. So. She has sent word that, should I accept it, I am to be . . . to be exiled."

"*Exiled?* From England?"

"Yes, instead of being burned. It sounds better, no?"

"A bit."

She sniffs. The weight and speed of this day's events are too great to be grasped.

"And will he accept that?" she wonders. "Sir Christopher?"

"Walsingham has devised a duty for Hatton that will take him north, to Suffolk, for a few days. And if by the time he returns, I am gone, then there is nothing he can do about it."

"A few *days?*"

"Five at the most. I am permitted to come to Mortlake tomorrow to collect that which I need, and then I must go— It is best to be safe than sorry."

"Tomorrow *night*?"

"If Hatton were to hear—" He need not finish the sentence.

Jane says nothing. She can scarcely look at him.

"It is not so bad," he promises. "I will go overseas. To Holland. Or elsewhere. And when I am settled, I will send for you. You have always wished to travel."

Both know this is pitiful stuff.

"Or it may be that Her Majesty will permit my return before too long."

"To what, though? You are utterly disgraced. There is nothing for you here now."

Dee nods. It is harsh, but fair, and she, of course, having been so long at court, knows of what she speaks.

"Whatever were you thinking of, John? With a new scryer and a count of Poland?"

"I know. I know. But Kelley has the gift, Jane, and in such abundance. I believe we had better contact with the messengers of God than ever did the prophets of the Old Testament. I have never seen or heard of anything like it. You should see my notes. Tables of the names of God's angelic spirits. And we are to prepare a book in Adamic, which will unify not just Christendom, but beyond, too."

She looks at him so sorrowfully that he cannot bear to tell her they only have forty days to complete it.

"And how is Arthur?" he asks.

"Very shaken to find you gone and the house so ill-used, but Nicholas gave him the parting gift of a rabbit, so that has kept him happy."

Dee feels his throat block with misery. Will the boy be permitted to see him off?

"I'm sorry," he tells her again.

"What is your plan?" she asks.

"I have friends. In Leuven."

"Though that is occupied by the Spanish at the moment," she reminds him.

A good point.

"And beyond. Prague, for example."

"*Prague?* But that is hundreds and hundreds of miles away. Months of travel."

He nods. He knows.

"Will you just trust me on this, Jane?"

She cannot hold his gaze.

"All will be well," he promises her, "on all that I hold dear. I know it sounds—I know it appears—odd, and not good. *Jesu*, bad, I mean. I know it appears bad, but you must trust me, please. It will work out. You will see. This is not an ever-farewell, I swear on my soul."

They talk more, and with each sentence Dee makes himself sound more ridiculous. He knows it, but he has nothing else to offer, nothing solid he might tell her, and at length they both need reminding that however bad this is, at least he is not to be dragged up to Smithfield to be burned as a conjurer.

Just before Jane leaves, he once again checks he cannot be overheard, and he leans forward and asks her to be very careful when clearing the ashes of the fire.

⊕

CHAPTER SIX

Gravesend, that morning, last week in September, 1583

"But still," Dee reminds them, "it could be worse."

It is dawn, and here they are, six men and a single woman gathered on a quay in Gravesend: Doctor John Dee with his servant, Roger Cooke; Edward Kelley with a woman named Joanna whom he swears to be his wife; and Count Olbrecht Łaski, the Palatine of Sieradz, his royal crimson hidden this morning under a fur-lined traveling cloak, with his servant from Winchester House and another who can speak no English. The shame of being deported weighs lightly upon the count's shoulders, Dee notes. It has happened before, of course, and perhaps he was given some small compensation?

No one says a thing. Each stands turned to the choppy broth of the spume-flecked sea, eyes clenched against the salt-laden wind whipping off the water to fill their noses with the smell of mud and fish guts, while below—worryingly far below—lie two low-gunwaled, open-decked boats, each twenty paces long, tied to the quay on straining ropes.

Around them are piled all the crates and coffers and tied bundles that Dee has managed to salvage from the wreck of his professional life: his astrolabes, his globes, his various cross-staffs, and about eight hundred books. To see them off is a thin, unwelcome crowd of locals among whom word has gotten out who Dee is, and what he and his companions have been doing, and the mood is ugly.

"Well," Dee says, "we'd best get the ships—Are they ships? They are scarcely better than punts—loaded."

"Might as well chuck all this straight in the water," Roger Cooke tells him, "and jump in after it ourselves," and Dee fears he may be right. Cooke has, very reluctantly, agreed to join him in exile, if only for the first three months, and even then, only if he likes it, and Dee senses he will bolt at the first chance. All it will take is a single thrown stone, which could happen at any moment.

"Nevertheless," Dee says, and he helps Cooke and Łaski's servants haul his boxes from the wagons and pass them down to the waiting boats. Dee tries to remember if there was ever a time he felt more desolate than now. When he was first arrested by Queen Mary's men and taken to the Tower? When Isobel Cochet died in his arms? When he was locked in the river barge and realized he would starve or drown or be eaten alive by rats? Time had softened each event, but this wound—exile from his Queen, his country, his wife and child—is still bloody and raw.

Still though: it could always be worse. Just.

Hatton has been gotten out of the city—sent to Suffolk, Walsingham told Dee, to try to inject some urgency into the building of a new gun fort in the town of Orford, which will have control of the river Alde, and thus access to the old Duke of Nor-folk's castle at Framlingham. Any news of Dee's exile has been suppressed lest anyone in Hatton's household hear of it and send word to their master, so Dee was able to fillet what he needed from his laboratory and library unbesieged by Hatton's men—or his creditors—and he and Cooke had left in the dead of a moon-less night, on two barges, which they loaded from the water steps at the end of the orchard. They were rowed eastward along the river to Southwark, to Goodman Fern's, a friend of Dee's who owns a pottery with a warehouse on the muddy staithe.

Here they unloaded Dee's possessions into two wagons and when the work was done, they were met by Count Łaski, who had discovered his own reasons for wishing to be away from South-wark without attracting undue attention—creditors, in the main; failed business ventures, too, as well as a possibly hefty bribe from Walsingham. They had rolled on through the night, ever eastward through Bermondsey, Deptford, and Woolwich, finally reaching Gravesend just before dawn. Here they found Kelley waiting for them, with a black eye and a wife, Joanna, whom he seemed to hate, and who seemed to hate him even more fiercely.

But still, of course, they all agreed it could be worse.

Now, though, as they wait to clamber down onto the slimy planks of already overladen boats, that may not be so true: Is it better to drown or burn? Or perhaps be stoned to death by some of Gravesend's finest, eager to get their hands on Dee's treasures, and on Łaski's cloak?

"We'd best be off then, I think," Dee decides, and down they climb, on rotting rickety steps, Dee and Cooke and Kelley in the first; Łaski, his two servants, and Kelley's wife in the second. The restraining ropes creak alarmingly, and the murky brown water laps at the gunwales, and when the master of the second boat unhooks the painter, it comes off with a springing twang and Kelley's wife screams as the boat sinks deeper into the water.

"We shall sink!" she cries.

"Nothing to worry about!" the young master shouts, but it's a shout born not from confidence, but from the desire to be proved right about something, and Dee supposes him to be of about fifteen winters, still with peachy cheeks, and Cooke nudges Dee's elbow and nods at the boy.

"Wonder if his da knows he's taking us out?"

It is a concern, Dee has to admit. The boy pretending to be master of the boat on which Dee finds himself is the boatman Jiggins's nephew, whom Jiggins claimed made his living smuggling Jesuits into England, "and always willing to take something back," while a friend of his is master of the second boat. Neither inspires confidence, in part because of their youth, and in part because when the first of them claims there is nothing to worry about, he is wrong, for there is: the stiffening breeze is keeping each boat pinned against the quay, and there seems no way to get out into the channel, and now the crowd of locals have come to line the quay above, looming over and staring down at them with expressions Dee can only describe as hungry.

"We will row!" he calls out, and as the two hands push off from the timbers of the quay, they must dip their oars into the split-flint waters and start to pull, and the reluctant boats are so heavy and low in the water that even the smallest waves threaten to breach the gunwales and it is then that the first stone is flicked, maybe kicked, maybe even accidentally, from above, and then there is a flurry as men, women, and children on the dockside stoop to pick up more, bigger, better stones, and soon they are rowing under a fusillade of pebbles and terrible blunt insults.

"Keep rowing!" Dee shouts. "Keep on!"

They inch out into the waters, opening up a gap of ten paces, fifteen paces, and still the stones come. One skitters across the deck and catches Kelley's shoulder and he drops his oar in the water and the master calls him something terrible and tells him his da will kill him, and that they will have to pay for it, but they are moving so slowly Dee is able to fish the oar out, and then behind them there comes an anguished cry from Kelley's wife, and then another, and, after a third stone hits Dee, he has had enough. It is time to resurrect his role of conjurer of damned souls and wicked hellhounds, and he sets aside his oar and turns to the crowd and spreads his arms for balance. He hopes he looks like a terrible, engorged bat, some satanic conjurer about to cast a terrible spell, for he knows them likely to be simple stupid superstitious folk, and he is right: seeing him like this they drop their rocks and their stones and as one they turn and flee.

Dee is part ashamed, and part delighted, and in the boat behind, Łaski laughs.

"Some power you have, Doctor!" he shouts, and they slow their rowing, and it is only then that they hear the deep rumble of swift-moving horses on the shore, and into sight above the line of the quay come the heads of men in helmets, moving fast. Horsemen, perhaps ten of them, in Her Majesty's red, clearing the stone-throwing locals from the dock. Dee's part shame becomes part relief, but his part delight now turns to consternation: Who are they, these Yeomen, and what do they want?

They mill around, turning their horses in tight, neighing circles, looking for further purpose now that the locals are gone, until a new man is seen, in a dark hat and cloak. He dismounts and comes to the quay's edge where he stands with his fists on his hips, and he watches them with his hard, grim expression on his face.

Hatton.

"Christ," Cooke murmurs. "What's he doing here?"

"He must have— Oh Jesu. Some accursed trick of Walsingham's, no doubt."

Dee salutes him ironically. He feels there's little chance this will not go horribly wrong. Hatton does not reply. He turns and shouts something over his shoulder at one of the horsemen, and a moment later the dismounted soldier comes to the quayside with an arquebus.

Dee's heart freezes.

"Row!" he shouts. "Row!"

And the makeshift crews set to, arms ringing, chests heaving as they dip and haul for all they are worth. Dee glances over his shoulder.

Jesu!

The first Yeoman has sparked his tinderbox, and his face is smogged in smoke while his tinder takes flame. A moment more and he'll be ready to light his fuse. Meanwhile other Yeomen join him, and they, too, have brought their guns and stands, and they're loading them with powder and shot, and if Dee and the boats are not out of range, then it'll not be stones they need to duck, but iron balls fired at terrible speed.

On they row, but by God the boats are like cows in the water, and they can still hear Hatton bellowing on the quay.

"Shoot them! Aim for the one in black! Do not let him get away."

Then comes the first boom of the first gun from the quay, and there is a wobbling thrum in the air and maybe even a blur of something dark that rips past Dee's ear and kicks up a pock in the dirty brown water beyond the boat's bow. The young master of the first boat laughs.

"Fucking wankers!" he shouts.

But the shot has passed through a length of rigging, which after a moment parts with a snap, and runs quickly through a block hoisted to the masthead, which comes down with a rattle, hits a battened hatch on the deck with a crack, and bounces smartly back to clock the boy on the side of his head with a hollow *clonk*. He falls slack, and only Cooke's quick grab of his collar saves him going overboard. The boat yaws.

"The tiller!" Dee shouts.

Cooke grabs it and straightens the boat. Another crack of powder, and another miss. Then another, only this time Dee sees the cloth tear on the ball of Kelley's shoulder, leaving a livid wheal in the flesh, and Kelley gives a great hiss of pain. Dee hears one of Łaski's servants bellow in agony, too, and sees him thrashing about on his thwart until Łaski pushes him off into the footwell. But the Yeomen's first fusillade is done, and in the precious lull while they reload, the sluggish current catches the first boat's bow and turns her downstream, and one of the hands scrambles to raise a small foresail, which fills with a clumsy fumble, and at last the boat seems to move of its own accord.

Cooke lets out a little cheer, but that is almost instantly drowned by a fresh crackle of gunfire from the quay. One ball hits something—not somebody—in the second boat, but the other balls pock the water behind and around, and one of the other boat's hands is on his feet hauling the mainsail. When that fills she, too, catches the current and begins to narrow the gap on the first boat until there is one last shot that punctures the sail, which splits from top to bottom and flaps violently until the mate can lower it again, and meanwhile they must all keep rowing for their skins.

On shore Hatton is bellowing again and pointing wildly downriver and the Yeomen are hurrying back into their saddles, hoping for another opportunity to shoot at the boats, but a glance down the muddy estuary bank is all you need to know there's nothing for them there. It is just leagues of gray mud, unspeakably desolate.

The two boats wallow their way out into the choppy broth of the estuary under rust-colored canvas, and the sun is rising at last and there is cause for hope. Dee can see Tilbury Fort on the north shore, and for a moment he wonders how accurate her gunners might be? Can Hatton have alerted them, too? Surely not.

He stops rowing for a moment, the others likewise, and everybody catches their breath, and the boy at the tiller seems brought back to life, and the wounds of Kelley and Łaski's servant in the second boat seem not as serious as first thought. Everybody looks around at one another and there are even some faint smiles at the relief of their escape, though it is not certain they all know *why* they were being shot at in the first place, but then, before they can celebrate too long, a new problem: both boats are sinking.

"Get bailing!"

So they set to, with whatever vessel comes to hand: a bowl; a cup; and Łaski must use his fur hat. Still the waves slap the boats' hulls and spill over into the bilges and fill them as fast as they scoop it out. The tide is taking them farther out to sea, where the water is rougher yet.

They will never make it across the North Sea.

"We have to go back!" Dee tells the boy. He accepts it now and nods tightly, his face gray with shame, his knuckles white on the tiller. Dee bets he cannot swim, but he has no time for sympathy, for he must keep bailing if he wants to save himself and his precious cargo.

"Doctor," Kelley calls. "Look!"

He points to the shore over Dee's shoulder, and Dee turns to see the Yeomen have found a smugglers' track or something, a little farther back among the dunes perhaps, and are riding in a line, nose to tail, with Hatton at the back, shadowing them along the line of the shore. What a welcoming committee they will make.

"What about the other side?" Dee asks the boy. He means the estuary's north bank. The boy grimaces and shakes his head.

They must keep bailing, but it is a battle they are losing in both boats.

"We have to go in," Roger Cooke insists. "We must get ashore!"

"What about Hatton?" Dee wonders.

"It's only you he wants to shoot. The rest of us'll be fine."

I will remember that, Dee thinks, but anyway, it is not true, is it? Kelley will be burned, too. Dee looks to the shore. It is the dreariest thing he has ever seen; all there is to enliven it is the sight of the Yeomen in their red coats, riding hard in order to shoot him dead or capture him so that he may be properly burned. But then a thought strikes, and he wishes he had one of his friend Thomas Digges's spyglasses about him now, because he believes he can see in the distance, over a league or more of mudflats, the turrets of what can only be Cooling Castle.

"Master Cooke," he calls, "does this remind you of anywhere?"

Cooke looks up from his bailing and studies the flats with a sour expression.

"Sheppey," he says.

"Exactly. The Isle of Sheppey. Do you know it?" he asks Jiggins's nephew.

The boy shakes his head.

"Have you ever even been to sea before?" Dee wonders. The boy is fat lipped and filled with guilt. He shakes his bruised head.

"Well," Dee goes on, "that need not matter, for if my calculations are correct—and they are—then if we can hold this course without sinking for three leagues, and then manage to steer due south, we should by and by come to the mouth of the river Medway, across which we can sail, while our friends in red will have to follow it all the way upstream to cross it on the bridge at Rochester. On the other side is Sheerness, where, pray Jesu, we will find some vessels a little more seaworthy, and be halfway to Holland before they manage the transit."

✛

And so it proves, though by Christ it is a close-run thing, and to achieve it they must ditch some of Dee's most prized possessions, the thought of which fills his eyes with tears. Books, in the main, since they are the heaviest, and when they reach the mud-stained dockside of the Isle of Sheppey, he is left with only half of what he set off with.

"Good thing, too," is Cooke's opinion.

"Nothing too vital I hope, Doctor?"

This is from Łaski, strangely concerned for Dee's baggage.

"So long as I still have the stone," Dee reassures them all, "and my notes from the Action with Galvah, then all shall be well."

He feels sick just at the thought of having lost Mercator's globes, but he sees them there, in their dedicated box. Then he pats his doublet and feels the by-now-familiar weight of the show stone that he plucked from the still glinting ashes of his fire in Mortlake, and he knows that he speaks the truth. That, for now, is all that matters.

"Unload what is left," Dee tells them, "while I—"

He nods to the only ship of any decent size that is moored at the dockside, at which they have all been looking since first they rounded the head and saw Sheerness. It is a Dutch fluyt. Dee feels there is something familiar about it, with its figure-head of a cleverly fashioned swan, and there is a bearded sailor sat by its gangplank on a sack of something, peeling the bark from a stick. When Dee tells him what he wants, he looks Dee up and down.

"I do not look in the first state," Dee agrees, "but nor would you if you had just more or less swum from Gravesend."

The sailor spits onto the cobbles and then calls up to someone within the ship.

"*Meneer!*"

A head rises above the gunwale, five feet above Dee.

"Eh?"

They fix gazes on each other. The man breaks into a smile.

"I know you!" He laughs loudly. "You are Doctor Dee! I was supposed to kill you!"

It is *Meneer* Willem van Treslong, who was indeed paid to kill Dee on Nez Bayard in Brittany nearly ten years ago. The years have been kinder to him than they are to most sailors, Dee thinks, for though his face is much lined, Van Treslong still has all his limbs and most of his teeth. When he comes down the gangplank to embrace Dee, he does not smell too bad, and he is still wearing a pair of much faded but still wondrously baggy breeches.

"Tell me," he says, "because I know: you stole those letters, yes? Was it you or your Walsingham?"

"It was a long time ago, *Meneer*," Dee reminds him.

"I knew it! It was you!"

He laughs again. He must be the happiest sea captain alive, Dee thinks.

"I knew I should have killed you!" Van Treslong continues. "Come! Take beer with me! Jens, there! Another cup for my friend the doctor! He is a conjurer, they tell me, and if you are not quick, he will turn you into an onion, so snap snap."

The bearded sailor trudges up the gangplank.

"What brings you to Sheerness?" Dee wonders.

"My ship!"

Again Van Treslong laughs long and hard for a moment and then stops and is serious.

"Seriously. The rudder. Again. Shot out by that same Spanish galleon. I think he is haunting me, like I kill his son perhaps, you know? So we come in straight line, unable to get back to Brielle. It is what I tell the searchers, anyway. You know it costs forty pounds if you want them to look the other way? Forty!"

Precisely what—or who—Van Treslong is paying the searchers to smuggle in while they look the other way is a topic for another day.

The beer arrives, pleasingly sharp.

"So you don't look crisp, my friend?" Van Treslong asks. "You look like shit. And your party, they look even worse. Save who is fellow in cloak? I like the look of him."

Leave it to Łaski to continue traveling in style.

Dee explains.

"*Exiled?*"

"It was that or the pyre."

Van Treslong slaps a hand to his tall forehead.

"Doctor Dee! What did you do?"

"It is a long story," Dee admits. "Best told at sea. Is your rudder fixed?"

"She answers, I think."

"Take us to Holland."

Van Treslong looks tempted and a fee is set, far too high. Dee consults Łaski. Łaski tells him he will pay, just as Dee had hoped, and he passes him a purse of brown leather, so new the ties are still square. It occurs to Dee to wonder where Łaski's newfound wealth is come from, but he thinks he knows: Walsingham. A bribe, probably, and he wonders again why it is that Walsingham never bribes him—Dee—to do things. Only tricks him, or black-mails him.

Van Treslong is sat eating cheese when Dee finds him again, and he counts out half the coins, which vanish into those huge breeches.

"But we have to go now, *Meneer*," he tells him. "Right away."

Van Treslong chuckles.

"I *know* you know how tides work, Doctor."

"Can we at least board?"

Dee means to lie low, and Van Treslong makes a "be my guest" gesture, and so the remaining coffers must be moved for the fifth time that day, but there are fewer than there were, and also they have an extra servant: Jiggins's nephew, whose father's old skiff now lies sunk in the waters off the dock.

"I'd be safer in Holland than in England when my da finds out."

So they load what is left into the hold of the fluyt, and while the others take to the cabin to try to sleep, Dee keeps watch on deck. There are only five hundred paces across the mouth of the river, but as many as a half a dozen leagues upriver to the bridge at Rochester, and then a further ten or so leagues back to Sheerness. A hard day's ride, but what if Hatton has his men requisition boats? No time at all, and as the afternoon wears by, the chains of unease tighten across his chest.

"How much longer?" Roger Cooke wonders.

Van Treslong peers over the gunwale.

"Half hour."

"You trust him, Doctor?" Cooke asks when Van Treslong has gone ashore to talk to the searchers.

"Not really. Look."

He points out two silver medals that hang from a nail above the door to the cabin. One is a half-moon on which is inscribed

"Rather a Turk than a Papist," while its fellow—round, like a seal, bears the imprint of the Lamb of God on one side, and Holy Mary on the other, just the sort that the pope oftentimes distributes— for a price—along with indulgences against sin. Each might easily be removed.

Van Treslong is unashamed when he returns.

"Is smart, no?"

And it turns out they can trust him, but only just, for it is just as the sun is setting and a pinnace is at last towing the *Swan* out into the Medway channel that Hatton and his mounted Yeomen come clattering up the track from the west.

"Keep down," Dee tells them all. "And say nothing."

And they lie on the decks, out of sight below the gunwales, their cheeks pressed to the planks, and a moment later the fluyt is out into the channel, and the towline is detached, and it is too late to turn back now, even if they wanted to.

Dee catches Roger Cooke's gaze, who starts to laugh.

They can hear Hatton shouting.

"You there! Master! Master there! Turn about! Turn about in the name of Her Majesty!"

And Van Treslong winks at Dee as he turns on the spot by the whipstaff and then gives Hatton a wave.

"Give my regards to your Queen!" he calls. "Tell her *Meneer* Willem Bloys van Treslong of the Dutch Republic will come calling next time he is in Greenwich! Tell her I will bring licorice!"

Dee cannot see Hatton, but he can imagine his face. He even imagines him stamping his foot. What he does not imagine is him giving his orders to his Yeomen to dismount and prepare a final, pointless salvo into the stern of the *Swan*. But this is what Hatton does, and that is what his men do: they spark up their tinderboxes and their fuses, and they load their guns and set them on their

74

stands, and they aim them as best as they can now, since the target is moving so slowly from them, and they touch their fuses to their powder and the powder explodes and expands and sends the balls in their barrels hurtling across the widening chasm between ship and shore, and this is an uncountably short time before Jiggins's nephew stands to shout something defiantly foul, only to be silenced by the meaty thwock of a ball as it tears through the soft tissue under his chin and then an inseparable gristly crunch as it breaks his neck.

His body falls among them, dead before it hits the deck, and he lies with his arms thrown out, head at an impossible angle, his face tilted to Dee and in his eyes an utterly baffled expression, and there is blood everywhere from his tattered throat.

"Oh sweet Jesus!"

Van Treslong is ducked, crouching by the whipstaff.

"Arseholes!" he snarls.

But there is nothing to be done, and not much to be said. They must stay their course, and when at length the *Swan* is obviously beyond gunshot range, they stand, one by one, to peer back at the Yeomen on the dockside, who do not know they have killed a boy and are congratulating one of their number on his marksmanship, and Hatton stands there, furious and unplacated, which is at least something.

A short moment later Van Treslong gives the order to raise sail and the ship's crew—bearded Jens and six others in leather jerkins and sailors' slops—set about it, and when first the bowsail then the mainsail is raised, the wind fills the canvas with a soil thump and the ship comes to life under them. Van Treslong sets a course eastward toward Holland, and Dee says a prayer over the body of the boy whose name they do not even know, and then between Cooke and Kelley and the two Polish servants, they lift the boy and tumble his broken corpse over the stern and into the freshening waters of the North Sea. Dee stares back at the coast of Kent as it disappears into the sea mist and wishes for a bucket in which he might wash the innocent blood from his hands, and he wonders why he ever, even for a single moment, thought it might end any other way than this.

PART | TWO

PART TWO

CHAPTER SEVEN

Receiving Room, Whitehall Palace, that evening,
last week in September 1583

Rain now, and a wind down the chimney, batting enough woodsmoke back into the room to make Lord Burghley cough. He is in black again this evening, as is Walsingham, as usual, while Her Majesty—somewhat recovered from her recent illness—wears velvet the color of old blood, the minimum of jewelry required for her station, and she rests her tired head on her cocked hand.

"Well?" she asks. "Any word of him?"

She means Sir Christopher Hatton.

"None so far," Walsingham admits.

The Queen emits a long angry sigh.

"You should never have told him," she says, and Walsingham and Burghley must freeze in silence, for it was not *they* who told Sir Christopher, but *she*.

It had happened the previous evening, during a curtailed

audience in Her Majesty's Privy Chamber, when it transpired that Hatton had turned back from his mission to Orford, having learned upon the road that there is plague all along the east coast, from Harwich to Happisburgh, which includes Orford, and, after a fourth hard day in the saddle, he had reached his house in Saint Benet's, only to learn from his barber that Dee had been released from the Tower at the Queen's say-so.

He had come straight to Whitehall, that instant, the soap still in his ears, to find Her Majesty in her Privy Chamber, still very weak, but managing a small beer and a honey-roasted quail and speaking to Walsingham and Burghley in a voice so feeble it would shame a child.

"I have sent my barber from me," Sir Christopher had announced, "because I presumed him misinformed?"

"No. Well, you'd better get him back," Burghley had told him, his voice croaky with suppressed laughter, because Hatton really was an ass, but Hatton had ignored him and wheeled instead on Walsingham, whom he blamed for this.

"You had me arrest him, Walsingham!" he snarled. "You sent me all the way to godforsaken bloody Mortlake to catch him conjuring and to drag him back to the Tower, and now you let him *go*?"

Had he been standing at a table he would have banged it with his fist, but Her Majesty's Privy Chamber was no place for such histrionics.

"Her Majesty has not let him go, Hatton," Walsingham had told him, more forcibly than was necessary perhaps. "She has sent him from her and banished him from the realm."

Hatton had been stunned.

"*Exile?* You are merely going to send him into exile? Since when was exile the punishment for conjuring? You wrote the bloody law,

Lord Burghley! And besides! That accursed pest will go only so far as Holland where he will offer his alchemy services to William the Silent, and every week he will petition Your Majesty to have him back! You cannot allow this, Your Majesty! He must be burned! To set an example! How will it look to other Christian princes if we allow such things in your realm, Your Majesty?"

The Queen held up a hand.

"Please, Sir Christopher," she had croaked. "I am not well."

And so the next few minutes had passed in emollient inquiries as to Her Majesty's health, which was bad again, until there was nothing more to say, after which Sir Christopher could not resist resurrecting the subject of John Dee.

"Hatton," Burghley had said, "we could not burn all three men, could we? One was a Polish count, for the love of Jesus, and we cannot just *burn* them."

"They have all gone together? Including that ugly little cozener Kelley?"

"What could we do, Sir Christopher?" Walsingham had reasoned.

"You could have let justice be done, and the law run its course!"

All of them had known how absurd this sounded. Justice is never done; the law never just runs its course.

"We know well how it looks, Sir Christopher," Her Majesty had told him, very faintly and uncharacteristically apologetically, "but it is not how it seems, and . . . and . . . there we are. Besides, the thing is done now and he has this night—"

Walsingham had coughed a warning and the Queen had stopped midsentence and looked at him with her mouth agape.

"He has this night *what*, Your Majesty?"

The Queen's eyes had swiveled to Walsingham.

"Jesu, Hatton, can you not see Her Majesty is unwell?" Walsingham barked, but that did not stop her finishing the sentence she had started.

"He has this night quit our realm."

Hatton had become furious.

"Dee has *gone*?" he'd snarled, at Walsingham, whom he blamed squarely for this. "You mean Dee has *already* escaped?"

"Oh, I do not know!" the Queen had mewed, helplessly, and then before Walsingham had had the time to intervene, the time to tell Hatton to leave the room for it was clear Her Majesty was not well enough for all this, he had been reminded that however vainglorious Hatton was, and however much a preening peacock he was, Her Majesty still felt great affection for him, and so he should not really have been that surprised when her next sentence had dribbled out.

"You must do what you think best, gentlemen."

And then she had begun to weep and a moment too late, suddenly from the shadows, Mistress Parry had appeared among them, a bustling, foursquare domestic tyrant.

"That is enough, gentlemen," she'd snapped. "Shame on you! Shame on you! Stooping to rancorous discourse while Her Majesty is clearly sick. Away with you, sirs! Be gone! One and all!"

And there had been no gainsaying her.

On the way out, back to their respective barges, Hatton had said nothing, but he had been bouncing with purpose and had vanished into the dark with no farewell or good night.

"I'd watch him if I were you, Francis," Burghley had said. "He means to see Dee burn."

Walsingham had dismissed the idea.

"Surely he'd never cross Her Majesty."

"She didn't tell him to leave Dee be, did you notice? She's still half smitten with the fool, of course. It's Hatton's calves, apparently: they drive women wild, though I detect a whiff of pederasty about him, don't you?"

"He is a very fine dancer," Walsingham had agreed, but there was as yet no evidence to suggest a penchant for boys.

"Well, anyway," Burghley had said, drawing his fur around his shoulders as he stepped on the gangplank of his barge, "I have some beautiful women to find, and no doubt you've got someone watching him, so I will bid you good night, Francis."

⊕

And that had been that until the short hours of the next morning, when word was brought to Seething Lane that Dee had made good his escape, on two barges, to Southwark, and then by wagon eastward, presumably to Deptford, or Gravesend or somesuch, and Walsingham had been pleased to have been woken to hear the news and fell asleep with a smile on his face. But he was less pleased to be woken again, a few hours later, to take word from a boy sent by Arthur Gregory, the man whom Walsingham had set on Hatton, to say that Her Majesty's chancellor and captain of the Yeomen of the Guard had personally taken a dozen troopers on horseback with him over the bridge into Southwark, in a hurry, and that Gregory was in pursuit.

Since then Walsingham has heard nothing of Hatton, nor of Gregory, nor of Dee, and now here he is again, with Burghley and Her Majesty, once more at Whitehall, to learn that although Her Majesty is strong enough to sit in the Receiving Room, she has forgotten it was she who told Sir Christopher Hatton that Dee was making his way overseas.

"It is unfortunate, Your Majesty," Burghley dares to suggest, "but John Dee makes for elusive prey, as you know, and good Sir

Christopher will be hard-pressed to search every port along the southern coast with just six men."

The Queen scoffs.

"You know very well Dee will have gathered up every book as he can, along with all his globes and staffs and whatnots, kissed that wife of his goodbye, and taken a barge from Mortlake to one of the docks before the bridge, and there loaded them into something more seaworthy to take him to Brielle or some such. It takes no genius to divine that."

Burghley and Walsingham both stare at the floor, for both know that that is exactly what Dee has done.

"And why was Sir Christopher back from Suffolk so soon?" Her Majesty now wheels on Walsingham as if it were his fault. "I thought you said he would be gone for a week or more?"

When he had sent Hatton to put the fear of the wrath of God into the work-shy masons at Orford, Walsingham had not banked on him traveling so quickly. The roads at this time of year were not bad, but still he reached Ipswich in two days, and then, when he was told there was plague along the coast, it took him only two to get home again.

"If Sir Christopher had managed to catch Dee before he boarded at Gravesend it would have been just after dawn," he reminds them, "and he'd have brought him back in triumph."

"But he cannot think to challenge our authority on this, can he?"

Burghley tweaks his ear, as he does when he has something sensitive to say.

"Your Majesty left it somewhat vague last night," he tries to remind her.

"We were ill, Lord Burghley. We hardly expected to be ambushed in our own Privy Chamber, and to have our word taken as gospel."

Nevertheless, neither of them says, that is what happened. And it is just then that word comes that Arthur Gregory is at the watergate with an urgent message for Sir Francis.

"Send him up," Burghley says, eager for distraction, but Walsingham is just as eager for escape, and anyway, he would rather see him alone. Also, he knows Gregory. The thought of the man in Her Majesty's Receiving Room is absurd. So he meets him down by the guardhouse and is once again impressed by the way in which his most reliable agent is able to emerge from any background and slowly manifest himself so that you see he was there all along.

"Oof," Walsingham says, for Gregory stinks of salt marsh, old sweat, and horses.

"Yes," Gregory agrees. "Long day of it."

"And?"

Gregory explains Dee's escape, and despite himself, Walsingham is powerfully relieved.

"And did you get a name of this fluyt?"

"The *Swan*, out of Brielle, captained by a Dutchie named Treslong."

Van Treslong! What was he doing in Sheerness? Dropping off some Jesuits, no doubt.

"And there is one other thing, though, Sir Francis."

"Oh?"

"I followed Hatton back. Force of habit, I suppose, and anyway, we were both going the same way."

"And?"

"And he didn't go home. He went to a house just off Saint Paul's Wharf."

"Not—?"

"Aye. Throckmorton House."

"Did he go in?"

"Around the back."

Jesu, what does that mean?

Walsingham thanks his agent.

"Now go home and take a bath, will you?"

Gregory scoffs and slips away into the shadows, leaving Walsingham with much on his mind. Throckmorton House is the home of Sir Francis Throckmorton, cousin of Bess Throckmorton, one of the Queen's ladies in waiting. Walsingham believes Throckmorton to be the courier of messages between Queen Mary of Scotland, the Duc de Guise, and Walsingham's old friend Monsieur de Castelnau, the French ambassador.

So what does that mean?

He will have to find out.

In the meantime, he must return to the Receiving Room to break the news of Dee's escape across the sea.

Burghley is astonished.

"Hatton *shot* at them? He actually *shot* at Count Łaski?"

There is a strong tinge of admiration in his voice.

"And to think I actually played bowls with the fellow," he goes on, meaning Łaski, not Hatton, with whom he would never play bowls for fear of being thrashed. "And I let him win, too. Well. Well."

Her Majesty looks at Burghley as if it might be time for him to retire, but then the old man bounces back.

"But it is perfect, for no doubt *Meneer* van Treslong and his crew will soon be spreading the story of their miraculous escape through every dockside tavern from Ostend to Alkmaar, whence it will soon reach the ears of those who matter. Yes. It has all turned out excellently. Congratulations, Your Majesty! Involving Sir Christopher was a masterstroke. It will convince everyone we meant to get rid of Dee one way or the other."

Walsingham almost laughs—that is how you retain Her Majesty's favor for so long, he thinks—and Burghley acknowledges his unmade point with a closed-eyed smile and a barely discernible nod.

"We must think of some manner of a reward for him," the Queen says, meaning Sir Christopher, her dancing chancellor, who once gave her a necklace with the specific instructions she was to wear it between her breasts—"the chaste nest of pure constancy"— which would be fine, in a girl of twenty, but . . .

"Very generous, Your Majesty."

Then she wonders, with a great long sigh, why Hatton and Dee so hate each other.

"It is mystery," Walsingham finds himself saying, though surely every other man, woman, and child along the Thames must know how Hatton forced Dee to sell him that ton of worthless ore? For some reason he cannot put his finger on, though, he does not tell Her Majesty this, nor does he share news of Hatton's visit to Throckmorton House.

But, he thinks, perhaps the time is come to reel in its owner.

⊕

CHAPTER EIGHT

Brielle, Holland, later that week, the last in September 1583

W hen the *Swan* is tied up, and the gangplank drawn out, Count Łaski is off the ship first and he stoops to kneel and kiss the dirt. Van Treslong stands at the gunwale, admiring the count's rear thrust in the air.

"Is very big, you know?" is his opinion, which he shares with Dee. "Like prize porker. But in Holland we have saying you need big hammer to knock in big nail."

He laughs. A little Van Treslong goes a long way, Dee has discovered over the last twenty-four hours while they have been at sea—in the first part making good progress through the night before a southwesterly breeze, until just before sunrise, when they became almost becalmed as the winds died and fogbanks bloomed along the Zeeland coast, shrouding the shore and the sea-lanes into Brielle—but now here they are and there is no denying the captain is a very useful man to have on your side. He is treated as a hero in these parts, and he knows whom to bribe—and how much of Łaski's money is needed—to get the searchers to look the other way while Cooke and Łaski's servants unload the rump of Dee's possessions onto the dockside. They are down to ten pine coffers and a balding horsehide bag. Dee still has those globes, though, and his astrolabe and cross-staffs.

Low clouds scud overhead, and a hundred thousand wheeling seagulls scream all at once, and everywhere along the quays men and boys are equally strident about their business: pulling, pushing, lowering, or lifting their loads, foreign tongues aclack with harsh consonants, and is it Dee's imagination, or is this part of the world harder underfoot than it is in England? Kelley does not seem to think so, but he has been very sick on the boat and is now a very dispiriting sight, hunched in his dirty brown coat and hat, blood on his arm from his wound, brushing his lank hair down over his ears and staring at the busyness about him through resentful eyes. He stands about three paces from his wife, Joanna, both looking away from each other, as if the other is the source of the strong smell that always permeates all such places as Brielle. Dee does not think they exchanged a single word or look all voyage.

When the searchers are paid off—thank you, Count Łaski—Dee must hire yet another boat to take them north through all the inland waterways, and he chooses someone older than him this time, with narrow shoulders, a long nose, and unsettlingly close-set eyes. He answers to the name of something like Sean, and he watches while they load the ship's hold.

"So what now, Doctor?" Cooke asks when it is done.

"Time and tide, Master Cooke, you know that. And wind."

There is a stiff onshore breeze blowing from the north that smells of iodine.

"No," Cooke says. "That's not what I mean. I mean: What are you up to now?"

Dee looks at Cooke and wonders what to tell him. That he has nothing particular in mind, and that he only wants somewhere safe to unpack his bags and finish his *Book of Loagaeth*? Or that he has some particular aim in mind, something that he must do, and then, when it is done, they can return to Mortlake, rich men, anticipating the rest of their lives at honeyed ease?

"Prague," he tells Roger.

"*Prague?*"

"Our destination. We are traveling there with Count Łaski."

"Bloody hell," Cooke murmurs. "Prague is thousands of leagues from here."

Dee acknowledges the truth of this, but does not tell Roger that the city is in fact farther than he thinks—five months' travel—for they must go the long way there, avoiding France. He wants it to sound simple, logical, inevitable, when in fact it is anything but that, and when he first mooted the journey to Łaski in the moments after they had heard the Queen was prepared to spare their lives, Łaski too had been reluctant. He did not see the point. There was nothing for him in Prague. Dee had to remind him what the angels had said: "He shall be helped here, there, and elsewhere, miraculously."

"I am convinced it means the emperor will help you with your claim to the Polish throne!" Dee had claimed.

Łaski had been rightly doubtful.

"The emperor will not even see me," he'd said.

"He will want to see me, though," Dee said, pretending certainty. "Surely?"

"He will think I am bringing him yet another Cornelius de Lannoy. Yet another Protestant spy, only this one sent by your queen."

"No, surely? I am exiled! In absolute disgrace. My reputation ruined. Her Majesty will not even see me. And you saw those men: they shot at us. They shot at me. They want me dead. I could no more spy for Her Majesty than you."

Łaski had shrugged then. Why not? he seemed to think. Prague is not so bad, is it? And besides: he had no better idea.

And so now while they wait for the right wind, they take rooms in an inn, the best available.

"On me," Łaski tells them, and later he catches Dee alone.

"We have time?" he wonders.

"What for?"

Łaski looks askance and shifts his weight from foot to foot; it's clear he wants another Action with the angelic spirits. He needs encouraging to go to Prague perhaps? But Dee has likewise begun to fret about the *Book of Loagaeth*, which they have a mere thirty days now to write before their names are razed from the number of the blessed, and so he, too, is keen to hear if the angelic spirits will perhaps grant them an extension on the deadline. Kelley, somewhat recovered having been on dry land for an afternoon, reluctantly agrees to conduct an Action in the morning, should they still be here.

⊕

They are.

They send out the servants and Kelley's wife—who actually does smell, it turns out, of fresh-split flint and distant sewage—to buy provisions for the voyage, and the men set up in readiness, though they have only one stone and are missing all the other paraphernalia.

"I will send letter," Łaski announces. "Demanding return of show stone. Was a gift, you know? From rabbi in Poznań."

When Hatton had arrested them he'd scooped up everything he found as evidence of their wrongdoing, including Łaski's show stone, but he had not checked the ashes of the fire, of course, for why should he? He had what he wanted, and so the day Dee was released, he searched the hearth, which Frommond had left untouched, and brought out the still warm and—hopefully—unharmed stone.

This they now have before them, on a small coffer, in an upper room of an inn called the Watergeuzen overlooking the marketplace of Brielle, and Kelley is at prayer while they wait. At last something seems to happen: the noise of outside's bustle seems to die away and Dee hears only his own breathing, his own heartbeat; the room seems to close in on them, and next to him Łaski is waxen once more. Kelley shuts his eyes and addresses an angelic spirit who does not name himself and cannot be seen, for what can be seen is a building.

"A castle," Kelley says. "Above a city. Gray stone. A huge cathedral. A cold wind and a frozen river below."

"Prague," Dee whispers.

But nothing further is said about the castle, or the city, and a new angelic spirit appears: Jubanladace.

"All is well," Kelley conveys. "God has numbered the days of your future. Before then, give good thanks unto God for delivering you from the perils of the ocean, take heart to endure unto the end of your task."

Dee asks how things stand in England.

"Her Majesty's wrath wanes."

"And my wife? My son?"

"I am no fortune-teller. Consult whom you may."

And that is that. Nothing more is to be extracted from Jubanladace other than there is to be no extension to the deadline of the *Book of Loagaeth*.

The room cools again, and the sound of the marketplace is heard once more, and Kelley is restored to them, much to both men's disappointment.

"Well," Dee supposes. "Perhaps we can try again this evening? Unless the wind turns."

Thank God it does, but not before Dee finds space enough at a table in the hall down the steps, where at one end an old and very strong-smelling sailor sleeps with his curly gray hair spilling onto the stained wood, to take out his ink bottle, pontayle, and note-book and set to writing a letter to Jane, the wife whom he left with tears on her cheeks at Mortlake with their son by her side. Before he can put pen to paper, though, he balks, for the page is too small to contain what needs be said, and then he wonders if there is a piece of paper large enough in all Christendom to contain such matters. And in any event, Walsingham or one of his espials will read it, so this is not the way to express his true feelings, so Dee opts for brevity, and he greets Jane and commends himself to her:

We are come to the port of Brielle, after no little trouble on our departure that saw the loss of half my books, but I am consoled to believe they will wash ashore on some lonely reach where an enterprising soul will establish a library in my name, and thus is the light of knowledge spread. All is well here. Master Cooke remains steadfast, but EK has brought his wife when he might just as easily have bought a stone to put into his boot. The Four Horsemen stalk the land, and all is dear, but Łaski has come by some money (probably a bribe from Walsingham), and the road ahead is smooth, in that we travel by water, so I send my blessings to our son, and this through a messenger in the hope that it finds you thriving, my entirely beloved Jane, and this comes with love from: your Δ.

He signs the letter in a mist of tears at what is said and unsaid, and then he diverts himself by slicing the paper to make a lock of it with a strip inserted into a slit, more to excite the interest and stretch the patience of Walsingham's espials than in the belief this will keep its contents safe. Then he seals it with good wax and an impression of his ring, which, if looked at under one of Digges's magnifying lenses, is an exquisite engraving of his monad, a gift from Jane.

He is about to give the letter to Cooke to take to *Meneer* van Treslong, whose ship the *Swan* has likewise been awaiting a favorable wind to take him back to England perhaps, but then he decides to go himself. Dee gives the captain the letter, and as he sees it tucked away in the Dutchman's doublet, he knows there is a vanishingly small chance of it reaching its intended destination.

"Out of interest, *Meneer*," Dee asks, "what were you bringing to England?"

"To England? Oh. A man. A gentleman."

"Any idea who?"

"I was paid not to ask. Not to speak."

"And which medal did you show? Better a Turk than a Papist, or—?"

Van Treslong laughs and points at Doctor Dee as if he has discovered a largely unobserved truth about him.

"Ha ha! I see you Doctor Dee! You clever man."

"And?"

"And— Yes. Other one."

So a Catholic then.

"And where did you drop him? Not Sheerness?"

"Farther east. Arundel. On south coast. I go back for him in five days, take him across to Dieppe."

Arundel? Well, why not? A Sussex Jesuit then, homesick for the Downs, perhaps. Dee thanks him and is about to leave him, but there is one more thing he thinks to ask, just in case.

"Do you ever have any dealings with the Hanseatic League?"

He means the association of trading cities that control the Baltic Sea trade routes.

"Sure," Van Treslong says with a shrug. "In this line of work, you have to."

"Bremerhaven in particular?"

"Of course Bremerhaven. Is good city. You want passage?"

Dee feels sure Van Treslong is about to offer him a good price for another leg of this trip, and he's tempted, but no.

"Not there," Dee tells him. "But back. One day."

Van Treslong tells him the name of an inn where the rope-makers go.

"If I am in Bremerhaven, that is where you'll find me."

Dee thanks him again, and they part, not precisely friends, but each reminded the other exists.

It is about then that the wind changes, and suddenly the quay-side is all abustle as ships and boats are permitted to escape. Dee summons his reluctant party, including a somewhat drunken Łaski, who has traded his servant Alexander's coat for a second bottle of Genever, "against the cold, Doctor!"

⊕

The boat is not as rickety as those that brought them to Sheerness, but it is the shape of a rich man's cupboard, and it lumbers and butts through the quick-running currents, and even before they reach open water there is much seasickness aboard, and Dee must keep his eyes on the distant horizon as they follow the river north-ward beyond Rotterdam, aiming to pass through Amsterdam and sail then to another port named Enkhuizen.

"When will we have the time for another Action?" Łaski wants to know.

Already? Dee wonders. It has been scarce a day since the last one.

"It's hard enough to take a shit on this boat," Kelley mutters in that soft voice of his, "let alone summon an angel."

Łaski looks at him as if this reticence is somehow unmanly, and later, while Kelley is doing just that which he finds so hard, Łaski complains to Dee: "He says God forearm me against all enemies. He doesn't tell me how to become king of Poland or of Moravia."

"Let's just wait. Till we reach dry land. Dokkum. In a few days."

"Tcha."

Dee sits and tries not to think about home for he knows he will draw attention to himself by weeping if he does think about Jane, and about Arthur, and about Mortlake in general. He thinks instead about Walsingham and his schemes, and he forces himself to think about how his application for a grant of exploration on behalf of the Fellowship for New Navigations Atlantical and Septentrional might be faring, and he wonders at length if perhaps he ought not to change its name to something more memorable such as—what?—the Atlantic Company? Would that be better? You'd be more likely to award the Atlantic Company a grant of exploration than you would the . . . the . . . Christ. He can't even remember what his own company is called now.

Dee sighs. And there is still his *Book of Loagaeth*, which he is gradually filling in with the correct symbols as described by Kelley during their Actions with the angelic spirits. It is painstaking work, least easily done on a boat perhaps, but time is passing, and he needs this done properly.

⊕

CHAPTER NINE

Throckmorton House, Saint Paul's Wharf, one week later

"Here he comes," Robert Beale, Walsingham's private secretary, announces. "And in a hurry, too. Good."

They are standing at an upper window in a house belonging to a silversmith just off Paul's Wharf Hill watching—as if through a squint in one of those country churches—Sir Francis Throckmorton returning to his house farther down the street. They believe, with good cause, that he has just been delivered of a packet of letters from the Queen of Scots and has a date with Monsieur de Castelnau at the French Embassy, although he does not look in any way troubled, or haunted, or marked for death, as he in fact is, but, still in his late twenties, he possesses those flush-cheeked good looks you associate with men on the fringes of English aristocracy.

"Comes from having beef in your bowl when you're a boy," Walsingham tells Beale, "and your parents born in different counties."

Throckmorton is accompanied by just one servant and is followed, less usefully, by a beggar with a limp, propped up upon a stick and trailing bandages, whom Walsingham and Beale recognize as Arthur Gregory.

"He's good, isn't he?" Beale asks and Walsingham grunts agreement. Fifty paces down the street Throckmorton and his servant stop at the gate to Throckmorton House whereupon the beggar tries his luck, with none, and then stumps off swearing and gesticulating down the road toward the river. Throckmorton and his servant exchange a look and watch him until he is out of sight, whereupon a porter opens the gate, and they disappear within, the porter checking up and down the street before following them in.

Beale lets out a sigh.

"Shall we?" he asks.

"There's no rush. Let's give him some time to settle down and get to work."

So they pack up their coats, bags, notebooks, pen, and ink jar and descend the steps, thanking the silversmith as they pass out on to the street. It is a rare fine day, and it is as if they are carefree and at their leisure, and yet Beale has noticed a tremor in Walsingham's hands, and he knows that this show of control is exactly that: a show.

"Do you ever wonder how he got into all this?" Walsingham asks as they stroll down the street.

"Throckmorton?"

"Mm-hmm."

"Well, born a gentleman into a Catholic family—his mother was caught taking Mass from a seminarian in '76, wasn't she?—in Warwickshire or somesuch? And wasn't his uncle the man who suggested Her Majesty should marry the Queen of Scots?"

Walsingham laughs.

"I had forgotten that. Cecil showed me the letter. How all wise men would wish one of them turned into the shape of a man, or something, so they might marry and unite the kingdom. Still not sure if he was joking."

"Well. It didn't happen, anyway, did it?"

"No, Robert. It didn't. That is a good point, well made."

They walk on a few paces.

"So come on then," Beale says. "Why Throckmorton?"

"Ahh. Yes. I bent him that way myself, do you see? His father—also a Catholic of course, though not so fervid as the mother—was a member of Parliament for one of those towns on the Welsh Marches, as you say, and he rose to become Master of Court of Requests, did you know?"

Beale does not, precisely, but he can guess the sort of thing Walsingham means.

"And then he made a mistake," Walsingham goes on. "He judged in favor of a relative and brought the Court into disrepute. So we dismissed him and landed him with a fine. A thousand marks."

"Tsssssss."

"Because by then we'd learned he'd racked up at least four thousand in debts to various scriveners, cobblers, tailors, and what-have-yous. He owed his wine merchant four hundred marks alone. So it was the Fleet for him, which, sadly, did for him, as it so often does, and which meant, of course, all his debts passed onto his heir."

"Francis?"

"Exactly. But it was not just the debt, was it? It was the shame of it. The family name tainted. Couldn't get any positions. No way of earning any money. Nothing but this house here, and one in Lewisham. And three needy brothers."

"So with nothing left to him, and in search of funds, so as to be able to hold his head high in the sort of society he is used to, with the advantages his upbringing has taught him are his rights, Francis takes money as a messenger for recusants and foreigners? But you are watching him from the very start."

Walsingham tips his head. Beale does not know whether to be impressed or perturbed. His doubt communicates itself.

"It was not me who spent all my money with the vintner," Walsingham reminds him.

It's a good point, but it misses a larger lesson: that if you break a man, shame him, and degrade him, then he's likely to act against you. That's what Beale thinks, and is about to say, but then realizes there are so many men broken, shamed, and degraded whom you cannot save, and who would turn against you, anyway, and whom you cannot know about, so why not add one more to that number, whom you *do* know about, and who will most likely take any of the dirty dangerous jobs on offer, so that you can keep an eye on what those jobs might be? Genius, in its way, but is it moral to ruin a family, just like that? Maybe not.

"Ah, here he is," Walsingham says. "Master Gregory."

The beggar is back, having lost his bandages and his stick, and there is another man with him, huge, with arms like portcullis chains, and carrying an ax stout enough to behead an ox.

"Sir Francis, Master Beale," Gregory greets them. "This is Nathan Mercer, a friend of mine. The others are around the back."

"Good stuff," Walsingham says. "How many chimneys?"

"Only three, but all smoking. The one to worry about is in the room to the right of the door."

"Got your gloves?" he asks Beale.

Beale has.

"Good. Right. Let's give him one moment longer, shall we, so he can get really stuck in, and then—"

Both draw their swords, and after a breath, Walsingham gives a wide-eyed nod to Nathan Mercer, who takes one step back and then swings the mighty ax to split the door in two, top to bottom, with a splintering crunch. They shove the planks aside and press into the yard, shouting at the porter—an old fellow more accustomed to bullying beggars than fighting armed men—that they are sent by Her Majesty and he is on no account to touch the knife he carries in his belt or resist in any way or they will kill him, and he throws up his hands and staggers back and they pass across the small courtyard and in through the front door into the hall.

It's gloomy, with small windows and a brick-built chimney; to one side is the buttery and so on, but to the south is the old solar, its doorway curtained in heavy red cloth, in which they hear a wailing cry and some frantic scrabbling. Beale shoves the curtain aside. Within, seated at a table, is Sir Francis Throckmorton, his face blood-drained, while behind is a woman bent and busy, and feeding papers into the fire below the very chimney Arthur Gregory had warned them about.

Both men shout at the two to sit down, show their hands, and not move a muscle because sound is important in these moments: the more, the better. Beale is around the table fast. He pushes the woman aside, and she screams as she falls but he ignores her and pulls what he can from the flames. He's glad to be wearing his second-best pair of gloves. Throckmorton pushes the chair back and starts shouting, too: some confected outrage that they should treat a woman so, but Walsingham shouts back at him to shut up now, and since the room is secured, with Gregory and Nathan Mercer at the door, a man outside each window, and Beale over the flames, things can begin to quiet down and individual words can be heard. Walsingham sheathes his sword with a satisfying finality.

"How dare you—" Throckmorton starts, blood back in his cheeks now, but Walsingham isn't interested.

"Oh shut up, Throckmorton, and see to your wife," he tells him.

There are papers all over the green baize table, along with all the paraphernalia of letter-writing, that are of much greater interest than Throckmorton's pointless protests. Throckmorton swallows his words and turns to his wife who is sitting up, unhurt, but her hoops all awry.

"What have you got, Robert?" Walsingham asks.

Beale shows him some black-edged papers covered in what looks like gibberish.

"Where's Phelippes when we need him?" Beale wonders.

"Here I am," comes a voice from the door and lo, it is Thomas Phelippes, Walsingham's chief decipherist: the son of a tailor, bent of back and short of sight, he speaks every language known to man, and some that aren't, and he is here today in faded black wool, carrying a leather bag that clanks when he places it on the table.

"You've no right," Throckmorton bleats.

"Oh, I think we have," Walsingham tells him. "Now: your ring." He holds out his palm.

"I shall not—"

"You shall."

Nathan Mercer steps into the room, that ax still in hand, eyebrows raised. Seeing him, Throckmorton's face writhes with fury but there is nothing to be done. He twists the ring off his inky finger and presses it into Walsingham's hand.

"God damn you, Walsingham," he snarls.

Walsingham merely smiles and turns to the sergeant of the Yeomen who stands clumped in the doorway: "Take him, will you?"

"The Tower, is it, sir?"

"Not the Tower. Not yet. Take him to the house of the Master of Her Majesty's Post on Saint Peter's Hill. Sir Thomas's servants know to expect you."

Walsingham will not risk Hatton's involvement at this stage, and so he has arranged Throckmorton a bed—probably quite comfortable—with Sir Thomas Randolph, a man who understands such things and is married to Walsingham's sister Anne.

"Can I at least say farewell to my wife?" Throckmorton asks.

She's standing now, helped to her feet by Robert Beale, and she's just a female version of him, really, save slightly horsier.

Walsingham sighs.

"Yes, go on then," he says. "But from over there. I can't stand the thought of you trying to whisper instructions as to the whereabouts of the stable door key. That horse has long since bolted, Throckmorton, and no amount of sliding incriminating papers under the Turkey rug will now help."

The Yeomen take him away after the Throckmortons have stammered their stilted farewells.

"Won't be seeing her again," one of them tells him—cheerfully—on their way out, and Beale is struck by it: it is true that every step brings a man closer to his end, but as Throckmorton walks out of the room, he is ceding yards of his life to death. He will never see this room again, never touch his wife again. Those are things lost, and what has he to look forward to now? A span measured in weeks, and most likely filled with terrible pain.

Lady Throckmorton knows this, too, and weeps.

"Take her to the buttery," Walsingham tells someone. "Sit her down with a pie or something, and give her a drink. We're not monsters."

When she's gone, Walsingham pulls back Throckmorton's chair and invites Phelippes to sit.

"Is there enough to go on?" Walsingham asks him.

Phelippes settles some powerfully thick eyeglasses onto his nose and then spreads out the burned pages on the table disapprovingly.

"Two papers," he commentates, "both very similar, on similar clean paper, and both sealed with a seal that is not here present, nor so far as our preliminary inquiries have revealed, in the ashes of the fire, so unless the suspect has swallowed the ring or hidden it about his person, we may conclude each paper to be written elsewhere, and the suspect is simply passing them on as a courier."

"But what about all this?" Beale asks, indicating the pens and paper; the ink bottle and the penknife, and the small stamp and sealing candle that litter the table. "And he had ink on his fingers, did you see?"

"One step at a time, Master Beale," Phelippes cautions. "I am just telling you what I see."

"But are they letters?" Beale presses. "Are they addressed to anyone?"

Phelippes pins Beale with a fierce glare over his chunky eyeglass.

"Should you not be searching the house for priests or some such, Master Beale?"

His insolence is tolerated as a genius's privilege, for each man knows Phelippes is, in his way, worth more than them.

"There is nothing to indicate," he goes on, "their nature on the outside of the unfolded paper, and since I have not yet had the chance to open them, I cannot say if they are letters. That being the case, I cannot say to whom they are addressed, if indeed they prove to be such."

Walsingham has a man who can lift a seal without leaving any mark, but Phelippes is no slouch, either, and he rootles in his bag and pulls out a leather roll of knives with blades so fine you would not know you had cut yourself until a week later, and he slices away the wax of the first paper.

"Any clue from the imprint?" Walsingham wonders.

"Nothing I recognize," Phelippes says. But then if you are sending a message you hope to keep secret, you do not imprint its seal with your signet, do you?

"It is like a mason's mark," he tells them, studying it under a formidably thick piece of polished glass. "Or one part of an unnecessarily complicated carpenter's scarf joint."

Then he unfolds the paper from quartered to whole and spreads it on the baize, studying it for a moment under the same circle of glass. When spread out, the paper is about the size of a man's palm. In the middle is a clutch of numbers and letters arranged in horizontal lines, and all the blank space around is scribbled on so that no one might add anything to what is already there.

"Well?" Walsingham asks. Phelippes ignores him and methodically opens the second paper: it is almost identical.

"And?"

"And nothing," Phelippes snaps. "It is a cipher that I cannot decrypt at a glance. Will that do you?"

"But is it this one?" Walsingham asks, indicating the three-quarter burned key that Beale plucked from the fire. Phelippes sighs and settles himself to compare the two papers with it. After a moment he says no.

Walsingham and Beale look at each other.

"So why *two* ciphers?"

"We'll know more when Phelippes has deciphered these."

"These two look simple enough," is Phelippes's first-glance opinion, "but my time would be more fruitful if spent uninterrupted by witless questions."

So they leave him to it and spend the rest of the morning searching the rest of the house—tapping on walls and cutting up mattresses—until Gregory appears with a sheaf of papers.

"Here we are," he says. "Look at these. Not even encrypted.

Found them upstairs under Thickmoron's mattress if you can believe it."

Walsingham and Beale share them, and it takes a moment before they realize what they're reading. A list of all the Catholic families in England likely or willing to send men in support of Mary Queen of Scots in the event of an invasion of troops financed by the Duc de Guise.

"We *must* be intended to find it, surely?"

Walsingham studies the list, looking for the obvious plant, perhaps, but there is nothing.

"No surprises there," is his opinion. "No one we did not suspect before, and none we suspect left off."

"Can it be—for *administrative* purposes?"

It seems incredible.

"But it's still not enough, is it? We could haul them all in and show it to them and they'd say, 'Well, so what?'"

Walsingham has to agree.

"What else is there?"

The next sheet is a list of ports and havens along England's south and east coasts. Walsingham frowns and tuts. It is not clear why. Disapproval at their carelessness?

And the third is a paper written by a Scottish bishop explaining the superior claim Mary Queen of Scots has over Elizabeth Tudor to the English throne.

Possession of this latter is enough to see Throckmorton hung, drawn, and quartered, and if that were their aim they might count the day a success and retire to the tavern, but now Phelippes calls for them.

"Simple enough substitution cipher," he says. "As I predicted: very low-level stuff."

"And?"

"And it's not signed, so it could be from anyone, and nor is it addressed, so it could be to anyone, but whoever has written it has done so to tell whoever is reading it that he is now very confident that he can raise money enough and ships enough to transport up to five thousand men and one hundred horses from Dieppe."

"*Dieppe?*" Walsingham wonders. "Why Dieppe? Why not Calais? Why not Dunkerque? Ostend even? Each is nearer Framlingham."

"Worried about the Sea Beggars sending in a fire ship to blow their fleet to pieces, perhaps?"

"That is a good idea, actually. We could have a word with our old friend Van Treslong."

Beale makes a note. It takes time to build a decent hellburner: you need a sound, seaworthy ship to start with, and then you need to line its hull with five or six layers of old tombstones, each edge sealed with lead so that the fire doesn't burn through the planks and sink the ship before it reaches its target, and you have to line the masts, too, for the same reason. Then you have to attach grappling hooks to the spars, to help the ship entangle with the rigging of any enemy boat, and you have to change the gunport hinges so they open from below and can be dropped at the last moment to ensure good airflow to the fire, but they can't be got rid of entirely, in case of high seas on the way to your target. Then you have to pack the hull with at least seven thousand pounds of good-quality powder and devise a mechanical timer that will deliver a spark to the charge when the time is right, and then you must seal all this in with yet more gravestones topped off with several layers of bricks and all the scrap metal that can be found, so that when your powder does explode, preferably hard-pressed to your target, the air becomes a whirling maelstrom of lethal missiles. Then you have to find someone to sail it.

"Go on," Walsingham tells Phelippes. "What else?"

Phelippes pushes him his decipher so that he might see for himself and Walsingham summarizes.

"If you are able to provide forty quarters of wheat and fifty tun casks of fresh-brewed ale as well as fodder for two hundred horses, *and* vouchsafe the proclivity of aforesaid safe harbor *and* provide all assurances as to the goodwill of the local commons, then, with God's good grace, we shall mount an invasion of England such as to make that of William the Conqueror's appear unto a—"

"What's that word?" Walsingham asks, pointing at the decryption.

"Couldn't work it out," Phelippes admits. "Too French for me. Thought you might know?"

Walsingham doesn't.

"By Christ," Beale breathes. "These are plans for a full-on invasion."

Walsingham nods. Perhaps it is the light through the window glass but he has begun to look very green.

"When, though? Does it say in the other one?"

Phelippes shakes his head.

"Identical rubric. Only different numbers. He wants fifty horses from whoever this is addressed to, but he does mention the supply of more gunmen as well as more wheat and ale besides."

"This has to be de Guise, doesn't it?" Beale says.

Walsingham nods.

"But who is he addressing?"

"We will bloody well find out. We'll pinch him until he squeals."

"But what was Throckmorton up to with his inky fingers?" Beale still wonders. "And this cipher?"

He indicates the tattered remnants of the burned key.

"Have a look at it, will you, Phelippes?" Walsingham asks. "See if you can make anything of it."

Phelippes looks doubtful.

"I need a bit more to go on," he says.

Beale has another look in the embers, just in case he can find what Throckmorton was writing. The ashes are still smoking, and there is nothing worth saving. He tries the chimney and his hands come away tar smutted and empty. Walsingham sits in thought.

"So he came from Salisbury Court, yes? From the French Embassy, and he brought with him these two requests for wheat and ale, presumably to pass on to the men whose names we will soon discover, and then he spent the morning *not* reading them, because they are still sealed with a seal that he does not have, but very obviously putting into cipher something else he'd—what?—learned while he was at the embassy?"

And now burned.

"Christ. Well. We will have to hope he talks."

"He will," Walsingham predicts. He is in a very dark temper.

"Who can he have been sending it to? It can only have been Queen Mary."

"Christ. That was the one thing we needed. Just a piece of incontrovertible proof that she is dealing with a foreign power that I could put before Her Majesty, and she would have had no choice but to agree to have her put to death. We would have her at last. And the bastard's gone and burned it!"

"It may not have been to Mary," Beale tries to console.

"No? Then who?"

Beale shrugs. It was most likely Mary.

"It is just endless," Walsingham says. "Endless."

"There must be something," Beale says. He now cannot decide

if he genuinely did not think there was more paper in the fire, or whether he has created a false memory of that being the case, but he cannot give up the notion there is still something to be found, and so they search the house again, top to bottom. Up every chimney, down the well, in all the outhouses, and among the roots of the newly planted hedges of the knot garden. There is nothing.

Christ.

It is only as the dark is rising, when Beale returns to the parlor to look through some papers and must move his stool to share some of Phelippes's candlelight, that he finds he has kicked something under the long skirts of the green baize tablecloth: a green velvet-covered casket.

"Gah," Walsingham says. "Always in the last place you look."

It is unlocked and must have been put there in a hurry, perhaps when Throckmorton first heard his gate shivered to pieces. They open it and within is a single slip of paper, folded carefully into a lock, and sealed with a blob of wax carrying the imprint of that curious stamp that they found on the table when first they entered.

Walsingham leans in to watch Phelippes go to work, and his eyes catch the candle flame like the darkest oil.

Phelippes cuts the lock. He'll fix it later and hide the cut under a new blob of wax. You can only do this if you have the time to make a reverse loss-wax casting of the imprint in the seal, or the original stamp, which he does, of course. He carefully unfolds the letter while Beale and Walsingham wait with their breath held to reveal a single, small page, covered in letters and numbers and a great many symbols the like of which neither Beale nor Walsingham have seen before.

"Ahhh!" he says, beaming with pleasure. "A proper cipher, this. Bring me candles, wine, and tobacco."

They are sent for, and brought, though the tobacco takes a while to find—from a Frenchman, found smoking a pipe down by Custom House—and Phelippes sets to.

"No one is to leave the house," Walsingham instructs.

The night wears by and Beale sits watching as Phelippes, befouling the room's air with the smoke of his pipe, goes through the code again and again, and again, until just after cockcrow something finally makes sense, and by ten o'clock he is done, and he passes the paper to Walsingham.

"There," he says.

It is a quick read, scarcely a hundred and fifty words, and Beale tries to infer its contents from Walsingham's reaction: it is not what he expected, but he is not completely downcast.

"Humph," he grunts.

"What is it?" Beale demands.

"See for yourself."

And he pushes the deciphered paper across to Beale. Robert reads it: "A Certain Gentleman says that the Mole has learned of where Balafré plans to land his troops."

"Who is the Mole?" Beale asks. "And who is Balafré?"

Phelippes laughs a cracked little laugh.

"Bound to be you; that is, Sir Francis," he says. "You look like a mole, don't you, with your hair all velvet and your black clothes. And forever digging up people's gardens."

"Shut up, Phelippes."

Phelippes carries on his mirthless chuckle while Walsingham strokes the back of his skull self-consciously, which is as close to an admission that he might identify as the Mole as he is ever like to make, and Beale cannot help but look at him, now, and yes, there is a likeness, he supposes, should moles ever wear ruffs and live long enough to go gray at their temples.

"Balafré could be the Duc de Guise's nickname," Walsingham suggests. "Scarface. He has a scar, like this, see"—he demonstrates—"down his cheek. Some skirmish or other with a German Huguenot. Wish to God they'd done a better job of it and sent him to hell."

The note goes on to say that even now the Mole "scrabbles in earnest to have his masons build a gun tower to cover the castle's approach, but the masons' work is bedeviled by delay, and now plague and three masons are dead and work suspended."

Beale looks up.

"Is that true?"

Walsingham manages a strained smile.

"Not so far as I am aware. In fact, Master Pughe has just this week written to say that he and his masons make great strides."

Beale laughs as he returns to the note.

"The Certain Gentleman cannot say how the Mole learned of the plan: possibly from the ship's captain who gave Master Mope passage from Dieppe, and perhaps learned of his true identity, or from an espial placed in the household of Roncherolles."

"Mope?" Beale asks. "Another nickname?"

"Not that I know of." Walsingham shrugs. "We'll have to find him, though, and this sea captain."

"And Roncherolles?"

"Ahh. That is Francois de Roncherolles. French. Catholic League zealot. He's the one who dreamt up the scheme to land the arquebusiers at Framlingham."

"So from which of them did you learn of the plan?" Beale asks, more out of interest than in any expectation of an answer.

"Neither," Walsingham says with a laugh.

Beale goes back and reads that this day also Count Łaski of Poland is sent from said realm in disgrace but likewise is Δ sent for the crime of conjuring evil spirits, but that far from being exiled, Δ is sent for reasons according to the purpose of the Mole.

"And Δ is who? Dee?"

Walsingham moues possible agreement.

"But is he? Dee, I mean? Working for you?"

"Of course not. He's a conjurer. Her Majesty would never permit me to employ a conjurer."

Beale wonders at that.

But the note has one last sentence.

"Therefore, Δ is not be trusted and is best declawed."

"Declawed? Christ. Does he mean that literally?" Beale has seen men with their fingernails pulled out. It is not something you forget. Nor they, of course.

"Could be," Walsingham supposes.

"But who is it from? I mean, yes, it must be Throckmorton who wrote it. But who is the Certain Gentleman?"

"Hatton," Walsingham suggests. "He came here last night, in a fury about Her Majesty not permitting him to put Dee on a pyre in Smithfield, and told Throckmorton everything, I expect."

Beale knows Hatton once swore he would be the one to escort Queen Mary south, holding her sword of state upright before her, down to Westminster to claim her throne, should its current occupant, Queen Elizabeth, have the misfortune to die suddenly.

"But this is base treason," he says. "And why ever would Hatton endanger Dee like that?"

Walsingham blows out a long sigh.

"Malice? A desire for revenge? Or— Well. He is not a total fool, is he, Hatton? He's a realist, I suppose, and has made his calculations and concluded—probably correctly—that we are done for, so he is just putting in place the things he will need to survive, and thrive in his usual style, when England has a new queen."

"A right bastard," is Phelippes's opinion.

While Walsingham has been talking, Phelippes has managed to relock the letter to his satisfaction, and he is now pressing into the fresh melted disk of wax an imprint of Throckmorton's stamp.

"But then—this message cannot be intended for Queen Mary. She's no interest in such details and nor could she organize for Dee to be declawed."

Walsingham agrees. That is what has disappointed him, but he is not as disappointed as he might be.

"But nor can it be de Guise, either," Beale thinks aloud. "Throckmorton came *from* Salisbury Court this morning, didn't he? So if he wanted to get this to de Guise he would have taken it to the ambassador then, in exchange for those we can only assume came from de Guise."

He indicates Phelippes's earlier decryptions, which he sees Phelippes has already tidied away into his bag.

"And nor would Throckmorton refer to de Guise as Balafré," Walsingham supposes.

"So—what does it prove?" Beale asks after a moment.

"It proves there is someone else involved. Someone else to whom Throckmorton has been selling secrets. And who that is, we shall have to discover."

"But you do not seem—*utterly* downcast?"

Walsingham sighs.

"No man can be pleased to discover that he has more enemies than he thought," he says, "but that is more than made up for by the knowledge that Hatton is spreading news about the stalled works at the gun tower at Orford. That above all else is what I wish de Guise know, so that he sticks with his plan—to land his five thousand arquebusiers at Framlingham—and only learns his mistake when his ships are blown from the water before his men can step ashore. And I am also pleased that Roncherolles will now believe his household compromised and will most likely purge it of perfectly decent people, leaving gaps into which we can insert our own."

"But?" Beale asks, for this was coming from the start.

"But. But I am less pleased he has included these warnings about Doctor Dee."

"Well, we have nipped that in the bud, haven't we? No more note: no more warning?"

Walsingham glances away, and Phelippes, who is carefully restoring the lock of the original message to its pristine state, looks up and pauses, tongue between lips, waiting for some outcome in their discussion, and Beale understands that he has missed something. Then it strikes him.

"Ah. You *want* this note to reach its intended recipient?"

Walsingham nods tightly.

"We need it to."

"But . . . we've arrested Throckmorton. The message isn't going to get where he wanted it."

"We've only taken him around the corner, haven't we?" Walsingham replies. "Not to the Tower. We leave this here"—he nods at the casket—"and see what happens."

Beale shakes his head to clear his thoughts. Perhaps it is the smoke from Phelippes's pipe, but there are too many imponderables and possibilities. Too many ifs and maybes. But meanwhile Phelippes has put the locked message back in the casket, closed it, and slid the casket back under the baize drape where he found it.

"Good man," Walsingham tells him. "Now let's get the wife in."

She comes, tearstained but proud, and Walsingham offers her Phelippes's vacated chair. On the baize before him are the list of English recusants, the possible landing sites of a French invasion, and the Bishop of Glasgow's treasonous claim that Mary of Scotland is better entitled to the throne of England than its current incumbent. Lady Throckmorton's gaze darts around the room. She is looking for something: the velvet-covered casket, of course.

"Lady Throckmorton," Walsingham begins, "we are not bad men."

"Yes, you are."

"We have not betrayed our country as your husband has."

"You've betrayed your God, which is worse."

"These lists are enough to have your husband hung, drawn, and quartered, Lady Throckmorton, and we will do that if needs be, but we believe him to have been in contact with Her Majesty's enemies; specifically, Monsieur de Castelnau, the French ambassador?"

She continues to look at them both as if they were turds.

Walsingham tells her that for her part in this treasonous scheme, she and her family stand to lose everything, but if she were to cooperate then she might save herself. When he says "lose everything," he really means "have her head chopped off," and it takes a moment before Beale understands that Walsingham is downplaying her jeopardy and underselling his offer.

Inevitably she scorns it, and them.

"Very well, Lady Throckmorton," Walsingham says, "we will leave you to your own thoughts, but please do not leave this house until we have finished speaking to your husband."

Even she is surprised by Walsingham's clumsy leniency, and there is a moment when Beale sees she believes that Walsingham favors her, for though, yes, she is horsey, she is undeniably attractive, and she knows it. She believes she has made a conquest, and it is with quiet pride, but also contempt, that she watches them troop out of the room, leaving her there alone with the casket.

Beale and Walsingham leave the house together and walk up

past the silversmith's and on toward the looming spire of Saint Paul's.

"Gregory can keep an eye on the house for now," Walsingham tells him, "and we'll go back tomorrow to tell her how it really is, and see, of course, if the casket's gone."

Beale stops and nearly puts his hand on Walsingham's arm.

"So . . . can it be that we've sent the message?"

Walsingham looks puzzled.

"Not us. Her. She'll find the casket, I dare say, or we'll alert her to its presence, and she'll pass it to one of her servants, who'll slip out the back and run to wherever it is supposed to go."

"Followed by Gregory?"

"Followed by Gregory."

"And what of Dee?"

Walsingham stops and turns.

"Dee?"

"That note condemns him to death."

Walsingham nods tightly and grimaces.

"Dee can look after himself, surely?" he suggests.

Another piece of careful wishful thinking.

"Not if it is believed he is working for us. He thinks because he is exiled he poses no threat, so will be left to . . . to wander about looking at the stars and consulting other . . . other men wandering about looking at stars, and meanwhile the French or whoever this note is intended for will believe him working for us. Working for you. And they will declaw him. Literally!"

Walsingham suddenly looks very tired. More so than from having been up all night. You can see the cords of his brain clench and unclench with every new thought. He's sick with something, Beale sees. A canker perhaps? Or perhaps anyone who'd had the last few years that he has had would look like this, too? The constant anxiety of protecting Her Majesty not just from lone assassins such as Hamilton, or groups of them such as the Guild of the Black Madonna, but against almost every prince in Christendom, and the pope to boot, and he has had to thwart them every single time, while they need succeed only once. Imagine that, he tells himself. Imagine saying at the end of a day: I can rest now, and sleep easy. You'd never be able to do it, ever, would you, because there is always something more that can be done.

"We must stop her!" Beale decides. "We must stop that message!"

"No!" Walsingham snaps.

"No?"

"No. Think about it. Stopping it won't help. Throckmorton has just come from the French Embassy, yes? Where he will have passed over another one of those locked messages, intended for de Guise, perhaps, telling him all that Hatton told him, so de Guise will soon know everything, anyway. Dee's disguise as an exile is already in tatters, and there is nothing we can do about it."

Beale cannot believe this.

"Then we must send word! Send someone after him, to warn him. Or he will wander into some town unawares and find himself taken up by the Spanish or the French, and he will be tortured half to death."

"Dee knows what he must do in that case. He is not without resource."

"What do you mean?"

Walsingham seems to gather himself for another costly effort, and he places his hand upon Beale's arm.

"Robert," he says, "we face invasion upon every coast; assassins around every corner, and an alliance of Her Majesty's enemies that stretches from Cadiz to Krakow, all determined to see her dead, and against this, it is just us. You, me, and a handful of others, each of us just doing the best we can. But we pay a price for every moment we survive: concessions and compromises are inevitable; sacrifices must be made; losses endured. Jesu, look at us, Robert: we make the Spartans seem self-indulgent, Horatio wavering in his commitment to the cause."

"So you are just—?"

Walsingham's grip tightens on his arm.

"There is nothing to be done, Robert," he insists. "We must place our faith in God and our trust in Dee. He will do the right thing, for Queen and country, I am sure of it."

Beale is left openmouthed as Walsingham turns and walks on, his head bowed, his shoulders, too, as if under the weight of the world, and Beale sees that he has traveled too far down the road with this plan and has lost all clarity.

He stands a long while longer, alone among the throng by the conduit below Saint Paul's and is filled with a powerful certainty that what is being done is wrong, for he knows and likes Doctor Dee, and he is certain that something can be done to save him, and even if Sir Francis is worn through to the bone, he, Robert Beale, is not. He is not yet ready to give up on Doctor Dee.

But what is to be done?

He walks westward, deep in thought, through Ludgate, where once Dee was imprisoned for his debts to some bookseller or other, but it is not until the short hours of the next morning, when he is safe at home and in his bed, that his eyes open in the dark and the answer comes to him:

"Mistress Frommond."

⊕

CHAPTER TEN

Dokkum, West Frisia, October 1583

After three days in the barge, Dee and the others are re-lieved to reach Harlingen, another one of those Dutch towns perched on the barest nub of reclaimed land and kept above the circling waters by ingenuity and willpower alone. Every bed in every inn is taken if not by one Calvinist fleeing Spanish op-pression and war in the south, then by two, or even three, and so they must stay in a tanner's house, at ruinous cost to Łaski's swiftly deflating purse, and sleep as one under the eaves, plagued by mice and the terrible smells from below.

Dee has promised Łaski an Action, if Kelley is willing, and he is—reluctantly, it seems—but as their journey has gone on Dee has seen his scryer become ever more bitter with everything and everyone around him, and most especially with his wife, Joanna, who has developed a thirst for the beer beyond all reasoning and would be drunk by midday if they did not ration her intake. Dee suspects she has also taken to lying with Łaski's servants Alexander and Emericus Sontag—one of them? or both?—if lying is the right word for what they do against walls as soon as her husband's back is turned, and when they start the Action, it is clear the trouble between Kelley and his wife has unsettled the heavens as well, for when the men finally settle to summon Raphael, he, too, appears in an apocalyptic, End Times mood.

"Thus, says the Lord, I am the God of Justice and I have sworn there is no one among them, nay not one soul, who shall live!"

And: "Every sin is noted! Every sin will be punished! Practice charity, and mildness, for it is better to refresh the soul with heavenly contemplation than to pamper to filthy flesh!"

As well as: "Look to thy servants! Share not thy quarters with those who harbor vice upon vice, whose drunkenness is abomination and whose diet stirs up fornication, for wickedness is among them and they fear not God!"

And even worse is: "These next five years shall be the Deliverance. I will plague the people and their blood shall become rivers. The earth shall be barren, and fathers shall eat their own children. The beasts of the fields shall perish, and the waters shall be poisoned and the air shall infect her creatures and in the deep shall be roaring and Great Babylon shall sit in judgment."

But it is not all bad.

"I shall reserve two kingdoms untouched and will root out their wickedness and I will be gloried by you and you shall have power. Happy are those who continue until the end."

Which must refer to Poland and Moravia, Dee supposes, but there is no further detail, and it soon emerges that Dee and the others have much more immediate concerns, for it falls out that Łaski has run through such money as Walsingham paid him to leave the country.

"We shall have to sell something," Kelley moans. "What about some of your stuff? Those globes? They must be worth a penny, even here?"

They stare out at the muddy fields and sodden reed beds and Dee wonders if that is what Kelley was doing when he was rifling through the house back in Mortlake: making an inventory of objects they might sell?

"They were lost overboard in that storm on the Zuiderzee," he reminds Kelley, whom he blames for their loss because he did not tie the baggage down properly.

"We just need to get to Lübeck," Dee goes on. "The count says he will be able to borrow money there."

Kelley remains furious, but Dee has no time for any further placating. He must get back to the *Book of Loagaeth*, which he has been quietly perfecting, hunched in a corner of the barge, listening to the thrum of the wind in the rigging and the gurgle of water against the hull behind his back as they are buffeted across the Zuiderzee and then along the coast to the town of Harlingen and from there on to Dokkum. He is pleased with the book so far: forty-nine tables of forty-nine tables, each table containing an Enochian symbol that can be translated into the language of the angelic spirits, if you know how, which no one quite does, yet.

Later he writes to Jane.

I commend myself to you and to Arthur, and confirm that we are come to Dokkum, a small town in a country where wind-mills outnumber men, but which might yet sink into the sea for the weight of Dutch Protestants escaping the war—and the Inquisition—in the south. I am sad to say, though, that disaster has struck and that in the crossing of the Zuiderzee, a storm blew up, and we lost much of our baggage owing to Master Kelley's poor knot-making, including, sad to say, all my mathematical instruments, by which I most especially mean the globes that Gerardus Mercator gave me when we studied together in Leuven. I am heartbroken, but contend God must have his purpose. Tomorrow we cross into Saxony and thence to Lübeck and beyond. EK still has the good ear of the angelic spirits, though I am daily less sure of Count Łaski and the success of his undertaking. I have sent word to Bess, and written to Thaddeus Hajek in Prague, and therefrom with God's grace I shall return before Saint John's Day next. I pray daily all is well in Mortlake with you and Arthur, and I think about you all the time, my entirely beloved Jane, and this comes with all love from: Δ.

⊕

CHAPTER ELEVEN

Mortlake, England, October 1583

I t has rained every day since John Dee left Mortlake, and Jane Frommond imagines her husband would have at least one explanation for the constant rain, if not two. One would be astrological—a sign of the imminence of the End Times was always a favorite—and one would be meteorological—some far-off ocean current will have shifted north, or south, causing some wind or other to warm, or cool, meaning there would be more, or less, evaporation and so denser, or lighter, clouds, and he will probably claim this phenomenon has a Greek name. Or he would simply put it down to the will of God and be done with it.

She has had new word from him, sent from the city of Amsterdam: a letter much abused by being opened and closed and read by a hundred eyes before hers, claiming that Roger Cooke is editing his collection of books according to those which float, and those which do not. He tells her he is daily petitioning Her Majesty to permit his return, but also that they are traveling to Prague by going northward, instead of eastward, which might seem logical, for the dangers of being recognized in France. The road, then, is to be very long and winding.

Dee adds as a postscript that Arthur's rabbit should not be permitted unfettered access to the herb garden beyond the laboratory, and particularly not the— But this word is lost in a water stain. And, anyway, it is too late for that because the rabbit has already been in the herb garden beyond the laboratory where it turns out Dee has been growing not only buttercups, foxgloves, and primroses—each deadly to rabbits—but also larkspur, columbine, hellebore, comfrey, poppy, periwinkle, monkshood, and deadly nightshade—all likewise fatal to rabbits—behind the protective cordon of an ivy-entwined privet hedge, cornered by a holly tree and a small yew, dotted with attractive red berries, all of which will also, again, do for a rabbit, and so it has proved.

"We can always get another," Arthur tells her. "And we could see my cousins again."

He's a somber little boy with soulful brown eyes, but he is unsentimental, and what he says is true: they can always get another, because her brother Nicholas's garden in Cheam is riddled with their burrows.

"I shall ask," she says, for they have both been in low spirits without Dee, and it would be good to be away from Mortlake, where she is daily subjected to a great weight of suspicion from the locals, and the almost constant knocking of creditors upon her gate. Before she can write the letter, though, there comes more of that selfsame knocking at her gate, and Sarah, her new maid, opens the gate to Robert Beale, whom Frommond remembers with some fondness from the months they passed together in Sulgrave Manor, attempting to educate poor Ness Overbury in the dress and manner of Her Majesty, with predictably disastrous results.

"Mistress Dee," he greets her, stooping to kiss her hand, very quickly, and shuffling into the property as if anxious not to be seen.

He has but one servant with him, when he should ordinarily be occupied by two or three, a secretary, and a half-dozen Yeomen. She notes he is in a tall-collared riding cloak that someone might have ordered to match the color of mud, and an unadorned and capaciously baggy cap, so that all that may be really seen of him is the beak of his nose, and his keen eyes. It is the same for Beale's servant, and Frommond feels rekindled within her that old fluttering worry, a prickling that something is afoot that should not be, especially as the servant stands in the gate, peering out, left and right, to see if by any chance they were followed.

"And so what brings you to our gate, Master Beale, if I may ask?" she asks.

He laughs, unreassuringly.

"You are ever to the point, Mistress Dee," he patronizes her. "And I thank you for it since I am somewhat harried for time. Is there somewhere we might—?"

He means "not be overheard."

"The orchard?" she suggests.

"Please, if you've a mind."

They walk in silence through the hall, out across the yard under the laden boughs of the apple trees. His preoccupation is contagious, and weighty, and yet thrilling.

"It is a welcome surprise to see you," she confesses, and he looks at her asquint.

"Not had many callers?"

"Hardly a one. Not since John left. Except creditors, of course. Though, do you know, we did have Lord Burghley. Is he quite well, do you know?"

Beale does not.

"He is getting on a bit," he supposes.

"He was talking about— Well . . . it was odd. Something he kept calling the Flying Squadron. He told me he was looking for beautiful women. I told him I did not know any. He hummed and hawed and wondered if he could count on my support if need be. I told him of course, though in what manner he could not say."

"Strange," Beale agrees. "Strange. And Sir Francis? He's not been to see you?"

She shakes her head tightly.

"No," she tells him. "That is it. Oh. A constable in search of Master Kelley. He is wanted for coining, did you know? And it is not his first offense, the constable said. Hence his ears."

She indicates, but Beale has no interest in Kelley.

"No. Well. I am sorry to hear Sir Francis has not been. He is— I hardly know what to say. Hard-pressed."

They walk on a bit, their toecaps darkening in the sodden grass and the air's dampness pills into little droplets upon their woolens. Down the slope the river brims very high, and the earth that covers the grave of Arthur's rabbit is very red.

"So," Frommond says, cutting to it, "you were saying?"

"Yes— Did John— Did your husband speak to you of his exile?"

"Speak of it? Yes. Of course. Sir Francis allowed me to visit him in the Tower, of course, though that was hardly satisfactory, and then gave him an hour to gather his belongings and bid us farewell, so yes: it cropped up."

Beale nods. His gaze is fixed on the ground for a few paces. Then he stops and turns to her.

"Did you know Walsingham sent Hatton here that night, knowing he would find your husband scrying with Count Łaski?"

She stops and stares. She can't believe it. Walsingham set her husband up?

"My God," she says, lost for better words. "Why?"

"He needed someone to go to Prague. To the court of Emperor Rudolf, for Her Majesty."

Frommond is simply stunned for a moment. She cannot place one foot before the other or believe what she is hearing.

"He could have *asked* him!" she finds herself almost shouting. "There is almost nothing John would have liked more than to be sent to Prague to represent Her Majesty at the emperor's court."

"Sir Francis was not certain he would go," Beale explains, though he does not look convinced, and she detects another level to this.

"And also," Beale continues, "there is good reason to believe that what needs be done in Prague cannot be done by . . . cannot be done officially. Your husband could only achieve what is necessary if he appears to be disgraced."

Frommond is now in a vortex, a whirl of swirling realities where up is now down, the past is now the present, and what seems to be is now in fact not. Through it all, though, she sees that though Walsingham might have been the prime mover in this scheme, it is Beale who is at hand.

"He *is* disgraced!" she shouts. "*You* disgraced him!"

Beale appears genuinely contrite.

"I'm sorry," he says. "It is as I say. We are at a breaking point. We face invasion from every quarter, assassins at every corner, and an alliance of enemies that will soon stretch from Cadiz to Krakow, and against this we are so few, and so poor, and so—so worn *through* . . . that we must stoop to— We must— We . . . must stoop to occasional sacrifices."

"Sacrifices?" she snarls. "That is my *husband*!"

Beale looks only made more miserable by his clumsy choice of words, but he is only being honest. That is what Dee has become: a sacrifice.

They walk on in silence for a while. Jane can hardly breathe and hears herself gasping and struggling for words. She does not even know where to begin.

"But there is a—" Beale starts, and then stops, leaving it hanging.

"There is a *what*?"

He explains his proposal, and she listens with a face that grows steadily more incredulous.

"I cannot send just anyone," he tells her. "I cannot overrule Sir Francis. But if you went? If you followed after him. To be with him, and at the same time, you can warn him that the French and the Spanish know that he is spying for Her Majesty. That would not be unnatural, would it? Sir Francis could hardly stop you?"

Well. He could of course. If he knew.

"So Sir Francis knows nothing of this? Nothing?"

"He knows nothing of my visit to you," Beale says in such a way as to confound every certainty.

She looks at him and remembers how he was with Ness Overbury that summer, and she understands that he is a good man, much better than many that stamp and strut through the shallows surrounding Her Majesty's court. But has Beale now perhaps gone out of his wits? Is this another scheme of his that will find all participants flirting with the headsman's blade? But while Frommond is thinking this, she is also thinking: *My God! It is the only thing to do.* It is the only thing she *can* do. It is the only thing she *must* do.

"But I cannot," she says. "I know nothing of this sort of thing. I have never been to France even."

Beale nods.

"It is no easy task, Mistress Dee," he admits, "and I would not think to ask it of any ordinary woman, save that—and I know I should not be telling you this—in his most secret drawer, hidden under a coffer in his office, Sir Francis has a list of those in this country on whom he and Her Majesty have decided may be absolutely relied upon for guts and ingenuity in any species of crisis. Special agents, Sir Francis calls them, and each has a number. There are eight names. Seven of them are men—one of whom is your husband—and one of them is a woman."

"So?"

"So that woman is you."

"Me?"

"You. Since you saved Her Majesty's life on London Bridge."

She says nothing. She thinks about what she did that day, and she believes no woman would have done otherwise. What a silly thing it is, to write a list. But Beale believes it means something.

"Which is why I have come to you," he tells her.

And Frommond nods, and thinks, and in a moment all problems are put aside the moment they arise: Arthur can go to her brother Nicholas's in Cheam; the household staff she can let go, save for a night watchman, and the house itself can be shut up. The only daunting obstacle is traveling alone as a woman in lands she does not know, and in a time of war between the Spanish and Dutch. By the time she has come to this conclusion, she finds that Beale has walked her back to the house, and the kitchen door hangs open, now candlelit from within, which was not so before.

"I have a man who might go with you?" Beale now volunteers. "To play the part of your servant. And to protect you, should anything—arise?"

She imagines some hoary old espial who will drink ale and leer at her all day.

"No, no. A young man. A student at Cambridge. A theologian, of sorts, I believe, though I am uncertain where he stands on that matter, but he is in training to pass himself off as a seminarian at Douai, until which time his hands are idle, and if there were ever a man for whom the devil will make work, then it is Christopher Marlowe."

"Christopher Marlowe? He is not one of Walsingham's men?"

"Not . . . yet."

"How young is he then? A babe in arms?"

"See for yourself."

Standing in the kitchen, shoulder to shoulder with Arthur who stands atop a stool, and just now adding a pinch of salt to the pot of soup that Sarah has been cooking all day, is Beale's servant. Hearing them, he turns and smiles and she guesses he cannot yet be twenty, but he is very composed and he looks to be one of those men to pass through any crowd without necessarily getting into a fight. What she notices about him, though, is that as he turns, he keeps ahold of Arthur so that he falls neither into the pot nor the flames. That is good, she thinks. It took her a year or more to develop peripheral care like that. He must have younger siblings.

"Mistress Dee," Beale introduces them, "this is Christopher Marlowe."

"Hello, Mistress Dee," he says in a voice enriched with a skeptical provincial twang, and he offers a hand that is small, smooth, cool, and yet not at all soft. He wears the ghost of an amused smile and his eyes are lively and polished conker brown.

"Boshed a bit too much salt in there now," he admits, nodding at Sarah's soup. "What you need is an iron nail. Bung that in, and you'll be right as rain."

Jane does not know why he is even in the kitchen, but Arthur is looking at the young man with adoring eyes. As is Sarah.

Beale takes his leave, and when he is gone, Frommond is left with a small purse of coins, and a hundred questions she wishes she could ask, including, primarily, what task is her husband actually carrying out for Francis Walsingham?

But Beale is gone, and here is Arthur, catching at her skirts.

"Is Christopher staying for dinner, Mother?" he asks. He still has an infant's lisp.

"If he would care to?"

"Much obliged," Marlowe says, with a reassuring, confirmatory nod at Arthur. "Don't get much home cooking."

He lives on a boat, and his father is a shoemaker.

"Always a steady supply of nails if you're a cobbler's son," he tells Arthur when they are sat around the table before the fire in the hall, eating that soup.

"What is so great about a nail?" Sarah asks.

Marlowe laughs.

"More or less the only thing in the world a man can rely on," he tells them. "You'll never go hungry if you've got an iron nail."

Frommond finds herself laughing.

"What *are* you talking about?"

"You wait and see, Mistress Dee," he tells her with a glimmer in his eye. "You just wait and see."

When she has put Arthur in her bed and reassured him Marlowe will be there when he wakes up, she returns to the hall to hear Marlowe now singing in a gentle voice, and Sarah sat in a settle, fast asleep by the fire. Jane feels no awkwardness being almost alone with him, and his frank gaze only spurs her to business.

"So Master Beale has told you what is proposed?"

"He has. I've been only as far as Munster before, but I speak Almain like a native. Well, a native dong farmer, if I'm honest, but where we're going that'll be what's needed."

"Where *are* we going?"

"Well, it's not so much where we're going as how we get there, what with Master Beale's purse being no deeper than a chicken's scratch."

Frommond had not fully understood how far Beale was taking responsibility for this task upon his own shoulders.

"And how will we evade Master Walsingham's searchers at the ports?"

"I know a bloke in Tilbury who'll find us a berth no questions. Won't be comfortable, mind, but it never is, is it, the old North Sea."

She has never been to sea, of course, and the thought of a sea voyage holds fears for her that she resolves to keep to herself. She feels, instinctively, that she will be fine, so long as he is there. And yet why? He is so young! In fact, she is just about to ask, when and why did he ever cross the sea? But he pre-empts her.

"Will Arthur be all right with you gone?" he asks.

"So long as I come back," Frommond tells him, "yes. He will be much happier at my brother's, if I am honest. I am heavy company at the moment, and he has his cousins there, and my brother will take Sarah, too, who has been like a sister to him in these last few weeks, which have been— Well. With John gone."

Marlowe understands.

"All right then," he says. "So. Tomorrow night it is?"

She agrees.

"Right then," he says, getting up. "I will wish you good night."

"You will not be staying?"

Marlowe looks surprised.

"I thought I'd take a look around the village. See what's what."

"What's what? It is ten o'clock. Every house will be shuttered."

"Well," he says. "There's usually something, isn't there?"

Is there? she wonders. But with that, he is gone, leaving Jane to wake Sarah, and both women are utterly baffled by his absence.

⊕

The next morning, Marlowe is not back, and after some long hesitation Jane takes Sarah and Arthur to her brother's at Cheam, and though the parting is terrible, she feels it more than he, for there is sunlight that day, and rabbits and cousins, and she only tells him a half truth: that she is going to get his father and bring him back home, and that they shall all three soon be reunited. And yes, Christopher will be there too.

Her brother is less pliable.

"I am happy to have the boy," he says, "for as long as you like, Jane; you know that. But it is you I fret for. You will not even tell me where you are going or for how long?"

She cannot. In part because she is promised to secrecy, and in part because she does not know herself. It could be weeks, months, even years. That she may never return is unthinkable. She borrows money and leaves him with the key to the house in Mortlake, "Against the day."

"And that is it?" he asks. "The house is all closed up and you are just—what?—going?"

"I have to be in Tilbury by dawn tomorrow," she tells him. "I will send word."

He lends her a horse and a servant to take her to the river, and he kisses her farewell, and then stands with Arthur by his side in the middle of the road; both return her wave as Frommond sets off north, her saddlebags plump, her heart winnowed.

A little while later Marlowe appears down the road, his hair awry, with a bruised cheek and a horse that she cannot believe belongs to him. He looks to have slept in a haybarn, yet smells of what? Is it *ambergris*?

"So you found what was what in Mortlake?" she asks.

He grins.

"Proper night out," is all he'll say.

✛

CHAPTER TWELVE

Tower of London, November 16, 1583

They rack Francis Throckmorton that morning.

"Just tell us who the messages were for," rackmaster Wilkins says, "and I can loosen this off right away."

Throckmorton is stretched so tight in the frame that if you were to flick him with a finger, you might get a decent tune out of him, and he breathes like a horse in labor, but still he will not tell them what they need to know.

To begin with, when they still held him in Sir Thomas Randolph's house, they had showed him the lists of recusants they had found under his mattress, along with the other of the suitable harbors along the south and eastern coasts, and the Bishop of Glasgow's arguments for Queen Mary's superior right to the English throne, and he had claimed never to have seen them.

"You must have foisted them upon me!" he had cried, so convincingly they had almost believed him, but they had not, so they kept pressing until he had admitted that a servant of his, Roger Nutterby, had written them.

"And where is this Nutterby now?"

"Gone over the sea."

"Ahhhh, isn't that always the way?"

The longer they made no mention of the green velvet casket, the more Throckmorton began to believe they had not found it, and that he might just have the slightest chance to come out of this alive. They even let him have his man of law visit him—he was in fact one of Walsingham's men—though there seemed little to discuss save his guilt. On the way out after their private conference, they had taken the man aside, and Phelippes had written upon the reverse of one of his papers—with a lump of coal taken from the fire so that Lady Throckmorton might believe her husband was being deprived of pen and paper, which in fact he was—a brief note in almost perfect replication of Throckmorton's hand that he should fain know the whereabouts of his green-velvet-covered casket, and if it being found unfound, it should be taken to the usual place.

"Should do the trick," Arthur Gregory had complimented Phelippes. "I like the word *fain*. Just the sort of thing a twat like that'd say."

And they'd watched the man of law bustle down to Throckmorton House, and then scarcely an hour later, just as it was getting dark, a servant had detached himself from the shadows at the rear of the house and set off toward Salisbury Court.

"See?"

And they had trailed the man—no more than a boy, really—up to Saint Paul's where they very nearly lost him in the early evening melee around the conduit because he did not turn left as they expected but went straight on up Paternoster Row not to the French ambassador's gate, but to that of the Spanish ambassador, Don Bernardino de Mendoza.

"Well, blow me," Gregory had said.

The next day they had moved Throckmorton to the Tower and the day after that they had found under his window five or six playing cards, from a pack they had lent him the day before, on which he had written instructions that he hoped would reach his brother, George, to get him to confirm that the lists found under his mattress were written in Nutterby's hand.

"Deserves to be racked, for that alone," was Gregory's opinion, but Walsingham had shaken his head and tried to fathom the man's unfathomable desperation. What did he *think* would happen to the cards? Blow into friendly hands? Unbelievable.

So they had arrested George Throckmorton, too, which they might well have done anyway, and now here they are, in the lower chamber of the White Tower, standing in a circle around that low oak frame, watching a man naked save for his braies being stretched to within a half inch of beyond endurance.

"Who is your contact at the French Embassy?"

And: "Does Queen Mary know you were plotting to put her on the throne?"

But they learn nothing. Or nothing that day. But nor do they necessarily expect to, for that is not how the rack works. Instead, after a while, they slacken the ropes and untie Throckmorton, and Wilkins helps him rub the blood back into his hands and feet, and they give him wine against the pain in his joints. After a while, they stand him up, steady as a newborn foal, and they take him back to his cell where they let him stew for a few days, letting his mind do the rest of their work for them; then, when they come for him three days later, to ready him for another session with the Duke of Exeter's Daughter, he cannot repeat his feat of bravery, and he spills his guts.

"By Christ," Beale groans afterward. "Percy *and* Howard?"

He means the Earls of Northumberland and Arundel, respectively.

"And not the French Embassy, but the Spanish!"

They are skirting Tower Hill now, near the gibbet—empty today—in thin gray rain. Beale is hungry; Walsingham less so.

"Not much of an appetite, these days," he admits.

This is the first time he has admitted aloud that there may be something wrong with him. Beale emits a flicker of concern.

"It's all the worry," he supposes.

Walsingham agrees, but really: it could be anything, couldn't it?

Still though: Northumberland *and* Arundel!

"I will leave it to Lord Burghley to break the tidings to Her Majesty," Walsingham tells Beale. "She will not be pleased and will most likely blame the messenger."

The Queen was—*is*—very fond of Arundel, who is one of those long-faced aristocrats of the sort who make Walsingham's hand clench into a fist.

"It is only a shame we could not press him on the message in the green casket," Beale murmurs.

Walsingham sighs.

"Yes," he agrees. "But that piece of mischief must play itself out in the dark. If Hatton knows we have read his message, he will find some other way to alert his Spanish friends that the information is tainted, and it will render such perils as Dee must endure entirely pointless."

Robert Beale says nothing. He kicks a stone. There is something amiss here, Walsingham thinks. He will set Gregory to watch Beale, perhaps? See that he does not come up with another scheme as he did with Ness Overbury. They walk on.

"Also," Walsingham adds, "Hatton is useful in this way. You can tell him something in strictest confidence in Whitehall at cock-crow, safe in the knowledge that it will be common knowledge in the Louvre or the Prado by sunset."

Beale says nothing. He does not wish to hear anything more about Hatton, and that confirms it, so Walsingham asks Beale to take a ride to Framlingham to oversee the search for this sea captain and this Master Mope.

"Take Arthur Gregory with you," Walsingham tells him, "and whoever else you like. Start with the searchers along the east coast. They are supposed to have an idea of who's coming and going, and if they don't, well, there you are. Any sudden unexplained wealth is usually the tell."

Walsingham knows Beale knows all this, of course, and feels he is gibbering, like a father fretful for a son about to embark on some risky enterprise. Anyway. They part, and Walsingham leaves Robert to be about his business while Francis himself walks on down to Custom House to take a barge up to find Lord Burghley in his house below the Strand.

It is late afternoon, and still light.

⊕

"Ahhh. Sir Francis. Glad you could come."

Burghley sits at his table in the library with his back to the south-facing window under an unusually fine hat that drips with pearls, and from which a peacock feather flutters to draw attention from his gray beard and fat and—that day—very florid face. Sitting opposite is a beautiful young woman in saffron velvet.

Burghley makes the introductions.

"Mistress Devereux." Walsingham bows.

She stands and reveals herself to be taller than Sir Francis by a couple of inches, and she stares at him through dark whirlpool eyes of the sort to make it seem she is in with you on some very fine but subtle joke. Walsingham wonders if this is Penelope Devereux or her sister, Dorothy? It hardly matters he supposes, for he has heard both are equally bright and beautiful, and both of what some might call a forthright nature.

"Sir Francis," she says very prettily, and he has to look away for fear of losing himself to gazing at her, witless and slack-jawed.

"Mistress Devereux is just leaving," Burghley explains, and that is that. They say their goodbyes and Walsingham sits while Burghley bundles her out with all sorts of fatuous nonsense. When he comes back, he is sweating and must mop his brow. He orders wine and it comes. Rhenish. Good.

"And how many recruits do you have so far?" Walsingham wonders.

"Only her," Burghley wheezes, "and she has already squeezed from me every last penny of this year's budget. Oh Lord, I am too old for this, Francis."

Walsingham laughs.

"It proves her talent, at any rate, and at whom will you aim her first?"

"I can't afford to aim her at anyone now that I have agreed to cover her dress allowance."

"So tell me where we stand with Master Throckmorton," Burghley instructs, though for some reason Walsingham is sure he already knows. How he knows, he does not know. Still, he is happy to oblige: modest where modesty is called for, proud where there is cause for pride, but as he proceeds to tell him about Arundel and Northumberland, he feels things crumble away and the lights begin to dim, and when he is done, Burghley has steepled his fingers and is resting his lip against the apex. He looks irrepressibly somber.

"She will not wear it, Francis, you know that?"

And this is what Walsingham most feared he would say. He had hoped Burghley would tell him that Her Majesty would wish for the Earls of Arundel and Northumberland to be taken up this very moment, and to be pinched, and have sweated from them not only confessions black-hearted enough to see each damned to the traitor's death, but each so incriminating that Her Majesty might order the instant arrest of both Hatton and Mary of Scotland, so that he can be done with her, and finally get some rest.

But no. Burghley is a shrewd judge of Her Majesty's limits, having strained them so often before, and if he says she will not give him permission to arrest these men—because they come from long lines of ancient nobility—and put them to torture, then she will most likely not.

"But by Christ," Walsingham groans, "it is like trying to shoot an arrow with no bowstring."

"She does not make it easy," Burghley agrees. "She only ever acts in extremis, you know that, and only ever when there is undeniable proof."

"How did you persuade her to behead Norfolk?"

The Duke of Norfolk was the Earl of Arundel's father, executed more than ten years previously for his part in a plot to replace Queen Elizabeth with Queen Mary, organized by a Florentine banker named Ridolfi.

"I think that was because Norfolk wished to marry Mary."

Is that true? Walsingham wonders. The Queen was simply jealous of her cousin? It is possible, he supposes, but she was perhaps also influenced by how it was seen in Paris, and in Florence, where the plot was supposed to be common knowledge, discussed at lunchtime in the squares and piazzas and whatnot.

"Well, what about Northumberland's brother, then? The seventh earl?"

"Ah. He was actually up in arms, wasn't he? He had to go. But I must say, Francis, in Her Majesty's defense, that I am not sure how good it is to chop off these fellows' heads, anyway. It stirs up resentment in their home counties and it doesn't seem to overly deter those they leave behind, does it?"

Both undeniable points. To most men, the Queen is a distant figure, while their local lord is, for better or worse, at least local, and it is natural to resent interference from so distant a planet as London. And also, even in London, even in Smithfield and upon Tower Hill, seeing a man hung drawn and quartered oftentimes provokes pity for the victim and disgust in the butcher.

"Will you at least ask her?" Walsingham asks.

"Of course. Of course. She may consent to their arrest if it can be shown they will slip overseas, but I would not live in hope of very much more. The Queen does not like to think of England's linen being washed in public squares, especially if those squares are in Paris, or Madrid."

"Perhaps then that is what you might tell her?"

Burghley nods.

"I will. I have an audience tonight and shall send word the moment she has decided."

"Thank you, William."

And Walsingham rises to leave, anxious to be away from his disappointment, and to be back on the river before it gets too dark to pay Mistress Dee a visit in Mortlake, but Burghley has one last question.

"About Łaski. Is all in hand? I have heard—ominous things."

"Such as?"

"That he's burned through all that money we gave him and has been cap in hand to the Earl of Friesland."

Burghley pulls a face and nods at a note on his desk.

"From the Friesland's secretary. Says Łaski is on his uppers, with not a penny to his name, and now traveling with a circus. Jugglers, clowns, professional bear wrestlers, and common fortune-tellers. Says he smells awful."

Walsingham tries to imagine Dee and Łaski as part of a traveling circus and finds he can, quite easily.

"Perhaps they'll help catch the emperor's eye? He is known to enjoy such entertainments."

Burghley grunts.

"Yes, well," he says. "Thank you, Francis. Now, if you see another Mistress Devereux out there, will you send her packing? Tell her I cannot afford her unless she is the same dress size as her sister."

⊕

Walsingham takes a common wherry from Burghley's watergate, and the man rows with the tide up toward Mortlake, passing Whitehall on the right where the candles are lit in the Receiving Room, and Walsingham can imagine perhaps that Hatton is dancing, with the Queen not quite well enough to join him but pleased all the same that he should be there paying court.

The lights on the riverbank become fewer the farther upriver they row until they reach Mortlake, to find Doctor Dee's house in darkness.

"You should have said you were after the doctor," the boatman tells him. "He's been gone weeks. Cleared out one night, all his books and magical wands and stuff and never been seen since. Took my nephew with him, too, and my brother's boat. Still not seen neither again."

Walsingham wonders what has happened to Mistress Dee.

"Likewise," the boatman says. "Left on the river only a few days later. Rowed her all the way to Tilbury meself, I did. Took me a week just to get the strength back in me arms. She gave me half a crown for it, mind. She's a generous one, that Mistress Dee. I shall miss her."

"Did she say where she was bound?"

"She didn't. No."

"You didn't ask her? Seems odd."

"I did ask but it is as I say: she didn't know."

"Ohh. But then—did she say why?"

"Going to find the doctor, she said. Make sure he gets home safe and sound. Determined, isn't she? Don't much like that in a woman, do you?"

Walsingham does not answer.

✠

CHAPTER THIRTEEN

Hamburg, Saxony, November 1583

That night Łaski lodges at the English House in the city across the Elbe in Hamburg, where he hopes to be treated as he deserves, while Dee and the others stay with a widow on this side of the river, under the sign of an angel, which Kelley does not feel is fitting, though it is all they can afford. Today is the first really cold day of what has so far been a mild autumn, and in their already road-worn woolens they are reminded of winter's fearsome pinch.

Dee takes the time to write another letter to Jane:

Dearly beloved Jane, I commend myself to you, and to our son, Arthur, too, as the angelic spirits have said that his rabbit is gone out of our world, and his passing is in some manner my doing. Our journey continues and we will soon reach Lübeck where Count Łaski hopes to receive sorely needed funds. My book is almost finished, for which thanks be unto

God, and in no small part to EK, though its purpose remains
as opaque as its meaning. I have written to Walsingham
about my homecoming and will receive his reply in Prague,
from Thaddeus Hajek, whom I hope will take us in to his little
house below the Bethlem Chapel, should you yourself wish
to send word, and so I go now, another day on the road, and
with this comes with all my love, my most entirely beloved
Jane, from: Δ.

By the time he's done, the candle is dead, but beyond the
window, the streets of the little township in which they find
themselves are waking up and there is, if he changes his place at
the table, light enough to let him return to work on the *Book of
Loagaeth*, writing out the rough notes he has taken during the
various Actions with Kelley and his show stone. Dee will not tell
Jane in a letter that might be opened by anyone on the highway
that properly understood, this book will grant the adept the power
to command everything in the world, and everything out of it,
too, even unto the angelic spirits themselves, and it may yet save
mankind from the coming apocalypse.

Until then they must press on, ever eastward, though they
are all already so weary, and Count Łaski is proving a mercurial
traveling companion: sometimes there, sometimes not, and with
a canny knack of finding himself either a bed where none seemed
possible, or the best if there is a choice. His servants—more so
Emericus Sontag, less so Alexander—suffer his lapses with phleg-
matic shrugs.

"He is either one thing or the other," Alexander confides one
evening when there is drink to be had, which provokes a heated
discussion between the two servants in Polish, which Emericus
later tells Dee concerned the possibility or impossibility of

there being only two things, especially when it came to human nature.

Dee likes them both and would greatly enjoy this discourse, but there are more pressing matters.

"Will the count manage to borrow any money from Lord Mecklenburg?"

"Oh yes." Alexander is confident.

"But will spend it long before we reach Prague," Emericus adds.

Before they leave to cross the river, they attempt an Action, in part because Dee wishes for more information on the *Book of Loagaeth*, and in part to bolster Łaski's faith not only in Dee, but in his own mission too.

"Will Emperor Rudolf help Count Olbrecht Łaski regain possession of his estates?" Kelley asks.

"Consider it," Galvah replies, which could mean anything, but before they reach clarity, Kelley loses his temper, and calls Galvah an evil spirit, and accuses him of speaking to him in Syrian. After that, they both refuse to have anything more to do with each other, so bringing the Action to a jarring, worrying conclusion, and Kelley will not be soothed even after he catches a long silver-skinned fish from the back of the barge.

"We'll soon be in Prague," Dee tells Łaski. "That should cheer him."

⊕

CHAPTER FOURTEEN

Kulmbach, Bavaria, late November 1583

I t is coming on toward sunset over the river Main, and Jane
Frommond stands in the bow of the sixth and smallest boat
they have boarded since leaving Tilbury more than a month ago,
and she watches Christopher Marlowe pulling himself up to, and
then letting himself down from, a rope that stretches taut from the
barge's stern to her mainmast. Jane is not alone. From his place by
the tiller the bargemaster watches, too, as do his three-man crew,
spread around the boat, for each has money on Marlowe not being
able to repeat this feat more than fifty times.

He cannot, of course, and at the forty-seventh time of trying
he falls and lies crumpled on the deck, dripping with sweat and
utterly spent. The master and his crew cheer, for they have won
their bet, but Marlowe, still with his head hanging low, holds up
his unblistered palms, and offers them double or quits, and they
laugh and agree, since the wager is not so very much—only a few
pennies—and Jane cannot stop shaking her head in wonder at

human folly for this is the sixth time she has seen this exact trick of his, and the sixth time that he manages—just, and with so much strain surely you'd believe he was going to die—fifty-one of pull-ups, and the sixth time she has seen him drop back down to the deck, a very marginally richer man.

It is not the only trick he has pulled to earn them their supper since they reached Nijmegen. On that first night, he had performed his much-vaunted iron nail trick to get them supper at the house of the childless widow of a ropemaker who had hanged himself in winter. Widow Vander Meerden had nothing to feed them, she said, despite herself being plump and her house smelling of well-cooked onion, and though they might have paid her, Marlowe was keen to demonstrate his trick and so they begged her for a pot of water, and a short spell over her meager cooking fire.

Then Marlowe crouched and watched the water come to the boil with eyes that seemed to shine in anticipation, and despite herself, the old woman—she must have been all of forty—was intrigued. When the water was seething softly, he produced from his doublet pocket the iron nail—two inches long, no longer sharp if it ever had been, and dark with rust—and he slipped it into the water with a satisfied smile. He waited, ostentatiously murmuring the *Pater Noster*, and then the *Ave Maria*, and then even the *Credo*, all of which he seemed to know by heart, and in which the widow joined, until at last he removed the pot of water and set it down upon the table with a broad and satisfied smile.

"Soppa," he said. "Soup."

Frommond almost laughed but the performance was not over yet. When he tasted it, he decided the soup was not perfect, and so he begged just the tiniest pinch of salt, and the widow, now transfixed, fetched it. Herbs followed. Then flour. Then the widow herself suggested some bread, which she had in a stone jar under the table and then there was even a fist of cured pork cupped with a finger's thick layer of lustrous fat, which in a stroke of genius Marlowe refused. That led the widow to slice it very finely and then cook it in a separate pan with a dab of butter and more of the herbs, into which she added some finely shredded leeks that Marlowe was about to put into the already by now quite thick sauce. Ground peppercorns followed and more bread was found and sliced to line the bottom of three bowls and then the soup was poured over the slices and then the pork shreds, by now crisp, and the leeks, now translucent, were placed in a heavy palmful on top of that, upon which were found—of all things—some pumpkin seeds that the widow toasted in a dry pan and scattered. When it was done, they all three sat at the table and looked at one another and laughed with delight when Marlowe extracted, and put away in his doublet, the rusty nail. Later he managed to get the widow to part with some beer, and at soup's end, he sang her a song about a sailor falling in love with a fish as big as Job's whale.

After that he went out, leaving the two women alone, and when he returned in the morning, he was dressed as a sailor.

"What happened to the doublet?" Frommond asked. Marlowe had bought it off someone on his way to Tilbury for a startlingly small sum, he claimed, and it had been deep burgundy velvet with slashes that revealed apricot silk; the sort of thing a courtier might wear on a Wednesday night.

"Yaaaargh" he'd said, as if he were careless of it. "Every girl loves a sailor, don't they, eh, Widow Vander Meerden?" and he'd given her shoulder a squeeze and she had blushed quite pink.

They left Nijmegen on a broad flat-bottomed barge under a great spread of rust-colored canvas that hung slack for two days while a succession of horses towed them upriver. The towns they came to were occupied with Spanish troops, and the atmosphere on the quays was sullen and threatening, and no man or woman went ashore unarmed.

"Could kick off at any moment, couldn't it?" Marlowe supposed.

They sailed on under vast skies through flat lands dished by sodden floodplains and only the occasional raised road, and Frommond learned that Marlowe seemed to need to stir up trouble to feel alive. Even before they'd left those Spanish-held lands, he could not stop himself shouting at a priest on a donkey waiting to take a ferry across the river. He called him a pederast and a wanker, right to his face as they passed, and a filthy Jesuit.

"Thank God he does not understand English," Frommond told him, but Marlowe's meaning was broadly clear, and the barge-master and his crew, already resentful at being so good-naturedly robbed by Marlowe's pull-up trick, looked at him in ways that spelled trouble, and so they changed barges the next opportunity.

"Didn't like that one anyway," Marlowe said.

More or less the same thing happened a few nights later, their first on dry land, in the hall of a tavern of a city where the cathedral had two equal spires, and where the regulars took exception to something Marlowe said or did and he told Frommond that if anyone came for them, she was to hit him with the earthenware jug.

"Just here, boom, and he'll go down like a hanged man."

"How hard?" she asked, for she did not want to kill anyone.

Marlowe laughed at her.

"Hard as you fucking well can," he said.

Later, on the smaller river they'd had to follow that would take them east, they'd eaten black bread and dense sausage and drunk wonderfully sharp beer in an inn below a church, when Marlowe—having traded his sailors slops for tight leather shorts held up by straps over his shoulders—took exception to the presence of five or six friars at a table nearby; he was soon gesturing and whooping and making all sorts of foul suggestions as to their proclivities. He even called them caterpillars.

"Please, Christopher," Frommond muttered. "We have no time for this."

She'd not once stopped fretting about John's arrival in Prague, him coming through the gates supposing everyone would believe he was exiled, and down on his luck, when in fact everyone would be waiting for him, knowing he was sent there by Francis Walsingham for some very specific, if unknown, purpose. In the short hours, she imagines they will take him at the gate and hang him from the walls for a spy. In the longer hours, she supposes they might watch him a little, to see where his schemes take him, and then hang him. That at least gives her a longer lease to save him, if Marlowe would but cease his endless risky games.

That night, in the inn, he had stopped mocking the friars out of consideration for her, but only for a while, for it seemed he could not help himself and soon he was back at it. The friars were unused to anything other than respect, and at first were mystified, then offended, then furious, and after a while their Christian forbearance gave way. When Marlowe went outside to relieve himself, Frommond was left to hear a furious discussion in their tooth-crunching tongue as to what they were going to do about it. By the time Marlowe was back, they had decided, and they came for him with beer mugs and stools, but Marlowe had guessed what would happen, and had—against all decency—slathered his palms with his own shit, and he came at them, dabbing at their faces and forcing them to flee. When they were gone, with Marlowe's laugh following them out of the inn, he wiped his hands on some straw, threw it in the fire, laughed again at the horrible stink, and thanked the Lord in whom he claimed not to believe that none of them were tanners, "for whom piss and shit is as bread and butter."

But again, it was prudent to leave the town that night, and they slept aboard a new barge crewed by men who claimed to be Bohemian.

"That's a good sign," was all Marlowe said as he drifted off, hands unwashed, and now, after nearly three weeks on the river they are finally at the town of Kulmbach, where the waters part into awkward unnavigable channels, and they have no choice but to hire horses to ride east toward Bohemia.

The horses are generally good, and the roads well-traveled, with frequent inns offering somewhat oppressive hospitality, but chained to every building is a startlingly fierce dog, on account of the bears and the wolves that come out of the forests at night, they are told, though Marlowe claims an affinity with bears.

Two days later they reach a line of forested hills, and they begin the climb while the temperature drops. Snow begins to fall and Marlowe is pleased to have traded those leather shorts for ordinary woolen breeches that are parti-colored mustard and plum that Frommond tells him make him look like a member of a players' company. They battle through the driving snow, half losing the track in the woods until at last they crest the peak and descend toward a small gray town on a swift-moving river where, to cross the bridge, they are forced to pay pontage to a man wrapped in matted gray furs.

That night at the inn, Marlowe nearly cries with chilblains, but the beer is even better than it had been in Bavaria and the son of the innkeeper is tall, square jawed, and blond haired, and he has spent his whole life in the mountains chopping wood. So Frommond is unsurprised when in the morning Marlowe tells her they will stay in this little village, in this little inn, until the snow has passed, but she has been visited in the night by terrible dreams of howling wolves and has woken terrified for Dee and insists they press on.

Outside the stables the snow is pressed with paw prints the size of plates, and the sad, huddle-shouldered innkeeper sends his son to ride with them until they begin their descent down onto the broad flatlands where the snow peters out, and the road becomes good again and there's a village every couple of leagues and a town every five. Then, after another night under the eaves of another inn, and another day in the saddle, when they are sodden and frozen and worn as old shoes, there, at last, ahead of them lies Prague: a spiky clutch of red-tiled roofs crawling up a hill upon which stands a formidably austere castle, and over it all, a pall of coal smoke.

"Thank Christ," is all Marlowe says.

And all Frommond can do is give thanks unto God that at least there is no sign of her husband's crow-pecked body hanging from the walls.

⊕

CHAPTER FIFTEEN

Orford Ness, Suffolk, December 1583

Robert Beale stands on the shingle spit with his face into an easterly wind that blasts off the cold North Sea and he wonders again for perhaps the five hundredth time that month why it is that they cannot just *ask* Sir Christopher Hatton who in the name of God Master Mope is? He understands that it is good that Hatton does not learn he is known to be a traitor, but is that so very much a *better* thing than having three men combing every shitty little muddy fly-speckled inlet along England's east coast in search of a mystery man calling himself Master Mope, of whom the only thing that is known for sure is that Master Mope is not his real name?

"They've never heard of him," Gregory says, his boots crunching on the shingle. "No one has."

"Where's next?" Beale asks.

"Bawdsey," Gregory says, indicating south. "But we have to walk back that way for two miles."

He indicates north.

"Where we left the horses?"

"No. That's just over there."

He indicates inland, two hundred yards away, to the little town clustered under the castle like children clinging to their mother's skirts. He and Gregory are separated from it by the river Alde, thirty paces wide when the tide is out, fifty when it is in, and across which they cannot get without a boat, which they do not have.

Beale says nothing for a moment, then: "All right. Let's get going."

And so they trudge northward, heads bowed, the wind paralyzing the right sides of their faces.

"Can I just ask, Master Beale," Gregory raises his voice above the wind and the pebbles, "and I may have already done so, save I do not recall receiving a satisfactory answer, but is there anything you can think of that might cause Sir Francis to send us to this godforsaken shithole on a wild goose chase?"

Beale shrugs again, and says nothing, for Gregory surely knows he will have nothing more to add to the answer he gave this morning to the exact same question Gregory had asked while they were retracing their steps after having reached an impasse in the leagues-wide swath of marshes that back the coast hereabouts. He knows Gregory is right, though: Walsingham sent Beale here the day after they first racked Throckmorton, and he did it in an almost fatherly way, meaning kindly; he had spoken softly, pretending this task of finding Master Mope was crucial to national safety.

"Her Majesty herself was asking after our progress in this regard," Walsingham had lied. Beale had understood that Walsingham knew he was up to something and feared it might be the same sort of thing as Beale's scheme with Ness Overbury, and that perhaps spending time, miles from anywhere, under Gregory's close watch might head it off.

"Well, at least it is not raining," Gregory supposes.

But they both know that is only a matter of time.

Later that afternoon they reach the village of Bawdsey, fifteen houses around a squat-spired church, just above the ferry on the north bank of the river Deben. Upstream are numerous fishing villages and little havens for coastal traffic, mostly boats carrying wool sarplers across to Flanders. No one knows of a Master Mope.

By the time they have asked up and down the river's north bank and have retraced their steps to the ferry, it is raining again, and the ferry is on the other side of the river. They huddle under some trees and stand for a while, their horses steaming and pulling at the wilted weeds below, and they watch the ferry inching its way back over the river toward them, fighting the forceful current of the plowed-field brown river. As it approaches, Beale and Gregory lead their horses out to the jetty to meet it, and Gregory catches the thrown rope and loops it over a stanchion. Four oarsmen need paying, but the master is good with the horses, and they walk aboard and stand calmly while they are propelled south across the turbid water toward distant Felixstowe.

"Don't suppose you know of anyone going by the name of Master Mope, do you?" Beale asks the ferryman, more in hope than expectation, and he—short-legged and sly-looking, faintly Dutch—pulls on his ear and considers the value of his answer before finding nothing in it and giving it for free.

"No," he says.

And Beale nods and turns away and ducks his head into his collar as the rain turns to sleet.

It will soon be Christmas, he thinks.

⊕

PART | THREE

CHAPTER SIXTEEN

New Town, Prague, Bohemia,
second week of January 1584

Snow on the ground still, and a thick mist rising from the river below, and they come to stop a hundred paces from its bank and drop their bags. Huge fires burn at both ends of the bridge, and in ordinary times this might be a cheerful sight, but the length of the bridge is choked with crowds of restless, milling men, and it looks like trouble.

"Is there another way across?" Frommond wonders.

"Might be a ferry," Marlowe supposes, peering doubtfully into the swirling darkness below. "Too much to hope for ice."

"We could try it?" she suggests, meaning the bridge. "There's no reason they'd not let us cross, is there?"

For once Marlowe is doubtful, and this should be enough to warn Frommond off, but she believes the house of Dee's old friend Master Hajek is within spitting distance, to which he wrote to say he was bending his steps, and dear God she is so tired and cold and hungry that this last gamble seems worth it.

"Come on," she says, and she gathers her cloak and hood tight about her, and she wearily hefts her bag over her shoulder just as Marlowe does with his, and they walk side by side down toward the bridge's western end, just two pilgrims perhaps. They are just about to step into the light of that first fire, to present themselves to the knot of men standing by the barrier across the road that consists of a tree trunk laid flat between two barrels, when the men see or hear something else, coming from the other direction, and they turn to face it: a cart, pulled by oxen and led by a man with a bull's-eye lantern, which when it comes into the light of the first fire, and is seen by those on the bridge, is greeted by a roar that spreads down the length of the bridge that sounds like burning wood but is in fact the sound of hundreds of leather mugs being beaten against hundreds of palms.

"Beer delivery," Marlowe tells her. "Should liven things up."

And it does. The men on the bridge surge to its end. They push aside the barrier and spill out onto the bank to cluster around the cart, mugs held upstretched to be sloppily filled by men in the bed of the cart dipping ewers into barrels and pouring them out in great long streams.

Frommond knows it is now or never, and they hurry down to slide through the tail of the queueing mob, passing through the melee of those at the rear, and then they are on to the span of the bridge—an ornate one, its parapets peopled by gloomy statues every twenty paces—and they hurry along against the flow, sliding out of the way of anyone they meet. They are nearly at the far end when a giant of a man looms out from behind one of the fires and calls to them in language that sounds like nothing so much as the strokes of a carter's whip.

"Run!" Marlowe shouts, and they abandon all pretense and

sprint from the giant and turn right at the end of the bridge, making for the shadowed lanes of the Old Town, where they are informed Hajek lives. If the giant decides to chase them, they're probably done for, but he doesn't. Instead they hear him laughing, taunting them perhaps, or boasting that he owns the bridge now, and that they are right to run from him.

Frommond hardly cares.

Into snow-choked lanes they go and they are swiftly lost in the rank maze of streets and alleyways. At last, though, after double-backing twice and finding their own footprints more than once, they find a new street with an austere church, its front banked with snow. There is no one to ask if this is the Betlémská Kaple, but it must be, they decide. They take their directions from it and find what they hope is the house of Thaddeus Hajek, and Frommond leaves it to Marlowe to knock on the dark-painted door. When he does, a small shutter opens at high head-height, and some question is spat at Marlowe, to which he replies in fluent Latin. There is a pause, as if for consideration, and then after, the shutter is closed.

There comes the sound of one, two, three, four locks being pulled back and then the door is swung open on greased hinges. A surprisingly small recessed figure ushers them in.

"Festina!" he says. *Hurry.*

They step in, and the door closes and the four locks are shot behind them, and it is like being gaoled, Frommond thinks, with gorge in her throat, remembering the time she spent locked in the hold of a river barge, but the house is warm and something good is cooking, and she steps aside to let the man shuffle past.

"This way."

They follow him along a dark corridor toward a light-filled, book-lined room where a man stands before a lectern, turned to them, feather in hand.

"Master Hajek?" she asks.

The man says something in the local tongue, which suggests he is as she says—a slender, child-bodied, adult-headed man of about fifty, with gray-speckled side whiskers and protuberant blue eyes—but who are they? Marlowe takes over in Latin and explains who they are and why they have come. The man has not been expecting them and knows nothing of them.

"You are after Doctor *Dee*?" he repeats, baffled, and then in strongly accented English, "He not come yet."

"Oh thank God!" Jane cries, and the relief that he is not actually yet known to be dead almost robs her of her last strength. It is as if her fears for Dee were all that was holding her up, and now Hajek must guide her to a chair, by the fire, where she sits and for the first time takes in her startled host's book-filled room and the unusual, probably cabalistic, drawings that cover the wall, from skirt to crown and across the ceiling, too: birds, fish, fruits, flowers, leaves and various symbols that she half recognizes from Dee's attempts to engage her in his work.

"But he's on his way?" Marlowe asks. "You know he is coming? You've heard from him?"

Hajek agrees with a hearty nod.

"He sends notes from all across Christendom! But what is happened in England? He is exiled? He is disgraced, he says. He means as joke?"

Marlowe and Frommond share a glance.

"He will tell you himself, I daresay," Marlowe tells Hajek. "When he gets here, that is."

Hajek must accept this, he supposes, and he expresses the desire to see his good friend the doctor seated there by the fireside. Until that time, they are to be his guests, he tells them, and he sends his servant to fetch something before apologizing for the unfriendly reception.

"You come at sad time for Praha," he says. "Much hatred and suspicion of people."

"Which people?" Marlowe wonders.

Hajek sighs.

"Ohhh. The usual. The Jews."

"So that's what was happening on the bridge?"

"You managed to cross it?" Hajek is amazed.

Frommond explains their good timing, and Hajek shakes his head. He is ashamed of his city.

"Is a dark shadow over us. Is this Spanish ambassador: Don Guillermo San Clemente. Bad influence on Emperor Rudolf, and emperor is . . . not here with us as emperor should be, and where he is not, someone else is, you see?"

"A vacuum," Frommond suggests.

Hajek is surprised and delighted that a woman should use such a term, and he credits Dee for this, of course, which to Jane counts against him, but after that journey it is just so good to be somewhere she is not having to negotiate merely to find herself. Meanwhile Hajek is telling her that he met her husband at Emperor Maximilian's wedding back in '63 or whenever.

"My sons," Hajek tells her, "they also study in England, and teach me what they can."

He is fishing for compliments about his English and duly gets them. Just then the servant reappears with a silver jug of wine and three cups. Hajek laughs.

"So much for little talk," he says, and it is true: they are into dark and weighty matters before they have even discussed the journey or asked after one another's health or any of the hundred and one other matters that might occur more naturally.

"But what's this Spanish ambassador got against the Jews anyway?" Marlowe asks, crouching to warm his hands on the glowing coals. "Aside from the usual, that is?"

Hajek blows out air.

"Wants Inquisition in Prague, in whole of Bohemia, in whole of Empire. Everywhere. But after Jan Huss and all the wars, we have Jews and Calvinists and Catholics living side by side, not noticing one another, and the emperor is— He wants nothing changed, so Spanish and the pope is rousing the people. Spanish pays crowds of beggars with beer to spit and shout and throw stones at Jews and then the pope say it shows people want Jews gone."

"But why are all your windows barred and that?" Marlowe asks. "Why the four locks and all the rushing us in and all that caper if you ain't Jewish?"

"Because as I say: ignorant fools is paid to throw stones and worse! Paid to throw shit at us and shout horrible things. And now there is been break-in. More than one."

"The filthy beggars!" Marlowe exclaims. "Was it them what came in and scrawled all over your walls?" He points to the cabalistic messages and the graffiti. Hajek frowns. He is not yet used to Marlowe's endless inappropriatisms.

"Everywhere is trouble. On bridge to castle always."

"No offense, Master," Marlowe starts, "but you look about as Jewish as my old mum. As Mistress Dee here."

Frommond supposes she is—what?—six years older than Marlowe? Sometimes he makes her feel thirty years older, and sometimes thirty years younger.

"Tell that to man who stand in street all day," Hajek tells him. "Out there right now. Watching house. You see him?"

Marlowe gets to his feet.

"He's out there now, is he?" he asks.

Hajek and his servant rush to stop him going to the window.

"We don't want trouble," Hajek insists. "It will soon pass."

Marlowe seems to doubt this.

But it is arranged that Frommond will take Hajek's room, while Marlowe and Hajek will share the library, and Hajek's servant, Edwin, and his wife will take to the attic. Frommond tries to refuse, but Hajek is insistent, out of respect, he tells her, for Dee.

"Any man who can make giant golden beetle fly is not to be disrespect!"

Frommond has almost forgotten that feat of Dee's, carried out long before she met him, when he was a student at Cambridge, but its fame has spread surprisingly far and wide.

Later, when she and Marlowe are alone, Marlowe tells Frommond that he does not believe Hajek.

"What? At all?"

"No. No. He's telling the truth, but he's got it wrong. The fella watching the house isn't doing it because he thinks they're Jewish. He's waiting for your doctor."

Dinner is taken early—headcheese in a brown sauce with saffron rice and rye bread, served by Edwin—during which Hajek tries to explain the character of the emperor without saying "yes but no" too often, but which he fails to do, for the emperor is never one thing nor the other but a wavering, havering mix of any two things, and obviously hard to describe. Frommond notices that whenever they talk of the emperor they gesture up toward the castle, and his presence seems to loom over the city, unknowable and slippery, and yet oppressive at the same time, a dark, sulfurous cloud.

"Have you ever met him in the flesh?" Frommond wonders.

Hajek almost laughs.

"No one has!"

"No one?"

"Well. He never sees anyone, and no one ever sees him. People wait in the palace whole lives. Never see emperor. He is every day in *Kunstkammer*."

"*Kunts-Kammer*?" Marlowe laughs. "Needs to see a physician about that."

"*Kunstkammer*," Hajek corrects. "You have heard this word? Emperor has a room in New Palace filled with things he loves—many, many manuscripts and books, yes, but also paintings—many, many paintings—and statues, of men and women and all sorts, from Italy, and Greece, and all over the world also, and these he keeps in his *Kunstkammer*. But you know what emperor loves most of all?"

Marlowe has a guess, but is wrong.

"Not quite," Hajek says. "He loves horses. He loves horses even more than women. And all things to do with them, too: saddles and harnesses, he has whole room of. Statues, too, obviously. His stables are bigger than most towns. But there is more also, you know? He loves things other people never seen, never know: skulls of dragons, rocks that bleed, a fish that has been to the moon. Such things."

Edwin, who really is closer to a secretary than a servant and eats with them, understands a little English but cannot speak it, and he now rattles off something very quick in their shared tongue that seems to annoy Hajek. Frommond would have ignored it, but Marlowe is less inclined.

"What's he to say?"

Hajek flushes.

"Edwin says that the emperor not only interested in horses."

"Really? What else is he interested in?"

"Emperor is in love with a French woman"—Hajek tiptoes carefully with his words—"but she is not French, yes? She is from

Land of Prester John, in Africa, and her skin is polished black by thousand days' tropical sun."

Marlowe whistles and laughs. Encouraged, Edwin tries his English on them, obviously gleaned from something cabalistic he has overheard, and probably in this very room.

"And emperor looks for Universal and Eternal Oneness," he says, "between her legs."

It takes a moment before they understand what he's said but when they do, Marlowe hoots and claps and Hajek sends Edwin from the room and apologizes to Frommond.

"Not a bit of it," Frommond tells him.

Soon after it they snuff the candles and go to their beds of fresh hay but too few blankets.

⊕

In the morning—very gray, with the threat of more snow before noon—Frommond hears Marlowe rise at cockcrow, and from a slightly parted shutter in Hajek's solitary room, she watches him go out onto the street and address the man standing there. It's a blade sharpener, standing with his cart under the arches of an arcade opposite, doing no business, but she now wonders if she did not see him the day before, when they arrived at Hajek's door? There is a knife sharpener in Mortlake who knows everyone's secrets, and makes up those he doesn't, and so she is ever careful around such men.

Marlowe and the knife sharpener disappear from view, and later Jane finds Master Hajek in his study, freshly barbered, stiffly dressed in black wool filigreed with gold silk, and extravagantly ruffed. He tells her he is due at the castle.

"To approve some astrological charts."

It turns out that is his job.

"May I come with you?" she asks. She cannot stand just to sit here if Dee is in danger. What good she might do she has no idea. She would at least have an opinion worth offering.

But Hajek is very doubtful.

"The streets of Prague are no place for a woman," he tells her. "Not these days. And you've seen the bridge."

"Can it be so bad in daylight?" she hopes.

"You won't be able to see the emperor anyway."

Just then Marlowe is at the front door, smelling of coal smoke and frost, and Edwin lets him in. Frommond sees there's a purple welt across his knuckles and blood in his hair. She takes his arm and they step outside, into the tiny courtyard behind Hajek's house.

"What did the knife sharpener say?" she asks.

"It's just as I said. He wasn't being paid to keep an eye on the place because he thought old Hajek's a Jew. He was being paid to watch for a tall man with a beard who looks like a magician. That sound like your husband?"

It does, sort of. *Jesu*, she thinks, so there we are: word of Dee's alternative purpose has reached Prague before him, but who is it who knows?

"Who's paying the knife sharpener?"

"A Dutchman: Arnoldus van der Boxe. Supposed to live up in that castle at the top of the hill. Geezer made him sound like some kind of official. Like he's got a job at the palace."

A courtier then.

"Master Hajek might know him," she supposes. "But does the knife sharpener know why he's been told to look for John?"

"He didn't."

"*Didn't?*"

"Done himself a bit of a mischief, hasn't he? With one of his own knives."

"You *killed* him?"

Frommond is horrified.

"Before he could kill me. He wasn't pissing about."

He points to his hair, where a nick is still bleeding. Frommond shudders. Marlowe's heart has many chambers, she has learned, and each is hard shuttered against the other, thanks be to God, but Jesu, she thinks: a man has already died in this.

"So now we need to find this Van der Boxhead," Marlowe goes on, "and sort him out."

"Will you kill him, too?"

Marlowe shrugs.

"If the occasion demands," he supposes.

Can it be so simple? she wonders.

They go back in to find Hajek about to leave for the castle. Marlowe insists on coming with Frommond.

"But is nothing interesting," Hajek assures them. "Just masons and carpenters only, and men like me shuffling paper. No horses. No emperor."

"Love it," Marlowe says.

Edwin shoots the bolts, and Hajek, Marlowe, and Frommond step out onto the lane. A thin layer of snow has fallen overnight, but already it is splattered with emptied privy pots and kitchen waste, and starving dogs hunt among peelings for bones. They look left and right. No one waiting. No one watching.

"Ha!" Hajek says. "He has gone."

Marlowe says nothing.

They turn right and make their way down to the riverbank where they turn right again. Ahead is the bridge, its statues rising up out of the river's mist, and above is the gray-walled flank of the castle, towers shrouded in the low cloud. There are still fires at both ends of the bridge, and in the daylight they can see signs painted on cloth banners that they cannot read for being in Bohemian but there are pictures: a crucifix, a gallows with a hanged man, a rat with a human face, a human with a rat's face, so they get the gist. There is less of the lawless menace of the night before, but even so, Hajek stops to study it for a while and is somewhat relieved.

"Good," he says. "There is one man who is usually here. A giant almost. His name Marek. He causes all my troubles, but not here today."

Frommond supposes it was him who shouted at them the night before.

The bridge is still a gauntlet to be endured, though, for the men at the barriers are suspicious and impertinent. They demand to search Frommond, who defies them with her stare, though dear God she is pleased that Marlowe is at her side, for he carries a strange energy that a certain sort of man seems to understand and fear. After a long time spent with Hajek pleading that they be let through unmolested, for they are personal friends of the emperor, they are, but even then they are followed up the length of the bridge by a small crowd of men and boys who are no better than thieves and cutpurses, who taunt them and shout in their faces.

"What are they calling us?" Marlowe wants to know.

"You don't want to know."

"I do."

"They calling us filthy Jews. And you, Master Marlowe, they will come for on Ash Wednesday, and they will string you up, upside down, and drain your blood to make a sausage that they will make your mother— You not want know."

Marlowe raises his eyebrows.

"What fucker said that?"

Frommond catches his arm.

"Please, Christopher," she hisses. "Just stay calm. Ignore them and keep going."

"But why'd they want to do that?" Marlowe demands to know. "What've I done to them?"

"Is because of what you did to Jesus at Eastertide," Hajek tells him.

"I didn't do— But we ain't Jews! Tell 'em that."

"They don't care. It makes no difference!"

After that Hajek refuses to translate anything else that is shouted at them. Halfway across, Frommond removes a hatpin, the use of which has saved her before. She stabs a hand that attempts to snatch her purse, another that tries to grip her breast, and a third her buttock, and so they gradually lose their escort and make it to the end of the bridge. There they must pass under the sour stares of those manning the cordon at that end, before they can begin up the winding path between the houses of the Lesser Town, and up to the emperor's looming castle in a little more peace.

"And that was a good crossing," Hajek says. "When Marek is there, is always worse. Did you see all the sticks and stones piled up?"

She hadn't.

"Normally they throw those. I've seen him push a man off into the river. They drown or freeze and the watch do nothing."

Hajek is swiftly breathless from the steps they must climb to reach the castle's East Gate, and at the top they pause to take a breath under the looming castle walls.

"Bugger me, mate," Marlowe says, "this is a palace, all right. He could be anywhere."

"Who?" Hajek asks.

"You know a fella called Van der Boxe? Arnoldus van der Boxe?"

The name is obviously familiar.

"The Dutchman?"

"Could be," Marlowe agrees.

"He is part of Spanish ambassador household."

Frommond and Marlowe look at each other quickly. If Van der Boxe sent the knife sharpener, and he is part of the Spanish ambassador's household, then it means the Spanish know Dee is coming, and that he comes not as an exile, but as a spy.

"And where would I find that?" Marlowe wonders. "This Spanish household?"

Hajek indicates the far end of the castle, beyond the cathedral.

"Is left over from days when emperor's mother lived here, but she back to Spain now. But anyhow, you never get in."

At which Marlowe smiles, of course.

The East Gate is blocked by a cart on which something like a huge painting is wrapped about in waxed canvas and strapped upright. The watch are asking questions of the drivers and their escorts, five men with halberds, who look to have come some way.

"You see?" Hajek says. "Another painting. They roll in every day. From Venice. Or Antwerp. Madrid and beyond. I wonder what is?"

"Ten to one says it's a picture of a horse." Marlowe laughs. "A white horse. Or some brass's Universal and Eternal Oneness."

At length the captain of the watch permits the wagon through, the guards recognize Hajek waiting, and all together they are waved through under the gatehouse arch. Once inside, enclosed within the curtain walls, it's as if they have stumbled upon another town entirely, an ants' nest of activity, for the whole bailey is a thronging building site, crowded with an army of masons and carpenters and hundreds of laborers, and the central square is given over to sheds and cooking fires and mounds of sand and stone. The lifts on the walls are so tall they are powered by teams of oxen in cages below and there is an enclosure of barrels so large each might house an entire family.

They follow in the ruts of the wagon with the painting, heading through the crowds toward a church almost as big as Saint Paul's, with decoration so ornate it gives you a headache.

"Emperor's new palace past there." Hajek points past it, down the length of the bailey, to where more halberdiers wait.

"But you never get in," he repeats.

Marlowe rolls his eyes again.

"Is he there now?" he asks, as if out of interest, really. "In his little *Kunts-kammer*?"

"His *Kunstkammer*," Hajek corrects.

"And anyway," Marlowe says, "who is this African bird—the African woman—that the emperor is so stuck on?"

Hajek sighs.

"Edwin talks out of turn," he says. "But her name is Kitty de Fleurier."

"Have you seen her?"

"A bit, tiny bit."

He pinches thumb and forefinger very nearly together, as if through a door or a keyhole.

"And?"

"She very beautiful."

"What's she doing here?" Frommond asks. It does not seem a stupid question, because she has experience only of Her Majesty's court in England, where people come to gossip and advance themselves, and though there are many beautiful women who come for wealthy husbands, she understands that the emperor is in fact already married.

Hajek has no answer.

"She just is," he says with a shrug.

They have reached a heavy door in one of the towers, where Hajek knocks and is let in by a gloomy halberdier without his halberd. Worn stone steps take them winding up past occupied offices until they reach one with windows pitched south over castle walls to give a view of the sprawl of the city and the length of the river that winds like a strap of polished iron beyond the city walls through the fields and the dark fir forests before blurring into the misted distance.

Frommond wonders briefly where it flows in to the sea and has no idea.

Desks and lecterns and banks of pigeonholes furnish the room, and there is a good fire of strong-smelling coal. Various beak-nosed men in black wool peer up from where they pore over papers, and they regard Frommond and Marlowe with the weary patience of men interrupted in work they believe important.

Marlowe asks Hajek to ask if any of them know the whereabouts of Arnoldus van der Boxe, and one of the men thinks he knows of him.

"Says he is one of chamberlain's men," Hajek translates.

"The chamberlain? Not the Spanish ambassador?"

There is some chatter, which Hajek distills as: "Both."

"And where'll we find this old chamberlain then?" Marlowe asks.

He obviously has a plan, Frommond thinks, fears.

Hajek points in the same direction as the Spanish ambassador's residence and opens his mouth to say something, but Marlowe forestalls.

"But we'll never get in, yeah, yeah. We know," he says, and he turns to Frommond.

"Come on," he says, and he cups her elbow, and they slip away, back down the steps and out into the courtyard. She finds she has, without thinking, picked up Master Hajek's heavy black cloak from one of the hooks. Marlowe has picked up someone else's.

"Very fetching," he tells her.

The halberdier at the bottom of the steps is already back asleep on his feet. Outside, Marlowe turns left, down toward the church. He has the confident swagger that may impress in Custom House, but it cuts no ice in the Hradčany.

"Walk behind me," Frommond tells him.

So he drops back to take up his position as her servant, and they follow the gravel road that the cart took, past a basilica on their right, and the cathedral, too, and into the gloomier depths of the castle courtyards, where the cold really bites. The masons are cutting stone blocks they move about the place on barrows with wheels padded against the noise, and there is an almost sacred sense of respect for some nearby deity.

"If he's as lowly as you say he is, we aren't going to find Van der Boxe around here," she tells Marlowe. "He'll be in the offices back there."

"Let's just see, shall we?" Marlowe says. "I'm feeling lucky."

They attach themselves to a throng of men and women waiting to pass through a gate, and Frommond recognizes them all to be dressed just as the Spanish ambassador and his household used to dress when she saw them at Whitehall Palace, and she suddenly experiences an aching pang of homesickness. What would she not give now to be sat beside Mistress Parry fiddling with her embroidery frame while literally nothing happens? Having said that, had she not always wished to travel? And now here she is trying to pass herself off as a Bohemian lady too proud to speak to a mere halberdier at the gate while she seeks a never-going-to-happen audience with her emperor.

"Nicely done!" Marlowe congratulates her when they are through and into another possibly more rarefied courtyard, where the doors and windows are taller and wider and the gravel underfoot deep and fine.

"In here," Marlowe suggests, and they duck into an open-doored guardroom, pass through it unchallenged, and are into shadowy, low-ceilinged corridors and unadorned rooms that give out the smell of men, coal smoke, and wet wool.

Approaching footsteps send them up some steps.

They are now in a very old part of the building, with walls of bare stone and flagstone floors and ceilings. The windows are small and barred but unshuttered, and must date from the days of crossbowmen. It is very cold and there is nothing very much to be seen. A dead end then.

"Well, nothing ventured," Marlowe says.

Frommond peers through the last window and is rewarded with a view of a small garden that appears to have been built out of the castle walls below. It is wonderfully ornate and newly planted, the hedges in some shape that is vaguely familiar from Dee's books—some astrological symbol, perhaps or something philosophical the meaning of which escapes her—and a large marble urn. Some trees fringe its edges, and it would be a pleasure to be here in the summer perhaps.

And then she sees them: two figures walking—though they are moving so slowly they are hardly doing that—arm in arm across a small patch of bright white stones about thirty foot below, making for the parapet with their backs to the castle. A man and a woman, the man in a short, ruby-red cloak and a broad gray cap, skinny shanks like knobbled sticks below and shoes that remind Frommond of the painting of Her Majesty's father in Whitehall. He gives an impression of some infirmity, or weakness, for he walks only with the help of a woman whose form is hidden, but also, somehow, accentuated, by the falling drape of a lustrous midnight-blue cloak that covers her top to toe from its hood to its hem.

"Christopher," she hisses, and he stops and comes back and peers over her head, down into the garden.

"Blow me," he says. "Is that—?"

"Must be."

"Old Hajek'll be fuming when we tell him we've seen him."

Frommond does not point out that the aim of seeing the emperor is to be seen, and heard, yourself.

"D'you suppose that's her? The French girl?"

She can only suppose.

The two reach the parapet wall at the end of the garden and stand a moment, looking out over Prague and Bohemia, until after a moment the emperor starts casting around, as if for a seat, but there is none. He raises his hand, and instantly two men appear from behind in short riding jackets, polished boots, and breeches. Courtiers, not servants. They bring a chair on handles and place it behind his knees and then another man, older, appears to help the emperor into his seat. All three hover solicitously before stepping away again, but Frommond has eyes only for the woman, who has turned to check on the emperor; though it is impossible to see her face properly for the hood, it is obvious that this is indeed Kitty de Fleurier.

"Bugger me," Marlowe breathes. "What a beauty."

After only a very few moments, the emperor seems unhappy, huddled up as if very cold, and starts looking about him for something. After one moment more he raises his hand in a peevish gesture, and the three men are there again, and this time they lift him up in his chair, and they carry him away, leaving Kitty where she stands, watching him go, as if she were watching an old man going for an afternoon nap. It is possible then to see how beautiful she is, the strength and character in her face. But after a moment, when perhaps the emperor has been freighted back in through the door that gives out onto the garden and it has been shut behind him, her face seems to sag in time with her shoulders, and it is suddenly clear how sad she is, how utterly devastated she is, and it cannot be by the emperor's departure, surely, but some other thing.

"Blimey," Marlowe whispers. "Cheer up, love: it might never happen."

"It looks like it has," Frommond murmurs, for the woman does look very miserable.

By now Kitty has turned her back on them, and they can see nothing save the angle of her shoulders and the droop of her head. She stays there, just like that, for some time longer, and then she leans forward and places her hands on the parapet wall and stares out over Prague and Bohemia beyond. It is easy to put all sorts of thoughts in her head, based on what you want to be in there, Frommond thinks, but really they know nothing of her, and anyway, they had better be getting back, if only to return Hajek his cloak, and to save him the worry. But she stays, rapt, and does not leave until at last Kitty straightens, gathers her spirits, raises her head, and sweeps back across the gravel to disappear out of sight below them.

"Come on then," Frommond says. "Let's go."

⊕

CHAPTER SEVENTEEN

———◆◆◆———

The Thames, below London, third week of January 1584

"I do not believe my scheme is working, Francis," Lord Burghley tells him, "though for the life of me I cannot say why."

They are in Burghley's barge again, under wondrously warm ermine, being rowed downriver through a light mist, but against a stiff tide, to Greenwich, where Her Majesty has retreated since Christmas in the unfounded certainty that the palace is warmer than Whitehall. Burghley is puzzled by the failure of his scheme to unleash the beautiful—and beautifully dressed—Mistress Devereux on the Earl of Arundel in the hope of discovering the secret of the identity of Master Mope.

"Perhaps you need to recruit a more diverse Flying Squadron?" Walsingham suggests. "Catherine of Medici draws upon all sorts, doesn't she?"

"But Mistress Devereux, Sir Francis? You've seen her."

He has, yes, and my God.

"But still, William," he says. "Some men—they are unmoved by such things."

"'Such things?'" Burghley laughs. "I think I know what you mean, Francis, indeed I do."

As he chuckles, his powdery cheeks quiver and pink, but does he *really* know what Walsingham means? Walsingham doubts it. He has, in any case, on his own behalf, more or less given up hope of gaining anything solid from the Earl of Arundel, who for now at least languishes in the Tower, but whom Her Majesty has refused to put to torture. When Walsingham was last in his cell, trying to cajole him into giving up the real identity of Master Mope in return for his own freedom, he had found scratched into the wall of Arundel's cell some idiotic drivel about how suffering in this world is rewarded in the next. Walsingham had offered him the chance to be racked—"think of the ecstasy to come!"—but Arundel was not *that* committed to heavenly bliss.

They arrive at the watergate and are conducted to the Receiving Room by a stout gentleman page whom Walsingham knows to be a homosexual with a taste in complex knots and simple sailors.

"You are looking well, Master Villeneau," he tells him, which makes Villeneau anxious, for no man with a secret likes to attract the attention of someone such as Walsingham. "Is Sir Christopher Hatton within?"

"Not joining you tonight, Sir Francis. He is come down with something, apparently."

Good.

Villeneau opens the doors and announces them to the room, almost empty save for Her Majesty, who has had her throne moved closer to the fire, and who also looks as if she has come back down with something. Her face, she tells them, aches; and even in the low light Walsingham can see her jaw is swollen. She's in black this evening and has lost so much weight over the last few weeks that her neck is like a stalk holding up her head, her red hair auburn in this light and topped off today with the lightest diadem of silver-linked pearls.

Elizabeth presses them for news, though, in a far more lively manner than in the recent past, and after the pleasantries are chugged through, she asks after the health of the Earl of Arundel.

"He remains unforthcoming, Your Majesty," Walsingham tells her through gritted teeth. "To the point of my believing he is enjoying the amenities of the Beauchamp Tower."

"So long as he costs us nothing?" the Queen approves.

Walsingham swallows his sigh.

"But might it not be more—ah—prudent to learn of the plot, don't you think, Your Majesty?" Burghley tries supposing, just as if he is new-struck by this unusual thought. "The one the earl was caught up in? If he has details as to the other conspirators, for example, then I for one would rather know their names, so as not to be caught out in future?"

The Queen does not bother to hide her sigh at this idiocy.

"I know you both wish him racked, Lord Burghley, Sir Francis, for I have heard your protestations all before, just as you have heard my explanation that my lord of Arundel is a peer of the realm and is not to be treated just as if he were of no account."

"Very well, Your Majesty," Burghley says with a bow.

"And what of my lord of Northumberland? Has he proved more forthcoming?"

"He has not, Your Majesty," Walsingham tells her. "Not since he was permitted to return home."

He says nothing of his frustration at Her Majesty insisting Northumberland was not charged, despite Throckmorton's confession. When she had told him this, Walsingham had asked then why he had ever put Throckmorton to the rack—no small thing to do, and not without its emotional costs for all concerned—if they were not going to make use of the extracted confession? Her Majesty had ended their audience abruptly, and Lord Burghley had winced, and afterward he told Walsingham that he was in his office, if "ever Sir Francis needed to talk."

"But he has not gone unpunished," Her Majesty points out. "We deprived him of the governorship of Tynemouth Castle."

Which Walsingham has to admit is true, but by Jesu, it actually hurts, sometimes, this, he thinks: the strains he endures, and the horrible things he must do in her name to men such as Throckmorton, who, when all was said and done, merely carried letters between the sorts of men Her Majesty is now protecting from the folly of their crimes against her, men who are far more complicit in only this latest plot to have her killed. Throckmorton has been stretched and now faces the traitor's death while Arundel—long-faced, wheedling, self-entitled Arundel—sits in his well-appointed cell, carving nonsense about his suffering on the wall, utterly indifferent to the suffering he has caused others. He is to be protected by the Queen from any consequence of his manifold wrongdoing, on account of his lineage, on account of the fact that once, a few hundred years ago, his forebear was the strongest and most ruthless among his peers and— Oh God. It was all so bloody pointless. Let the Catholics come. Let them put Mary on the throne in place of Elizabeth. Did it matter?

"Sir Francis? Are you quite well? You are muttering."

"Sorry, Your Majesty. Forgive me. I am—a touch of ague. Brain fever. From being upon the river in this cold."

She signals with her eyes that one more log is to be placed on the fire. Burghley does so, puffing with an old man's exertion.

"Most generous, Your Majesty."

There is a long moment of silence, as if a page were being turned, a scene reset, before Her Majesty asks after news of elsewhere, specifically she means the Duc de Guise.

"Ah," Burghley says. "Yes. The duke is on the move, we hear. He closed up his house in Fontainebleau just after Christmastide and has set off east. He has a house in Metz, and so that is where we may suppose he is bound."

"Strange time of year to take to the roads of northern France?" Walsingham supposes.

"Indeed," Burghley agrees, "and do you know what? He is even taking with him two pairs of very fine—and I am given to believe they are *extraordinarily* fine—horses that he has had brought over from Arabia at vast cost and no little trouble."

"They will feel the cold," Her Majesty imagines.

"He has had coats made for them, of course. In crimson wool!"

Burghley finds the whole thing absurd and amusing, but Her Majesty is wondering why she has nothing of the sort.

"I will see to it," Burghley assures her, though God, how much would that cost?

"And what news from Prague, Master Walsingham? Every week you promise us something, and yet we have learned nothing of the Duc de Guise's whore beyond her name and the color of her skin."

"I am working on it, I do assure you, Your Majesty. If the emperor's court were livelier, then it would be easier, of course, but he is obsessively secretive and passes his time locked in a tower, dabbling in the arcane, so we must rely on Doctor Dee to inveigle himself into his circle, and then—act, as he sees fit."

Walsingham is almost sorry that Hatton is not around to hear the Queen remind Walsingham and Burghley that John Dee is as valuable to her as her very eyes.

"We only regret the manner in which we sent him from us."

She might almost shed a crocodile tear, Walsingham thinks.

"I shall have a haunch of venison sent to his wife," Burghley announces, and the Queen approves. It should go some way to make up for the disgrace—and absence—of Mistress Dee's husband, she tells them, and that he—Burghley—is to send her comptroller the bill for the meat and she will ensure that it is paid, and Walsingham believes he may scream. He does not tell them that Mistress Dee—whom he still thinks of as Jane Frommond—has left the realm, almost certainly to join her husband, and he wonders why not? It is because he actually wants Burghley to send the Queen a bill for a piece of fucking venison.

"Sir Francis? You are mumbling again."

"Sorry, Your Majesty."

"And how fare the preparations at Framlingham? We had a dream two nights ago of masons building a stout wall, but it was of cheese or somesuch?"

Burghley and Walsingham exchange another covertly weary glance.

"Your dreams are ever very revealing, Your Majesty," Walsingham tells her, "for it has been found that the tower is built with the wrong type of stone. Chalk, Your Majesty, which is found not to be strong enough to take the guns, and so the tower is to be taken down and rebuilt in stone brought from Portland."

The Queen's anger at the masons is much tempered by her delight in the power of her dreams, and she dismisses Walsingham and Burghley, generally pleased with their work. They walk in silence from the Receiving Room, both men wondering why it is they have to lie to the Queen to protect her, for they both know she will now summon Hatton from his sickbed to tell him all about the power of her royal dreams, and, by the by, the disastrous state of the works at Orford, which Master Pughe has written to say will, in fact, be topping out in the next few days, weather permitting.

Afterward, just as they are about to step out into the dark where it is now snowing great fat fobs the size of rabbits' scuts, Walsingham makes a point of introducing Lord Burghley to the gentleman page Master Villeneau.

"You might just bear him in mind," he says later.

⊕

CHAPTER EIGHTEEN

Old Town Gate, Prague, last week in January 1584

"He who arrives hungry arrives happiest, hey, Doctor?"

They are by now and at last perhaps only two days from Prague, and Doctor Dee is as hungry and footsore as he has ever been, and by now very fed up with Count Olbrecht Łaski and his sayings. What had once seemed charming—imagine piloting yourself through a world according to such simple axioms!—now seems childish, unhelpful, and even dishonest.

"He who arrives—?" Roger Cooke mutters by his side. "It just doesn't make sense."

"Try not to think about it," Dee suggests, though that is easier said than done: when he had to sell his astrolabe to a dealer in Hamburg, for an eighth of its value, just so they might eat that night, Łaski had later toasted him over some expensive wine and told him that "he who travels lightest travels happiest," which still has the power to jerk Dee awake just as he is about to fall asleep. Łaski had gone on to tell him they would soon be in a position to buy a new astrolabe—"Two of them! Twenty of them!"—when he is king of Poland.

"And why do we go so far, Doctor?" Cooke goes on. "I know I have asked before, but your answers are vague, and get vaguer still the farther we travel, and we have been on the road for months now, and I know less now than I did when we started out."

It is the longest speech Cooke has made in some time, Dee notes with some sympathy, and in answer he might once more repeat the details of Count Łaski's plans to raise money for an army in Prague and to seize Poland's throne, but he does not now, for as time has passed and the journey has gone on, it has become clear—for no single identifiable reason—that such a plan will come to nothing. It is something to do with Łaski, for despite his great height, and the size of his beard, and his booming voice, and his bonhomie, there is something lacking in the man. Occasional truths about him also have leaked out in occasional comments from Emericus Sontag: that he has already burned through the fortunes of two wives, and that he once kidnapped the wife of another count and kept her in ways Emericus would only hint at—"but you would not wish to find your wife kept that way. Not by another man at least"—until a ransom was paid.

So he reminds Cooke that all will be well when they reach Prague, which is almost within sight now, and that though the journey has been a bad one, it shall soon be over, and they shall soon be sat over a dish of fine stew in the warm kitchen of Dee's old friend Thaddeus Hajek, and after a night of uninterrupted sleep on hay-stuffed mattresses, they will wake refreshed, to reassess their prospects with more hope in their hearts.

And so on they go, and it is Dee's and Cooke's turn in the cart while the others walk, and they sit with their feet hanging out of the back, and, like their boot soles, they are utterly worn through, cushionless, and they feel each wagon jolt in their molars.

By Jesu, Dee thinks, it has been a terrible journey, hasn't it? He can laugh at it now, at how he had found Brielle chill, when here in Bohemia the earth—when it could be found under snow and ice—rang like iron and the winds were blistering furies from the east. They'd had to sell more of Dee's books along the way—for an absurdly low price—and bought any furs they could find for sale at inflated prices: fishy, imperfectly cured pelts of dog, cat, goat, or anything, really, and boots that left footprints in the snow the color of blood. By Christmas the rivers were solid ice and outside the town of Konin they had to cross an enormously long, enormously rickety wooden bridge over a river the name of which no one who had not spoken Polish from birth could pronounce, only to find that towering ice cakes had broken the bridge and were now the only thing keeping it in place. God knows what would happen when the ice melted come spring. Outside the town of Poznań the snow was so deep they had to pay—using almost their last reserves—twenty men to clear the road so they might get the wagons through. On the left and right of the roads were impenetrable, trackless forests in which wolves could be heard day and night, and each town and village was almost exactly a day's ride from the next, so any delay or hitch during the day could prove fatal.

⊕

But now here they are, at last, just after the three o'clock bell, under an endless steel gray sky, on the road's final bend, and ahead lies Prague, and each man and the woman must now believe that they have survived, and that all will be well. Dee is not sure what he hopes for—a meal that is not nine-tenths water, one-tenth cabbage, perhaps, seated beside one of those tiled stoves the Germans so love while drinking a wine that does not hurt the teeth—but really, he is so weary of this constant grind that merely to stop for a day, to lie still, and not to try to hold on to the hope that all will be better in Prague would be enough.

The city gates remain open, but they are manned by a handful of very watchful men in bundled fur, gathered around a smoking brazier. Each carries a fearsome halberd, and a sword, and there are axes to hand, as well as half a dozen of those terrible fierce dogs snapping at whoever on strained chains; and above, on each snow-capped roof of the watchtowers, a hundred crows are gathered as if they are witnesses to an execution.

"Jesu," Łaski mutters. He is become very nervous, but he must climb out of the wagon, where he has sat in privilege next to the carter at every turn since Hamburg, and walk—openhanded to show he comes in peace—the last hundred paces toward the watchmen, and it would not totally surprise Dee if they set on him with those dreadful blades and hacked him to pieces and left him to die in the snow while they went back to warming their hands over the brazier.

Do they recognize him? A giant with a huge gray beard is not so rare in these parts, Dee supposes, even one in a bottle-green coat with wolf-fur collar and cuffs. A long conversation follows that none can hear, but after a moment, Łaski gestures to them.

"He needs something to sweeten the deal," Emericus tells Dee. "Otherwise they will not let us in."

It is Cooke who tuts most loudly, but Kelley who spits and Joanna who moans.

"What have we got left?" Dee asks.

"Just your book on navigation," Cooke tells him.

"No," Dee says. "He can't have that. Tell him to give them his cloak. Tell him that, Emericus."

Łaski is furious, but he has no choice, and eventually he removes his cloak, to reveal his much stained but still crimson doublet, and he hands the cloak over to the captain of the watch, who alone seems pleased at least. Then Łaksi gestures—come, then—and he makes to go in through the gate.

"At last," Dee breathes. "At last."

But it is not so simple.

The watchmen detain Łaski. He must be on a list somewhere.

"You can't," Dee tells the men in Latin.

They can.

Dee feels everything begin to slip. They've come all this way and now Łaski is *arrested*?

"Some mistake, Doctor," Łaski reassures him.

But you can see in his face that he knew this was always going to happen.

"If I can explain everything to the emperor," Łaski goes on over the heads of the guards, "I am certain he will forgive me."

The guards bundle him away, heading toward the castle, and an appointment with the emperor's chancellor who will perhaps have questions about his relationship with the Dutch fraudster Cornelius de Lannoy.

"All will be well, my dear doctor!" Łaski calls over his shoulder. "All will be well! Trust in your Łaski!"

Dee watches, with the taste of ash in his mouth.

To have come all this way—*Oh Jesu*.

At last he sees the others are standing staring, bags at their feet, shoulders down, almost dead from fatigue. He would not have let them through his door, he thinks. He gathers himself.

"Right," he says, and he leads them along the close, snow-girt streets toward the Old Town Square where he had been looking forward to showing them the astronomical clock—the *orloj*—that he hopes is still working, because it is almost on the way to Hajek's house, and when they reach it, he is reassured that it is at least still turning. My God, he thinks, standing before the clock, staring up at its clean and certain intersecting circles, marveling afresh at its ingenious mechanism, at least there are some things that may be relied upon.

"The triumph of science," he tells Cooke. "A glimpse of the future, when superstition is finally vanquished."

"Tell you what, Doctor," Cooke mutters, "unless we get some food and warmth into us, we'll all be bloody vanquished."

Good point, Dee thinks, for he is weary beyond belief.

"Well," he says, "Master Hajek's house is just this way: down here."

Dee leads them into a broad lane, with arcades on both sides, and traders staring out over their wares, and he wonders why until he stops, and looks at his little party of companions, and he thinks, Jesu! look at us: a desperate lot; they were utterly disheveled and threadbare, unfit to walk the streets, let alone to hope to be admitted past the dark-painted door of Thaddeus Hajek's little house on this lane below the Bethlem Chapel.

"Well," he says. "We are here now."

And there is nothing else for it. He is on his last legs. If he is denied now, he fancies he will subside into the snow and die.

He knocks, feebly.

After a moment, a hatch opens at around head height.

"Is Master Hajek at home?" Dee asks in Latin.

"Who wishes to know?"

When Dee announces himself, the hatch snaps shut, the four locks are shot, and the door is opened.

"Come in," a little man says. "Quick."

Dee is wavering with exhaustion now, and he staggers down the corridor to the light, knowing he is on his very last legs. The front door booms shut behind them and he hears four locks deployed, but ahead he hears voices. A man asking a question, and a woman replying in a tone that reminds him of—

"Jane."

✛

Dee wakes into if not heaven then a version of it. A minor heaven, perhaps, if such a place exists, for he is in a bed, with sheets and blankets up to his chin and on the whitewashed ceiling are written words that he agrees with, and next to him the warm weight of his wife.

He sits up in terrible fear.

"My book!"

He means the *Book of Loagaeth*.

"Is safe," she tells him. "As is your show stone."

"And my bag?"

"Likewise safe."

"You've touched nothing?"

She shakes her head.

"We left it as it was when you fell through the door."

"Thank God," he says, and he lies back down and sleeps again, and when he wakes it is to an even better heaven, and she is still there, and he looks up at the words on the ceiling and he smiles.

"What do they mean?" Frommond asks. She is lying above the blankets, fully clothed in a dress of mustard wool, and she has been watching him read the words, with a smile.

"It is a warning," he tells her, "that our art is a game for a boy, or for women."

"Our art?"

"Alchemy, I think," he tells her. "I suppose it is to remind whoever wakes in this bed that—well, look, it says that no one can collect the fruits of our elexirs, unless by the entrance of our elemental stone, and if you seek another way, you will never enter or reach the path."

"Fair enough," she supposes.

They are silent for a long while.

"How long have I been—?"

"Four days. Master Hajek's physician wanted to bleed you, but I refused. You need nourishment, not your humors balanced. Look at you. There is nothing on you."

He laughs gently.

"It has been quite a few months."

"Roger has told me about it. There's nothing on him, either. On any of you."

"I do not think I would go back the same way, I have to admit."

Now she laughs, too.

He asks after Arthur. She tells him about the boy's rabbit, how they found it stiff under a tree.

"It was all swollen up and— Well. I did not wish him to see it."

"I wish I had been there," Dee tells her. "I could have done something for it."

"Well, we buried it in the orchard," she tells him.

He squeezes her hand.

"And so—what in God's name has brought you here?" he asks.

Frommond tells him about Robert Beale, and how he could not stand by to see Walsingham abandon Dee to walk unknowing into whatever trap the Spanish have set.

"Or the French. De Guise. He will know, too, by now, if he did not before."

There is a long moment. Dee considers the implications. He tells her he is sorry.

"I could not tell you. Francis Walsingham came to me when I was at the Tower and offered me this instead of the pyre."

She nods.

"He set you up, you know that?"

Dee closes his eyes.

He'd suspected. Couldn't believe it was true sometimes, and at other times he knew it for certain.

"But to let the Spanish learn that you are about his business?" she wonders. "That is unforgivable."

Dee manages a shrug.

"Perhaps he knew what Beale would do? Or perhaps Beale was not straight with you? Perhaps Walsingham actually sent him?"

He's had a lot of time on the road to think about this, though he has come to no conclusion.

"But they are waiting for you," she tells him. "They posted a man outside. We got rid of him, but he was put there by someone in the Spanish Embassy. And Master Hajek says he is these days followed wherever he goes."

"When you say 'we'—as in 'we got rid of him,' as in 'we came by boat up the river Rhine' and 'we buried it'—who is the 'we'?"

She asks if he has heard of Christopher Marlowe. He has not.

"You are in for a treat."

He asks if any word has come of Count Łaski.

"None so far, why?"

"I need him," he tells her, "to get me an audience with Emperor Rudolf, but the count has been arrested. I hoped—I clung to the hope—that the emperor had merely sent for him. Not to put him in irons, but because for all his failings, Łaski is a fellow philosopher. I hoped he'd tell the emperor about the *Book of Loagaeth*."

She shakes her head.

"Master Hajek says it will never happen. He says the emperor sees no one."

"Łaski has to manage it. It is why he is here. Why I brought him all this way."

Frommond tells him about her own expedition up to the castle.

"You saw Kitty de Fleurier?" he asks.

She is surprised that he knows of her. He tells her about *L'Escadron Volant* and she actually chuckles ruefully.

"So that is what Burghley was going on about! He came to me. Asked if I'd like money to buy a pretty dress. God, it made me laugh. I thought he wanted me to be his mistress! Imagine! He then started talking about visiting cities over here. Mentioned Prague and Dijon and Bologna and all sorts of places. I was very tempted."

"I'm glad you didn't," Dee tells her.

"Ahhh," she says, "but I did not say I didn't, did I?"

"Is that why you are here? To seduce Emperor Rudolf?"

Again she laughs.

"I told him to try to recruit either of the Devereux sisters, but not even they can hold a candle to this Kitty de Fleurier."

Dee thinks for a bit before asking Frommond how she would stop Kitty de Fleurier persuading the emperor to back de Guise.

"I'm glad you asked *me* that," she says, "and not Christopher. He'd just try to kill her just as he killed the knife sharpener. He went out on our first morning and that was when he learned about Arnoldus van der Boxe having set him in wait for you, but I think he had to kill him to find it."

Dee sighs.

"Well," he says. "We shall have to come up with something to stop her. Kitty de Fleurier, I mean."

And he feels her looking at him very closely.

"Could you really kill a woman?" she asks, and he is sure he has told her a hundred times about Isobel Cochet, about her death in the sands outside Mont Saint-Michel.

"Never," he says. "Never if I could help it."

Which doesn't really mean as much as all that, he knows. He changes the subject.

"Prague," he says. "It seems different. More dangerous. It is not the Prague I remember?"

"No," she agrees. "Master Hajek says it is a new thing. He says—Well, you must talk to him, of course, but he believes the Spanish ambassador is fomenting it, paying the crowds to cause this trouble, and then the pope is putting pressure on the emperor to eject the Jews and permit the Inquisition."

There is a depressing logic to that, Dee supposes.

He gets up, slowly, weak as a kitten, and is pleased to see his belt curled atop his newly laundered clothes, and later, after he has greeted his old friend Thaddeus, he meets Christopher Marlowe.

"All right?"

Dee thanks him for looking after Jane so well, but Marlowe claims it was the other way around and that, anyway, he would not have missed it for the world because his Jane is a diamond and if there's anything else he can do for Dee, then he need only say the word.

⊕

A day or so later, when Dee is feeling stronger, he does.

"I hoped you'd come with me to the Old Town," Dee says. "To buy a pair of gloves."

Marlowe looks at him with some surprise, wondering if that is a euphemism, perhaps, but then says: "Why not?"

They stand in the upstairs room—Dee in an unaccustomed

grass-green coat and red cap—and they search the lane in front of Master Hajek's house. There is nothing to be seen of the back of the arcades opposite, however, where a whole army might shelter out of view, so then Marlowe leaves first and turns left up the lane. Sure enough, a man emerges from the shadows to follow. Blue coat, black hat, no sign of a sword but he's sure to have a knife.

"Damn it," Dee says. "He's back."

He means the knife sharpener. Or a new one, at any rate.

They wait several moments, by which time Marlowe has walked around the block and reappears at the other end of the street, just in time to meet Edward Kelley as he steps out of the door—wearing Dee's black cloak—and turns right. They pass on the street and nod. Another man steps out of the shadows of the arcade to follow, and the two trailing men dither as they pass, but they keep on.

"Two of them," Dee murmurs. "Surely two is enough?"

A moment later Dee watches as Hajek leaves, accompanied by Edwin. No one follows.

Two is enough.

Good.

Dee hurries down and out of the door, leaving Frommond to lock it behind, and he turns right onto the river's bank. It is another bitterly cold day, and the streets are blue with ice and frozen snow, and Dee shivers even in his new coat. A moment later Marlowe appears at his shoulder. He's lost his trailing spy. They walk for a bit, past the Bethlem Chapel, hoping to avoid passing the bridge, though Dee is anxious to see if all he has heard of the rioting mob is true. Before then, though, he needs to know something else.

"How is it that you know Master Beale?"

"Bobby Beale? Old family friend he is. Sort of, anyway."

Dee notices that Marlowe oftentimes changes his voice, but he cannot decide if it is his courtier's accent that he exaggerates, or his dockside accent, for he is yet to discover what he is hiding.

"But you were working for Francis Walsingham?"

"Odds and ends. Keeping an eye on some types in Cambridge."

"And what do you make of Thaddeus?" Dee asks.

There is a slight waver in Marlowe's next pace.

"Of Master Hajek?" he checks. "I thought he was a friend of yours?"

"He is."

"Ahh. But—?"

"Exactly."

Dee supposes Thaddeus will be passing on to someone in the castle the same sorts of odds and ends that Marlowe himself had passed on to Walsingham while he was at Cambridge. He supposes Thaddeus will be speaking to someone in the chamberlain's office about his new houseguests, and Dee asks if either Marlowe or Jane have been at all indiscreet?

"About what?" Marlowe wonders.

"About my reasons for being here?"

"What are your reasons for being here?"

Dee smiles.

They walk on in thought through shadowed lanes, their breath smudges before them, their boots loud on the dirty, frozen snow.

"Suppose it's the life you lead isn't it, as an exile? Always on the hop. Landlord a government agent and your friends paid to spy on you."

"There must be quieter lives," Dee agrees.

They turn back toward the river and emerge to the north of the bridge, where they stand and stare up at the castle louring over the city, with its steel-gray flanks and towers lost in the low cloud. Dee thinks of Łaski up there, and he tries to imagine him talking his way out of some dungeon or other, and into the emperor's company; and despite everything that he has heard about the emperor, he finds that he can imagine just this—the big man talking his way past everyone and throwing himself at the emperor's feet and somehow, somehow, laughingly achieving forgiveness—and this thought experiment cheers him.

"Quite a river, isn't it?" he wonders idly. "Wider than the Thames at Mortlake, and still hundreds of miles to flow before it reaches the North Sea."

Marlowe grunts.

"Nothing on the Rhine," he says, having just seen that. "What's it even called?"

"The Vltava. It runs into the Elbe, north of here. Useful little river, but not, as you say, the Rhine."

Dee's eye drifts across the sluggish waters, opaque with ice, as if it might freeze over at any moment, as the Thames sometimes does. He feels a pang of homesickness.

But his attention is caught by the knots of men idling on the bridge, who are hanging about in that way that you know means trouble. It is worse than that, though, for they have made it like an occupying army's temporary camp: rough hurdles for barriers against people crossing; as well as foul signs; piles of sticks and stones; and a wagonload of beer barrels.

"Some fucker's rented a mob, haven't they?" is Marlowe's opinion. "Whoever's paying for the beer."

Just then a man appears from the lanes leading to the Jewish Quarter and approaches the bridge with two heavy leather bags and tries to negotiate his passage. He's a small, hunched fellow, a grandfather, in a long dark coat. A mercer, you'd think, with business over the other side. But he's stopped at a barrier, and the men on the bridge swirl toward him, and Dee can see this will not end happily. Words are exchanged, but any negotiation is ended by a massively tall, well-built man stepping out from the crowd to cuff the man, who drops his bags and wheels away clutching his ear.

"That must be Marek," Marlowe tells Dee. "Old Thaddeus is scared stiff of him."

Another man—a lesser demon—comes out from the group to hit the old man with a staff, to ragged cheers, and then while his back is arched, a third man kicks him to send him staggering to trip and land on his face. Marek walks over, slowly, to rest the sole of his boot on the old man's buttocks and forces him to fuck the ground, provoking much laughter, until he grows bored and makes a great show of wiping his boots on him, and then walking away. After a moment the man rises cautiously to his hands and knees, checks his face for blood, of which there is quite a lot, and then he stands and straightens himself as much as he is able and turns to find his bags.

"Please," Marlowe groans. "Don't go back for them."

But he does.

And the crowd is waiting for him and as he comes toward them, they begin a rhythmic chant that can only mean one thing, and while some men and boys run to line the bridge's north parapet others stand and clap as the man they know as Marek picks the mercer up and hoists him up above his head. The crowd grab at the mercer, to try to snatch his purse or anything else they can, and then Dee hears them begin a low moan, like cattle in need of milking; they clear the way as Marek marches to the southern parapet of the bridge, still holding the wriggling man above his head to turn him in a spin, with quick strong hands. People dance around and the lowing grows into a crescendo that ends with a great cheer as the mercer is hurled over the parapet to take his chances in the freezing water below. While the giant preens and flexes those mighty blacksmith's muscles, the crowd surges to the north parapet to see if the mercer surfaces, and when he does, flailing, after he's passed under the bridge, they hurl rocks at him, and there is a great cry of pleasured satisfaction as he is evidently hit not once but often, for they are obviously good at this game by now. And then after the flurry, the rocks stop and the mercer is seen no more, and the crowd turns back. Dee can easily imagine their rage when they discover while they have been enjoying themselves the man's bags have been salted away by those with a more mercantile disposition, and they are left mulish and unsatisfied and in search of more pleasure.

"You ever been a shepherd?" Marlowe asks, seemingly out of the blue.

Dee has not.

"Why d'you ask?"

"I spent some time in the Weald once, when I had to get out of town for it being too hot, if you take my meaning, and they carry these long sticks with a sort of scoop at the end, which they can fiddle a stone into, then flick, like this"—he demonstrates—"and the stone smacks into anything you like, a hundred feet away. It's how they control sheep when they're driving them to market: shoot a stone over the flock and ping one of the fuckers on the noggin if he looks like he's taking the wrong turn. You know."

"Ah. And you think—?"

He indicates the men at the end of the bridge, particularly the giant.

"Be like David and Goliath. Smack that Marek right in the face all the way from here and then they'd be all oy! Did you throw that fucking stone and you'd be all, what stone, mate? It is just me and my stick here, walking along enjoying the fucking sunshine if you don't mind, not that it is any fucking business of yours, and not that there is any fucking sunshine."

Dee looks at Marlowe quizzically.

Marlowe shrugs.

"Always had an overactive imagination," he admits.

"Just another thing on our to-do list," Dee says. "Which is about to get very long indeed, but anyway. Look. We'd best be off. I think they've taken against my coat and hat, and we are yet to find those gloves."

The giant is pointing at them, and a group of about ten men have begun sidling off the bridge toward where Dee and Marlowe stand. They carry sticks and stones.

"Oop," Marlowe says. "They'll certainly break your bones."

Dee and Marlowe turn and break into a gentle trot, shouts and footsteps matching them behind. Dee expects a stone any moment.

"Up here," he says.

And he leads Marlowe around a corner, where they put on a burst of speed.

"Jesu," Dee cannot help murmuring for it is as if they have stepped back a century in time. All the houses are boarded up or abandoned and more than one is smoke stained, as if it has hosted a proper fire. A roof is pulled down here, and the drift of broken tiles acts as stepping-stones in the stew of wet filth underfoot. The snow is gray with soot, stained with God knows what, and it stinks of rot and shit and there's no one about. Dee remembers how it was: streets thronging with people, pulsing with life, a happy and prosperous place, but now?

"Like a plague village," he tells Marlowe when they have slowed down, though there are some signs of life going on behind the shuttered windows and doors. Cooking fires seep smoke from chimneys and vents, and there is the occasional shuffle and clink of stealthy, wary movement. Within moments they are lost within the maze of streets, but then they emerge into a small clearing around a synagogue in front of which someone has stuck a pig's head on a post.

"Nice," Marlowe says.

"This way," Dee tells him, and they dip into a narrow alley as if he'd been looking for it all along; they can only walk in single file, and at the end is another small square, where a market is being held, patrolled by halberdiers provided by the various guilds, and it is as if they have stepped through the gate into a different and infinitely more civilized town.

"Here we are," Dee says.

There are a few used clothes stalls—so called fripperers—but also some of a better quality, including Prague's finest glovemaker.

"All that just for a pair of gloves?" Marlowe asks.

Dee laughs.

"Two pairs, actually."

⊕

Later, when they are back at Master Hajek's house, there is good news. Very good news.

"He's done it!"

Well, almost: there sits on Hajek's table an invitation sent to Dee, with a covering note from Łaski, summoning him to an audience not with the emperor—the world does not turn at such speed—but with the emperor's chamberlain: Octavius Spinola.

"It's a trap, isn't it?" Frommond supposes.

But one into which he must step. Dee reads Łaski's scrappy cover note, and he cannot help but smile ever more broadly.

"Master Kelley!" he calls. "A word if you please."

There is silence, yet he knows Kelley is home. He finds him in

Hajek's library, with his nose in the only book he can find that is written in English: George Ripley's *Bosome Book*, which concerns *chrysopoeia*—the transmutation of base metals into gold.

"Łaski wants us to conduct one last Action," Dee tells him.

"I don't think I can manage that," Kelley replies. It is odd, Dee thinks; since arriving in Prague, Kelley has also begun speaking with a very soft Irish burr.

"One last one," Dee tells him, "and that will be that. I have asked Count Łaski to attend us here tomorrow at noon. You may use Master Hajek's oratory for prayer." Kelley groans and puts the book aside and leaves with no further word. Dee hears the locks being pulled, and the door slammed, and he is left wondering. A moment later, Frommond appears. She, too, has noticed Kelley's changing accent, and manner, too.

"As if he is likewise trying to transform himself from base English metal into something altogether more exotic."

Dee gives Jane a pair of the gloves, wrapped in pale silk.

"A present," he tells her.

"Whatever for?"

"For coming all this way and saving my life," he says.

"*Gloves?*" She laughs when she's opened the wrappings. "Wherever did you get them?"

"Prague's finest glover," he tells her with a smile.

When she tries them on, they fit perfectly, and she is delighted.

"Ha!" she says, holding out a hand.

⊕

CHAPTER NINETEEN

Hastings, England, February 1584

Heavy rain on the shingle beach and Robert Beale feels he is wading in treacle. He's alone now, with Arthur Gregory feigning some illness back at the inn in Rye, and still looking for a ship's captain—no, he doesn't know his name—but a few months ago—no, neither does he know exactly when—who gave passage across the Narrow Sea—but to and from which ports he isn't sure, though, yes, he does see that would help—to a certain Master Mope, about whom the only thing he can be absolutely sure about is that this is not the man's real name, and can you help?

He is usually met with bafflement that yields to scorn and then—if the catch has been good, or the sea is calm but the wind steady—good humor, but sometimes, if the day is none of the above, it is irritation that he should be wasting their time on this load of old bollocks.

"Get out of here! I've got fucking work to do!"

When Beale asked these questions in Essex, he took with him

two of her Majesty's Yeomen to try to bolster his authority and to ensure reasonably civil answers. They were somewhat heavy-handed, though, and now both men lie under the care of a surgeon in Brightlingsea, lucky to be alive, after provoking the fishermen of the local fleet to go all in to defend one of their own.

So now he works alone, walking from boat to boat in all weathers, in every harbor and hard, and along every beach, as here in Hastings, where even the gulls screech that he is a fool, and the answer to the question that he must always write down in his book is always the same: "No."

"Be of good courage, Robert!" Walsingham had written from his fireside in Seething Lane. "You need only to find one man to say yes, then all will be proved to have been worthwhile."

Which is true, he supposes, but it does not happen this day.

Nor the next.

Nor the one after that.

And still it rains.

⊕

CHAPTER TWENTY

Prague, early February 1584

The next day it is warmer, or, really, less cold, and a low cloud sits above the unhappy city like a lid, sealing in its coal smoke and its tensions. Just before a dull noon, with Kelley locked in Hajek's oratory, Count Łaski comes, accompanied by two servants whom Dee greets affectionately enough, and five of the emperor's halberdiers, in steel breastplates and helmets sprouting red and white dyed ostrich plumes.

"Mistress Dee!" Łaski cries. "What brings you to Prague?"

Before she can answer he carries on, telling her how astonished he is to find that the wife of such a humble philosopher as Doctor Dee, "for all his attributes," should be so beautiful, and he kisses her hand once, but for a long time. Since his beard is somewhat greasy, Frommond is pleased she is not wearing her new gloves. Then he kisses her left cheek twice and her right cheek once, which he claims is the Bohemian way, and then he professes a fascination for every detail of her journey, without ever asking a single question, and that is that.

"How do you think he got so fat?" Marlowe asks Frommond after Łaski has disappeared with Dee into Master Hajek's library where they are to conduct the Action. She is sitting with Marlowe in Master Hajek's back hall, shoulder to shoulder, peeling mangelwurzels with Edwin's wife who speaks not a word of English or Latin. It's a good question, she supposes, since all the others who survived the journey through Poland are withered almost to the bone.

"Just one of them sorts, I suppose," Marlowe concludes, without meaning it.

They peel on for a bit in silence, and then he asks how she feels being excluded from the Action in the library.

"I've no interest in it," she confesses. "I don't think I'd ever be able to separate the voice of the angels from that of Master Kelley."

"Even with his new accent?"

They both laugh.

Frommond hates the Actions if she is honest. It is not merely the manner in which everyone else in the household is excluded from these conversations; it is their covert, furtive nature that makes her uneasy: seeing her husband act as if ashamed of what he is doing, and that shame is contagious.

In any event, she is relieved when the Action is done, and though Master Kelley will not join them, the others come and Master Hajek sits with them at the table to eat the mangelwurzel roasted with some goose fat and chicory. Łaski does Master Hajek the honor of staying for it, though it means they run out of butter and cheese and then wine, and when that is all gone, Łaski uses the last of the bread to mop up such juices that are left in the serving dish. After that he regales them with how he managed to get out of the emperor's guardroom and into the emperor's receiving room—"no mean feat, my dear Mistress Dee!"—he tells them about a new thing that he has seen, come from Krakow.

"It is a mixture between a spoon and a knife, so you can scoop like this, and pin like this."

He demonstrates.

"Like a small pitchfork?"

"A table pitchfork but with three prongs."

"It will never catch on."

But Dee is impatient with all this and wants to discuss what was said during the Action. This is unusual, she thinks, for he is usually so secretive about this, and she wonders why he wants to talk about it now, but Łaski only sighs.

"The angels no longer talk about Łaski's two kingdoms," he tells her. "They talk only of terrible things."

"It was not very cheering," Dee agrees, suspiciously cheerfully. "An angel-faced woman will fall ill, they say."

"I had terrible fear it was you, Mistress Dee," Łaski says, gallantly enough.

"But do you remember the words?" Dee asks. "'As red as the beet; as dry as the bone; as blind as the bat; and as hot as the hare.' That is what Galvah said."

"None of which apply to you, Mistress Dee," Łaski adds, with another unwantedly gallant laugh.

Dee appears unusually mystified and repeats it all again.

"She will become as red as the beet, as dry as the bone, as blind as the bat, and as hot as a hare. You must admit, that is quite the picture."

Frommond stifles a yawn, but Dee presses on.

"What does it mean, do you think, Count Łaski?" he asks. He is being much more considerate of others' views than is ordinary, but Łaski is hardly flattered by Dee's interest and instead chews the last crust like a cud, before telling them that the angelic spirits want them to know a beautiful woman will soon be red as a beet.

"And so on."

Across the table, Marlowe rolls his eyes, but Dee repeats the description for a third time, and Frommond is perplexed. This is now very odd. Whatever is he talking about?

"What's the use of that?" Marlowe asks. "Some brass's going to be ill. So what? Be more use if the angels'd tell you how to cure her, wouldn't it? That'd be worth the candle."

"But they did!" Dee is quick to tell him. "They did. Did they not, Count Łaski? Did you not hear what they said?"

Łaski looks doubtful.

"I—ahhh. Was it prayers? Special prayers?"

"It *was*," Dee confirms. "Special prayers of an *angelic* nature."

It seems to Frommond that Łaski is also mildly baffled by Dee's insistence on this, and perhaps if he cared to think about it much longer he might disagree, but Dee goes off on one of his sprawling, elusive explanations of angelic intercourse, and very soon there is nothing left to think or say. At length, Łaski rises and tells them that he must be across the bridge before nightfall, for after that the beer will really flow, and not even the great Łaski will risk that.

Dee thanks him fulsomely for all he has done and all that he will do—he is referring to tomorrow's audience with Spinola—and Łaski admits that it was nothing really.

"Spinola very keen to meet you, Doctor!"

And when he is gone, Dee sits exhausted, resting his head on his hand.

"What was all that about?" Frommond asks. "The angel-faced woman who is as red as the beet?"

"It is what they said," he tells her with a shrug, but she is not convinced. She's seen him perform before and knows he is up to something. She feels she is standing at the edge of a fogbank, knowing that something within is taking shape at a gathering pace, but only able to glimpse occasional disembodied movements from without.

⊕

The next day is the audience with Spinola, the emperor's chamberlain, and in the morning, Marlowe appears in the library and claims to have been to a fripperer and bought Frommond a dress.

"Just jumped out at me, it did."

Green silk, with blue silk-shot sleeves, suspiciously new, and clean, and smelling of meadowsweet as if from a lady's wardrobe and very obviously stolen. He overcomes her protestations by promising he will take it back the next day.

"She will not even miss it," he says, "and look: it fits perfectly."

It does. *My God*, she thinks, *he must have trawled all of Prague looking for the right woman to follow home.*

Dee is astonished.

"You look as you did when we first met," he tells her, which was when she was a lady-in-waiting at Whitehall Palace, in the days when she needed to look perfect every moment of the day. Before Arthur, before Mortlake, before Dee. Dee himself is in midnight velvet—likewise from Marlowe's "fripperer"—and she winks at him and tells him he looks like a well-to-do conjurer.

He laughs, but is jumpy and tense, and his eyes find shadows, and entrances, and exits, and she knows he is either scared, or up to something.

"Wouldn't it be safer to go as Her Majesty's ambassador? You would be accorded some protection and honor on that account alone."

Dee acknowledges her point.

"But the emperor would never bother to see me if he thought I came from Bess," Dee claims. "And I want to appear before him as me: a fellow natural philosopher."

Is the first bit true? Possibly. But the second bit: Why? Why does he want to appear as a fellow natural philosopher?

"I hope to persuade him not to align with de Guise," he says, as if it is just that simple, and it makes her laugh.

"De Guise sends a beautiful woman and Her Majesty sends you?"

"That is cruel, Jane," Dee says, acting offended. "But what I lack for in pulchritude, I make up for in philosophy."

There is a book on the table—one of his, the one about the mystical power of the monad—which he now pats. She has tried, she really has, but she is yet to make it past a single page of a single one of his books.

"And I also have something that the emperor will value above all other things, even above Kitty de Fleurier."

"And her Eternal Oneness," she cannot resist adding to his bafflement. "And what is that, this thing?"

"It is Master Kelley," he tells her, and she lets out a hoot.

"I'm serious," he says.

"You're going to give him Kelley? Like a slave?"

"If only," he says. "No. I am taking him with me to see if Rudolf will join us in an Action, so that he may communicate with the angelic spirits."

"Aahhh. And so was that the plan all along?"

A flicker in Dee's eye alerts her to an evasion.

"One of them," he admits. "Or part of one of them, anyway."

Frommond sees his eyes dip to the book on the table again, and she is about to shake her head and say something to suggest that perhaps he knows what he is doing, when she sees he is not looking at the book, but at what is next to it: a slender box of silver-inlaid sandalwood.

"And what is that?" she asks.

"Ah," he says, instantly evasive. "Another present."

"Who for?"

"For Kitty de Fleurier."

"What is it?"

He is awkward now, all elbows and knees.

"A pair of gloves," he says.

"Another pair? May I see?"

"They are just gloves."

"Nevertheless," she persists.

He opens the box, and unfolds some pink silk, and holds the box up to reveal a most beautiful pair of gloves, silk-lined, and of camel skin, she thinks, dyed butter yellow: the single most luxurious thing she has seen in five years of marriage to Dee.

"I am certain she will love them," she says, for they make her own, which up until this point she treasured, look shabby; she sighs inside and says nothing more as he carefully folds the silk over, and closes the box, and she vows to never think about them ever again.

"Jane," he says, "I hope you know that if I could have bought two pairs of these gloves, I would?"

And she tells herself that his buying her a pair to soften the blow of seeing him give these beauties to another woman makes him a decent, kind, and thoughtful man, but dear God how she wishes he had not done so.

She squeezes his shoulder and thanks him again, and he lays his hand on hers.

"Sorry," he says.

But there is nothing to be sorry for.

"Are you quite well, John?" she probes. "You seem—"

"I am a bit taken up with things," he admits. "I feel as if I am about to stick a sword in a wasps' nest."

"And are you?"

After a moment's hesitation, he nods.

"And what sort of wasps are you talking about?" she wonders.

"Spanish wasps. And French wasps."

"Ahh. And is there—anything I can do?"

"Pack your bag," he tells her, "and stand by with a swat."

⊕

Later Frommond finds Dee, Marlowe, and Hajek at the kitchen table eating bread and butter, and it feels as if it is in preparation for something, as if they are lining their stomachs for a night's drinking. Dee looks very pale and distracted. He makes space for her and Marlowe passes her the bread. Master Hajek is worrying about getting across the bridge.

"That Marek is a fucker, isn't he?" Marlowe says.

Hajek nods.

"And do you hear," he says, "there is to be something he is calling a Day of Rage?"

"What is that? A Day of Rage?"

It sounds, Frommond thinks, very bad.

"Two weeks' time," Hajek goes on. "On Ash Wednesday. A Day of Rage to show they want Jews of Prague gone."

"Christ. And do the Jews know that?"

Hajek shrugs. It has not occurred to him to wonder.

But now there is a commotion, and Dee leaps to his feet.

It is Edward Kelley. He is shouting and throwing things— books, pots, a sextant—on the floor of the library, and he is kicking the furniture, because he has just learned that despite yesterday's efforts in the Action, he is not invited to the audience with Spinola, and Dee springs to his feet and has to do all he can to calm him, which he manages, eventually, with extravagant promises of audiences to come, and how once he has *his* feet under the table, he will ensure Kelley gets his taste, which is all Kelley keeps demanding—just his "taste," "which is his right"—and more besides. Just when everything is calm again, and Kelley soothed, he learns that Marlowe is to come with them, even if only as a servant who will not even be permitted into the room with Spinola anyway, and the whole thing starts again with Kelley demanding he should go in Marlowe's stead. On it goes, around and around, and Joanna Kelley joins in, and it is only when Marlowe clips Kelley on the back of the head, and tells him to shut his cakehole, and then punches Joanna as she attacks him, knocking her out cold, that there follows a moment of stunned calm.

Which is when there is a booming knock on the door and Frommond sees Dee's hand go to his knife. Marlowe looks concerned, but no more, and she wonders how much Dee has told him of his plans?

Master Hajek looks to Edwin, who trots to the front door, and opens the hatch, and they listen, their breath held, but it is only Emericus Sontag, come in one of the emperor's chamberlain's carriages to see them safe back across the bridge.

"Thank God," Dee breathes.

"But is it safe to leave him alone?" Frommond wonders, pointing to where Kelley sits in the corner, rocking to and fro, every fiber of his being clenched in fury.

"He'll be all right," is Marlowe's contention. "Edwin'll keep an eye on him, won't you, Eddy?"

Edwin strokes his mustache nervously.

"If he moves, knock him out with a pan or something?"

Edwin doesn't have a choice.

"What about her?" he asks, pointing to where Joanna Kelley is coming to.

"Her too."

They gather in the gloomy hallways while Edwin shoots the bolts, one two three four, and then they must launch themselves out into the gray daylight, and the icy slurry underfoot, to find the coach farther down the lane to the right, on the road above the river's bank. The usual urchins and thieves are held at bay by six beefy guards in scarlet with feathered helmets and halberds on which you would be able to spit-roast an ox. The horses stamp and fret, as if they know they will have to cross the bridge again.

They climb into the coach, Dee and Frommond with Master Hajek shuttered within, and Marlowe on the back with one of the halberdiers. Dee closes the door, plunging them into almost total darkness.

"Is better this way," Hajek says. "You see."

The carter touches the lead horse with his switch and they set off with a rackety jerk along the bank. They must wait as the guardsmen negotiate to cross the bridge and Dee is peering through the window to see something, and Marlowe calls down that that fucker Marek isn't here, luckily for him, because Marlowe would have killed him. Then after a while the barrels are rolled aside and the tree trunk swung away, and they are permitted to cross, for they are the emperor's guests, after all, though still faces are pressed against the linen of the windows and incomprehensible obscenities are shouted. Hajek shakes his head with disgust, and Dee takes Frommond's hand in his, though she wonders if it is for his own sake, rather than hers, for he is very jumpy, and even when they are across and through the worst of it, he becomes ever more taut and tight-strung, as a greyhound in its traps.

At length they are nicely pressed backward into their bench and Hajek leans forward and they hear the carter apply the whip as his horses begin up the hill to the castle's West Gate. Through the linen Frommond can see more milling crowds gathered before the gates, but there are halberdiers and footmen to keep a channel, and at length the carriage is permitted through the iron gates and into the castle's first courtyard where Marlowe jumps down and opens the door and helps Frommond down.

"You make a very fine servant," she tells him, and she is suddenly struck by the thought—almost a certainty—that she will now meet the woman whose dress she is wearing, but Marlowe is looking about the place, as tense as Dee, and does not answer.

"Well?" Dee asks from within the carriage.

"Nothing," Marlowe says.

And Dee steps out, as anxious as she has ever seen him, and he looks around as if expecting attack from any and every quarter. But nothing comes. Everyone is busy about their own business.

"Is this the wasps' nest?" she asks.

He has almost forgotten she is there, and he starts when he catches her gaze. He lets out a long, relieved sigh.

"It seems not."

He is clutching his book, and the sandalwood box of those gloves.

After a moment, he decides he can let Marlowe go.

"Make sure Kelley is safe. And for the love of God do not let him near Thaddeus's wine cellar."

Marlowe touches his cap, and turns to go, leaving them to Hajek, who finds a footman to escort them up the steps into the palace, and to the threshold of a cavernous receiving room, where the walls are painted blood red and are covered—even the ceiling—with vast and gloomy paintings of martyrdoms: so many flayings

and crucifixions and immolations and breakings on wheels of gro-
tesquely contorted men and women, each vast and almost naked.
Each reminds Frommond of the cadavers she sometimes saw
hauled from the river at Greenwich, and soon she begins to feel
dizzy and sick and disorientated, and so she must concentrate on
the crowd that fills the room below. The people in it are as small as
dolls in comparison, but mercifully dressed in dark, somber cloth
cut in the austere Spanish style so out of favor at home in England.
She sees and hears Łaski at the same time, his laugh booming and
his head looming above all those around him, over by the fire, in a
new crimson doublet, exuding the instantly recognizable energy of
someone trying to borrow money.

"Doctor!" he growls when he sees Dee, pushing his way
through the crowd as if the thought of him is the one thing that
brought him here. "Mistress Dee!"

The same kissing rigmarole and then, in an aside that is boomed
over all heads so that all know, he confides in Dee—and the whole
room—that he has seen the emperor and spoken *in person* to him
about the Action with Kelley and the angelic spirits, and the emperor was fascinated by the details, and wishes to know more, so
he—Dee—had best have his finest suit brushed and ready for the
summons.

"Do not say your old friend Count Olbrecht Łaski ever lets a
man down!"

Dee is very grateful.

"You spoke of the Action? All the details?"

"Every one of them! Even the stuff about the beet being red and
the hare being hot! The emperor was *most* intrigued. Come! Let
me introduce you to Octavius Spinola."

Dee thanks him.

"For I have brought him things that I think he, too, will find of interest."

"Ahhh, books. Excellent. Spinola loves books."

"And something to express my esteem for Mademoiselle de Fleurier."

Łaski throws his head back and roars a laugh.

"Aha!" he cries. "You remember her? You sly fox, Doctor, but that chicken already very much taken."

Dee feigns flustered denial, and Frommond, who stands at his elbow, has seen this before, and she cannot help but roll her eyes, at which Łaski laughs ever more, though she cannot say why. He turns and leads them through the crowds to a low dais behind a velvet-covered rope at the far end of the room, its social center, on which stands a taut, fiercely Spanish man in typically Castilian black, with a tidy silver-streaked beard, close-cropped hair, and a pair of those very dark, piercing eyes that all English children are taught to fear. His ruff is starched and at his waist, a thin-bladed sword in a red velvet sheath; he can only be the emperor's chamberlain. Behind him stand five or six others, dressed likewise, but turned away from the crowd, in a huddle with their heads bent over some document.

The footman announces Łaski first, and Łaski strides across the roped-off area to greet Spinola.

"Excellency!" he growls, just as he always does, and for a moment it looks as if he will take Spinola into one of those all-encompassing bear hugs, but he restrains himself and limits his greeting to a double-handed handshake, which Spinola tolerates with unbending formality, and his rigid bow gives little away.

What is more interesting is that as soon as Łaski's name is mentioned, the small crowd of men who had been standing in a knot behind Spinola all look up. They are all alike with their dark eyes, dark beards, dark Spanish cloth, and dark Spanish swords, save one, who is taller than his fellows and has the paler eyes of a Hollander. It must be Arnoldus van der Boxe, Frommond thinks. What chills her most, though, is that the men are looking not at Łaski, but over his shoulder: at Dee.

And so this is it, she thinks. He has walked right into their trap, if it is even worthy of being called a trap. Did they just wait for Dee to come and find the emperor and now the only thing that will save him is courtly propriety, for surely no one will try to kill him in the emperor's receiving room?

But what about afterward? she wonders. Does Dee have a plan for that?

Meanwhile Łaski has stepped up onto the dais and is standing alongside Spinola, almost putting his arm around his shoulder and pulling him close, and he's telling him that he has brought with him to Prague the most esteemed friend, the peerless English alchemist and philosopher Doctor Dee, whose fame has spread throughout all Christendom, ever since he made a magical beetle fly, which was a feat that Łaski claims he saw with his own eyes "and many such other things besides and since."

Dee's jaw clenches at that, but now he steps forward, and though Spinola looks at him with grave suspicion, Frommond's husband breaks into fluent and perhaps unexpected Latin. Even if Spinola's bodyguards remain implacably hostile, it seems the chamberlain himself is won over by Dee's eloquence, for after a moment he takes the book that Dee presents him with something like gratitude. He leafs through its first few pages a moment before handing it to one of the men behind as if a promise that it will be read later. When he turns back to Dee, though, he is reluctant to take the gloves that Dee forces on him, suggesting perhaps that it is too much, or that it is not for him to accept such a gift, but Dee is insistent and so after some good-natured wrangling, Spinola takes the gloves with a conceding smile and passes them very deliberately to the man whom Frommond has identified as Van der Boxe.

Van der Boxe passes them behind, to another man, more obviously a servant, along with some terse instructions and a nod toward a door in the paneling at the back of the hall. Frommond notices Dee watching him go, relaxing when he has gone, and she cannot help wonder how much he spent on the gloves.

After that, and at last, she is introduced, and it is a stern old business, for with women Spinola resumes his previous haughty demeanor in the belief that it is dignified and aristocratic. Frommond laughs inside to think what Marlowe would say of that, and then with nothing much to say herself, in part for not being able to speak Latin or Spanish, she is excused any further role. At the first chance she absents herself, as she has learned in Whitehall, and she finds herself adrift among the crowds awaiting their turn for an audience.

Frommond makes her way through the crowd toward the windows, in part in search of escape, and in part because she is suddenly taken over by a powerful overflow of emotion. There are musicians in a slender gallery above, playing tunes she does not recognize to people whose language she does not speak, and the awful pictures and the blood red walls crowd in on her. She feels suddenly very oppressed and low, and she tries to think of happier things. Then she remembers Arthur, her son, poor dear Arthur who had wept at finding his rabbit dead in the orchard, stiff and with a great quantity of sticky froth in her jaws, and now he is alone without his mother hundreds of leagues distant and though she is sure all will be well in her brother's household, she feels a great pang of sickening self-sorrow.

"Jesu," she finds herself muttering, and her cheeks flush, and her eyes blur and she feels such a wrench of emotional weight within that she must get out of here, out of this wine warm room and out into the air. So she leaves the audience without telling anyone. She slips away along corridors thronged with servants and halberdiers, all waiting on their masters and mistresses, and she hurries past a guardroom where she glimpses more beefy men in red cloth sitting playing cards at a table. Ahead she feels a cool breeze soothe her cheeks, and in a moment she is through a door and out into a formal garden that ends in a parapet wall with a view over treetops and Prague itself. She knows instantly where she is, for she has had almost this exact same view from the windows above, when she came looking for Arnoldus van der Boxe with Marlowe and found Kitty de Fleurier with the emperor.

She rests her hands on the wall, almost exactly as she had seen Kitty de Fleurier rest hers, though Frommond, for having come from a different door, is farther along the wall, under a leafless chestnut tree. She breathes deeply of the air that is only faintly tainted by the smell of the alleyway that runs thirty foot below, and she does her best to gather herself and suppress the maternal undertow to see her child, to hold him again, and smell the back of his slender neck, but *Saints!* It is hard.

Frommond gives into it, even allowing herself a few tears, but then she knows she must not allow herself to slip further into self-sorrow, and instead she concentrates on the city below, a jumble of red-tiled roofs, spreading from the castle's ramparts down to the river. She tries to see where they had come from, which roads they took to get up from the bridge below, but it is all a confusing warren of roofs.

After a long moment, she feels ready to return to that strange room and those strange men and she takes one last long deep breath and is about to turn when she hears the voice. A woman. Speaking urgently in French. Frommond turns.

It is Kitty de Fleurier. Come sweeping out into the garden, back in that lustrous cloak again, pinning Frommond in place with no retreat. Has she noticed her? No. She is talking to another woman over her shoulder, white-skinned, perhaps half as beautiful, but still very beautiful, who bobs anxiously in her wake, evidently trying to soothe her. Frommond slides very slowly farther behind the tree's trunk and waits, and in another time and in another place perhaps she might not be interested in what was being said, but she is human, and far from home, and her French is very good and so she listens.

Kitty de Fleurier is very upset, her voice tearing out of her throat.

"Did you know?" she cries. "Did you know? He's just told me that de Guise is coming all this way from France, but he is leaving my sister with his mother in Lorraine! He has left her there with that disgusting old woman and all those servants who are always unkind. They pinch her, you know, as if she is not real. I have seen it! Marks on her flesh. And he promised! He promised he would bring her here. That is the only reason I carry on with this! He promised!"

The other woman continues trying to soothe her, and it is less easy to hear what she is saying, but Kitty replies very heatedly.

"I know it is a long way! We came here ourselves, remember? And he is bringing those horses, though, isn't he? He cares more about their well-being than my sister's!"

Murmur, murmur.

"It *is* true! I know it. He keeps me here like this—and my God! What I would do to be free of this. To be back home. To have never come to France. That man is the devil. I wish whoever cut his face had cut his head off."

More murmuring.

"Two weeks! He will be here in two weeks to collect his stinking money but I will not see my sister for months! If ever again! He promised! He promised me I could take her and go free as soon as he had his money! He promised!"

She breaks down into racking sobs and the other woman tries to soothe her with more words Frommond still cannot hear clearly, and she sees she is rubbing poor Kitty's back but Kitty is now weeping more or less uncontrollably.

"I hate it! I hate it!" she moans. "And I hate Van der Boxe! The way he pushes and pulls me like I am a cow! I hate the way he locks me up when I am not with Rudolf. And I hate to think he is listening when I am. And I hate his questions afterward!"

And the noise is so heartbreaking that Frommond wishes that she too might come to comfort her, to tell her that all will be well, but of course what does she know? Perhaps it won't?

"And look at what he has sent me! As if they would soften the blow!"

She holds up her hands, palms turned to her, and on them: Dee's beautiful yellow gloves.

"He told his servant to tell me that he bought them for me because he knows I love gloves!"

Frommond nearly steps out to tell her the gloves are not from Van der Boxe, but from her husband, from Doctor John Dee, and how dare she—but then she thinks well, yes, they are a gift from Dee, but could she explain his intentions? Not really. Nor her presence here behind the tree.

"But I hate him!" Kitty wails. "I hate him! I hate him and his gloves! So a curse on him and a curse on his stupid gloves!"

And now Kitty rips the gloves from her hands. She balls them and hurls them out over the roofs below, and then she subsides into more of those terrible racking sobs. Frommond remains behind her tree and waits for the tears to dry, for dry they must, eventually, surely? And so they do, and after a good long while where there seems nothing can be said, the other woman says something to the effect, perhaps, that the emperor will be wondering where she is. Kitty tells her that she does not give a damn for the emperor, and that he can fiddle with his own penis for a change while he waits for his precious horses.

At this the other woman raises her voice, and for a moment it seems she might slap Kitty. She settles instead for gripping her shoulders and shaking them and snarling into her beautiful face that she is to shut her mouth and open her legs if she ever wants to see her sister again, and that she is a black-skinned whore who deserves no better. Kitty screeches and breaks free and runs back across the garden and in through the door she came from. She slams it behind her, leaving the second woman alone breathing deeply for a few moments, trying to calm herself, before at length she does, and she stamps after Kitty and follows her through the door.

Frommond is left alone, her eyes very wide, searching, despite herself, for the pale dots of the gloves on the tiles below. No luck. Shame, she thinks, absently, trying not to think about what she has just seen, for they really were beautiful gloves. Someone else will benefit from them, she supposes, although then she wonders what will happen if one person finds one, and another the other?

She feels benumbed by what she's seen, by Kitty's sorrow and her anger, and the foul words that the other woman spat, and she cannot tear herself from where she stands until, after a good long while, she starts to shiver and knows she must return to that awful room. She retreats back into the palace and back to the threshold of the receiving room, which is blood warm now, and steamy with breath; there she finds Dee hemmed into a corner by four of the men who had stood behind Octavius Spinola on that dais. She sees that each has his arms crossed, with his right hand hanging loose, and very near the hilt of his sword, and any moment now they will take Dee by his elbows, one on each side, one before and one behind, and bundle him out of the same door by which Van der Boxe's servant left.

After that: he's done for.

Dee has noted them, too, of course, and she can see him pretending to be fascinated by the conversation of the sort of man whom he oftentimes finds at these sorts of occasions, and in whom she usually has very little interest. This time she goes over. The more of them there are, she thinks, the less the Spanish can do.

Dee greets her with animated pleasure and insists she is introduced to his companion, though they have no language in common, and the man's name hardly touches the sides of her memory, but Dee explains in lengthy detail that the man is the business manager of a certain William of Rozmberg, who owns much of southern Bohemia, and that he has come to confirm the final details of a deal he has done with a certain Duke of Brunswick-Lüneburg—also in the room somewhere—regarding his lord's sheep, which are ready to be put on a barge and sailed downriver the very moment the ice melts.

"Master Krcin here says the Valachian sheep is perfect for the conditions typically found in the Harz mountains," Dee translates. "Which belong to the duke."

"Do you have a plan to get out of here?" she asks in the exact rhythm and tone of the sentence "Oh really? And what are these conditions?"

"I was wondering," he says, "if Count Łaski might also be

interested in hearing about these wonder sheep? If he came over perhaps? They would not dare move against him, I think."

She finds Łaski unsuccessfully petitioning a fat choleric man for money, and when Łaski sees Frommond, he takes great pleasure in turning his back on the fat man as if he were of no consequence.

"There is a man here to whom my husband owes money," she lies, "who has set men on him."

She nods at the Spaniards in black, who are now pressing in on Dee. Łaski grasps the situation instantly and laughs without opening his mouth.

"And who is the man to whom the good doctor owes this money?"

Frommond points to the most unpleasant-looking man in the room.

"*Julius*?" Łaski murmurs. "He owes money to *Julius*?"

Frommond nods.

"Do you know what Julius did to the last person who didn't pay him back? No? Ask your husband about Anna Maria Zieglerin."

"I will. Only—?"

"Of course, my dear! Wait. Who is he talking to now? Ach. Jacob Krcin. Christendom's foremost water bore. Come!"

And he sweeps across the floor, all six foot five of him, with his huge beard spread across his gut, and he gathers Dee up under one arm and engulfs him in a lot of nonsensical expressions of great bonhomie. He bundles him away across the room with Frommond bobbling behind, and Dee bent under his arm, and the crowd parting before them, and there is nothing the swordsmen can do to stop him, and in a trice they are out into the courtyard, where Łaski stops and releases Dee.

"Nicely done," Frommond says.

Łaski bows.

"My thanks," Dee says, "but now, I think, we had best be gone."

"Remember!" Łaski calls as they set off. "Anna Maria Zieglerin!"

They go the way they came, but on foot, hurrying through the gate to the castle stairs and leaving Łaski blocking the door like a dam, talking nonsense about not wishing anyone to leave the party because it has all been such fun and he is roaring with laughter, but he can only hold the crowd for so long, because at least some of them are armed with swords and are extremely determined.

"This way," Frommond says. She had seen a path, while standing in the garden earlier, which doubles back under the castle ramparts and runs down through the Lesser Town to the bridge.

"I'm trying to think what I prefer less to running from men with swords," Dee tells her.

"You should try it in a dress."

Ahead drops a long, cobbled ramp that follows the castle's ramparts. It's walled on both sides, and its descent is broken in places by series of steps. They have to get off, she thinks, or it'll be too easy to follow them down to the bridge and trap them there. There are footsteps behind, and she can almost imagine those blades slicing through air and then flesh.

"Down here, look," and Frommond grabs Dee's arm and tugs him to the side: a low archway onto a flight of rough uneven steps down into a gloomy lane and a path that loops back and then divides in two. At least it will throw some doubt where they've gone. She goes right. He follows.

"Have you been here before?"

She did look down from the garden, it's true, but she couldn't see this: a bakery. Deserted now, but still warm on the outside where the oven must be and a little farther along, in the gloom under an arch, hangs a rope pegged to the wall.

"Stop," she says.

She's seen these before at home, in the kitchens of the palace. The rope leads up through a pair of trapdoors in the underside of the arch above, and it will have a series of loops on it onto which the miller's boy attaches a sack of flour, and then he hauls it up through the doors of the hatch to a block attached to the roof above. When the sack's through the doors, they crash closed below, and the sack drops back onto them for the baker's boy to haul it to one side and wait for the next.

It's only ten feet or so, but who looks up?

"Quick."

Frommond grips the rope, her boot through a loop. Dee hauls on the other end and up she goes. He is much stronger than he looks in his velvets, or the block above is doubled or something, for she shoots up and cracks her head on the underside of the shutters and almost lets out a cry. She flies through and only just manages to stop them thundering shut behind her with a boot in the gap. Another suppressed cry.

Now they have to get him up. She should have thought! But he is so slight after his journey and startlingly agile—"for a conjurer"— or again, perhaps it is the doubled block above which is so efficient, but when she hauls on the rope, he seems to sail up and would have gone back down again if she had not lowered the hatches in time. He lands light-footed on them, and they look at each other in total silence a moment until she says: "The rope!"

Dee hoiks it up through the hatches with no time to spare before they hear urgent footsteps running below. There's a call. A countercall. A curse. Retreated steps.

They remain stock-still and silent, just staring at each other in the fading light, waiting until they hear two more pairs of feet hurry under the arch below, and then when they are gone, they risk a smile. She can only see her husband's teeth and eyes now. The smell of flour is thick in the air but the room is warm and dry, and both start laughing at once.

"Do you know," he says, "this is the first time we've been alone since—"

"Wait! I have something to tell you—"

But he is, for that moment at least, not interested.

⊕

Later, they lie in the warmth above the bakery, and Dee tells her that he will never think of bread in quite the same way again, but they should be going now.

"Though there is the bridge to be negotiated, and then the night watch—"

"And there doesn't seem to be much sign of the baker."

They both laugh, and he kisses her again, and she sneezes for each movement they make causes dust to rise.

Then Dee remembers she had something to tell him, and she tells him about Kitty, and what she said about de Guise, and as Frommond speaks, she feels Dee's flesh transform from postcoital languor into that of a river-banked eel, and he is on his feet in a single leap.

"When was this?" he barks. "When was this? And you saw her with the gloves on? Jesu! We need to be back at Thaddeus's house now. We need to see that Kelley is restored to his wits."

"*Kelley?*"

"The emperor will send for him, for us, first thing. Come."

"How do you know?"

"Trust me," he says, and he helps her up and into her clothes.

"What about de Guise?" she asks.

"We've got two weeks before he comes," he tells her.

"To do what?"

"To do all we must, all we can. Everything. Come."

They adjust their clothing and find what they are missing by fumbling in the floury dark, and then when they are ready, they open the hatches, stealthy as they can, and lower the rope, and he goes first this time, dropping nimbly to the ground ten foot below. She follows on the rope and is dropped into his arms.

"Ha," he says, and he kisses her once more before putting her down.

Above them, the cloud is scraped back, and the moon is out, and they are bathed in its eerie light, and they hear a bark. Dee stiffens and turns, and there standing in the thin moonlight is the baker, at the door of his shop, staring at them, mouth open, and frozen into place. He remains wordless as Dee removes his hat and tells him he is much obliged to him for his unwitting hospitality, and that he is sorry if they have caused any inconvenience, and that his purse is irritatingly empty just now, or he would of course compensate the baker for any troubles incurred, and/or indeed buy a loaf of the baker's no doubt excellent bread, but sadly things being as they are, the baker will have to accept some other recompense, which Dee suggests might take the form of him putting in a word for the baker and for his wheaten services to the emperor—or, failing that, the emperor's chamberlain, whom he now believes himself lucky enough to count as a friend—but until then . . . And this having been done, Dee can do little more than reassure the baker of his continued and indeed increased regard for him, and his products, and all through this the baker stares in open-mouthed silence as Dee hooks the rope back on its peg, bows to the baker, and off they go, back down the hill toward the bridge.

"Strange," Dee murmurs. "He looked at us as if we were ghosts."

And Frommond laughs and beats her forearm with a palm, and in the moonlight a cloud of flour rises up and they stop and look at each other and see they are covered in it, head to toe, and only their mouths and eyes are anything but alabaster.

"You look terrifying," he tells her.

"Perfect," she says. "Let's see what they say at the bridge."

And they set off quickly down toward the bridge, where the evening's excitements are passed, and the fires now burn low, and the cold has winnowed the less hardy among them, and the few men and boys who still linger are too drunk or startled to say anything to the two glowing figures as they walk hand in hand through their midst, but cross themselves and cringe back into the shadows to let them pass.

"The superstitious mind," Dee says, when they are across the bridge. "It—" And he indicates to suggest it is unknowable.

"Fuck me! There you are," Marlowe says when they knock on Hajek's door. "Been looking all over for you. It's Kelley. He's gone off his noggin."

He stops for a moment and gives them a second look.

"Hey!" he says. "Why are you all covered in flour?"

⊕

CHAPTER TWENTY-ONE

Arundel Port, West Sussex, February 1584

As Robert Beale walks along the beach toward the group of fishermen crouched over their nets, they all turn to stare at him, and then he remembers why.

"Mistress Devereux, please. Just stay behind."

She beams at him from her saddle, and it is clear she intends to ignore him.

"Oh nonsense, Master Beale," she tells him. "I've known plenty of fishermen. Young and old. All sorts. I love them and their little boats. And the stories they tell."

She gives an unexpectedly throaty laugh, as if remembering some—*what?* Tumble behind the boat sheds? And even the thought makes him blush.

She is, though, a very fine horsewoman, using a new saddle she claims is French and was invented, she says, by Catherine de Medici. It allows a woman far greater control and also lets her show off her very fine ankles, careless of the distraction they cause.

"They are my ankles, Master Beale," she had told him, "to do with as I will, and if by looking at them you are given the wobbles, or incited to commit an offense, then that is your problem and not mine."

"Then why do you not also show your knees?" Beale had asked.

"Because I do not wish to show my knees."

Beale had stopped himself asking why not. Though, God, why not?

They have been together three days now, ever since Walsingham brought her to the village of Angmering, in West Sussex, where Beale had been staying in the best—only—bed in the inn, recovering from an ague picked up after a ferry capsized under him and his horse in the middle of the river west of Shoreham.

"Brought you someone to replace Gregory," Walsingham had told him with a curious smile. "As a favor to Lord Burghley, really, but she might be of assistance."

Beale had propped himself up on his elbows.

"*She?*"

Walsingham had laughed.

"We will see you below, in the hall," he'd said.

Beale had gotten up, washed and changed, and come down, and there she had been, at the table, eating a sausage and drinking from a mazer of ale: Mistress Devereux, in emerald silks under a midnight-blue cloak, with her blond hair in a pearl and silver net. She was negotiating with a one-eyed man to buy a pair of red fingerless woolen gloves, and a knitted cap of the same.

Walsingham had made the introductions.

"How fetching do you think this will look?" she had asked, putting on the one-eyed man's cap, straight from his head. God, I would not do that, Beale had thought, but he said, "Very."

For she did.

"Good," she'd said and had turned to the one-eyed now hatless man and offered him her hand.

"Then we have a deal."

After breakfast Devereaux had told him that she had known she could have beaten the old man down to almost nothing, but what she had given him would keep him in ale "probably for the rest of his life," so her conscience was clear.

"Quite something, isn't she?" Walsingham had whispered when she was out of earshot, dealing with her three servants, who were to follow along behind with all her luggage.

"But why?" Beale had asked. "Why have you sent her to me?"

And though Walsingham explained about Lord Burghley, and the Catherine de Medici's *L'Escadron Volant*, Beale knew this was a further punishment: Walsingham knows about Mistress Dee, he thinks. He knows I have paid for her to save her husband, and he remembers Ness Overbury, of course.

"So we must now show Her Majesty that she has such a thing," Walsingham had gone on, "though of course we can afford to send her no farther than West Sussex, and only then for a week, tops."

They both turned to see her dismissing her servants as if they were nothing to do with her and ride back to them on that astonishing saddle on a very fine horse.

"And I guarantee she will send us the bill for the hat and gloves."

Which she did, and Beale, later, thought, Well, why not?

So now they are approaching the fishermen and their nets, and the fishermen only have eyes for Mistress Devereaux and her ankles. They answer Beale's questions about Master Mope only very absently, and negatively, of course, but at least they are not rude to him, so there is that.

After noting down that none in that village know of a Master Mope, they ride on to the next, the name of which is contested, but it is on the east bank of yet another of those rivers that must be crossed, and into which Beale feels he is now like to be tipped again, and the ferryman tells him there are three or four families that fish from two or three boats out of hereabouts.

When they disembark, they stop at the first house, overlooking the river mouth, and though there are no boats moored, there are stanchions sunk in the ground, so perhaps the boats are out at sea? Set back from the shore are three stone shacks, thatched roofs over low windowless walls in which someone has sunk row after row of flints, and against one of which sits a bent old boy in a long-knitted smock. He's gutting mullet, and the smell is strong.

"What is the name of this river?" Beale asks, and the man tells him old folks used to call it the Tarrant.

"And now?"

"Arun," he says, his eyes fixing on Mistress Devereux, who sits very handsomely in her saddle. Beale makes a note in his book and sets to with his usual questions and he gets the usual answers. After he is done, Mistress Devereux turns her horse about, so that the man gets a glimpse of those ankles, though in truth today they are in sturdy mud-spattered boots, but a man's imagination is a powerful tool, and the fish gutter wishes she'd linger a moment longer.

"Our boat is too dainty for a crossing to France, Mistress," he tells her, not Beale. "But try upriver. Young John Halter. He's always coming and going, he is, and just this last month he came by—just there—in his father's boat only with a new sail. Not patched, mind. New."

Is that significant? Who knows. Over these last few months Beale has written so much of this sort of nonsense in his book he is neither surprised nor bored by any of it. When Gregory was with him, they would discuss it at night, in various inns along the coast, but Gregory hadn't been able to stand it any longer, hence the feigned sweating sickness back in Rye, and since then—for the last seventy miles or so—it has just been Beale with no one to talk to at night, and no way to judge what he had, or had not, learned.

He wonders if Mistress Devereux in her red knitted fisherman's cap will sit with him in the evening to speculate on such niceties?

"And how should we find young Master Halter on this fine day, sir?" Mistress Devereux asks. "Is he in harbor or out at sea?"

"Aye, he's up there all right," the fisherman growls, nodding up river, disapprovingly. "Came in last night with his fine new sail. Cargo of paper out of Dieppe. French paper."

The fisherman spits and then slices the belly of the hand-sized fish with—what? Just his thumbnail?—and flicks the guts on the cobbles by his side.

"How far is the harbor?" Beale wonders.

"A league or more," the man tells them. "You'll be going that way, anyways, if you want to get across."

Now he nods to the river's far bank. Beale looks about for a ferry. There is none.

"What's the next village along?" he asks.

"How should I know?" the old man says.

Beale sighs. Nobody knows anything.

"And where will we find this bridge?" he asks.

"Up there."

He means: follow the river. Fair enough. As Mistress Devereux thanks the fisherman, Beale mounts up and they set off north along the river's eastern bank through marshy flat lands. Emerging from the distance, though, is a hill, the first of the Downs, and as they approach, Beale can see it is flanked by an old castle. He stops to rest his horse, and she stands by him, staring at it from under a flattened hand.

"Do you know it?" he asks.

"Of course I do," she tells him. "It is the Earl of Arundel's castle."

"Arundel? The old Duke of Norfolk's son?"

"The very one."

"I thought he had his castle at Framlingham?"

Devereux shrugs.

"You know what these families are like, Master Beale," she says. "Anyway, we should go and see if he's in. I hear he's been let out of the Tower."

Beale had not heard this, but he is not surprised. The whole shabby business of Throckmorton's racking still bothers him, in greater part because of Walsingham's willing sacrifice of Doctor Dee, but in no much smaller part also the Queen forbidding them to pursue the real traitors because they were old families, to whom the laws seem not to apply. It is a game, he thinks, and he wonders how long it will last.

But Mistress Devereux is asking him a question.

"Do you know him?"

"Arundel? Yes. I've met him."

"Tell me: What did you think of him?"

Can he tell her he wanted to punch him on sight?

"I wanted to punch him on sight."

She half laughs, half gasps.

"Me too!"

She grips his forearm as she laughs, and they are very close. She is in tight-cut, faded green wool today, from which he can scarce take his gaze, with ballooning blue corded skirts, and still in her fisherman's hat. Beale knows this is probably how she will appear to him tonight in his dreams, and tomorrow morning he will be unable to look her in the eye, again.

"But do you know," she confides, "I think he may be a sodomite."

Beale concedes that is possible.

"Because on Lord Burghley's orders I absolutely threw myself upon him," she goes on. "And there was nothing. Not a thing. And this was when he was in prison! Can you imagine?"

Beale says nothing. He keeps his eye on the castle. If he looks at her mouth, her lips, her curiously white teeth, the dimple—

"Come on then," he says. "We'd best get going if we are to find an inn."

"And our mysterious merchant adventurer with his brand-new sail."

She says this as if it is an amusing mystery. Beale tuts.

"It will come to nothing. Some age-old feud between two rival fishermen."

"I think it sounds wonderfully intriguing. I mean, how do you set about getting a new sail?"

See if you can guess, he thinks, and after a moment she giggles, because there ahead of them is another one of those low, flint-dashed houses in a clearing, and in it a man sits on a stool with his knees covered in a broad spread of red canvas and between thumb and forefinger a curled steel needle and length of waxed twine. A sailmaker.

"Aye," he says when Beale asks. "And not before time."

"How did he pay?"

And now the man hesitates, unsure whether this is anybody's business but his and Halter's.

"I'm here on behalf of Her Majesty's principal private secretary," Beale tells him, which cuts no ice.

"Sir Francis Walsingham," Mistress Devereux clarifies, at which the man starts.

"Right," he says. "Right. Well. I did think it were odd, but John Halter is oftentimes to and from France, so look."

And he plucks from among the various coins in his purse two

worn silver French *testons* and he holds them up for inspection between his fantastically calloused fingers.

"Silver is silver," Mistress Devereux supposes, and the sailmaker agrees.

Does it mean anything? Beale wonders. If Halter, as they all agree, oftentimes sails to France for business?

"We could ask the searcher," Beale tells Mistress Devereux. He means the man employed to search every ship or boat that leaves or enters a harbor, in search of contraband in any form.

"Hah!" the sailmaker snorts. "Good luck finding him in harbor. He's taken up trade of his own accord now. Come into money he has. Can't think how."

And he says this with such a twist that Beale starts to feel the most extraordinary sensation that he might actually at long last have found the trail of the man they know only as not being Master Mope.

⊕

CHAPTER TWENTY-TWO

Prague, February 1584

The fight between Kelley and Łaski's servant Alexander had perhaps been a long time coming, ever since Kelley caught Alexander with his wife up against the wall behind the *Watergeuzen* in Brielle, but it had spilled over in the early evening, with Kelley already unsettled by not being invited to meet Octavius Spinola, and then Alexander appearing at Master Hajek's door in search of Joanna, with whom it appeared he had arranged to pass some time while they believed her husband would be at the castle. No blood had actually been spilled, or not very much, but a sword had appeared, and terrible threats made, and it had all taken place out in the lane in front of Master Hajek's house, so the night watch had been called. There was now the danger that news of it would reach the emperor's chamberlain, if not the emperor, and that he would refuse to even meet Kelley, let alone trust him.

"By the time I got back he'd already worked his way through most of old Thaddeus's cellar," Marlowe tells them, "and he was ranting and raving about this that and the other, and fuck me, you should have heard some of the stuff he was shouting. Threatened to cut old Alex's head off he did! Alex ran away in tears!"

Dee is surprised at that and wonders if Alexander should perhaps have considered something like this outcome before he ever tupped Joanna.

"Where is he?"

"Asleep in the outhouse."

Letting him sleep it off is all they can do.

"He'll freeze to death you leave him out there," Joanna says. "Going to get cold it is tonight. Colder than anything we ever saw in Poland."

"How can that be?" Roger Cooke asks, and it is a good question.

"Do you feel these sorts of things in your bones?" Dee wonders, but it is in her waters that she feels them, she tells him.

"And they is turned to ice, for there is more to come!"

Dee looks up at the stars, which are fiercely bright in the deepest blue, and he thinks of the Great Conjunction in the fiery trigon and he wishes he were back at home, in his orchard perhaps, studying the stars with the prospect of eating alone with Jane, and drinking wine, and going to bed with her, but no: here he is, in Prague, with a comatose Kelley, and the thought of what is now to come.

"Well, let's give him a blanket at least then," he tells them, "and everyone, we must be up at dawn, and ready for developments."

Dee does not sleep that night but lies awake and thinks of de Guise. In the small hours, Jane turns to him.

"What is it?" she asks. "You are thinking of Isobel Cochet?"

He is, sort of. Thinking about how de Guise has done the exact same thing to Kitty de Fleurier as he did Isobel: stole the one thing that mattered most to her—her sister, in this case—and bent her to his will in order to save it. A cynic would applaud, he supposes: If something works, why try something else?

⊕

The next morning, Kelley is still alive, but it turns out that Joanna was right: it has turned bitterly, bitterly cold, and there is ice rime on the lock of the outhouse door and crystals of it in Kelley's hair, too, when they get the door open, and Kelley's skin is the color of goose fat.

"Silly old fart's gone and died," Joanna says.

But he's shuddering under his blanket, which Dee takes to be a good sign.

"Get me a bucket of water and some soap," Dee tells her.

When she's gone, Dee bends and look closely at Kelley. He smells very strongly as if he has shat himself—he has—and vomited on his boots—likewise he has—but Dee ignores all this. He has found a stick, about a hand's length, and with it, he prises apart the hair clumped around one of Kelley's ears.

"Ugh," he says to himself. Kelley's ears have been clipped: the punishment for someone who shaves the edges from coins back in England. No wonder he hides them. But what does that make him? Dee shakes his head. It hardly matters now, anyway, and if he is a cozener, then he has become very good at it, so perhaps that is enough?

He backs out of the outhouse and tosses the stick aside just as Joanna comes back with a pail of warmed water, which she empties on her husband with a gleeful cheer. Kelley is roused and flails around as if fighting off bees.

"No soap to be had," Joanna tells Dee.

"Oh come on," Dee moans. "He can't go before the emperor like that."

Hajek appears.

"Even if he was dressed in gold, the emperor would never see him."

"We have to get him up."

"Give him some ale in which you have doused a glowing poker, and an egg," is Marlowe's suggestion and for a moment it seems to work, and Kelley is able to eat some pig's liver, which Edwin swears is restorative, and they leave him to Joanna to wash. Marlowe has found him a doublet of undyed hessian that suits him, but Dee will not let him put it on.

"Why not? I'm freezing."

"Because—"

Just then Kelley expels the liver and the ale all over himself.

"Christ."

Another bucket, another egg, and more ale.

"But no more liver."

A little later, Kelley is standing, and a little drunk, and Dee lets him have the doublet, and a moment after that there comes a thunderous knock on the door, and Dee cannot help but smile.

"What is happening?" Hajek cries.

"The emperor," Dee tells him.

And outside in the lane is a company of the emperor's lancers, with studs in their beautiful horses' hooves, escorting an empty carriage, and at Hajek's door is an officer, discernible by his fine bearskin hat, and his worked breastplate and fine scabbard and boots, with a sergeant of sorts, there to thump the woodwork with a fist like a ham.

"Doctor Dee?" the officer asks.

Dee nods.

"Come quick, sir: the emperor needs you."

⊕

The bridge is cleared completely as they thunder across at exhilarating speed, though Dee sees some men still linger at each end, gathered around their fires and watching the lancers and carriage pass with unreadable expressions.

"So much for the Day of Rage," Cooke says.

"They'll be back," Dee is sure.

There is hardly a change of pace as they start up the hill to the castle.

"I'm going to be sick," Kelley says.

"Don't you fucking dare," Marlowe tells him.

He doesn't.

They hurtle up the cleared streets, through the West Gate and swing around to draw up before the same steps they'd used for Spinola's audience, but this time the door is wrenched open by another captain of the halberdiers almost before the carriage stops. The halberdier helps Frommond out, and Dee follows.

"This way," he says in English. He has long gloves, and tall boots, and a curved blade in his sash, and he leads them hurrying up the steps, cleared of snow.

"Hurry!" he calls over his shoulder.

Two halberdiers click to attention as they pass, and within the palace the corridors are deserted and deathly quiet. They cross the hall, and pass between two more halberdiers, before turning right, then left then right again. More halberdiers. A hall with a roaring fire minded by a single glum footman, and at the end of another long corridor is gathered a knot of men and women in black, who stand and turn to face them as they come. Their hostility is unmasked, and Dee recognizes among them at least one of the swordsmen from the other night, and for a moment he wonders if he has misjudged this.

But then there is Łaski, fighting his way through the ganglion of courtiers to greet Dee before bowing his thanks to the captain of the halberdiers and placing an arm on Dee's shoulder again, so he might whisper fragrantly—of bacon—into his ear: "The emperor is with her now. I would escort you myself, but I am not permitted for I am—they say—too loud."

Dee notes he has been weeping.

"Why summon me, though?" Dee asks, so that all about might hear. "I am no physician!"

"It is what you said. At the Action at Hajek's house. You remember?"

Dee frowns.

"About the angel-faced lady falling ill?"

"That was not me. That was Galvah."

"Even so. I told the emperor. Come."

He ushers the courtiers out of the way as if they were children, and they part reluctantly. Łaski stops to greet Frommond, with a hurried kiss on the hand, and he nods at Marlowe, Kelley, and Cooke but no more, before returning to whisper in Dee's ear.

"I could not tell emperor that Kelley is the scryer."

"We've given him a wash, and a new doublet," Dee tries.

"Even so," Łaski grumbles. "Emperor would never forgive Count Łaski if I put Kelley before him."

They march on.

"Is very bad for Mistress de Fleurier," Łaski tells him over his shoulder. "Emperor hates any kind of illness in others. You know type?"

Dee does.

They are at two broad, ornately carved doors guarded by two captain halberdiers in sashes.

"Is Doctor Dee," Łaski tells them. "And attendants."

The door is opened from within.

"I leave you here, Doctor, but ask that I might come in when time is right. I will be not too loud, I swear on the head of Saint Vojtěch!"

Dee agrees, and he thanks Łaski.

"Don't thank me, Doctor. Save her, and you will have the emperor's ear. Also: do not get separated. You will see what I mean. Julius's men are everywhere."

Julius? Ah. Yes. The Duke of Brunswick-Lüneburg; Frommond had told Łaski he was the man to whom Dee owed money.

Through the doors is another large hall. Between each window stands a halberdier, sword unsheathed, and there on various padded benches about the room sprawl yet more men and women in their somber Spanish fashions. Dee recognizes at once all the signs of that mind-rotting, spirit-crushing boredom he associates only with the worst sort of courtly life. The floor is covered in the largest Turkey rug Dee has ever seen, and all over the walls and again on the ceiling there are more of those paintings that had so overwhelmed Frommond at Octavius Spinola's audience room: a flayed Bartholomew with his flensing knife, just blood and sinew, with his eyes raised to heaven; Lawrence's killers turning his cooked side up upon a glowing iron grill; a nameless woman being trampled under the hooves of a vast and careless horse. Dee feels the warmth on his face of two fires in their places, and in the center of the hall stands not only Octavius Spinola, the emperor's chamberlain, but also Arnoldus van der Boxe, and a beautiful woman with a skeptical hitch to her eyebrow that lends her the impression of intelligence that Dee has an uneasy feeling will prove to be borne out.

"That's her," Frommond whispers. "Kitty's minder."

All three are very drawn, and tense, and none are pleased to see him.

"You are Doctor Dee?" Spinola asks, just as if he had not met Dee two days earlier.

Dee nods, somberly, as if already at a funeral, and bows.

"My wife—" he starts, intending further introductions.

"Come," Spinola interrupts.

And he turns now and leads Dee through a maze of further doors and along further corridors, and at almost every corner is one of Arnoldus van der Boxe's swordsman, or someone very much like him, and each man watches Dee with the look of someone marking whom they are next going to kill. Dee counts seven of them before they reach what must be the inner sanctum of Rudolf's palace and he knows he will never find his way out of here, without help, without being murdered.

At last Spinola stops before an especially grand set of doors made from rosewood or some such into which is carved a tableau that at first glance looks like one thing, but on second forces those seeing it for the first time to do a double take, for closer inspection reveals a number of men and a number of women coupling in every way imaginable, though when Spinola's gentle knock causes the door to be half opened, the coitus is interrupted.

"Ha!" he hears Marlowe exclaim with some pleasure.

"His Highness's *Kunstkammer*," Spinola explains.

Even warmer and richly pungent air uncoils from the darkness within, and Dee hears strange rhythmic prayers being chanted by deep-voiced men in time to the beating of some great cosmic heart and another deep voice from within bids Dee enter. Every hair stands upright and every sense and nerve jangles, for there is surely something unearthly within.

He steps forward.

"Just you, Doctor," Spinola tells him. Dee glances around. Eight of Van der Boxe's men stand ten paces up the corridor, waiting.

"I must have my assistants," Dee lies.

"No."

"Yes."

There is a long moment when it looks like he might be sent away, but they need him, he knows.

"Very well."

And the door inches wider to admit Frommond, Roger Cooke, and Kelley, who is suddenly reluctant until gently propelled by Marlowe, and then Marlowe himself, and in the light that the open door lets in, Dee sees the shapes of many hooded monks kneeling and chanting the prayers in time to a swinging censer that billows a pale, bitter smoke. He gets no sense of the size of the room, for the walls cannot be seen, only there are at least two fires, and many, many umber-flamed candles in sconces all around. When he steps in, the air is thick and damp, and breathing it in feels as if he is making himself complicit in some intimate act.

He stands stock-still. Slowly his eyes adjust to the gloom, and he sees that a thickly curtained bed, as big as a poor man's house, sits in the middle of the room, while to one side is a double-height dais, couched with banks of candles, upon which is set a throne under a cloth of state, and, on the throne, a figure.

Dee bows as low as he can.

"Your Majesty," he says.

And he feels for a moment as if he may be talking to God himself, but a moment later a low raspy, raised-voice speaks in fluent, unaccented Latin.

"An angel-faced woman that waxes red as the beet, as dry as the bone, as blind as the bat, and as hot as the hare."

Dee stands now and opens his hands.

"The angel Galvah," he says. "He spoke these words to us not two days ago. We had no idea what they could mean."

"But they were prophetic," the emperor goes on, "as our liege-man Count Olbrecht Łaski has told us."

Dee cannot be sure if this is a question or not. He cants to one side and glances at the bed, hoping the emperor can see more of him than he can see of the emperor.

"May I see the . . . the patient?" he asks.

"You may not."

Dee had not anticipated that.

"Then how may I serve you, Your Highness?" he asks.

"Ask the angelic spirits to cure our Kitten," the emperor tells him.

Dee is beginning to feel dizzy with all the perfumed smoke, and the doctored warmth, and the unsettling chants, and the great, grand peculiarity of addressing the emperor of all the Germans, the king of Hungary and Croatia, the king of Bohemia, and the archduke of Austria, in the near dark, and he feels he cannot get his thoughts straight, and he is gripped by a powerful need to run, to be out in the cold air, breathing free.

"The angelic spirits cannot be summoned in such circumstances," he tells the emperor.

The emperor is silent for some time, waiting for Dee to change his mind, to see it his way; but Dee needs only hold his nerve, only to imagine that he has no stake in this odd game. He needs only to forget that everything he has done in the last six months—all the hardships, the risks, the troubles he has put his wife to—and the fate of Bess, and of England herself, are come down to this one moment: how this one man reacts.

At last the emperor sighs.

"What is it they need?" he asks, his voice blurred and dulled by his ill-matching teeth.

"They need light, Your Highness," Dee tells him. "And air that is clean. And silence. They abjure crowds."

Particularly of monks, he almost adds. The emperor continues to stare. Long moments pass during which Dee is again invited to yield, but still he doesn't, in part because what he says is true: the angelic spirits come only after prayer and fasting, not during this sensuous, ungodly performance that reminds him most of the time he provoked that beetle to fly to Jupiter, in the play in Cambridge, only here magnified and amplified a million times.

At last the emperor signals—a short flick of a weak wrist—and Dee now sees that he has been bracketed all this time by a small army of black-clothed attendants, one of whom steps forward to bend his ear to the emperor's command. A moment later there is a swirl of activity in the darkness, after which the chanting stops amid some confusion, and thick curtains are drawn back from broad, many-paned windows in which are set glass doors through to gardens outside, and cold light spills into the vast hall to reveal a hundred bleary-eyed men blinking as if woken from wine-fogged sleep.

Some are priests, others physicians perhaps, while others are mere courtiers: all look at Dee and his party with competing expressions of rage and contempt, but Dee ignores them all, for he only has eyes for the emperor, who remains seated on his throne, and when a gust of frigid air from a newly opened window stirs the smoke, Dee at last has his first proper look at him, and he has to admit he is disappointed.

The emperor is a strange, warped, and obviously unhappy little man, like a prematurely aged child with pale blotchy skin, a patchy auburn beard, and red-rimmed eyes. He seems to lurk within his voluminous, camouflaging cloak of richest crimson velvet, peering out from under his baggy cloth-of-gold hat that is pulled low against the new-brought light, and at his side, bolted to his chair on a silver chain, frets a restive and equally unhappy monkey.

Dee bows again, for the sudden light makes him feel as if he has only recently entered the room, and the emperor lifts a slender finger in acknowledgment of the situation, but from behind him his attendants—of a Spanish stripe, every one of them—stare at Dee with unmasked malice, but whether this is because he is a Protestant Englishman come for an as yet to be divined purpose or because of how he appears to be usurping their influence on the emperor, he cannot tell. Both maybe. Dee does, though, notice three men in long black scholars' robes have not left Kitty's bedside, but stand guard, and he welcomes their simple professional jealousy when he sees it.

When the monks are ushered out, the candlewicks are pinched, and the windows are opened to cool and freshen the room that is easily fifty paces wide, and sixty long, with its distant walls and even its ceiling hidden by more of those awful paintings of terrible, fraught deaths. In this room there are statues, too, all over the black-and-white-checkered marble flags, of naked well-muscled men fighting one another, or tigers or lions or snakes. And so many horses, too; some are life-size, in marble, bronze, onyx, and even amber. One of them rears up, forehooves thrashing, with an ebony-skinned rider pinning a writhing marble dragon snake with a lance. But Dee's eye is drawn to the various display cabinets, of which there must be a hundred, holding coins and corals, and books and rocks and what looks to be the skull of a dragon, and various other stuffed animals, including a unicorn, in ghastly tableaux of their death throes. He knows the emperor is also a collector of scientific instruments, which he will be interested to see, but in the middle of all this there remains above it all the great bulk of the red curtained bed, like a blood-soaked meteorite sent from another planet.

"Tell us how to save our Kitten," the emperor now mews, looking mournfully at the bed, and the monkey lunges at it, baring its teeth and making the silver links of its chain sing. Emperor Rudolf holds up his arms, and men lift him to his feet, and he pads softly across the rug and descends to Dee's level. He is very short, Dee sees, and his chin is as big as they all say it is, and Dee cannot help thinking that were he not Holy Roman Emperor, he might be thought a fool and sat upon a stool in a fair where men might compete to toss coins into the gap between his teeth.

"Tell Kurtz what else you need," he says, "and he will see it is fetched."

Dee knows the emperor means Jacob Kurtz von Senftenau, his chancellor, who must, Dee supposes, be one of the black-clad attendants. Hajek has said he is a decent man, of their way of thinking, and, Dee is hoping, most likely to want to join them in an Action.

What Dee says—or doesn't say—now is of every importance. Everything comes down to his judgment on the sort of man the emperor is.

"Thank you, Your Highness," he tells Rudolf. "We require nothing but privacy to summon the angelic spirits, and silence to hear their voices."

The emperor gives him a look that in another man might be described as beady, but whatever his eyes imply, his hanging jaw gives him a moronic mien, and Dee realizes it is going to be impossible to judge him by his facial expression alone. What else then? The monkey? It has climbed onto the throne and is crying in grotesque imitation of the emperor. Perhaps that is it? There are stranger things.

"You wish us all gone?" Rudolf asks.

Dee regrets it, but yes.

"The angelic spirits can be capricious," he tells the emperor, and he seems to accept this, for why wouldn't they be capricious? They have defied all Rudolf's previous attempts to contact them. But the man Dee assumes to be Kurtz leans forward and speaks for the first time, in precise, clipped Latin.

"Yet they spoke with *Łaski*?"

It is clear what he thinks of Łaski.

"They did not speak to him," Dee lies. "We asked if they might tolerate his presence at an Action, and after no little time, they agreed, and they now favor him."

The emperor is too startled to understand he has been expelled from his own hall, in his own palace, in his own castle, so it is left to Kurtz to ask: "Might you not ask them if they would"—he hardly likes to say the word *tolerate* of His Highness the Emperor, who is exalted above all men perhaps, but he is talking about angels here, so—"*tolerate* the presence of His Highness?"

Dee makes a show of confusion.

"We can only ask."

The emperor blinks. Dee wonders when he was last refused anything he wanted.

"And the physicians must leave, also," Dee presses, for he needs the physicians gone as soon as possible if his plan is to succeed.

"But they are Mistress de Fleurier's physicians," Kurtz objects, on behalf of the emperor.

"She shall have no need of them, with divine intervention."

Rudolf nods, grudgingly, and Kurtz signals to one of his underlings, who crosses to where the gray-bearded physicians cluster about two cloth-covered tables covered in unguents, powders, flasks, and so on, all the implements of their trade. The scene fleetingly reminds

Dee of Jesus clearing the moneylenders from the temple, but here they must leave what they cannot carry: some dishes and pestles and mortars and a small brazier that is too hot to the touch. By the time they are expelled, traipsing through the door pursued by overladen assistants, the room is cold, with the windows open, and a courtier slips a fur around the emperor's shoulders.

"What else did the angelic spirits say about our Kitty?" he asks.

"Nothing further, Your Highness. In the most recent Action we talked of other things. Of a book, for instance, that the angelic spirits have bid me write out for them, and their purpose in doing so."

"A book?"

The emperor's attention is piqued, but Dee remains elusive and vague.

"I cannot speak of it, Your Highness," he tells him, "for its meaning is as yet ungraspable to my feeble intellect, being written in what I believe to be the lost language of Adam."

The emperor opens his mouth, closes it again. It is almost, Dee thinks, as if he were a fish—a lugubrious old carp—swallowing a fly. Will it hook?

He changes the subject.

"And it would be better," Dee says, "if the paintings were taken away, or shrouded, or perhaps turned to face the wall at least."

Those on the ceiling must stay, he supposes, but Jesu, how they loom: hulking, bearded prophets grappling half-naked, wide-eyed virgins; male fingers indenting female flesh, lots of ripped cloth; contorted limbs, rolling eyes, and nipples, lots of nipples.

All this while Jane, Cooke, Marlowe, and Kelley have stood in a tight circle, a little to one side, and Kelley is simpering at the emperor, and the effect is repugnant. Even at a moment like this Dee is struck by how unknowable Edward Kelley is, so uncomfortable, ill-defined, and strange. He remembers his ears and cannot even begin to imagine what he is thinking at any one moment. Even now in his new—to him—doublet, Kelley appears to melt at his edges, to blur with the air around him, to crumble, fade, reappear as something else. Perhaps that is what makes him the scryer he is?

Jane is meanwhile looking to the curtained bed. She is worried about Kitty, of course, and when Rudolf's messenger had told them that is why they were summoned, it was Frommond who had been the most upset, but also the most surprised.

"Why do they wish to see you?" she'd asked Dee. "You're not a doctor."

"It was what the angelic spirits said," he'd told her. "About the angel-faced woman."

Dee had been able to see her mind spinning then, looking for handholds, and it had occurred to him that she had never quite believed in his scrying, had always believed it to be hocus-pocus. But now here was solid proof: the angelic spirits had predicted an angel-faced woman would fall ill with certain symptoms, and lo! So she had done.

"In the absence of any physicians," Dee now says, "my wife will see to Mistress de Fleurier."

The emperor finally risks his eyes to look at Dee's party of assistants. His gaze does not settle on Kelley, mercifully, but on Frommond, who is extremely presentable in her stolen dress, and also, though to a lesser extent, upon Marlowe, who bows alongside Frommond's dip, though far more extravagantly, at the emperor's attention.

Emperor Rudolf is doubtful. Dee and his party have expertise—perhaps—in summoning angelic spirits into crystal stones, not ministering to very ill women. Anything Dee says to reassure him—that Frommond was once at the court of Queen Elizabeth, for example—will only make him suspicious. Rudolf is about to say he cannot leave

Kitty unguarded for he does not know these men and woman. Nor can he guard her himself: with her ill, he cannot risk his own health.

"But perhaps we had best be making our preparations," Dee hurries him. "Doctor Kelley must pray. And fast. And we must have the windows restored."

For it is now bitingly cold. At a nod, the servants set to, replacing the frames.

"And another log on the fire," Marlowe adds.

Dee turns his body so that the emperor knows it is time for him to leave, but Rudolf is still caught in two minds until at last he nods curtly at Jane.

"Your wife may see to her," Kurtz interprets. "See that she has all that she needs. And if anything else is wanted, I will put servants just beyond the doors."

He indicates to the pornographic doors, which are even worse from this side, the private side, and—*Jesu!*—that handle! There is no polite way to grasp that.

"May we have Count Łaski sent?" Dee asks. "The angelic spirits respond very favorably to his presence."

The emperor takes a hissing breath. He is not pleased. Dee knows he takes a risk involving Łaski as witness but how else will Rudolf ever learn of what is said in their Actions but through Łaski's incontinent boasting? Rudolf would never believe Dee if he told him what the angels said, because he would be so sure Dee was lying for his own benefit. Not only that, Łaski's involvement is both a lure to the emperor to join, and a rebuke that he has not already done so.

With this in mind, Rudolf hesitates, before finally giving the nod.

"I will pass on your invitation," Kurtz tells Dee, and so at last, with one lingering look at the bed, the emperor turns and shuffles off out of the pornographic door, which closes with a startling click behind him, so that the handle might put your eye out. Dee and Frommond, Roger Cooke, and Kelley and Marlowe are left alone by the fire to look at one another in a species of amazement.

After a moment Marlowe whistles in admiration.

"What just happened there, Doctor?" he asks.

For it does feel as if they have staged some sort of coup, or revolution. The five of them are alone in the *Kunstkammer* of the Holy Roman Emperor, the heart of the Empire. The room is now gripped in the cold, scientific, almost Protestant light of northern reason, and there is scarcely a moment to be wasted.

"Quick," Dee tells them. "Turn those awful paintings around and block the doors, all of them, and Jane, please, will you see to Kitty?"

⊕

CHAPTER TWENTY-THREE

Arundel Haven, Sussex, February 1584

Robert Beale runs a finger around Mistress Devereux's left nipple and wonders how she can lie there and read without speaking the words aloud, or even moving her lips. He also wonders how she can lie there with all this glory before her—by which he means her naked body—and not be constantly playing with it.

"I would," he says.

"Would what?"

"Nothing."

It is raining again—he can hear it on the roof, scarce six foot above their heads—and the gulls are screeching again, which suggests that a catch has come in. Perhaps it is time to leave her alone, and go and see what there is to be seen. He hauls himself from the bed, adjusts himself, and begins to dress, but she is still frowning over some detail in the letter from Master Walsingham.

"He seems obsessed with all these works at Orford," she says.

"Always going on about how badly the masons are doing their job and how the gunners will never be able to sight their guns in time."

Beale laughs.

"He means the opposite," he says.

She frowns at him over the top of the letter and he laughs again, for Mistress Devereux needs eyeglasses to read, which makes her owlish.

"Why?"

"In case anyone to whom it is not addressed reads it."

Such as her, he might add, for he should never have shown it to her, save how could he resist?

"But won't they know he means the opposite?"

"They might, but they'll never be certain. They'll pass along what they have read and someone, somewhere will presume he means it. It is human nature to trust what is written."

Is that true? he wonders. Possibly not.

"But why does he want them to think the gunners at Orford cannot sight their guns?"

"He wants whoever reads this—apart from you, apart from me—to believe that Framlingham is still vulnerable. Still the best place to land five thousand Spanish tercios."

Devereux is perhaps the only woman in England who knows what a tercio is, for the moment, at least.

"But it's not?"

"Not anymore. Now they've built this tower in Orford. It overlooks the river that leads to Framlingham, from which even a blind gunner could hit a passing ship."

"Should you be telling me this?"

Beale thinks about it for a moment.

"No," he agrees.

She puts aside the letter, takes off her eyeglasses and stretches, and oh Jesu, he can scarce control himself, but she is having none of it.

"Come on," she says. "Master Halter will be back from France, I am certain of it, and time's a-wasting, and we do not want to miss him again."

Which is what happened last time Master Halter was in port, when they ventured a fruitless diversion to Arundel Castle, hoping to find the earl there, with no luck, for he had gone, his steward said, to Petworth and was not expected back for a week at least.

They dress now and Beale might almost weep to see all that beauty sheathed in linen, but she is with her back to him, and less enamored of him than he of her, and they go for breakfast in the hall of the inn where they eat ashy bread and drink strong march ale. Continuing their conversation, Mistress Devereaux asks Beale why they are flogging their guts out down in Arundel if they already know the tercios are to land in Suffolk.

He does not want to tell her that he is sent here on this almost hopeless task to find Master Mope, in part as punishment and in part to keep him out of the way. He does not want to tell her that he no longer has Master Walsingham's trust and is in part disgraced. He does not want to tell her that she is sent to him not to learn from him, but to keep an eye on him, and as a challenge to him, which he has—what? Failed? Well. That has been worth it, at least.

"It is due diligence," Beale tells her, coining a phrase.

"That doesn't sound very exciting," she says.

"Talking to a hundred thousand fishermen about a man of whom the only thing we know is that he is not called Master Mope?"

"Yes. That. Whyever are we doing it in the first place? And how do we know he's not called Master Mope?"

"Because," Beale tells her, scarcely recalling it himself, "Master Mope is what they called him in the letter we discovered in Throckmorton's casket. We know only that he has another identity. Once we find him, we can find his other identity."

"But to what end?"

That is a good question, Beale supposes, for he, too, has almost lost sight of the importance of the man who is not Master Mope.

"Mope isn't the real name of the Duc de Guise's agent, who is supposed to be dealing with three English lords, in preparation for an invasion by five thousand Catholic mercenaries. If we can find this—this—this *anti*-Mope, then we can find the three lords, and put a stop to any invasion."

She nods slowly.

"But then what will we do if we do not find him?"

"Well," he says, having given this a great deal of thought, "we still have two hundred miles before we reach Plymouth. A village every mile, say, means we have—well, you can work that out. But there is also Southampton and Portsmouth to consider, both large towns, and the home of many, many seafarers, so there is every chance we shall run him to ground by and by."

She looks at him very skeptically.

"But if we don't?"

He smiles at her, very broadly, very unconvincingly.

"Then we start again."

⊕

"Glory be!" Devereaux exclaims. "Look!"

They have been in Arundel haven waiting for a boat with a new sail for what has seemed like weeks now, with no proper luck, but this morning there is a boat they have not seen before, roped to the quay, and wrapped about its mainmast is what they have come to recognize unquestionably as a new sail. On board a man is unloading a quantity of waxed-linen-wrapped parcels to a boy on the quay under the watchful eye of another man in a striking blue coat.

"Are you Master Halter?" Devereux asks the man in the boat, and he stops in midpassing to the boy.

"Who wants to know?"

Beale tells him, using Walsingham's name. He notices the man in the blue jacket take a step back.

"Who are you?" Beale asks the man.

"No one," the man in the jacket says, and Mistress Devereux laughs.

"You're Henry Waddle," she tells him. "The searcher for this port. We've been waiting for you, too. And that, by the way, is a very fine coat."

Devereux can cost a man's cloth in an instant, over and above a certain price point, and Waddle's coat is expensive enough to reach that. You can see Waddle wishing he had not worn it this day.

"So," Beale says, turning back to Halter. "What do you know of a Master Mope?"

And for the first in four months' of asking the same question a thousand times, he receives a different reply.

"What of him?"

Beale almost gasps with pleasure. He can feel his face flushing, and it is as if his head will burst. Halter, on the other hand, wishes he might dive overboard.

"Where did you pick him up, and where did you drop him?"

"Well," he says, passing his parcel to the no-longer waiting boy. "I can't exactly remember that, can I?"

"You better had," Devereux tells him, "or it'll be to London with you. The Tower."

She makes it sound fun, but still Halter shakes his head.

"Oh Jesu," Beale mutters. He looks at Halter: an old man. Wiry probably from all his exercise, but still. Beale draws his blade theatrically.

Devereux and Waddle step back. Halter holds up his hands.

"Now steady on, young fella," he says. "I didn't tell you I wasn't going to—"

"Just tell me where you picked him up, where you dropped him, and his real name."

Jesu! Holding a sword is wonderful!

"Dieppe," Halter admits. "Last August sometime. I was over there delivering some boards for old Ainsley, London merchant. A bloke I know over there—a Frenchman, he is—introduced me to a man named Wattes, who asked if I'd bring another over. No questions asked. I mean: none at all. Wasn't even allowed to look at him. I was to bring him over. And then take him back. Normally I'd not do it, of course, upon my honor, like, but I had more boards to take over, and a fardel of paper to bring back here anyways, and—"

"And they offered you seven pounds to do it," Waddle added.

"He gave you forty, so you can shut your fucking mouth with your new fucking coat!"

"*Forty!*" Devereux exclaims. That is an enormous sum of money, even in her books.

"We'll come back to that, Waddle," Beale tells him, before turning back to Halter. "Go on about Master Mope."

"Right. Yes. So. I brought him over. Easy enough passage, though my God, he was seasick, and then he asks me to take him up to see old William Davies at Patching."

"Where's Patching?"

"Just over a league thataways." He nods eastward.

"So you did?"

"Aye. Him and his servant, aye."

"A servant? So he was a gentleman?"

"Oh yes. You could tell that straight off."

"And did you speak to the servant?"

Halter shakes his head.

"Not overly friendly like."

"Is seven pounds a lot to bring a man over?" Devereux wonders.

Halter and Waddle look at each other anxiously.

Beale has not yet put his sword away.

"Aye," Halter admits.

"And do you oftentimes carry gentlemen? With servants?"

He is a bit less sure about that.

"Sometimes."

"But in such secrecy?" Beale presses.

Halter agrees it was unusual.

Beale feels his senses tingling.

"But let me get this right," he says. "You do not know who Master Mope really was?"

Halter shakes his head.

"But we know a man who does," Devereux says. "William Davies, at Patching: here we come."

⊕

When Beale and Devereaux have ridden about half a league eastward, following one of those roads left by the Romans, she slows to let him catch up and she tells him they should give up this work for Walsingham and Burghley and become searchers at one of Her Majesty's ports.

"We shall take such bribes as you would never believe and live in squandering luxury." She laughs.

But then she turns serious and tells him that come what may, at the next opportunity, she shall buy herself a sword.

"Great God in heaven," she says, "I shall look so dashing. I cannot *think* why I didn't think of it before."

⊕

CHAPTER TWENTY-FOUR

Hradčany Castle, Prague, March 1584

Jane Frommond peels back a fold in the velvet brocade curtains that surround the bed and she peers in. The bed is roofed in the same material, to keep the cold out, and so it is very dark within, and startlingly warm. She opens the curtain wider, to let out the steam, and the smell of the poor woman, and to admit air and light, and in it she can see Kitty lying in the mattress's very middle, a small stretch of human in a broad plain of mattress, covered in sheets and blankets and quilts from which she has struggled to free herself. Her physicians have covered her in a powerful-smelling unguent, and she has strapped to her forehead a broad, flat, semi-translucent amulet of the sort cunning women offer the credulous or the desperate in childbirth. Jane thinks Kitty's eyes are open but cannot be sure.

"Mistress de Fleurier?" she says and extends her head into the gloom. "Kitty?"

And Kitty moans and turns and her eyes are open but it seems she cannot see who calls, and she says nothing intelligible but shakes her head as if to remove the amulet. Her face is terribly swollen, most of its beauty at bay. Even as Frommond becomes accustomed to the gloom, she cannot decide if Kitty's face and arms are red from such light as seeps through the curtains, or are actually red, or are their natural color, but this puzzle is solved when Dee opens the curtain behind, much wider, and peers over her shoulder.

"Jesu," he murmurs, and he almost crosses himself. "Pray to God we have not left it too late."

Kitty flinches from the light and thrashes her head aside, as if it hurts.

"Will she be all right?" Frommond asks.

Dee looks grim.

"Get some water," he tells her. "We must cool her down."

"She is safe to touch? She is not contagious?"

Dee hesitates midstride, caught in some machination of his own making, before telling her that if Kitty is suffering what he thinks she is suffering, it is not contagious, "not like the plague."

So Frommond turns and opens the curtain, and slides in, and pulls it shut behind her. The bed is so big—enough for six or seven, perhaps, in comfort—that she must climb onto the mattress and shuffle forward on her knees to be able to touch Kitty—just her arm, where it lies on the blankets—and when she does, she draws her hand back sharply in surprise. Jesu! The girl is so hot! And her flesh dry and powdery, like a crone's, but swollen and drum tight.

"Kitty?" she whispers. "Kitty."

Kitty does not answer.

Frommond hears the men moving the paintings, grunting with the effort for some of them are vast, and she hears Dee's steps hurrying on the marble flags beyond the curtain and the bark of his orders. She realizes he is close to panic.

"Christopher," he calls, "cold water, fast. Take it to Jane with a cloth. Roger, get the brazier going, and clean that mortar. It has to be spotless. Master Kelley: prepare yourself for an Action."

She can hear her husband fiddling among the paraphernalia the physicians have been forced to leave on the tables, the clink and tap of earthenware on glass.

"All is well, Kitty," she soothes. "All is well."

Marlowe's arms appear, hands holding a ewer of water and a linen napkin.

"She decent?" he asks before he puts his head through the gap.

"Christ," he says, "it's roasting in here. No wonder she's so selsey."

Sometimes you do not have to know the meaning of each word Marlowe uses to understand its sense. At other times it is a mystery.

"Selsey?" Dee queries.

"Selsey Bill," Marlowe explains with a frown to suggest Dee is somehow deficient not to have heard of the Sussex peninsular. "Ill."

Frommond cannot help but smile though this fades when she applies the soaked cloth to Kitty's forearm; she would swear there is a small sizzle and a puff of steam. Marlowe climbs up onto the bed, careless of the blankets in his muddy boots, and cuts away the bed's canopy to let the heat out, but the light streams in and Kitty flinches from it, so Frommond places the wet napkin over Kitty's eyes and soothes her with gentle words.

"Christopher," she says. "Fetch some beer, will you? And some more ice. Snow even. That would do."

There's some on the windowsill.

Kitty's breathing is ragged and pained, each breath a hardship. Her hair is dirty, and her skin is powdery, and she smells very rank, but despite her heat, she does not sweat.

A moment later Marlowe returns with the beer and icy snow in a jug and then she drips it between Kitty's cracked lips. Her tongue seeks it out with a sighing gasp.

Then Dee arrives back with a dish of soap and hot water and he looks more closely at Kitty.

"Roger!" he calls over his shoulder. "Roger! Quick! We have little time!"

"I'm going as fast as I can!" Cooke calls back.

"Come on!" Dee mutters. "Jesu! Come on."

He takes Kitty's hand and almost drops it.

"Red as the beet, hot as the hare," he says. "Oh Jesu! Come *on*, Roger!"

She has scarce seen him so nervous.

"She's drinking," Frommond tells him. "Surely that's a good sign?"

He nods.

"But not too much, please," he asks. "We need her thirsty."

Frommond thinks she'd drink a bucket and still be thirsty.

"Here it is, Doctor," Cooke calls, and he passes through the curtains a small white mortar of a pale pulp, which Dee then stirs with a short length of glass. He shuffles forward and settles with a sigh by Kitty's head, and then with a murmured Latin prayer, he takes a smear of the pulp from the mortar and puts it on her lips.

She moues with distaste and her tongue—almost white—sticks out.

"More honey, Roger," Dee calls.

Cooke passes in a small earthenware jar and Dee spoons some into the dish, and he stirs it, still very carefully, then tries again. This time the mix is more acceptable. He waits until it is all gone and does the same again. And again.

"Will she live?"

"Only if she swallows all this, and even then—"

"What is it?" she asks.

He does not look up.

"A panacea."

"A panacea?"

He nods and smears more on to Kitty's lips.

"Do such things exist?" she wonders.

"We had best hope so."

There is something he is not telling her.

"When will we know?"

"I think— I am no expert, but soon, though."

When the mortar is empty, he summons Cooke with another dish, this one of warm soapy water, and he begins very carefully and thoroughly to wash Kitty's hands with a cloth, and when he is done, he tells Cooke to take it and empty it out of the window.

"As far and wide as you can."

Cooke takes the slopping water.

"Are you happy to stay with her?" Dee asks.

Frommond is.

He climbs off the bed and disappears. A moment later she hears him murmuring with Kelley, in that particular secretive voice they use for their Actions.

She soaks the bandage in the water and blots Kitty's skin again.

"I thought we wanted her dead?" Marlowe whispers. "That she is an agent for de Guise?"

She tells Marlowe what she heard in the garden, principally that Kitty is being forced to work for de Guise. Marlowe stares at the poor swollen, red-tinged woman whom the angelic spirits predicted would fall blind and go mad, and he shakes his head as if to clear a thought.

"Lucky your doctor had that panacea, eh? Do you suppose the angels told him to bring it?"

⊕

Dee is wandering around the display cabinets in the emperor's *Kunstkammer*, less interested in the coins and corals cabinets, and baffled by the unusual skeletons of dragons and so on, but when he reaches the cabinets devoted to astrolabes, dioptras, sextants and clocks, and other scientific things, he knows what he will find— and there it is: one of Mercator's globes, identical to the one he lost in the waters of the Zuiderzee. He nearly smashes the glass to take it, and is perhaps about to, when Roger Cooke appears at his elbow to whistle at it.

"What a beauty, eh, Doctor? Not thinking of nicking it, are you?"

Dee denies it, but Cooke doesn't quite believe him.

"Anyway, what do you think?" he asks. "Reckon she'll live?"

He nods to where Kitty de Fleurier lies abed.

"Pray to God," Dee tells him.

"And what about them beans you bashed up in the mortar? What about them, eh?"

Ah. Cooke saw him do that, did he?

"Just a panacea," Dee tells him.

"*Just* a panacea? Just a panacea that you happened to brung from England?"

Dee sometimes forgets that Cooke is no fool.

"Just a panacea that you brung from England," he goes on, "that no one has ever heard of, and that you have been keeping ever so safe in a cutout in the middle of your book on navigation what you know no one will ever open, let alone read, along with a vial of something else that has since been bunged away? That panacea?"

Dee looks at him.

"Yes," he says. "That panacea."

And Cooke says nothing more, for what is there to say?

At that moment there is a crash, and one of the emperor's priceless paintings lies on the floor. Someone is pushing at the door behind. Marlowe is there in a flash, blade drawn.

"Who is it?"

There is no reply. The door keeps being forced, the painting moved.

"The fuck is it?" Marlowe demands again.

Still no reply.

Marlowe steps onto the canvas painting, which tears, and he bends his head around the door. A moment later he stabs the sword through the gap, and there is a cry and another sword comes at him and rips his doublet. This seems to enrage him more than Dee would have imagined, and there is a great squall of cursing, as when cats fight, with Marlowe stabbing and slashing through the gap. Then Cooke lumbers over and leans his weight against the door, trapping two blades, which are hastily withdrawn before they can be broken.

"Spanish fuckers," Marlowe says. "Look what they did!"

He holds out the slash in his doublet.

"Looks like you did worse to them, though," Cooke says.

There is a sleeve of blood on Marlowe's sword. He holds it up and looks at it with a growing smile.

"Who were they?" Dee asks. "Apart from being Spanish?"

"Those fellas in black," Marlowe tells him. "Hanging around earlier. I thought we were here with the emperor's blessing?"

"We're supposed to be. And he's supposed to have sent us some halberdiers to guard us, but Van der Boxe will be desperate to get Kitty back, and keep her, at least until de Guise gets here, and he'll not have taken kindly to us snatching her from him. Here, help me with this."

While Cooke keeps the door shut, Dee and Marlowe clear the fallen painting—"just a little tear"—and shove one of the horse statues across the floor to butt it up against the door.

"Another?"

"Just in case."

The amber one is a bit lighter than the marble one, but they'll come down with a crash if they try this door again. They have just gotten them in place when on the other side of the hall, the handle of the pornographic door shakes against the rim of the painting they've jammed under it.

"I always do it three times afterward, too," Cooke tells them.

Marlowe and Dee run for it.

But it is only Count Łaski.

"Are you alone?" Dee calls through the door.

Łaski does not answer for a moment.

"Sorry," he says. "Yes. Just looking at door. You know? I think one of these women my mother."

They let him in and are quick to close the door behind and jam the door with a pair of what might be narwhal tusks and the petrified corpse of a pigmy horse.

⊕

At length Kelley is as ready as he will ever be again, and though they still have not managed to have made the altar of two cubits cubed, painted with symbols and certain words in yellow oil, and nor have they found any of the seals or the red silk they were supposed to rest it on, they have set up an altar of sorts in a far corner of the emperor's *Kunstkammer*, near the fire and away from the windows. After his introductory prayers and incantations, Kelley manages to summon the angel Galvah.

Dee is mightily relieved, for although Kelley has purged himself—violently, twice—that is not the same as fasting, and he feared his drinking would have disgusted the angelic spirits so that they would not appear, or if they did, they would be those malign spirits, or shout at him in Syrian, as they had in Hamburg.

But that is not to say Galvah is happy with him. In a deep, pained voice, Galvah calls Kelley unmeet, accuses him of living with a harlot, and tells him that he shall inherit the rewards of fornication and adulterers; he says as well that a threefold door bar, stronger than any iron, shall be placed to stand between his eyes and understanding.

"I am the true medicine of such as put their faith in the God of Hosts!"

Dee writes all this down, and then asks Kelley to ask Galvah on his behalf if there is a particular cure beyond prayers for Kitty de Fleurier's sickness.

Galvah tells them that physic is the true and perfect science of the natural combination and proportion of known parts but is beyond the capacity of those who use it just to make money.

At this Dee cannot resist the slightest of smiles.

"Yes, yes," he says, "go on."

Galvah tells them that Kitty's disease is the result of a malign spirit that has entered her womb, and as a result her digestive functions have become corrupted. Which is all very interesting.

"But what is cure?" Łaski demands.

The cure comes haltingly. They are to take a pint of wheat, a live pheasant cock, eleven ounces of umber, and an ounce and a quarter of turpentine. The pheasant is to be plucked and roasted and broken into parts; the umber is to be ground in a mortar; and all the ingredients are to be put in a gallon of red wine, distilled twice, and then divided into three jugs. Kitty is to drink the first jug—a little at a time—and the rest is to be taken as a sauce thereafter, in secret.

"In secret?" Dee queries.

"In secret."

Dee shrugs and writes it down.

"Is there anything else we should know?" he asks.

"Many devils and witches are risen up against her, and one comes of the west leading two stallions, who has taken from her that which she most cherishes on this earth. But she shall not be alone in her sorrow."

Kelley is sweating as he relays this, and Dee supposes he might soon vomit again. He needs to move things along.

"And what can be said regarding the life of the emperor himself?" Dee asks.

"Many witches and devils have risen up against this stranger," Kelley starts, and then adds, "also."

"And may he be here present at any future Action?"

There is a moment when Kelley's eyes flicker, or change shape slightly, and there is an infinitesimally longer pause than is usual, and then Kelley gives the reply.

"Those that are of this house are not to be denied banquets therein."

Dee sits back, glances at Łaski. Łaski's face betrays nothing, as why would it? He had not been in Mortlake to hear those exact same words spoken about his joining the Action back in England.

"And what can be said as to our duties to the *Book of Loagaeth*?"

"Keep it safe, guard it wisely, for its hour is at hand. My spirit shall dwell within you, and in the works of your hands shall you receive comfort."

After that the angelic spirit falls silent, or the connection is broken, for Kelley's face is now sheened with sweat and has turned a waxy gray green. Dee sends him to sit by the window while he tidies away the show stone and writes out a fair copy of his rushed notes.

"What will you tell the emperor?" he asks Łaski, and Łaski sits like the sad bear he had been when Dee first met him, and he blows out a long sigh, before looking up at Dee with a cold hard eye.

"Whatever you want," he says.

What is it, Dee wonders, that I have done to you that you did not do to yourself? Nevertheless, the pretense must be maintained.

"I wish only that you tell him that which he wishes to know."

It is easy to find yourself speaking as the angelic spirits do.

"And nothing more."

Łaski nods, understanding everything.

"Although I would esteem it an honor," Dee continues, "if the emperor would ensure we go undisturbed by such as Van der Boxe's men."

Łaski is surprised.

"Van der Boxe's men? I thought they were Julius's?"

"Julius?"

"Julius, Duke of Brunswick-Lüneburg? Your wife, Mistress Dee, she said you owed him money? It is why I rushed you out of the audience with Spinola: I thought they were after you, and I did not wish to see you end up like Anna Maria Zieglerin."

Dee has heard of Anna Maria Zieglerin. She was one of the very few women alchemists, who ended her career as alchemists tend to, in disgrace and failure. Zieglerin, however, was made to pay a terrible price by this Duke Julius of Brunswick-Lüneburg, who believed she had defrauded him: she was first flayed and then burned alive while chained to an iron stool.

"That is . . . very kind of you, Count Łaski," Dee admits. "But the

Duke of Brunswick-Lüneburg may be the only man in the world to whom I do not owe money."

Jesu, he thinks, is that true?

"So who are they, these men? I see them all over the palace. Dark looks they give Count Łaski but I tell them he is not so bad a fellow."

Łaski tries a brave laugh, but he is sad, really.

"As I say: Van der Boxe's."

"Oh, Doctor, what have you got yourself into?"

Dee can't answer that, and after a moment Łaski shuffles off—hopes dashed, thoughts confused—and Dee can only hope he will pass on to Rudolf all that has been said and done.

When Dee returns to the bed, it is to find no change in the patient, but he did not expect it. Jane has removed the amulet from Kitty's forehead and continues to keep her cool with chilled water.

"It is all we may do for the moment," he supposes.

Frommond and Marlowe look at him just as Cooke did, in a curiously hostile manner, as if they know that he is somehow responsible for all this. That it is he who has led them all this way, for reasons they do not know or like. It makes him feel very wintry, and he walks to the windows and peers out through a wavy glass pane to the snow-covered roofs of the city below. The river is frozen over, and he can see figures scurrying to and fro, and he wonders if this has not come as a release to the citizens, who no longer have to negotiate their way across the bridge past Marek and his mob.

✦

CHAPTER TWENTY-FIVE

Patching, Sussex, March 1584

Wurthermore illiam Davies lives behind the small, flint-faced church, the spire of which is modeled upon a bodkin head—or vice versa—of the sort to tip the arrows that Beale's grandfather—well, his tenants, really—sent across the lines and into the Scots at the Battle of Flodden. It is a handsome but modest house, and his servant answers the door at their first knock.

"Is Master Davies in?" Beale asks.

He is.

An old man, as Master Halter had suggested, and loose in habit, with only a couple of teeth, and very poorly shaved, and when he sees them at his door, he begins trembling and murmuring to himself.

"No," he says. "No. No, I never. It weren't me."

But it were, you can tell that from his servant's face.

"Who was he?" Beale asks when they have sat him upon a low stool in his damp, dark, and dirty little kitchen. Dried herbs hang from the rafters, and a ham, too, though it blooms with mold, but

Beale wonders how he would ever eat meat with teeth like that anyway?

"No one," Davies quavers. "I never met him. Don't know what you're talking about."

He smells fungal, and if nothing is done about him, he will soon revert to the soil of his own volition anyway. But before then they need to know the real identity of Master Mope, and Beale has not come all this way—from Cromer, in Norfolk, via every harbor and mud-slicked inlet along the coast—to be lied to so obviously. He cannot draw his sword and flourish its blade under Davies's chin, however, for he has, against his better judgment, lent it to Mistress Devereux; she looks just as dashing with its belt wrapped around her narrow waist as she'd predicted.

He sighs and looks around.

Everything is as expected, save there is, against a wall, a very serious-looking coffer, of dark cherrywood, perhaps, into which has been carved a horn-of-plenty motif. Its feet have been sawn off, though, sometime recently, and it sits ground-bound upon the tamped earthen floor. Beale glances at it and then sees the maid following his gaze.

"Do you mind?" he asks.

He feels Davies's rheumy old eyes follow him as he saunters toward the coffer, pushing aside a hanging bunch of dried sage, he thinks, on a nail in the rafters. On the coffer is a small tray, and on the tray some pewter: a plate, a jug, and a cup. Not the best quality, but a step above anything else on display in the functionary cupboard. He picks the tray up, watched very closely by Davies and the servant, and carries it to the table, watched in silence.

Then he returns to the coffer, and the silence and stillness is oppressive as he opens the lid.

Ha.

Another tray, fitting within the coffer, holding folded linens this time, with carved handholds at each end, and made to be lifted out, to expose the bottom layer. But there is an oddity: the coffer is cold. A cool draft blows up from around the edges of this second tray. He smiles and lifts it out, and a cool breeze flows unimpeded from within, carrying the earthy scent of a storage cellar.

Devereux is by his shoulder peering down, her eyes ablaze with pleasure.

"Oh, how marvelous!" she says, and she claps her hands with glee.

Beale has always prided himself on his ability to sense the whereabouts of a priest hole—he once found one in a house in Herefordshire that you had to lift the stair risers to access, though it was, thankfully, empty at the time save for a yellow-crusted piss pot and a rosary with half its beads missing—and he is happy his gift has not deserted him in front of Devereux.

He looks down into the darkness and it is impossible to gauge its depth, but it is very much deeper than the coffer, and there is, at the hole's bottom, a shape covered in what might be waxed linen. A sliver of gray light falls on it from some breathing hole or other on the outside wall.

"Come on," he says. "Game's up."

The shape moves, twists, and a moment later Beale is looking down into the eyes of a thin, vaguely haunted young man. A priest? A Jesuit? Or Master Mope himself? There are four or five steps, and the man below slowly climbs them. Beale steps back to let him step out of the coffer into the kitchen.

"Bit awkward," Devereux says.

"Who are you?" Beale asks.

The man hesitates before saying anything. He's beardless, narrow-shouldered, very young, and thin and pale, with an almost demonically intense glint in his eye. And so Beale is not taken completely unawares by the sudden thrash of his limbs and the appearance of a long, thin dagger, aimed straight at his eye. Beale rocks to the side and feels the blade scorch through the skin at his temple and he moves to grapple with the man, but he is so thin and quick and whippy that he has ducked under Beale's embrace and slipped his wrist from his grip. Beale is left staggering forward, past the boy, and he knows the boy will stick that dagger in his kidney and dear God what a depressing place to die.

But the man/boy has reckoned without Devereux.

She moves beyond all possible speed as she draws the sword and slices the blade through the air to chop the man/boy's wrist and divert the fatal strike down into the meat of Beale's buttock. Still the pain is amazing, but it is not him screaming: it is the boy, who has dropped the dagger and is clutching his severed wrist to his chest as the blood splashes from it, all over his dark jerkin and breeches.

Devereux has cut the man/boy's hand clean off, and it lies under the table, twitching, and all are looking at it save the man/boy, who has turned and staggered out of the door into the herb garden beyond, a splashy trail of bloodied footsteps in his wake.

Devereux stands with the sword still pointing at the ground, her eyes and mouth three perfect circles, and then she drops the sword, wheels away, and vomits copiously into the glowing embers of the fire.

⊕

By the time Beale is able to think straight, the man/boy has left the herb garden and taken to the road. He has not gone far though and is easy enough to follow; five hundred yards up the road they find him toppled in the long grass, bled out into the prints of horses' hooves in the grit. Beale bends over the dead body and begins to go through his purse. A single coin: a silver French *teston*.

"Well, well," he says. "I think you killed the right man."

Devereux says nothing. She is ethereally pale and he leads her back to Davies's house, where they find the servant gone, and Davies sitting shaking in what might be his final, shock-induced death throes. Beale himself is beginning to feel the loss of blood, too, and so they sit in the grubby kitchen and finish the bread they find, and all the ale that's left over, and they wait for the bailiff or the reeve to come to inquire as to the dead man.

"Who was he?" they ask the old man, but he just shakes his head, and Beale cannot believe he will ever be able to be made to talk sense.

"I killed him," Devereux keeps saying.

"You saved my life," he tells her.

"But still I killed him."

"Only to save my life."

"But he's dead because of me."

Beale nods. There's only so far they can go with this conversation.

So that is that, he thinks. Their only lead gone. What will Walsingham say to that? He is wondering what story to tell about lending Devereux his sword when she gives a soft yelp of disgust and pushes herself back from the table and points at the floor.

"The hand," she says.

He'd forgotten about that. It is still lying there under the table. A dog'd've had it ages ago, he supposes, but Davies has no dogs. Beale hooks it out with his boot and is about to kick it to the door for the pigs, perhaps, when he sees on one finger, the blood-rimed shape of a fine gold signet ring.

"Ha," he says.

⊕

CHAPTER TWENTY-SIX

Hradčany Castle, Prague, March 1584

Three days later, and at last Frommond calls from Kitty's bed. "John," she says. "Come."

And he is on his feet in a moment, caught in a maelstrom of terror in case his plan has not worked and that Frommond summons him to see Kitty not recovering, but dying. He tries to judge her tone of voice, but cannot, and in the end, of course, there is nothing else for it.

He pulls back the curtain, and Frommond gives him the faintest of tight smiles.

"Oh thank God," he breathes.

"She's cooler, isn't she?" she asks. "I think she is."

Dee presses his fingers to Kitty's forearm.

"Yes," he says. "I am sure of it. And her skin. It is less flushed."

And her pupils are no longer the size of buttons, either, but of beads. That is an improvement, he is certain, and he almost grips her in a hug, but he contents himself instead with a squeeze of Frommond's hand.

"Thank you," he murmurs, and by Jesu he means it, though Frommond brushes his thanks aside, for if Kitty had died—well, it does not bear thinking about. Expiation would hardly be the start of it. Frommond has past the last few days been dousing Kitty with iced water, and feeding her small beer all, helped in spells by Marlowe, who has proved an unexpectedly useful nurse, while Edward Kelley has ignored them all and burned through a dozen good candles poring over Ripley's *Bosome Book* and brushing up on the twelve gates of alchemy. Dee meanwhile had paced the floor in a fever of anxiety, constantly checking the doors, and thinking that Kitty is at least getting no worse, and that the fire still burns, and so the hours have inched past. He has tried to occupy himself applying the last flourishes to the *Book of Loagaeth*: a stroke of red ink here, green ink there, to help clarify the wonderful diagrams he has concocted. Sometimes he tries to understand what is written and is gratified when he cannot, and he is growing ever more convinced that he has penned a work of rare and beautiful genius.

"Has the emperor sent word?" Frommond asks.

"He has asked after her health," Dee confirms, but there has been nothing else. He has not yet taken Dee's bait, and if he does not do so, then the whole scheme—every single thing he has worked for over the last eight months—will have been for nothing. It would have been better had he never left England, never have set off from Mortlake.

Still though.

Kitty will not die.

He will not have that on his conscience.

He gives weary Frommond one last squeeze of the hand, and later he stands by the windows and scratches a monad in the ice. It makes him smile.

The clouds have come now; they are thick and gray and filled with yet more snow.

Dee thinks about de Guise and wonders where he will be now. He hopes he is having a miserable time on snow-choked roads.

⊕

Late afternoon, early evening, and the emperor has still not sent for Dee.

He puts another log on one of the fires and kicks Kelley's foot where he sleeps over Ripley's *Bosome Book*.

"You are snoring, Master Kelley," he tells him even though, for once, he was not, but Kelley needs to know the twelve gates of alchemy by heart if this is going to work.

To and fro Dee paces, around and around, back and forth until, just as it is properly dark outside, he hears a knock on the pornographic door.

"Who is it?" Marlowe asks, sword drawn.

It is a servant, he is told, knocking on behalf of His Excellency Jacob Kurtz, the emperor's chancellor, who waits without. Dee gives Marlowe the nod, and Marlowe opens the door with lingering, prurient pleasure.

Greetings are exchanged, and Kurtz first asks after the patient. "May I see her?"

"Of course," Dee says. "She has taken the medicine the angelic spirits prescribed, and we have said the requisite prayers, but we do not claim to be her physicians and have no claim to her person."

If Kurtz notices the bed is significantly less curtained than once it was, he says nothing, but stands at its foot and studies Kitty de Fleurier where she lies covered in a sheet and two blankets, with a cold cloth across her eyes, and Frommond sat beside her, cross-legged and anxious.

"Does she respond?" Kurtz asks.

"We believe so," Dee answers in case Frommond says no. "Slowly."

Kurtz crosses himself.

"Thanks be to God," he murmurs.

"Oh, amen," Dee agrees. God did, after all, provide the Calabar beans, even if he planted them in a somewhat inconvenient spot.

"I will be pleased to report her progress to the emperor," Kurtz tells them, "who will be pleased beyond measure."

Dee feels the smile fixing to his face.

Yes? And?

"And he has sent me to summon you unto him, Doctor Dee, for a private audience, if that is convenient to you?"

He feels inundated with warm relief. At last.

"Now?"

"If you've a mind?"

Dee nods tightly, as if it is inconvenient.

"Keep the doors very locked," he whispers to Marlowe.

"Very?"

"You know what I mean."

He does.

And so Dee sets off, following the chancellor through the pornographic door where a company of halberdiers wait to escort them to the emperor. They are big men, in lavish uniforms and extravagant mustaches, and probably not as effective as once they were, or in tight spaces, but they carry a certain weight, and the corridors clear before them. Dee sees one of the black-clad Spaniards slip aside and down a corridor like a rat. Damn, he thinks, he will be off to alert Van der Boxe.

They stamp along behind the halberdiers along broad, stone-flagged corridors, up and down which two horsemen might comfortably ride abreast, and then out into the square where the snow has not been permitted to settle and across toward a building that has unmistakable elements to remind one of a stable: half doors and fodder troughs in copper gone green. Candles burn within, and fires, too, and there are more halberdiers at the doors. They are opened as the men approach and the halberdiers wheel in front, leaving Kurtz, who has not had much to say on their walk, to lead Dee through the doors and into a vast sand-strewn, triple-height arena, the sides of which are lined with actual stables, from the upper doors of which peer the finely sculpted heads of a score of beautiful gray horses, each with a colorfully dressed stable lad standing in attendance. The smell is extraordinary: horses; leather; beeswax candles; apple wood smoke; and sand washed in rose oil.

A hundred candles are lit, and there are braziers and sconces everywhere, and across the sand another elegant, high-stepping horse that Dee guesses is probably Andalusian is being exercised on a long rein by a slight but muscular man for the entertainment of the occupant of a throne upon a dais that sits alone in the middle of the sand: Emperor Rudolf, of course. He makes a small movement, a come-hither tapping of his fingers and thumb, and Kurtz advances, leading Dee across the sand that is as fine as flour.

"How is our little Kitten?" the emperor asks without taking his eye off the horse.

"She responds well to the angelic spirits' physic, Your Highness."

"Is she well enough to stand?"

"Not for some time, Your Highness. She is still very weak."

"When will she be well enough to see us?"

"I cannot say, Your Highness, not being a physician. I am a humble philosopher who possesses nothing save such gifts as God grants."

Dee is about to go on, to mention further supplication to the angelic spirits, but he has lost the emperor for now, and he waits for the horse to ride around behind him, watching Rudolf's eyes as they follow it, and then the emperor looks back at Dee and Kurtz as if he has forgotten why they are there.

"What?" he says.

"Perhaps Count Łaski told you of our recent Action during which the angelic spirits told us?"

"Oh, Count Łaski. Yes."

He says no more, and Dee is left at a loss. It was the emperor who summoned him. What does he want? But Dee knows royalty loves to test the world's patience.

"Łaski, he tells us great many things," Rudolf says eventually. "He tells us of your Actions with the angelic spirits, and of your scryer, Doctor Kelley, who summons them into his crystal."

"That is so, Your Highness. Doctor Kelley's connection to heaven is extraordinary. It is unlike any enjoyed by mortal man since the death of Enoch."

The emperor nods.

"Łaski tells us that he has seen it with own eyes. And that the angelic spirits had messages for him."

"The angelic spirits did likewise say they had certain and specific messages for you, Your Highness, should you ever wish to honor us with your presence at one of our Actions."

The emperor gives him a hooded-eye look, and the meagerest nod of acknowledgment, and then he glances away to watch his horse again, and to leave the matter unresolved for now, for the angelic spirits' invitation presents the emperor—and his advisers—with a complicated question of precedence. All men are equals before the crystal, and should Rudolf join Dee and Kelley, he must do so as a guest at a commoners' table and inevitably undergo a strong dose of lèse-majesté.

The horse passes behind Rudolf's right shoulder and he returns his gaze to Dee.

"When we spoke before, you mentioned a book. A book that is being dictated to you by the angelic spirits?"

"Oh," Dee says, feigning shock. "The *Book of Loagaeth*. Forgive me, your Highness. I—should not have said anything. I spoke out of turn."

"Tell me more of it."

Rudolf is looking closely at Dee, waiting.

"The angelic spirits say it is written in the language that God gave Adam before the Fall," Dee is forced to admit. "And in which he named all things, and which was last spoken upon this earth by Enoch."

"Go on."

"But should any man now learn its secrets, and come to speak it himself, then that man will be granted dominion over all things on the earth, even unto the seraphim and cherubim."

A horse thunders past Dee's shoulder, but this time Rudolf does not take his eyes from Dee. He stares openmouthed, although that means nothing, and he says nothing, and just waits for Dee to continue.

"But its comprehension is the work of a lifetime," Dee tries to put him off. "And none save the very finest scholar will ever even begin to grasp its most basic tenets."

"And you have this book?" Rudolf asks.

"It sits unfinished," Dee lies. "The angelic spirits are yet to hand down the last words, the final details, and then it shall be complete. I am not certain to what purpose they wish it put, for its great power is far beyond my meager understanding, though Master Kelley seems to grasp its fundamentals if not its specifics."

Rudolf manages to lick his broadly parted lips. Dee sees why he prefers to conduct his business in the dark, for he is a strikingly odd-looking man. The horse has come around behind Dee's shoulder again, and still Rudolf looks at him.

"We should like very much to see this *Book of Loagaeth* when it is completed," Rudolf says. Dee rounds his eyes, and bows, but says nothing. Silence stretches. The emperor waits.

"It will be so, Your Highness," Kurtz speaks for Dee.

And with that, Rudolf sits back and returns his attention to the horse once more. After a moment, Kurtz taps Dee's arm to indicate the audience is over, and they must retreat backward out of the arena.

On the way back to the *Kunstkammer* they walk shoulder to shoulder between the halberdiers, and Dee feels curiously companionable, as if they have been through an experience together, and he asks Kurtz if that was an in any way unusual audience with the emperor.

"One of the best," Kurtz thinks. "Sometimes he has two horses running, and he looks at you not once."

"He loves his horses," Dee says.

Kurtz nods.

"Is he getting any more, do you think?" Dee asks.

It is a strange question, of course, and Kurtz looks at him strangely.

"Why you ask?"

Dee lets out a long sigh.

"It was something Mistress de Fleurier said in her sleep," Dee lies. "And something the angelic spirits mentioned also: about a man coming from the west, bringing horses from the south, and I wondered if—well, I wondered what it meant."

Kurtz knows this is nonsense and half guffaws, and Dee tries to explain his clumsy question.

"You heard what I told the emperor. Too often I do not know what the angelic spirits mean."

"You mean the Duc de Guise, Herr Doctor Dee. It is obvious." Kurtz is not a fool.

"Do I?" Dee asks, all innocence.

"He is coming here at Mistress de Fleurier's request. He is bringing two Arabian horses, he tells her, as a gift for the emperor."

"Ahhh," Dee says. "That makes sense now."

"Hmm," is all Kurtz will say.

They walk in silence for a moment, then Dee asks if Kurtz knows de Guise.

"Only by reputation."

"Do you know why he comes?"

Kurtz shrugs.

"To borrow money?" he supposes. "Is usually the thing. Or to sell something, like you have."

"Like me? I have not come to sell anything!"

Kurtz gives him a long level look.

"Your book of Log-whatever? That is not for sale?"

Dee feigns a loss of words. He comes to a stop and the halberdiers behind nearly crash into him. Meanwhile Kurtz has walked on. Dee must trot to catch him up.

"It is not for sale," he announces.

"If he offered you—what?—ten thousand silver thalers, now, you'd not take it?"

"Absolutely not. It is—"

"—Worth much more than that?" Kurtz laughs. "You do surprise me, Doctor!"

"Well, yes, it is, but it is not for sale. I have not come to Prague to sell it."

"Then why are you here, Doctor? Once upon a time there was no Doctor Dee, and now there is only Doctor Dee."

"I was exiled from my own country," Dee reminds him. "Expelled. And Count Łaski invited me to come with him, and that is that."

"So you wash up here, in Prague, at the court of the emperor whom you know to have a weakness for philosophers and kabbalists, and alchemists and so on?"

"What would you have done?"

"Done? It is not a question of what I would have done. It is a question of what I would *not* have done."

"Which is what?"

"Not have conjured spirits when that was against the law."

Dee is silenced for a moment, and they walk on.

"I don't blame you, Doctor," Kurtz explains. "A man such as yourself must make a living."

It always astonishes Dee how proud people are to have inherited their wealth, and how they sneer at those who have not. It's like a scab, he thinks, to protect a wound.

"But you have roused some powerful enemies," Kurtz goes on. "Trodden on some very sensitive toes."

Dee nods.

"Van der Boxe's men have been trying to break into the room the emperor gave us," Dee tells him.

"I thought he might. He wants Kitty back under his control, and if he can't have her, he wants to be certain you can't, either."

"He might *kill* her?"

Kurtz shrugs.

"I thought he had tried, with this poison—"

Dee stops again.

"*Poison?*"

Kurtz stops and turns to face him, puzzled.

"Yes. Of course, poison," he says. "Surely you must suspect it?"

Dee feels himself flushing.

"Well," he says. "I suppose it crossed my mind."

Kurtz sets off again, talking over his shoulder, knowing Dee will catch up with him.

"But then I could not work out why Van der Boxe might do such a thing, since she is de Guise's only link to the emperor. Anyway, things are getting to the point now: Van der Boxe can't let Rudolf's attention stray before de Guise arrives in Prague next week."

Dee comes to a stop again.

"Next *week*?"

Kurtz nods.

"He has already reached Pilsner, to the west, but means to be here by Ash Wednesday, he has written, for this so-called Day of Rage."

This news is so alarming that Dee will have to postpone thinking about Kurtz's mention of poison, and of the Day of Rage, and devote his thoughts to what to do now: his scheme had relied on some time at least between Kitty's recovery and de Guise's arrival. Without that—

But here they are, back at the pornographic door again.

"I will post more guards," Kurtz tells him. "And instruct them to yield to no one but myself."

Dee thanks him.

Marlowe opens the door with a smile. The room is dark and cold, and there is frost on a broken window.

"Had another little intrusion," he says, holding up his other sleeve, ripped in two places. "Worse than moths, ain't they?"

He has obviously seen them off, but that does not explain his good cheer.

"Come and have a look," Jane calls from the bed.

It is Kitty.

"Jesu!" Dee cannot help exclaim, for it is as if there is a different woman in the bed. The swelling is down, the color rectified, and when he touches her wrist, she is no longer a furnace.

"She's been talking," Jane tells him. "Murmuring really, in her sleep."

"Keeps saying the same thing," Marlowe adds. "We reckon it's a name. Emily or Amelie or something."

"Must be her sister," Frommond supposes.

"Well done!" he congratulates them. "Well done."

"It is not our doing," his wife tells him, and there is an accusatory edge to her words that brings him up. He avoids her eye. One day there will be a time to discuss the Calabar beans, but later, perhaps. Later.

"How was Rudolf?" Marlowe asks.

When he tells them that de Guise is coming sooner than expected, and that when he does, he will retake control of Kitty and they will lose their reason to be in the palace, they are silent, and they look to the patient.

"But why are we here anyway, Doctor?" Marlowe asks, after a while.

And both look at him expectantly.

Perhaps it is time? he thinks. Perhaps he should now tell them? It has been a plan he has kept so long to himself that he can hardly now tease it out, for it is become like a crumpled letter, clenched in his fist, and then swallowed to be kept from prying eyes. Now though, with the news of de Guise's infinitely more imminent arrival, it needs updating, urgently, and if he takes Jane and Marlowe into his confidence, they might have some better suggestion than that which he has hit upon.

Only there are already elements to this scheme that from the outset have brought him sleepless, shame-filled nights, and which, if he is honest, he has prayed he need never think about again. The thought of confessing them—above all to Jane—makes him sweat, and bilious to the core.

"I had thought," he begins. "I had *hoped* to deter the emperor from giving de Guise the money he needs for his invasion of England."

They nod. This is obvious enough. They all know this.

"To do that," he goes on, "I had, at the very least, to get an audience with him, during which my aim was not only to divert him from giving the money to de Guise, but also in the longer term distract him from concerning himself in the wider struggle in Christendom."

"Why don't you just stab him or something?" Marlowe asks.

"Because firstly Bess—Her Majesty—will not countenance procuring the death of fellow princes, and secondly, the emperor's heir is his brother Matthias, who is staunchly Catholic and will do anything his uncle King Felipe of Spain tells him. It would be like replacing the Archbishop of Canterbury with Torquemada. And thirdly, I am not an assassin. I have never knowingly, willingly, willfully killed anyone."

"All right," Marlowe says, in a tone that suggests Dee is being unreasonably sensitive.

"Now since it is well known that the emperor has an almost unhealthy fascination in what the unlearned might call the esoteric, my scheme was to use any audience I might get to tempt him into joining one of our Actions with the angelic spirits."

"And what good would that do?" Marlowe asks.

"I hoped he would listen to the angelic spirits, who would turn him against de Guise, and in favor of England, but also to describe to him the power of the *Book of Loagaeth*."

"The *Book of Loagaeth*? That thing you have been scribbling in all this time?"

He cannot help but give Marlowe an exasperated look.

"I have not been scribbling," he tells him. "I have been writing down that which the angelic spirits have told me to write."

"Can we see it?" Jane asks.

Dee is about to say no, but then he thinks, *Where is the harm?* He finds his bag, hidden under the physicians' covered table and brings it to them. It is a great lump of old vellum he'd bought from a stationer in Moorgate before they left, and it is gathered loosely, yet to be stitched, let alone bound. Some pages are ordered and ruled: tables of tables; sixty-four rows and sixty-four columns, each square filled with a tiny symbol, or letter, or number. Other pages are filled with Enochian text, and diagrams that he has attempted to draw after Kelley's oftentimes lurid descriptions of plants, and flowers, strange beasts, even humans going about their business. Sometimes, depending on where they were on their journey, Dee had access to different colored inks—green, red, blue—and he used them to draw the things Kelley described.

"It is astonishing," Jane says. "But what is it?"

Dee manages a laugh.

"That is almost exactly the point," he says.

"Fuckin' looks the part," Marlowe says, flipping through it.

It is sometimes not easy to remember that Marlowe can even

read, but then again, reading would not help understand the *Book of Loagaeth*.

"But what does it all mean?" Jane wonders.

"That is the very question I hope the emperor will ask."

There is a long silence while they all look at the book. Kitty lets out small moans. Kelley is asleep, slumped across a chair, the *Bosome Book* on the floor.

"So you came all this way to put this before Emperor Rudolf," Marlowe wonders, "in the hope that he would . . . what? Dedicate the rest of his life to decrypting this?"

Dee cannot help but beam at him.

"*Exactly*," he says. "The angelic spirits say that whosoever can understand this book will understand God's secret levers and will have dominion over all the earth, even unto the heavens. He will understand everything, you see? How the stars move; how fish breathe; why the plague came among us. He will be able to control everything: tides; winds; elephants; his friends and his enemies. With such powers, there is nothing a man might not achieve."

Marlowe bobs his head.

"I like it," he says.

"And you forget that the Great Conjunction in the fiery trigon portends some great change, this summer, when one ruler shall rise above all others. So."

And Dee feels warm self-congratulation ease through his system.

"But that does not solve the problem of de Guise's mustering of support for his invasion," Frommond reminds him.

"No," he agrees, feeling suddenly less pleased with himself. "No."

"Do you have any ideas?" she asks.

He looks at her very carefully.

"I have one," he says.

"But?"

"But it is a low thing," he says. "A very low thing."

He does not tell her how very low he has already stooped. He never will. He looks at Kitty. She is snuffling now. Perhaps she is hungry after producing all that heat on beer alone? Meanwhile Frommond has tilted her head back and flattened her eyes to look at him askance down the length of her nose.

"Go on," she tells him.

"Now I am not saying this is the *only* thing to be done. I am just saying this is one thing that might be done. *A* thing that might be done."

"What is it then?"

"She—Kitty—is de Guise's only link with the emperor, isn't she? Without her, de Guise *might—might—*get an audience with the emperor, just as I did, in the stables, but if Rudolf has already taken our bait with the *Book of Loagaeth*, de Guise might not even get that. With Kitty under the duke's control and advancing his case, though, not only will he get an audience, he will get his money, for Kurtz says she has Rudolf wrapped about her finger."

Marlowe starts to laugh, a bitter, incredulous snicker.

"You want her *dead*?"

Dee throws up his hands.

"No! No! *Jesu!* No! I promise."

He can see a thunderhead of disgusted fury roiling up within Frommond, but he means what he says: No. He does not wish Kitty dead. If he did, he would not have gone to all this trouble with the beans. It is true that that was Sir Francis Walsingham's first suggestion when he came to the Tower that night after Dee had been arrested, and that this evening, when Kurtz told him that de Guise was due within the week, it had likewise been the first thing that occurred to him. But from the moment back in Winchester House, the first time Dee had met Łaski, when Łaski told him that de Guise had somehow managed to turn Kitty de Fleurier to his own purpose, he had guessed how the man might have done it: by snatching someone close to Kitty's heart, and keeping him or her from Kitty until Kitty had done what he wished of her. It was what he had done to Isobel Cochet, after all, and it had worked, hadn't it? From that moment Dee had sworn he would do anything not to kill her. He owed that to Isobel Cochet, at the very least.

And with that in mind, he had even been relieved when Jane overheard Kitty in the garden, for it confirmed his suspicions, and justified some of the risks he had taken, which he'd done so only because he could not bring himself to plot to kill anyone. The memory of Isobel, drowning in the sands off Mont Saint-Michel, will never leave him, and he would never willingly bring about anyone's death. It is why he brought with him the distillation of belladonna and various other plants that he had carefully grown in the herb garden behind his second laboratory back in Mortlake. He'd brought a vial of the poison, carefully concealed in a cutout in a book, with which he coated the insides of those beautiful butter-yellow gloves, knowing that whoever next wore them would be brought to the very threshold of death's door.

But he had also brought with him a handful of slowly wizening beans that had been given to him by Sir Francis Drake, who had brought them back from Calabar, in the Bight of Benin, where they are primarily used in witchcraft trials among the Chamba peoples, and which, if taken in too large a dose, are poisonous, but if taken in the right dose, actually reverse the effects of poisoning by belladonna.

What was that Paracelsus's dictum that Łaski had quoted in

Winchester House all those months ago? *Sola dosis facit venenum.*
It is only the dose that makes it a poison.

"But so long as de Guise has Kitty's sister, he has Kitty,
doesn't he?"

This is from Marlowe, and then he sees something that not
even Dee had seen, in part because of the practicalities: "You mean
to kill the *sister*?"

Jane claps her hands to her cheeks, aghast.

"Of course not!" Dee tells them both. "Of course not. I would
never— Jesu! That would be even worse."

"Well, what then?"

He takes a breath and then: "We must *tell* her that her sister is
dead."

They both sit back, and all three gaze at Kitty lying there in the
bed, almost within touching distance. She is better, yes, but still
far from well, still far from out of the woods, and would not such
a shock kill her? Jane shakes her head.

"She is just come back from the brink, and you want to tell
her . . . that her sister is *dead*?"

That is better than actually killing her sister, Dee almost reminds her; better than actually killing *her*.

"If we tell her that the sister has died in some accident, that it
was painless but that it was the fault of de Guise, then she will turn
the emperor against him. That is all we need. Then we admit we
made a mistake. Or we let her discover it."

"What, like a nice surprise?" Marlowe asks.

"Something like that."

"No," Jane says. "That will kill her for sure. You did not hear how
she was when she learned the sister was not coming. I do not use the
word 'heartbroken' lightly. And that was a mere delay. She is already
weak. Telling her that the poor sister is dead will be the end of her."

Dee lifts his hands.

"What then? What else can we do? De Guise will come and force Kitty to persuade Rudolf to give him the money, and it will no longer matter if he subsequently becomes too distracted by the *Book of Loagaeth* to join the crusade against England, because there will, for all intents and purposes, be no England."

"There must be something else," she says.

"I am bereft of ideas," he tells her. Because he is. The last few months have taken their toll, he can feel. This is not what he is meant to be doing. He should be at home in his laboratory, or in his orchard studying the scheme of heaven, or attempting to raise money for his voyage to find the Western Passage to Cathay, but instead he is here, in Prague, a tolerated invader with a shortening lease, arguing with his wife about whether or not to kill an innocent woman or her sister.

At that moment a knock resounds on the pornographic door.

It is word from the emperor: he wishes to join an Action in the morning.

Dee feels such a rush of relief he must sit.

"Praise God," he breathes. "Praise God."

⊕

CHAPTER TWENTY-SEVEN

Seething Lane, City of London, March 1584

"She was a *what*?"

"A woman."

"You killed a woman?"

"I didn't kill her. And we didn't know she was a woman. Until later. When we searched her body more thoroughly and discovered her sex. And also this ring."

He indicates the ring that sits on a square of undyed leather on his desk. Beale has cleaned it, as best he can, and has discovered it is imprinted with the seal of the Paget family, who are notorious recusant Catholics.

"So you discovered—by killing her—that Master Mope was in fact a Mistress Paget?"

"*A* mistress Paget?"

"Mm-hmm," Walsingham confirms. "You know there are at least a dozen of them?"

"Really?"

"Maybe not quite that many. But still. We shall have to find out, I suppose. Where is the rest of her? The part you did not cut off?"

"In a cart, on its way up from Sussex, salted and packed with some herring. She should be here within the week."

Walsingham pulls a face.

"Well, that is something to look forward to, isn't it?"

"At least it is not too warm out." Beale need hardly remind him, and Walsingham goes "brrrrr" and rubs his arms, for London is in the grip of a late frost, and there are fears the river will freeze over again.

"Well," Walsingham says, returning to the ring. "It would have been better, if you absolutely had to kill someone, to have killed one of the brothers in her stead. If it'd been Henry—though isn't he dead already?—or Thomas, or Charles, or Edward even, then I'd knight you myself, right here and now. Still, though. Hmm. A Paget sister. It'll send a message, won't it? Show them we aren't messing about."

Beale supposes there is that.

Walsingham tugs on his beard, lost in thought for a few moments, and then asks himself what a Paget sister might be doing hiding in a priest hole in Sussex.

"Strange, really," he says, "because Lord Paget wrote to me only last week from Paris, offering to betray some Jesuits in return for a pardon for some as yet unspecified crime."

"Perhaps it was she who was committing that crime? You don't hide in a priest hole for fun, do you?"

Walsingham nods and slips back into thought. Beale does likewise, but he is thinking of Devereux, and of how she likes to sleep holding his cock.

"We shall have to call in one of the brothers to identify her when she gets here," Walsingham supposes, "but they are scattered all over the country. Who can we ask? Hmm. Aha. Yes. Thomas Paget's wife, the dead woman's sister-in-law. Nazaret Newton. Lives in Norfolk somewhere. Perhaps I could ask you to—?"

Beale sighs. He is tired of being on the road.

"Can we not send word?"

"I think not. She is a grand old lady, Robert. It will require skill to coax her down here."

"Sister-in-law? Not mother-in-law?"

"A large age gap. I think Thomas is her third husband. Stole all her dead husbands' fortunes, of course. He has, I mean. From her."

"Still. There must be someone else," Beale pleads.

"No, no. I think you should go. See this through."

This is another punishment for— What? Well. Everything.

"Thank you, Robert," Walsingham goes on. "I am most obliged. I will dig out the details. Hang on."

He starts going through a book of addresses.

"And what is Arundel like?" Walsingham asks after a while.

"The place or the man?"

"The man, I know," Walsingham reminds him. "We had him in the Tower for a month, remember, until Her Majesty ordered his release."

It still rankles.

"The place, then, is . . . well. Built on a hill over a river. Fine castle with a good view over flat farming land to the south, and the Downs to the north. You can see the sea from the turrets, and there are five or six fishing villages along the coast. Shingle beaches. Handsome houses, faced with flint. What else?"

Beale tries to think. The fact is that he spent so long in bed with Devereux that his memories are dominated by sensations that even now require him to adjust his braies, and he can hardly remember the town itself, nor much about the area elsewise.

"We didn't linger overlong," he tells Walsingham, "because Arundel himself wasn't there, and by then we had wind of Master Mope."

Walsingham sighs in exasperation.

"If indeed the man mentioned was Master Mope."

"If indeed it was Master Mope."

"And so where was he?" Walsingham asks. "Arundel the man?"

Beale frowns. That is a good question.

"I can't remember," he says. "Gone for a week or more, the steward told us."

"Hmm," Walsingham says. "I'm supposed to have someone down there watching him."

And he starts rummaging through papers in a broad bank of pigeonholes, looking for a letter perhaps from an espial down in Arundel, the town. The light through his window is very good, Beale notes, and he wonders who his glaziers are. Hollanders probably. Then he remembers where Arundel the man was.

"Petworth," he says.

Walsingham stops his rummaging and stares.

"Petworth?" he repeats. "Arundel was at *Petworth*?"

Beale nods.

"I think that's what the steward said."

"You know where Petworth is? No? Or, really, do you know *what* Petworth is?"

Beale doesn't.

"Northumberland has his house there."

"*Northumberland?*"

Beale sits. My God. Now he sees it. The two men whom Throckmorton had implicated in the plot, both of whom are now free, have been meeting to do what? Hunt? Fish? Play the harp? No. Conspire. And they both have properties not near Framlingham on the east coast, but near Arundel, on the south, near which he and Devereux unearthed—and then killed, it has to be said—a woman who is a member of a notoriously Catholic family, and like to be the linchpin in any plot against Her Majesty, whose brother is in Paris, and who herself may well have come hotfoot from the Duc de Guise via Dieppe disguised as a man in the hold of Master Halter's boat.

Walsingham is staring at him, absolutely stilled.

"That's it," he says after a long moment. "That's it. Oh Jesu, what a fool I have been."

Beale is still at a loss.

"They mean to land in Arundel haven," Walsingham tells him. "It is obvious. It was obvious all along. Oh Jesu. And do you know what this means?"

"What?"

Apart from the obvious: that an invasion of five thousand French mercenaries is imminent in an utterly undefended county of England.

"All that work in Orford: wasted."

"Ah."

"And worse than that. Not where it is needed. We will have to pay to take it down and pay to transport every stone and every gun to Arundel haven and pay to rebuild it there. It will cost . . . thousands. Thousands more. Thousands that we do not have. Thousands that we never have had. And Her Majesty. My God. What a fool I have been."

⊕

CHAPTER TWENTY-EIGHT

Hradčany Castle, Prague, March 1584

Tthe next morning is even colder, with frost blotting the window glass, but Jane Frommond is in no mood to overhear the Action, which has suddenly become as repugnant to her as listening to someone being garroted, so she leaves the emperor's *Kunstkammer* for the first time in five days and is escorted into the snow-girt garden by five halberdiers assigned to her by Jacob Kurtz.

"You'll be all right, Mistress Dee?" Marlowe asks. "You won't freeze to death?"

He holds out a new cloak that she realizes is Kitty's, the beautiful one that she had been wearing when first they saw her from the windows above. Frommond hesitates, but then she has been with Kitty so long she has come to think of her as some sort of sister, and she supposes Kitty might think the same, and not mind lending it to the woman who has nursed her and changed her linen for the last five days while she has slowly returned to life. Frommond takes it, and Marlowe helps her on with it.

"I'll come with you, if you like?" he asks.

She doesn't mind. Christopher is easy company, and she is used to him by her side, though she still has no idea what he will do next.

Through the frost-rimed doors, the snow in the garden is still frozen hard as rock underfoot, and Frommond feels curiously tall as she walks across it. The five halberdiers spread throughout the garden, stopping at certain strategic points perhaps, where they can see anyone coming. They are all reassuringly large men, in their red doublets and steel breastplates, each with a fearsome halberd and a sword at his hip. She is grateful for their presence, for despite the constant cold, she can see footprints in the ice crust to show there have been men in the garden, and she thinks of those Spanish assassins peering in through the windows and wonders where they are now. Watching from above? Probably. She looks up. All the windows are shuttered hard against the cold.

Frommond shivers and gathers the cloak about her and retraces those steps she took the night of that first audience with Spinola, which seems like months ago now, and she goes to stand by that tree where once she hid from Kitty.

She stands awhile, breathing in the icy air, which is a change at least from the *Kunstkammer*, and she looks at the city below: its towers; steeples; churches; halls; synagogues. Its bathing houses, and quays, and its broad slew of more modest, snow-covered roofs below. Something big is burning in the Old Town, in the Jewish Quarter she thinks, and a plume of gray smoke blots the sky to the east. It is strange to see the river iced over. Without that constantly moving fissure in the city, Prague is become still, hermetic, sealed in among its ice-rimed forested hills, capped by a dense layer of snow cloud.

Marlowe tells her he prefers London but is not sure why, when you look at it, "because London is a bit shit."

She agrees. Prague is a striking city, angular and odd, but it is not home, and she thinks then again about soft, dreary Mortlake, and her dear Arthur, and she wishes they were at home again, and she even misses dear old Roger Cooke pottering about the laboratory, breaking things, and all the people coming to see John, and then leaving again, utterly confused by his latest scheme or discovery.

She thinks about the last few days, and how many hours she has stayed awake with Kitty, mopping that brow, those bare forearms, and her taut throat with iced water, dribbling honey-sweetened beer between her lips, and forming a picture of the woman that is more a tribute to her own imagination rather than reality. Frommond tries to remember when she began to believe Kitty would live. The second morning after the second dose of the panacea that John had brought. That was when Kitty began to cool under the touch, and her swelling was suddenly less alarming. Jane had called John, who had come scuttling, and he had almost had tears of relief when he, too, could convince himself that she was past her crisis.

But then he had ruined everything with his complications, and what had seemed so simple—the recovery of a woman—now became drear and perplexed and fraught with moral danger, and even physical danger.

Dee had been elated when the summons had come from the emperor, and he had rushed across to shake Edward Kelley awake, and then sat with him all through the rest of the night, constantly going over things in advance of the morning's Action.

Frommond hopes it is going well. She hopes it has all been worth it. She hopes, above all, to be able to go home soon.

She looks below, at the Lesser Town, and her eye seeks the bakery where she and John hid from the Spanish assassins, and she thinks she can see it, for its roof is cleared of snow, thanks to the heat from the ovens, and after a moment, her eye registers a speck of yellow.

"Ha!" she says, pointing. "Look. Kitty's gloves. She threw them there the night we came to the audience with Spinola. The night Kelley went mad."

Marlowe peers.

"Beautiful gloves they were," he says. "Cost a fortune."

She agrees.

"And look: there's the other one."

It is on the roof, just across the alleyway.

Marlowe grunts.

"Shame to let them go to waste," he says. "You hang on here, and I'll go and get them."

⊕

Emperor Rudolf sits on a silk cushion set upon a leather cushion set upon what might be a gold stool, his head a little above both Dee and Kelley, and he watches Kelley with a curious, slightly incredulous disgust, for which Dee blames him not one jot, for Kelley is an unprepossessing sight. He is kneeling, in his now-stained russet doublet and greasy sag-kneed hose, about which they can do nothing, bent before the little altar they have cobbled together, endeavoring to summon the angelic spirit Anachor.

"In the name of the blessed and Holy Trinity," Kelley says, "I do desire you, good angel Anachor, that if it be the divine will of him who is called Tetragrammaton, the Holy God, the Father, that you take upon yourself some shape as best becomes your celestial nature and that you appear visibly here in this crystal."

Dee watches with his breath stuck somewhere in his lungs. He cannot bear this. He cannot bear the fact that everything has come down to this moment, and that it all depends on Kelley, who, even before they set off from Mortlake last year, was hardly the most reliable of men. It has taken every ounce of patient machination to get him to this point, and if Kelley forgets that which he is supposed to say, it could all still come to nothing.

"Answer our demands," he begins in a low voice, "in as far as we shall not transgress the bounds of the divine mercy and goodness by requesting unlawful knowledge, but that you will graciously show us such things that are most profitable for us to know and do, to the glory and honor of this Divine Majesty, who lives and reigns, world without end. Amen."

"Amen."

So, Dee thinks, well, that was not so bad, but now we come to the meat of the thing, and he is suddenly filled with a high-strung terror of failure, for he feels nothing that he once felt in Mortlake. He does not feel the room grow unnaturally cool, nor unnaturally hot, nor does he feel his heartbeat in his ears or any of the other manifestations he takes to be typical of the Actions. He feels a sharp stab of panic and allows himself a look in the reflection of one of the seals and sees the skeptical outline of the emperor, and he detects the slightest element of restlessness, and he wonders if he ought to interrupt now, to say that Master—*Doctor*—Kelley is not well, or not ready? This is their only chance at this, and if Kelley fails to convince the emperor—well. It cannot stand to think about it.

Dee is about to speak up, to stop this now, to tell Rudolf he must come back later, or they will come to him perhaps, for this room is not propitious, when Kelley hears a voice.

"Now the time has come," he relays.

And Dee feels an elemental thrill course through his blood, and he starts writing.

"A white horse is the beginning of your teaching," Kelley tells them, in the voice of Uriel, from whom they have not heard for some time, "and the word of God. Ten and nine are nineteen."

Dee watches as the emperor leans in; he seems about to open his mouth to ask a question, but Kelley as Uriel goes on before he can.

"Do not doubt it for I am a servant of God. I am a witness of the light. I touched him and he became a prophet."

Dee asks Kelley if he means Ezra, the Hebrew prophet.

"Chapter four, verse nine," Kelley tells him. "There shall you find the prophecy of this time and this Action."

Dee cannot call that verse to mind. He hopes Kelley can, but before Kelley need go any further, he is presented with a vision.

"I see a sea, like quicksilver, with a harbor and two rivers running into it. And there is a giant, standing with one leg in the sea and the other in a river. One leg is of gold, the other of lead, both of the substance of the rainbow."

Rudolf is transfixed, and Dee forgets his doubts about Kelley, for this, he thinks, sounds very promising.

"He has a face with many eyes and noses," Kelley is going on, "though they are indistinct, and he has a body like red brass. His right arm is the color of silver and the left is black, and twinkling. The head is quicksilver, like the sea. A voice is calling to him. Telling him. Telling him to measure the water and he tells them that it is a cube twice doubled in himself in a straight line. The fourth in the third and three in himself square, which is the age of nature."

Rudolf is utterly stilled, and Dee is silently begging Kelley to remember to mention the *Book of Loagaeth*. Mention the *Book of Loagaeth*! And Kelley does!

"A new spirit comes," he says, and his eyes widen. As do the emperor's.

"I am named Nalvage," Kelley says. "And I have given you the *Book of Loagaeth*, which in your language signifies 'Speech from God' and in it are forty-nine tables, and in those tables are contained the mystical and holy voices of the angels dignified and in state disglorified and drent in confusion which pierce heaven and look into the center of the earth: the very language and speech of children and innocents such as magnify the name of God and are pure. And unto me are delivered five parts of a time wherein I will open, teach, and uncover the secrets of that speech which is known as the Cabala of Nature, and in all parts may it be known and this being achieved, the son of God shall be known in power, and establish a Kingdom with righteousness in the earth and then cometh the end."

It is transcendent performance, and the emperor's eyes burn with the scholar's light of insatiable curiosity, and Dee wonders how he could have ever doubted Kelley for a single moment?

When it is over, Kelley collapses into an apparent dead faint, and Rudolf summons servants and demands they do everything for him.

"Make him comfortable; bring him a bed, a bath, and when he wakes, the finest food, and wine, and many new clothes. Refuse him nothing, do you hear? We wish him to prosper, and to keep him close about our person, for he is blessed by God."

Rudolf is now strutting about the hall, so filled with purpose and energy it almost makes Dee laugh. After a moment, he summons Dee over, and for once the emperor is alone, with no attendants within earshot.

"The *Book of Loagaeth*," he says.

Dee nods. He can feel his heart thundering.

"May we see it?" Rudolf asks.

"It is a rough, unfinished thing," Dee tells him. "No sight for an emperor."

"Please."

"And I make no claims as to its meaning. I have merely done as the angelic spirits commanded."

"Doctor. Please. We would see it above all things."

Dee's hands are trembling as he unwraps the rough-bound pages but they are steady when he holds the book up for the emperor's inspection. Rudolf gazes at it, tilting his head to see it from different directions.

"May we touch it?" he wonders, finger outstretched. "It is not sacrilegious in any way?"

Dee permits the emperor to touch it.

"May we see a page?"

Dee shows him one at random: a continuous circle of Enochian text surrounding four flasks and some quicksilver in which the sky is reflected. It could have been better, but it could have been worse. The emperor bends and peers and Dee feels a strange thrill: the emperor's eyes seem to glimmer with lustful greed. He wants this book, and there is almost nothing he will not do to possess it.

That is enough, Dee thinks, and he feels breathless with incredulous relief. His job is done. He has pulled off his great task. He takes the book away and wraps it with enormous and unnecessary care and places it in his bag. Of course, Rudolf *might* steal it. He *might* have Dee thrown off the battlements. But the book is no good to him without the angelic spirits, and the angelic spirits are at the command of Kelley, who is, for now, at the command of Dee.

He hopes.

Emperor Rudolf is left watching—and licking his lips.

"Would you like to see the patient now, Your Highness?" Dee wonders, and the emperor lurches almost back to the here and now; he remembers his dearest Kitten, who has so recently come back from the very brink of death and should, surely, be more on his mind than a book?

"Yes, come, Doctor," he says. "Come and let us see our patient."

The emperor strides to Kitty's bedside to gaze down at her and murmur soft endearments that are best left unheard, and she raises her hand to him, and he takes it and bends to kiss her wrist and when he straightens up, his face is flushed with such love and joy that Dee momentarily forgets what he has done.

After a moment Rudolf summons Dee, and together they smile down at Kitty de Fleurier, who is washed now and lies among sheets and pillows of new-laundered linen. Under soft gray wool, she is restored to her almost astonishing beauty, with dark eyes, high cheekbones, and a smile that is so broad that when she smiles—not often at the moment, but Dee saw it once, perhaps, directed at Frommond—it is as if the sun has broken through the clouds.

"You both look very pleased," she murmurs, speaking in French, and Rudolf replies that they are.

"Both of us," he says, clapping a hand on Dee's shoulder, "and with good reason."

But he does not tell her what that reason is.

"How do you feel?" Dee asks.

"Restored to life," she tells him. "Thanks to you, and your wife."

"And the angelic spirits, my dear!" Rudolf laughs, and Kitty's gaze slips away, as if she is not so sure about that.

"Our Kitten is tired!" the emperor exclaims. "Come, Doctor, let us leave her. You and I have much business to discuss. Much business."

When she sees her lover turn away from her, Kitty's expression is hard to read, but Dee feels a fleeting stab of sorrow for her. The emperor's affections are fickle, as is well known, and they burn bright, and fast, and then are no more. Perhaps Kitty realizes this? But is she altogether sorry? Perhaps not.

The emperor's hand still lingers on his shoulder, and Dee is aware of being done an almost impossible honor, and he is basking in self-satisfaction at having achieved what never looked possible, when the doors to the garden are pulled open, and in stamp two halberdiers, faces mottled with cold, and behind them come Jane and Marlowe, and both are laughing at something, and then when Jane sees Dee looking her way, she smiles happily enough at him, in a way he has not seen—for obvious reasons—for some time, and she holds up her hands for him to see, and he feels a riveting stab of searing, unbearable terror when he sees she is wearing those bright, butter-yellow, camel-skin gloves.

⊕

It comes like nightfall, in slow and sooty accretions gathering in the corners where the shadows are already deepest, but then it comes fast, and the darkness spills out, and out, and out until it is everywhere, and there is nothing but it, and the great roaring heat that swells within her core.

"It is happening!" she tells them, and she feels the heat blowing up within, not unlike when she was pregnant with Arthur, save the heat grows much hotter, and she feels her body swelling in all parts within her clothes, as if her skin will surely split.

There are always hands upon her, and each finger is like a molten tong.

"Get off me!" she cries. "Get away!"

She suddenly cannot stand it. She must be away. Her head is burning. Her breath will not come. She runs. She hits something, hard, and is granted merciful release.

⊕

CHAPTER TWENTY-NINE

Tower of London, London, March 1584

G ray skies, and a strong marine smell in the air.

"Delivery's come for you, Master Beale."

It is the cart, come up from Worthing, with the dead Paget in the back. They should have pickled her in brine, he thinks, and kept her in a barrel. Lady Paget will not like this. Nor will Sir Francis.

And nor will Devereux, of course. He has not seen her for more than a week now while he has been on that familiar road north to find Lady Paget in her park in Woodrising, just this side of Norwich, to break the news to her that her sister-in-law was dead.

"Which one?" she'd asked.

"Well, that is it. We don't know."

"Any would do. All would do. The brothers too. I curse the day I first heard the word 'Paget.' They are an evil family and I hope whichever one it is rots in hell."

"I see."

She had not wanted to come down to London, of course, for the journey is long and she is old, but Beale had used all his authority, and some personal money, to ensure she came, on condition that he did not call her by her married name but by her given name.

"Nazaret Newton," she had repeated. "I cannot think why I ever gave up such a name."

And so now here she is, holding on to his arm, hobbling across the great court of the Tower of London to where Sir Francis Walsingham waits next to a humble cart, pulled by oxen, and— praise Jesus—there she is: Devereux, today in silks and sarcanet, lawn and cypress, with the homespun hat and gloves long gone, and of course with no sign of the sword.

On the bed of the cart is the body, wrapped in waxed canvas, and the smell is not yet so bad until Walsingham nods to a servant, who pulls back the canvas. The smell billows, and they all step back for fear of breathing in the miasma.

"You probably do not have to see this, Mistress Devereux," Walsingham calls.

Lady Paget does have to see it, though, and she steps up and peers very closely.

"Poo-hoof," she says, wafting away the smell.

"Seen better days," Beale agrees.

"Well done, my lady," Walsingham says through pursed lips.

"I am a countrywoman, Master Walsingham," she reminds him, rightly proud of her ability to look a rotting Paget in the face. After a moment she steps back.

"That's one of them, all right. They have that Papist look about them, even after death it seems."

"But which one?" Beale asks. There are, what? Five Paget daughters? Six? Seven even? No one seems to know for sure.

"Oh, I don't know. Etheldreda? Or Eleanor? Or perhaps Anne? No! It is Grisold! That's right. Awful name, awful girl."

Who'd name a baby Grisold? Beale wonders.

"Or is it?" Lady Paget wonders on further reflection. "Maybe one of the others? There are so many of them."

Walsingham gives the nod, and the servant flaps the canvas back.

"I'll let the family know we have buried Grisold in one of the pits beyond Smithfield," Walsingham confirms. "And if by any chance we have the wrong Paget, and Grisold is still alive, then perhaps she will let us know."

Later, after Walsingham has broken the news that Beale must now conduct Nazaret Newton back to Norwich, he takes him aside, out of all earshot.

"When you've done that, Robert, will you ride to Orford for me? Speak to the master mason. Anthony Pughe is his name. Ask him how much it would cost to take the gun tower down, and to pack it up and transport it to Sussex. He can hire a boat. Two boats. Whatever it takes. And whatever he says, agree to it. Tell him to start work as soon as he is able and ask him to send the bill directly to me here. It must be to me. Only me. No one else. And order the gunners to unsling their guns, or whatever it is they do with them, and bring them as swiftly as they are able around to Arundel haven in absolute secrecy. At night. No one must ever learn of this. Her Majesty must never learn of our mistake."

Beale agrees.

"Should I take Mistress Devereux with me? She knows the situation well."

Walsingham looks at him, his brown eyes damp and frank.

"Are you certain that is for the best, Robert?"

He is not, of course, but so what?

"I will ensure she kills no one new."

Walsingham laughs, a bitter, faded, autumnal laugh.

"So long as she confines herself to Pagets," Walsingham says, "then I do not overly mind."

⊕

CHAPTER THIRTY

Hradčany Castle, Prague, March 1584

J ohn Dee asks himself how it has come to this.

An oversight, yes, obviously. He could not have guessed what would have happened to the gloves after Kitty had worn them, but perhaps he should have?

But there is no point in again going over all this.

There is no point in doing anything at all if Jane does not live.

"What about your panacea?" Marlowe asks. "All gone is it?"

They are sitting on the bed, Dee taking his turn to mop Jane's brow and soothe her beet-red skin with iced water, and he cannot even look at Marlowe, let alone confirm there is none left, for all he ever had were the few beans that Drake brought back from Benin, all of which he has used to save Kitty's life, but he knows that all of this Marlowe knows.

"I did not mean for this to happen," Dee tells him.

"'Course not," Marlowe agrees. "But it has, hasn't it? And so here we are."

And Marlowe's voice—all plangent and urban now—spits the words out at him that are like nails to pin Dee out and expose him for his iniquity.

"Wondered why you needed them gloves," he says. "I thought you knew something about our Kitty here being partial to fancy togs and suchlike, and I thought: fair play, Doctor Dee does his schoolwork. But then the next day, after your Action, down at old Thaddeus's, and you were going on and on and on about the angel-faced woman being red as a beet and whatnot, I thought you'd lost your marbles, but now I see you were just ramming it into old Łaski's ten-inch-thick skull, weren't you? So that he'd remember it and recognize the symptoms when he saw them in Kitty, whom you were planning to poison that very afternoon, weren't you? With those magical bloody gloves of yours."

Dee denies nothing, admits nothing.

"So then when our Kitty comes down with the aftereffects of what I guess must be something a bit stronger than belladonna, and shows all the signs of what your angels had foretold, why, there you'd be, ready and waiting for the emperor's nod with your astonishingly large bag of tricks, from which you would—unbeknownst to those who might wonder what it is you are up to—pull the cure, which you had with you all along. Is that about right, Doctor?"

"I had to get an audience with the emperor," Dee tells him.

"You couldn't just ask?"

"He'd've never seen me." Dee is firm about that. "And if he had, he'd've never trusted me, anyway. Not enough."

"Not enough for what?"

"Not enough for me to stop him giving de Guise the money."

"And how were you ever going to do that?"

"There is no *one* thing," Dee tells him. "Of course there's no one thing. There are things. Kelley. Kelley is one. He will tell Emperor Rudolf that the angelic spirits see his future in the east, conquering the Ottomans. And I had hoped to turn Kitty de Fleurier against the Duc de Guise and persuade her to persuade the emperor to do likewise."

"How were you going to do that? Oh. Yes. Cure her. Have Mistress Dee whisper sweet words in her ear?"

Dee shrugs. He had thought that, yes.

"I hoped to create an obligation," he admits.

"And what about the sister?" Marlowe asks.

Dee can say nothing about her. She is the one moving part too many in his plan.

"If de Guise had brought her," he supposes, "then Kitty could have insisted on seeing her."

He imagines Kitty wresting her sister from de Guise. He knows it is weak.

"Which is why he went and left her with his mother," Marlowe supposes, "in wherever she lives."

"Lorraine," Dee tells him.

"And so how does this"—he indicates Frommond, lying broiling in the bed—"affect your scheme?"

Dee has not even thought about it and does not know.

"In no way that is good," he admits.

⊕

Later—though how much later Dee cannot say, for he has lost his grasp of not just the hours, but even the days. Kitty de Fleurier returns in saffron silks, with one servant—Dennis, from Benin, Dee guesses, and he wonders if . . . ? But there is no chance—and she sits at Jane's bedside just as Jane had sat by hers, and Dennis passes through the cordon of halberdiers to fetch ice and snow for the water and beer, with which she carefully, dutifully, returns the favor that Jane did her.

Every so often Kitty looks up at Dee, only to dart her eyes away and return to dampening the cloth over Jane's eyes and running ice along her swollen, scarlet forearms. Dee cannot help but choke on his own shame and guilt every time he considers that surely she must have seen him wrench those gloves from Jane's hands and throw them in the fire, and then force her back outside into the snow to scrub and scrub those hands, with Marlowe looking on as if he were mad. Frommond cried out and tried to wrench herself from him, but he'd used all his strength to keep scrubbing until Marlowe shoved him over, telling him that Mistress Dee was not enjoying it, and even though they are husband and wife, that it is not right, what he was doing.

But then they saw how intensely bloody serious he was. And then they understood what he'd done, and she was mute and pliant when he grabbed her wrists again, just as she was about to clap her hands to her face, and scrubbed them in the snow again.

Afterward Frommond sat in horrified, disgusted, shocked silence until . . . until she gave notice that the poison was in her system, for she could not focus, she said, and her head had begun aching as in a vise and, dear God, look at her skin! It is becoming the color of a rose and then a beet!

And so as that first night fell she set off on her journey alone into the darkness, far away from them, and far from the shore. All they who remain in her wake can do is to keep her mortal body cool while her tortured spirit rages into the night, to heaven's threshold, and to hope and pray that she hears their voices, and that she comes back to them.

But Dee fears she will not, not without the beans from Calabar.

And where is he going to find such things in Prague?

Nowhere.

So: prayer. And ice. That is all he can offer. He cannot hold her hand for it seems to burn her, and she flinches from all touch save with ice, or iced cloth, and beer dripped from ice into her ever parched lips.

"If only she would sweat," Kitty says.

"Do you remember it?" Dee asks.

She shakes her head.

"What is 'it'?" she says.

He tells her he does not know.

"The infection," he lies.

"You are not scared of catching it, just as she was not?"

He has no words to describe his shame when he says "No."

"I consulted the angelic spirits," he tells her, and he hardly bothers to note the familiar flinch that women usually display when he talks of such things. "They say that this is a trial heaven-sent, to test those whom God most loves."

"As gold in the furnace?" Kitty croaks, showing she knows her Book of Wisdom.

"Something like that," Dee says. And as he says this, he catches Marlowe's gaze, and Marlowe holds it awhile, then lifts his lip and turns away. Dee wishes he could turn away, too, but he cannot. He has gotten them to this stage, and now he must get them out, or get them beyond it. He cannot just sit here and feel bilious with self-pity.

"So," he says, turning to Kitty. "How is it that you find yourself in Prague, Mademoiselle de Fleurier?"

She might ordinarily sneer at him as if he were a common barber, he supposes, asking stupid questions, in his wearied velvet robes and strange French accent, but their proximity and common endeavor have brought them together, and besides, she is not unkind.

Kitty lets out a long sigh, a silver plume in the cool of the room, and she tells him that she came at the behest of the emperor. Dee knows this is only half—a quarter—true, but he is not interested in a confession. He knows her situation. He remembers Łaski chortling with lascivious pleasure at the thought of the women of Catherine de Medici's *L'Escadron Volant*, at the thought of the services they provide and what they'd do for a man, but facing her now across the broiling body of his wife who might die at any moment at his own hand, he cannot condemn Kitty, even if he wanted to.

We each have a master, he knows, whom we must serve to the best of our varied talents.

Dee wishes to get Kitty to tell him about Arnoldus van der Boxe and the woman Jane had seen insult Kitty in the garden, who must be de Guise's agents here in Prague, but as luck or ill luck would have it, before he can ask, Łaski appears at the pornographic door, his belly like a galleon in full sail; he is very bright-eyed and filled with a kind of excited awe. He has heard nothing of what has happened to Frommond.

"What have you done, Doctor?" he breathes. "What happened at the Action? The emperor says it was greatest experience of his life! He told me he felt presence of the divine."

Dee rubs his eyes. He has almost forgotten the Action. It feels so long ago.

"Yes," he admits. "Kelley—he made a very good connection. As good as I've ever known."

Łaski laughs to cover his envy.

"Bravo!" he says, clapping Dee on his shoulder. "Bravo! You

have made Łaski very proud man! I bring you here, see? And you delight the emperor. Means Łaski delights the emperor."

He is about to perform another bellow of laughter when Dee grips his arm, just above the elbow, and twists, hard, and Łaski is silenced by the calculated jolt of pain. He rubs his elbow and looks hurt until he sees Jane and takes the radically altered temperature of the room.

"My God, Doctor, forgive me!"

Dee waves him aside.

"Forget it," he says.

Łaski does.

"But I am here at express wish of emperor," he whispers very loudly. "He has entrusted your Łaski with delicate mission. Łaski is to be his ambassador."

He would roar with more irritating laughter, but he eyes Dee's crablike pincer and restrains himself.

"What is it?" Dee asks, too tired for much more nonsense.

And now Łaski adopts a conspiratorial whisper and leans in, as if to thwart an eavesdropper.

"He was so impressed by the angels predicting Kitty's illness, and then with the Action the other day, that has asked me—no, begged me—to ask you to sell him—*sell* him—your *Book of Loagaeth.*"

Dee hardly blinks. In other times, he would be well pleased to hear this, for it is the very thing that he set out to achieve, but with Jane on her deathbed, all joy is turned to ash in his mouth, and he barely manages a smile.

"It is not for sale," he says.

Łaski ignores him.

"Emperor told Łaski about it," he says. "Łaski never seen him so excited. And Łaski seen emperor excited, believe me. He wants it, Doctor. He wants to buy it. He will pay good money for it. Silver thalers. A thousand. He says he must have it. It is not just for his *Kunstkammer*. He says it more important than all this other stuff he has collected—"

He breaks off when he sees how Marlowe has rearranged Rudolf's *Kunstkammer*, like an iconoclast at a household sale, or an eviction, with everything piled this way and that across the doors and windows.

"—put together," he finishes lamely.

"It is," Dee agrees, "but it is not for sale."

"Everything is for sale, Doctor," Łaski reminds him. "For fifteen hundred silver thalers."

"It is not the money," Dee tells him.

"Of course it is the money: two thousand silver thalers! Please, Doctor. You do not know him. He will get it one way or another. He is— You cannot stop him acquiring things that he wants. Ask Kitty."

He gestures to the bed, where Kitty continues to mop Jane's brow. She ignores them both.

"And I have never seen him like this. That book. It will become everything to him. I nearly choked when he told me it was one you were scribbling away at all that time, yes? On boat. The one I nearly threw in the Elbe, yes?"

Łaski takes off his hat and runs a palm through his long sweaty hair.

"I can't sell it," Dee tells him, "because there is still so much that I do not understand about it. And without Kelley on hand to help interpret what is already written, and what else the angelic spirits say, it would be unfair to sell it to the emperor, even for twenty-five hundred thalers. Will you tell him I cannot in all honesty do so?"

Łaski splutters incredulously.

"You are not going to sell old book you've written yourself for what—three thousand silver thalers?"

"It would be a waste of his money."

"So *what*?"

"Keep your voice down!"

"So *what*?" he whispers urgently. "He is Holy Roman Emperor! The king of Bohemia and Hungary! Jesus, Doctor! He has pots of money! And you can always write a new one! Come on! This is silly. You need money. I need money. He has it."

It does not surprise him that Łaski intends to take a cut of any deal negotiated.

"But I cannot," Dee tells him again. "In all conscience. It will be wasted on the emperor unless he has with him a guide. Someone who is able to consult the angelic spirits in search of greater under-standing of what has been written."

Łaski takes a step back as if to gain the whole view of Dee, to really take him in, as if afresh and for the very first time, and then he gives Dee his shrewdest look.

"Such as? You? You wish to stay in Prague?"

Dee shakes his head.

"Not me," he says.

Łaski's eyes roll around his sockets, and then he sees it!

"Kelley!" He laughs. "*Kelley* wishes to stay in Prague?"

Well, Dee thinks, it is more that *he* wishes Kelley to stay in Prague, but Kelley will go where the money is. They both glance over to where Kelley is asleep again, undisturbed by hearing his name exclaimed; snoring softly by the fire with the *Bosome Book* on his lap, he looks like a dog that most households would put out at night.

"If the emperor wants the *Book of Loagaeth*," Dee explains, "he will need thirty-five hundred silver thalers, and his Mercator globe, but most importantly he will need a guide to help plumb its Enochian mysteries, and there can be none finer than Doctor Kelley. But the fact remains, Count Łaski, that the *Book of Loagaeth* is not for sale."

Łaski is perplexed.

"But you," he says, "you wish no part in this? You go home to England? You homesick? Yes. I see it. Have you heard anything from your Queen? From that man Walsingham?"

Dee shakes his head. He has heard nothing from either, but he must perhaps have somehow communicated his desire to return home in some unintended way? Or perhaps it is understood that an exile always yearns for home, even if home does not seem to yearn for him? And mention of home almost brings tears to Dee's eyes. He thinks of his son, and the boy's dead rabbit—another unwitting victim of his scheme—and of Mortlake, and of quietly pottering in his laboratory, or walking in his orchard by the river with Jane, whom he loves above all others in this world, and he thinks of all the things he has left unfinished: his calendar reform; his application for a grant of exploration of the Northwest Passage, both of which hang in limbo. He wants, too, to be away from Prague, from its harsh, unforgiving cold, its mercilessness, and the terrible sense of failure it has given him. For a moment he believes if he could somehow go back to England, he could go back in time, to any moment before he poisoned Jane.

But what of her?

If she dies— He cannot go on, not even with that thought.

And Łaski is still there, watching his expression changing as each of these thoughts occurs, and after a moment the big man places a big hand on Dee's shoulder and pulls him into one of those hugs.

"All will be well, my doctor," he murmurs. "All will be well. You see. Jane will live. You will sell your book. Then you go home to your boy. All will be well. Łaski will see to it."

And Dee almost believes him. He almost believes him.

⊕

In the evening he goes to Jane's bedside to relieve Kitty de Fleurier and her servant Dennis, who have been there all day, and he looks down at his wife, and sees her condition is unchanged. Is that good? Bad? Who knows. At least she is not dead, he thinks. At least the poison has not killed her straightaway. Perhaps the body can survive the shock and come back stronger? He feels for the pulsing vein under her wrist—it is almost obscured by the swelling, and his hands burn from her heat—but it is there, tapping so fast it is almost a constant, and so then he wonders if it is the body's reaction to the poison that will kill her? Her heart will surely wear itself out, beating so fast, creating so much heat out of nothing more than ice-cooled beer? He applies more wet cloths to her arms and face and legs and settles in for a long night of prayer.

⊕

Later, when all are asleep, Marlowe comes to him by Jane's bedside.

"Doctor," he says. "I've got a bit of an idea."

⊕

The next day when Kitty de Fleurier comes bustling in with the dawn, she finds Dee still awake, still on his knees by Jane's bedside, still praying that the poison would not be so strong as it had been when Kitty plunged her hands into the gloves, and that it might be diluted by the meltwater perhaps, that it might be . . . be . . . be anything.

"How is she?" Kitty asks.

"No worse," Dee tells her, which is true.

Kitty orders the doors open, despite the cold, and fresh ice brought in.

"What is that noise?" she asks from the doorway.

"A drum," Dee tells her. "It has been going on all night. From down on the bridge."

They stand almost shoulder to shoulder at the doorway, looking out over the snow-laden garden, listening to the steady deep boom of a drum from the town below.

"What does it mean?" she asks.

Dee shrugs.

"It is the prelude to tomorrow's Day of Rage," Dee can only suppose. "Jesu. Imagine hearing it if you are a Jew of the Old Town."

Kitty crosses herself, which is ironic, Dee thinks.

"It is not so cold, is it?" she asks.

"A thaw's on the way," Dee agrees. He thinks of Marlowe, and the plan that he had proposed that he is even now trying to carry out; Dee feels happier about him than he did.

They step aside to let the shivering servants back in.

"Where is that boy?" Kitty asks. She means Marlowe.

"Gone," he tells her.

"Good for him," she says. "I wish I might be gone, too."

"You do not have to stay here," he tells her. He pretends he thinks she means at Jane's bedside. "I will carry on."

"No," she says. "It is a relief to be here. Besides. What she did for me—"

He nods.

"She would do for anyone," he says.

Kitty understands him to mean that Jane is saintly, which is what he meant.

"She is a good woman," Kitty says.

"The best," Dee tells her.

"Then we had better make sure she gets through this, hadn't we?"

She laughs, and even such a soft, brave laugh like that is lovely to hear, and Dee takes his heart in his hand. There is no other way to do this than come clean.

"Your sister," he says, and Kitty is instantly stilled. Her eyes become beads, fixed on Dee.

"What of her?"

"You mentioned her, when you were— In your sleep."

He sees her relax a mite.

"Amelie," she whispers.

"Yes. Amelie," Dee repeats, affirming. "I know where she is being kept."

Hearing this she looks at him as if she might at a wild animal come into her room late at night.

"Who are you, Englishman?" she asks.

"I mean you no harm, I promise on my wife's life. I came here to stop the emperor joining the Duc de Guise in a plot against my Queen and my country, and I know you, too, are caught up in the plot, but I sincerely believe you are reluctant, and that the duke has forced you to act in this way against your will."

Kitty is looking at Dee now with contempt, and he feels he has misjudged her, but he holds her gaze, and she his.

"I have come across the Duc de Guise before," he goes on, before she can give voice to her thoughts. "And I know how he forces women to act on his behalf by taking their children or their loved ones hostage. He will never have spoken to you of Isobel Cochet, but he kidnapped her daughter, Rose, and he forced Isobel to steal a document and kill a man. I could not save Isobel, but I saved her daughter. And I swore an oath that I would not fail in any such matter ever again, and I will not now, upon the life of my wife."

He holds Kitty's gaze while he places his hand solemnly on Jane's. He dares not stop looking at Kitty, but Jesu, he thinks, Jane's skin is surely cooler than it was. Her breath, too, sounds easier. He is desperate to look down at her, but Kitty is still staring, her eyes so glossy her gathering tears might be rose oil.

"What are you saying?" she asks, her voice almost a whisper.

"You asked after that boy," he reminds her. "His name is Christopher Marlowe. He is an extremely resourceful and capable young man, as my wife"—he risks a glance down at her now, and she is no longer beet red, but rose red—"will testify. He knows France and the French well, and he brought Jane here himself with no servants, all the way from London risking every kind of peril: pirates, wolves, thieves, priests, murderers, rapists, Germans. You name it, he evaded it."

A frown creases Kitty's brow. He is losing her, he can see, but dear God! He moves his hand to feel the pulse under Jane's wrist. It is still fast, faster than it should be, but no longer thrumming as it was.

"Why are you telling me this?" Kitty asks.

"Because," Dee tells her, "because Marlowe set off last night for the dowager Duchess de Guise's château, in Bar, in Lorraine. He is going to find your sister. He is going to find Amelie, and he is going to get her back. He will take her wherever you wish."

Kitty looks at him for a long time, and later, much later, if he ever needed to remind himself not to get too far ahead of himself, Dee would force himself to recall her expression and remember how it gathered slowly from a distant confusion to harden over the time it takes to say the *Ave Maria* into an expression of such towering, incredulous fury that he will never forget it.

"He has done *what*?" she snarls.

Jesu! She is going to attack him!

"Your sister will be free!" he reiterates. "Freed from de Guise's mother. It means *you* will be free! Free to go wherever you please. Free of de Guise!"

"You fool! You don't know what you have done! You don't know who I am. You don't know my sister. You don't know anything about us, and yet you presume *to save us*?"

It had all sounded so simple when Marlowe had proposed it the night before. Now though—*Jesu*. But he remembers what Jane had overheard about Amelie. And though he may not know everything about her, or Kitty, he knows de Guise.

"I do know you!" he says. "I know all about the Flying Squadron. I know all about Catherine de Medici, and I know de Guise. I know his mother's servants pinch your sister. I know she is not happy. I know you are not happy. And I can help."

Kitty is lost for words, and stares, stuck dumb.

At that very moment there is a gurgle from below.

They both look down.

Jane has moved her hand and, with it, moved the cloth from across her eyes.

They are very slightly open.

"I am burning," she says.

Praise Jesu! She will live!

⊕

Later, after much distracted thought, and a long conversation with Edward Kelley, Dee finally sends word to Count Łaski to say that on account of a change in personal circumstances, and on further reflection, he has changed his mind. He writes: the *Book of Lo-agaeth* is for sale, for five thousand silver thalers, and Mercator's globe, on the understanding that the services of Doctor Kelley are retained as the emperor's personal guide to the realm of the angelic spirits.

Within fifteen minutes the emperor is there, presaged by a great booming knock at the pornographic door, and Dee is pressed into unexpected action pulling aside the narwhal tusks and the petrified pony. He has had no time to insist on Kelley washing himself.

"What is all this?" Kurtz asks, pushing his way into the room. Behind him comes Emperor Rudolf—in a drooping cloud of red silks—and behind him file in today's selection of courtiers all in sober black, save Łaski, beaming in crimson, led by the emperor's chancellor, Octavius Spinola, with a "let's put an end to this nonsense" expression on his face. With him also—Dee sees with a lurch—are Arnoldus van der Boxe and the woman with the hitched eyebrow, whom Jane identified as Kitty's gaoler, here, no doubt, to reclaim their charge.

Meanwhile the emperor is almost panting with pleasure, his eyes glistening as if with oil.

"Doctor Dee!" he says. "Doctor Dee! You cannot imagine the excitement we have been feeling since last we communicated with the angelic spirits! Our mind has been awhirl. And to hear that you are prepared to share with us the secrets of this *Book of Loagaeth*, we are for words lost!"

Dee wishes him joy of it.

"I only pray you will have more success in learning its meaning than my feeble efforts have thus far afforded me, Your Highness."

"Pish! Doctor, your learning is renowned throughout Christendom, and beyond I dare say it! Everybody knows your book."

Books, Dee nearly corrects.

"Where is it?" Rudolf asks.

Dee fetches the book, walking past the bed, where Kitty de

Fleurier stands—even she would not dare sit in the emperor's presence—and this is when the emperor finally sees her.

"Oh, there you are," he says. He does not call her Kitten, or summon her to him, as he might once have done, and his attitude is— What? Merely distracted? Or actively cold? Dee feels a pang of sympathy for her, standing there, being judged by all the courtiers, who have perhaps been placing bets on when she would fall from grace, actively conspiring to this event, even. But it is always so with royal mistresses, he supposes: their lease as favorites is necessarily of uncertain duration and likely to be terminated suddenly, with no warning or appeal. To lose out to a book, though! And to Master Kelley!

"And how fares Mistress Dee?" Kurtz asks, the only one to do so.

"She is better this morning," Kitty answers. "Bone broth and eggs and some fresh beer will give her strength."

It is an order from someone used to having her slightest whim fulfilled, but this morning there is that telling hesitation, and all eyes click to the emperor to watch how he will react, before Kurtz signals to a servant to see to it.

Emperor Rudolf actually wiggles his fingers as Dee approaches, bearing the fruits of his last six months labor wrapped up in a piece of the bed hangings. When he has handed it over, a courtier approaches, honored to relieve the emperor of all burdens. He might ordinarily be expected to take the book and carry it to whichever lectern the emperor wishes, but today the emperor will not relinquish it. He wishes to carry it himself.

"Where shall you put it, Your Highness?" Łaski booms proprietorially. "In pride of place, I hope?"

He means in which cabinet of the *Kunstkammer*, but the emperor shakes his head.

"No," he says, hugging the book to his body. "We shall keep it in our new tower, which we shall clear of those worthless scholars and work-shy mathematicians, and from henceforward, the tower shall be dedicated to investigating the hidden messages contained herein, which is a task that we shall from now on call our Great Work. The tower shall be reserved for the exclusive preserve of our most esteemed Doctor Kelley, who shall be afforded everything he desires, and in this way we shall—as our dear Doctor Dee has prophesied—have dominion over all things, from the fishes in the sea even unto the cherubim in the heavens above."

Which is not quite what Dee had done, but he has no wish to argue. Kelley has appeared and executes a deep bow of pleasure at being called to duty. He disgusts most of the courtiers, but that does not matter. With all the money the emperor will give him, he will clean himself up, Dee supposes, and even magic himself a new pair of ears.

And talking of money, here comes a servant bearing three bags of silver thalers, more money than Dee has ever had in his entire life, to place them in his hands. He cannot carry them, of course, for being too heavy, and he must place them by his feet with the cold clink on the marble flags.

He does not mention the Mercator globe. He will sort that out for himself.

"So then," the emperor says, "let us to our Great Work then, Doctor Kelley," and he extends an ushering hand and turns, to guide Kelley through the door, and it is as if he has put everything else out of his mind: Kitty de Fleurier; John Dee; Jane Dee; his *Kunstkammer*; and his empire, even. There are many rounded eyes and alarmed expressions among his courtiers, and his panicking chancellor steps forward.

"But Your Highness," he says, "we have— We are expecting . . . a visitor. An important visitor. He comes this very day."

It sounds so limp, surely even in the chancellor's ears, and the emperor turns to him, his face screwed into a petulant child's.

"Today? Of all days? When we have so much to do. Who is it that comes?"

"The Duc de Guise, Your Highness. From France."

The emperor tuts.

"We have no time for him," he mutters. "He wants only money."

"But he is bringing with him two very fine horses," Van der Boxe pipes up, and the emperor starts and pulls a face. He does not expect to be spoken to by such minor figures as Van der Boxe, who is there to watch and applaud, not to contribute.

"What are two very fine horses to us?" the emperor asks himself. "We already have so many."

"And one of which is already lame," Kelley says, in his softest, noblest Irish accent yet, and the emperor does not consider how Kelley might know this, and Kelley does not seek to explain. But when attention has returned to Rudolf, Kelley catches John Dee's eye, and lifts an eyebrow. It is perhaps his way of saying farewell, and Dee forgives him most things.

"Yes, yes," the emperor mutters. "The Duc de Guise and his two horses, one of which at least is lame. Tell him if he insists we are to have them, then he should leave them with our Master of the Horse, who will stable them with our others and we will look at them by and by."

"But—" Van der Boxe starts.

"But, Your Highness," the chancellor interrupts. "It is the *Duc de Guise*. He comes as a representative of the French king."

Rudolf laughs at this, for it is well known that the Duc de Guise and the French king are near mortal enemies, and that the duke's visit is almost certainly not sanctioned by his king. And so now the chancellor is trying to appeal for help from Kitty de Fleurier, who has until recently been the duke's champion.

"The duke is very anxious to honor you, Your Highness, isn't he, Mistress de Fleurier?"

And Kitty opens her mouth, but whether to agree or disagree is never learned, for perhaps she catches sight of the threatening glares that Van der Boxe is shooting her over the emperor's half-turned shoulder, for she shuts her mouth, and defiantly lifts her chin, but by then, anyway, the emperor is paying her no mind.

"Perhaps Galvah will take a view on whether you should see the duke?" Dee suggests, and this is a much more appealing prospect for the emperor.

"Aha! Yes. What do you think Doctor Kelley?"

"The heavens mirror the earth," Kelley tells them all. "As above, so below."

"Quite right!" Łaski booms.

Dee almost laughs.

"Come," Emperor Rudolf says, and he turns decisively now, and the crowd of courtiers part to let him pass back out through the pornographic doors with deep bows, and then they follow him out, leaving behind in *Kunstkammer* only Count Łaski, Van de Boxe, and the clever-looking woman.

Van der Boxe and the clever-looking woman are quickly across the room to Kitty de Fleurier.

"Go after him!"

"Get off me!"

"Go after him!"

"Get your hands off me!"

Dee is across swiftly.

"Get away from her," he says.

"Or what?" the woman asks. "You'll cast a magic spell will you, Jew wizard?"

Dee is taken aback, but he laughs properly this time.

"Don't tempt me," he says.

Łaski approaches.

"Arnoldus!" he booms. "What is going on here, eh?"

Van der Boxe is in no mood for Łaski's bonhominous buffoon act.

"This has nothing to do with you, Count," he snaps. "Go away and leave us in peace."

"No," Łaski says. "You stand by the bedside of my esteemed Mistress Dee, who is still not well enough to listen to you shout at a woman."

He is suddenly enormous, towering over even the Dutchman Van der Boxe, whom he pushes suddenly and sends him skittering backward. Van der Boxe has a sword, but for the love of God, this is the emperor's *Kunstkammer* and you cannot go spilling blood here, can you? Especially not a count's blood, and anyway Dee has found the narwhal tusk, which in a fair fight would never match a sword, but it is enough to make Van der Boxe hesitate. By now the halberdiers that Kurtz had designated guard the room are gathering and Dennis, Kitty de Fleurier's servant, has appeared, and Van der Boxe and the clever-looking woman who turns out to be an anti-Semite are in retreat from Jane's bedside, and the battle—skirmish—is won.

When they are gone, Łaski wipes his brow.

"Phew," he says. "They are gone, Doctor, but I know them: they will be back, and with more swordsmen. And now that the emperor has taken to his tower—"

He need not go on.

Through the open doors they can hear the drum beat from the

town below, and with Rudolf's withdrawal into his tower with Kelley, they know its lawless intent will soon pervade the palace.

Dee turns to Kitty.

"De Guise will be here before the day is out," he tells her. "And when he learns that you have for whatever reason lost your place in the emperor's affections and can no longer guarantee him an audience with Rudolf, let alone the money he has come all this way to collect, he will not be merciful. He will punish you in exactly the manner in which he threatened, and he will do this as an example to any other woman he forces to do his business in future."

A glossy tear streaks Kitty's beautiful cheek, and next to her Dennis rumbles enigmatically.

"Come with us," Dee continues. "Both of you. Escape while you can. Master Marlowe has a full day's ride on whoever de Guise sends to deal with your sister, and Master Marlowe is— Well, he will not be caught. And we will find him with your sister, eating cakes, I daresay, somewhere in Holland, or in England, and he will have her safe. I have already sworn this on my wife's life."

Jane is watching, listening, from her sickbed. She raises a hand. Kitty is by her side instantly.

"It is so," she manages, her voice like teasels in the wind. "He is— If Christopher says he will do it, he will do it. No force on Earth can stop him."

Kitty clasps Jane's hand.

"Come with us," Jane goes on. "Come with us. Back to England. Or wherever. I cannot promise comfort, but there is much else besides—"

With that she falls asleep.

Kitty shakes her head and widens her eyes. She cannot decide. This is madness, you can see her thinking, but then—what else has she?

"I will come," she says. Then she turns to Dennis.

"You can stay, if you like," she tells him. "And I would not blame you if you did."

He chuckles, a deep and powerfully reassuring sound they all take to mean that he is coming with them. Dee is more relieved than most.

"Łaski will find carriage," Łaski announces grandly. "Take you over border."

Dee thanks him.

"That would be a favor that I hope to return in some way, should we meet again in more leisurely circumstances."

And Dee must endure one last embrace—powerful and lingering—before Łaski releases him, bids the others farewell, and retreats through the pornographic door with a promise to meet them in the castle's courtyard.

"The sooner we are gone, the better," Roger Cooke mutters. "That infernal drum's getting on my nerves."

Dee agrees, and he does not tell them they have not a moment to lose, for it is now late afternoon. It is not the ideal time to be taking to the road perhaps, but better now than later, and it cannot be long before the Duc de Guise arrives, and when he does, and he discovers the turn of events, his vengeance will be swift and bloody.

"Quite so," Dee says, and they hurry to gather up all their things, and soon are dressed and ready at last to leave the emperor's *Kunstkammer* for the first time in what feels like weeks.

"How do we look?" Frommond wonders.

"Merely unusual," Dee suggests, though he is lying, for they look absurd: a shabby magician; a sick woman in a ripped doublet (left by Marlowe) who is scarce able to walk one step; a beautiful Black lady in a dress she has swapped with a servant; a Black giant; and a sorrowful-looking laboratory assistant, each of them swagged about in every piece of cloth they have managed to find against the cold. Strangely, it is a look that suits Dennis, who is standing by the pornographic door, waiting to pull aside the barricade to let them through.

"Right then," Dee says. "Follow me."

Out they go, Dee carrying the thalers and the emperor's globe, which Dee believes he rightly took from the cabinet. He supports Jane, while the others follow behind, stared at in wonderment by the halberdiers who've done the barest minimum to keep them safe.

"I'd tip them," Cooke says, "if I thought they deserved it."

Dee guides them through the corridors back to the courtyard where he very first arrived in a carriage for Spinola's reception, pleased his memory is so good, as he turns left, right, right again, and then straight through two halls where courtiers languish waiting for audiences that will never happen and who stare aghast as Dee's party stagger through.

But as he crosses the third and final hall, the one that gives out onto the turning circle between the palace and the castle walls, Dee sees between the wide-flung double-doored doorway, across the broad swath of the cobbles, that coming through the towered gateway is a troop of cavalrymen leading a carriage, and from the carriage fly the complicated but instantly recognizable flags of the house of Guise.

They are too late.

He comes to a stop and the others stop behind him and stare as the courtyard fills with the clamor of the arrival of de Guise's party: ten carriages—one of them gilded and another made for transporting horses—and some fifty horsemen, easily. There are even buglers. A celebratory show of strength.

"Damn," Dee mutters.

"Think we can get past?" Cooke wonders.

"We are hardly inconspicuous, are we? And look!"

There is Łaski, swanning about in some official capacity, preparing to welcome de Guise on the emperor's behalf, having forgotten all about finding Dee and his party a carriage.

"Quick," Dee says. "Back to the *Kunstkammer*."

⊕

CHAPTER THIRTY-ONE

Newmarket, Suffolk, England, March 1584

It is a hundred miles from London to Woodrising in Norfolk, and ordinarily Beale would hope to cover these in three days' hard riding, but with Lady Paget—Nazaret Newton—with them, they scarce manage ten miles a day for all the stopping and starting and the bad roads and her bad carriage. Beale would not mind, save that since they are traveling with Nazaret, Devereux will not sleep with him.

"She knows my mother!"

The truth is, he sees, their time together is a mere diversion for her, whereas he has, in some distant part of his mind, been totting up his income and savings with a view to proposing marriage.

And nor will she ride with him on the journey.

"It is unladylike," she tells him.

"What about your sidesaddle?"

"Oh yes!"

She had totally forgotten about it.

"Anyway, I left it at home. So I will share the carriage with Nazaret. She knows my mother, did I tell you?"

Waltham Abbey, Stansted Mountfitchet, Saffron Walden, Linton, and now Newmarket. Beale rides alone, happily enough, he supposes, sometimes remembering if not these exact roads, then roads very much like them when he was trying to recruit Ness Overbury into his scheme to— Well, perhaps the less even thought about that, the better.

He supposes they are perhaps halfway. Another fifty miles to Woodrising, which is five nights, and then one at Lady Paget's crumbling hall, where he is fairly sure Devereux will still not come to his bed, but after that, he will have her to himself for the rest of the way to Orford, which he has been told must be about fifty miles, and then they will surely have to wait a few days at the very least while he makes arrangements with Master Pughe the mason, and for the gunners to unsling their guns. He supposes he will have to find them a ship, of course, but dear God, he knows every mariner in every port along this coast and can name ten off the top of his head who would jump at the chance to serve the Queen.

And the weather has not been so bad for March, has it? So, all in all, he cannot say he is unhappy at his near to immediate prospects.

⊕

CHAPTER THIRTY-TWO

The Lesser Town, Prague, Shrove Tuesday, March 1584

"What are you doing?" Kitty asks.

"Just stripping the bed," Dee tells her. "Like any good guest."

While Dennis pushes the barricade back across the pornographic door, the others stand and watch, like refugees from some disaster at sea, and Dee knots the sheets from Frommond's still warm bed into a double-stranded rope about twenty foot long.

"You're not thinking of climbing down?" Frommond asks. "From here?"

She manages a weak nod to the garden.

"We need to get to the bridge," he tells them.

"The bridge?" Cooke says. "Now? In the dark? You can't mean it? Listen!"

The drum booms on, more menacing than ever now that the light is going, and there is the promise of a long, violent night ahead, but Dee has not time to argue. He glances over to where

Dennis has his ear pressed to the pornographic door. Nothing yet.

Yet.

But it will come, they all know: the sound of marching boots, for when de Guise discovers what has happened, the reverse he has suffered, he will be incandescent with fury. He'll send his men with Van der Boxe's while the emperor is distracted poring over the *Book of Loagaeth*. He'll have them all killed and then throw himself on the emperor's mercy. Sometimes it is easier to seek forgiveness rather than permission.

Just then, Dennis looks up, his eyes very round, and he points through the door.

"Company," he says.

They snatch up what they can: the silver thalers, the bag with the Mercator globe, a narwhal tusk, and Dee leads them out into the garden where it is already dark now, the snow heavy and glassy underfoot.

"But there's no way down from here," Frommond repeats. "It is just a cliff."

Dee is unfazed.

"Christopher managed it," he reminds them. "Without a rope."

Though he did not see this for himself: if he had, he would have stopped him fetching those cursed gloves.

"Come on," he says, his eyes getting used to the snow-lit dark. "A cliff is fine, isn't it, Roger? We don't mind a cliff."

Cooke cannot suppress a groan.

"You do know I am supposed to assist you in your alchemical experiments, don't you?" he asks. "That's *all* I'm employed to do."

"And this *is* going to be an alchemical experiment," Dee tells him. "Come on. It won't be so bad. We have all these sheets. They are all we need."

"How far is it?" Cooke asks.

"Twenty feet?" he hazards.

It's thirty feet.

Thank God it is dark, Dee thinks. It is warmer than it has been. The freeze is over. The air smells of coal smoke, and that drum is beating loudly from the bridge below. Dee ties one end of the snaking rope of knotted sheets around the girth of the tree, the one behind which Frommond had hidden.

"You go first, Roger," Dee tells him. "Wrap the sheets about you like this, and you will be able to skip down the cliff as if it were a church path."

He shows Cooke how to do it, wrapping the rope over his shoulder, down his back, up between his legs.

"Go backward," he tells him. "Brace your feet against the cliff. Let friction slow your fall, rather than the hand's uncertain grip."

He tosses the end of the sheet rope over the edge into the alley below and Cooke closes his eyes as he backs over the precipice. He prays loudly, verses from the Bible concerning walking in the valley of death.

Dee peers over the edge.

Halfway down Cooke slips, screams, but holds on and his shoulder swings against the wall with a crunch, and he's all right.

"Keep going, Roger! You've but a few feet left."

Cooke drops with another scream and lands with an ankle-twisting sprawl.

"All right?"

He can imagine Cooke down there, mournfully at a loss to know which part of his body to rub, but Dee's sympathy is scant, for here comes Frommond. He shows her how to wrap the rope around her, but then Dennis arrives from the *Kunstkammer*.

"I will lower the mistress," he says.

So they make a loop, and tie a swing for her, very pale and beautiful, and she steps to the edge, and Dennis lets her down, her soles braced against the wall, and he makes it look easy.

They start at the crash that resounds from the pornographic door of the *Kunstkammer*. Dennis throws the loop over Kitty next and lowers her over in the same way he did Frommond.

"Your turn, Doctor," he says when she has gone.

"No. You go, Dennis."

Dennis frowns.

"I have no time or wish to argue with you," Dee tells him. "Your place is with Kitty. Besides, I will have need of your strength below."

Dennis bobs a reluctant nod as something else crashes to the floor in the *Kunstkammer*. There's a scrape of the door being forced against the weight piled against it.

"Go!" Dee shouts.

Dennis does, with Dee helping him loop the rope over his shoulder and between his legs.

"Hold tight," is all he can think of to say and Dennis gives him a grin and then disappears backward over the edge of the cliff. Dee hears the linen rope creaking, but a moment later there is a low call from below.

Then it is Dee's turn. He bends to fiddle with the knots around the tree, slackening their grip, and then he flips the rope around himself and steps back, feet wide apart, knowing all the while that the rope will give.

As it does, when he is halfway down.

The knot around the tree unravels, and Dee is left to slide and fall fifteen feet into Dennis's arms.

"Thank you," he says, and Dennis lowers him to the ground. Dee throws the rope into the shadows and they set off, limping down the alley, moving as fast as the slowest can manage, just as the first guards arrive on the parapet above them in a babble of angry shouts.

They follow the path Dee took with Frommond, turning off to the right and ducking this way and that through the narrow ways, under the baker's arch, and then down through the cramped lanes of the Lesser Town to the bridgehead, where fires and torches are already lit against the early evening and the drum beats like a heavy pulse. When they get there, the mob is two or three hundred strong, gathered on the far end of the bridge, chanting something foul and threatening in time to the thumping drum, and there is something already aflame in the Old Town, from which black smoke billows above the roofs. Dee looks for Marek and fancies he sees him, strutting about the bridge, bald head catching the light of the torches, a bully forever on duty.

But then Dee allows himself a smile.

For he notices two things: the ice on the river is broken.

And there, on the far side of the river, comes the beer delivery, and the crowd of men surge along the bridge toward it, and Dee cannot help but feel a thrum of excitement unconnected to the beating drum.

This might—*might*—just work.

"Come," he says, and he leads them reluctantly toward the bridgehead.

"Doctor? The way! This is the road out of Prague!"

This is from Roger Cooke, he's pointing westward.

"Have I ever let you down?" Dee tries to laugh, but this is no time for flippancy and Cooke shies away, like a horse pulling for home. Frommond is looking very weak, too, and Kitty not much better. Dennis is looking tense.

"We must get on the bridge," Dee tells them.

"But the crowd," Cooke tells him, pointing to the far end of the bridge where he can now see the mob have erected a gibbet and have hanged a doll. "They'll kill us!"

"They might, it is true," Dee has to admit. "But look: *they* will definitely kill us."

They turn to where he is pointing. In the gloom along the road that sweeps around and down from the castle trot at least twenty of de Guise's fifty horsemen, some of them carrying pitch torches. And then out of the alleyway they have just come from emerge a dozen or so of those Spaniards in black: Van der Boxe's men, likewise with flaming torches; and in the flickering lights, their swords are already drawn.

"So we are caught between two rocks and a hard place," Dee tells them. "Or a rock and two hard places if you prefer. All moving rapidly in our direction."

"For the love of God, Doctor!" Cooke groans. "What are we going to do?"

"Trust me!" he repeats. "Trust me and do as I say."

And he hesitates a moment, scanning the river beyond the bridge.

"But how are we to get home?" Frommond murmurs. Her voice is very weak, and she can barely stand. "How are we to get back to Mortlake? Back to Arthur? Have you a plan for that?"

Dee takes her in his arms.

"I have," he says. "But first things first. We must get out of here, my love, and to do that you must trust me, yes? And do what I say when I say it. Do you understand?"

They all stare at him and before any can voice any sort of doubt in his sanity, there comes a sustained roar from the direction of the bridge, and the drum skips a beat, and then resumes, twice as fast, twice as loud, as if there are two drums and four drummers, and the muddy ground beneath their feet seems to tremble.

On this side of the bridge the horsemen are perhaps a hundred paces away; Van der Boxe's men, fifty. Both parties approach cautiously now. They are confused, perhaps, or leery of the mob at the other end of the bridge. Dee imagines they will speed up at the last moment, when they are certain of their prey, and come at them with blades drawn in some sort of triumphant charge, but before then—

"Come on!" he says, and he turns and he leads his party of stragglers hobbling up the bridge, through the frayed edges of the mob, the men who are too drunk to do very much save prop themselves up and stare.

"Stay close," Dee tells Cooke. "And Dennis. Be ready. Understand?"

They must navigate through a few more drunks now, and the energy of the mob at the Old Town end of the bridge can be felt as a kind of hellish heat you would ordinarily run from, yet on they must go, forcing themselves forward, as if into a trap.

Dee risks a glance back over his shoulder down the bridge.

The horsemen are there, turning their mounts in circles by the bridgehead, waiting for something or someone perhaps. But the Spanish swordsmen are more intent and are coming quickly.

"John!" he hears Frommond bleat. "John! This is madness."

At that moment, someone in the mob sees them, and the crowd turns, almost as one organic being, and from their midst emerges the bald giant Marek. The mob start bashing sticks together and chanting some horrible, predatory chant, and they start to march toward them.

And now Kitty has seen something else.

"Oh my God!" she cries. "Look! It is him! He has come!"

And she points back to the castle end of the bridge where the horsemen have parted to let a single rider through. A slight man, his grim expressionless visage indistinct in the falling dark, he rides a pale horse and is instantly the focus of everyone's attention. Dee feels a strange lurch, as if some element of his own destiny were falling into place, for he is sure the man's eyes are locked on his own. It is Henri, Duc de Guise, come on to the bridge like the fourth rider of the apocalypse.

Kitty is gibbering now though Dee cannot decide whether it is with fear or rage.

"Roger," he manages to mutter out of the side of his mouth, "take these and stand with Dennis against the parapet wall."

He passes his servant the thalers and Mercator's globe, and he indicates the bridge's southern parapet.

"And be ready."

"For what?"

"To jump. And when you do, be ready for us."

Cooke looks at him as if he is mad, as if trying to piece the meaning of the words together.

There follows a long, strained moment, then Dennis speaks.

"Ahhhh," he says. "I see."

He springs up onto the parapet. When their pursuers see him up there, there is an instant reaction among de Guise's Spaniards, who start running. The drunken mob, too, seem to clench purposefully around Marek, who strides forward, shouting something that Dee does not care to hear or cannot hear over the beating of the drum and the thundering of the sticks. He feels the hooves of de Guise's horsemen's horses on the bridge now.

"Ladies?" Dee says, addressing Frommond and Kitty. "The moment is come, I believe, to make ourselves scarce."

He guides them away from Dennis and Cooke, to whom they had looked for some protection, with more force than they might ordinarily expect and across the bridge to its northern parapet.

The two bands are still a hundred paces apart, closing in on them, about to crush them, and when they are fifty from each, Dee turns to Dennis, who is helping Cooke up on to the parapet where he straightens and looks back at Dee, wide-eyed, waiting—waiting—and then: Dennis nods, takes Cooke by the arm, and turns and drags him off the parapet into the darkness of the river.

Frommond screams.

But Dee has bent and catches her knees and flips her sideways so that she's lying across his arms and then he hefts her up onto the parapet and she screams again as he bundles her over, and she tries to cling on for dear life, to stop herself falling, but there's nothing to cling on to, for Dee is already turning to do the same with an astonished Kitty, just gathering her and dumping her over the edge of the bridge into the night.

Too late, the Spanish swordsmen have realized what's happening; too late, the Duc de Guise on his pale horse; too late and too clumsy, the mob, for then Dee leaps up onto the parapet, suddenly agile, and he stands a moment before he leaps out into the darkness—and is gone.

⊕

CHAPTER THIRTY-THREE

Woodrising, Norfolk, March 1584

"It's no good," Beale admits. "I have to go."

He knows Devereaux has been playing with him, and he hardly blames her, but the time has come. He needs to fulfill his duty to Sir Francis, which he has already extended for a week—two weeks?—longer than he was supposed to, and now he must ride to Orford to tell Master Pughe to stop his masons topping off the gun tower and to explain to the gun master—whose name he does not know—that he must load his guns into a barge and set sail, for he is wanted on the south coast, on the river below Arundel.

"But we are having such a good time," Devereux tells him.

He is not even sure she is—embroidery with Nazaret, walks with Nazaret and her dogs, eating Nazaret's horrible food—but he knows he is not. There is almost nothing he wants to do here in Nazaret Newton's house in Norfolk save re-create the long days he spent in bed with Devereux while they were trawling for Master Mope along the south coast. Perhaps it was the thrill of the chase that so excited her? Perhaps it was the relief of getting away from having to visit her husband in the Fleet? Or perhaps she changed after killing one of the Paget sisters?

Either way, Beale feels he has lost her, unless he can come up with one last thing.

"What will we actually do in Orford?" she asks as he is packing up his saddlebags. He tells her again.

"I wonder what it is like to fire one of those guns," she says, "from the top of a tower?"

⊕

CHAPTER THIRTY-FOUR

Somewhere on the river Elbe, March 1584

J ane Frommond had forgotten much of the night they jumped—or were pushed—from the bridge in Prague, while she has lain almost unconscious with fever for two days and two nights, recovering from the strain put upon her already weakened body, but now that they have changed boats and are gathered in the stern of a hugely long barge with perhaps two hundred perfectly limbed tree trunks heading north along the river Elbe, she has begun to remember. She remembers the sensation of falling and then the sensation of being caught in Dennis's strong arms, and instantly being passed on to Roger Cooke, who helped find her space among the sheep that crowded the barge, and she was so disorientated that she did not mind what she sat on. Nor did Kitty, even, when Roger put her aside and went shoving through the ewes that crowded the barge to make sure Dee had landed safely in the barge as it passed under the bridge.

"How did you know about the sheep?" she had asked him that

third day, when unknown to her they had surged through the union of the Vltava and the Elbe and were well on their way north, to Dresden where they were to find this new, less stinking boat that would carry them onward north to Bremerhaven.

"It was Master Krcin, remember?" Dee told her. "You met him at Spinola's reception. He is the Duke of Rozmberg's business manager, and he was collecting the money owed by the Duke of Brunswick-Lüneburg for a flock of his master's Valachian sheep. We kept in touch, naturally. Did you know he is an expert on the building of freshwater ponds?"

She had nodded and looked away. There are parts of the scheme that both know are best left interred. A thin sun is shining, and after a while Frommond raises her very pale face to it, and she is still for a long moment.

"And what will we do in Bremerhaven?" she asks later, which gives him another chance to smile.

"You wait and see," he says, laughing.

⊕

CHAPTER THIRTY-FIVE

Framlingham, Suffolk, early April 1584

They have stopped at inns in Attleborough, Diss, Bedfield Long Green, and now Framlingham.

"We've been on the road a month," Devereux complains, "and I have spent more time studying the rafters of more inns than I ever knew were built."

"You should close your eyes," Beale tells her.

"What? And think of England?"

"Think of firing that gun from the tower in Orford."

She tuts.

"It is only a few more miles," he tells her, because after all this, he wants her to be happy. Last night they fell asleep in each other's arms and did not move until the morning. He is beginning to prefer the smell of the back of her neck to the smell of anywhere else.

⊕

CHAPTER THIRTY-SIX

Bar, Lorraine, early April 1584

A lawn is a rich man's thing, to show the world that he has so much land, he doesn't need every inch of it to grow vegetables, or run cattle, so Marlowe—finally here after countless days and countless leagues—is impressed by the great green skirt of grass that surrounds the château, but not so much that he will not ride his horse straight across it and pick up the girl—Amelie— whom he is watching playing on it, as if lawn were the most natural thing to find under your feet in all the world.

Should he do that? he wonders from the shadows of this little copse across the river.

Just snatch her up and explain later?

He thinks not.

Better to wait.

He watches as the gates are opened down by the lodge, and a mud-splattered messenger is permitted into the estate.

"What's your game?" he wonders aloud.

The man rides a knackered horse, fast, as if he is careless about wearing it out, and Marlowe thinks to himself, Oh my God, can they have caught me? He had at least two days on them, but they are messengers. Messengers, plural. Each one can ride twenty miles on a fresh horse and pass the message on to another man willing to ride twenty miles on a fresh horse.

So . . . snatch her up and explain later it is.

Marlowe spurs his horse—roan this time, which he calls brown—into the river and across the water, and then up the bank and thundering across that smooth grass, and as the girl looks up, he reins the horse in, throws his leg over the saddle, and drops to the grass, where he performs a quick rolly-polly, then another, then another, to come to a stop crouching before her so that they are eye to eye, and he says:

"Amelie, darling, you do not know me. My name is Christopher. Not such a bad name if you think about it. He was supposed to have carried Jesus across a river when he was a baby. Did you know that?"

The girl looks at him with saucery, swimming eyes and nods.

"Anyway," he goes on, "we can talk about that later, if you like. But in the meantime, your sister sent me. Kitty. She doesn't like that old bag whose got hold of you. She wants you home. So she's sent me to get you, to bring you to her."

Again she blinks, slow and sweet.

"So are you with me?" he asks. "Or against me?"

He hears men running. Someone in the house calling her name.

"We shall take that as a yes, then," he says, "shall we?"

And he is gentle as he can be, but this needs to be done fast, and he picks her and her doll up, and he puts her up in his saddle, pulling the reins and retracing his prints back to the river.

A man appears before him, holding up his hands.

"Stop!" he cries.

"Oh, behave," Marlowe says, and he directs his horse to send the man diving out of the way.

Within a few moments more, they are across the river, and back on to the far bank.

"Hang on a tick," Marlowe says, looking at her closely. "Your name *is* Amelie, isn't it?"

The girl laughs, and Marlowe kicks on.

CHAPTER THIRTY-SEVEN

North Sea, April 1584

Very heavy weather: high seas, hard southerly winds, and a vomit-slicked deck.

"Verdammt!" *Meneer* van Treslong keeps shouting. "Verdammt!"

The captain is wearing oilskins as he stands over the whipstaff, gripping it as if he is stirring a pot of mash. Over his shoulder, four or five hundred yards behind, is the same damned Spanish galley that has seemingly forever dogged his wake, which has shot out his rudder on two separate occasions before. It came from Antwerp this time, he tells his passengers and had the weather gauge from the start.

"Verdammt!"

Sometimes they lose her. Perhaps only behind really big swells, but even though the galley is a cow compared to the swift fluyt, the *Swan*, the galleon's captain is a masterful navigator and has a knack of putting himself exactly where Treslong wishes him least: in this instance waiting in the sea-lanes out of Bremerhaven.

"Verdammt! How did he know I was in Bremerhaven? You tell him, Doctor? You tell him that we arrange to meet third Sunday of April? Spring tides and all that?"

"Hardly," Dee replies. Why would he put himself in danger like this? Treslong will not let it lie, though.

"What about that lump of Polish person?"

"Why would he?"

"Money? A fat reward from Spanish captain?"

Dee shakes his head and stops listening, and Treslong continues his swearing, until after a while he stops that, too, for there is nothing much more to say other than prayers. Opposite Dee, Kitty de Fleurier is rolling with the swells, her eyes closed, her lips moving, while Dennis seems unaffected, and stands with his legs athwart, peering back, with seawater and rain pouring from the tip of his pointed beard.

"A natural sailor!" Dee shouts.

"What?" Frommond asks, not even bothering to look up, for she hardly cares about the answer and is just then overcome by another spasm of painful dry heaves.

"Never mind," he shouts. "We shall soon be home."

He sees her shake her head, but she is wrong to doubt him, for with these winds, cold though they are, the crossing of the North Sea is fast and furious, and it is only just after noon that one of Treslong's men signals from the bow where he has been keeping watch, and Treslong turns to Dee and shouts and points.

Dee follows his finger.

"Engerlond!" Treslong shouts. "You hear me? Engerlond!"

Dee stands, gripping a stay, and peers westward. A low flat line of land. England. Dear God. It does not matter that it is not much to look at. It is England. He wonders where? Essex? Suffolk?

Before he can think much more there is a sudden crack, and

then a throbbing rush overhead and a hole appears in the *Swan*'s jib sail.

"Verdammt!" Van Treslong calls again. "Verdammt!"

And he hauls the whipstaff, and the fluyt lurches, and on they go, hard as they can.

Another crack of gunfire and this time the cannonball skips across the gray green heaving waves and hits the *Swan* in the stern, scarcely missing the rudder. Van Treslong screams with rage and frustration, but then orders are bellowed. The crew scamper to trim the sails and Van Treslong sets to once again, eking every ounce of power from the *Swan*'s tattered sails, but still the galleon seems to be gaining.

They've no cargo left to jettison except their five passengers, but the fluyt has a shallower draft, and is designed for shallow seas, so Van Treslong hopes if they can just reach the lee shore of England, then the Spanish must shy away.

Crack. Another ball. This one to the starboard.

He shouts to a crew member something that Dee does not understand, and the crew member makes his way to the bow, and then up the bowsprit where he shields his eyes from a nonexistent sun. After a moment he signals back to Van Treslong. To port. To port. And van Treslong makes the adjustments.

The coast rises before them now. Low trees, even a church spire. A fishing village, a small town beyond a shingle spit, and then . . . what is that? A gun tower?

Where are they? Dee wonders.

Another crack of the Spaniard's cannon and this time the ball slices across the deck. How it misses everyone God only knows. The man in the bowsprit is pointing harder to port, harder to port. He has seen something he likes.

Van Treslong still won't take the sail in. They are hammering hard toward the breaking waves, and the rocks below. He turns to look at the galleon. She is frighteningly close. Dee can see her captain, see her gunners running out the cannons on the bow. Has he taken note of the shore? The fluyt is infinitely more maneuverable than the galleon, and Van Treslong is courting disaster even as it is, so what the Spaniard is thinking, Dee cannot guess.

The man in the bowsprit is shouting something, but his hand is stilled, in midair, and he's looking down at the water as if privy to some secret, and all the other members of the crew—three of them—are poised by their line. As the captain gives the word—now!—they let go their ropes and the sails billow and the fluyt instantly drops her speed as Van Treslong hauls on the whipstaff and the boat turns on what feels like a sixpence to drift with the ingoing tide up a turbid, brown-watered river. It is as fine a piece of seamanship as Dee has ever seen, and he would clap the man on the back, maybe even offer a bow, perhaps, except there is another crack of gunfire and the gunwale is shattered by the passage of a cannonball and the air around Dee is suddenly filled with splinters and one catches his wrist, but that is it. What is more remarkable is that the galleon has performed precisely the same trick as the fluyt, and despite Van Treslong's neat piece of seamanship, they have not lost the Spaniard. The galley is still on their stern, and they are at its mercy now, drifting very slowly together up a river on an incoming tide and the galleon's guns are being reloaded, and the underarmed fluyt, all her crew and her passengers, are, to all intents and purposes, dead in the water: the galleon's guns will now be able to slowly pound her to matchsticks.

"Oh, verdammt," Van Treslong whispers.

⊕

CHAPTER THIRTY-EIGHT

Orford, Suffolk, April 1584

"Thank you, Master Pughe, yes. A terrible business, but it cannot be helped. You have done a magnificent job, I can see that. Portland cement? Yes. I do see that is going to be difficult to knock down. Would it be easier to start again, do you suppose? Well, you tell me. It is the cost of the thing. And the speed. That is the key."

Master Pughe is an extravagantly handsome young man with very pale eyes, quite as short and blocky as one of his well-dressed building stones. He's unhappy that no one appreciates what a terrific job he and his masons have done with this tower. It is a thing of beauty, which Pughe tells him justifies its existence, and all other matters are irrelevant.

"I dare say you are right, Master Pughe," Beale agrees. "But we are at the whim of our superiors."

He is consciously marching Pughe up the turning steps to the tower's gun platform, where he is certain Devereux will have gone straightaway to try her luck with the gun master, and sure enough, there she is, in a coat of her own design made of midnight-blue, very fine needle cord that fits very narrowly to the waist but allows her to ride like a man, should she wish. She has already started her charm offensive on the gun master, who is showing her which of the various diameter cannonballs fit the various caliber guns. She has her eye on the largest, of course, about the size of a giant's head, Beale supposes, which lies on a carriage next to a huge gun oriented almost southward over the length of the river Alde.

Such is her enthusiasm and her beauty that the gun master is prepared to use up some of his black powder and even that precious ball, though he hints he'd like Beale to reimburse him. Pughe says something about that being one way to take everything back down again after having gone to the not inconsiderable trouble of bringing it all up in the first place. Beale wishes he would be quiet and not spoil the moment for Devereux, who only wants to fire a cannonball from the top of a tower, for the love of God, which is not so very odd a thing to wish to do, is it?

And then they can get on with the serious business of dismantling everything they've built and packing it into boats and shipping it along the south coast to reerect it above Arundel, just as if there never was anything here at all.

"So I tamp the ball in with this thing?"

"Aye," the gun master says. "That'd be. Like this. Right hard like, but not too hard."

Devereux laughs her dirtiest laugh and the gun master is outmatched, and Beale steps up onto the parapet and looks east out to sea. It is rough out there, he thinks, with water the color of split flint and restless under a gusting wind. Then he looks south, stops, starts, and looks south again.

"Then wadding," he hears the gun master telling Devereux, "and then you've got to ram that home likewise."

But Beale is no longer listening. Down the length of the river, two ships: one familiar, a fluyt, Dutch, probably, and much knocked about; the other, a galleon and surely Spanish.

"Not too hard, and not too soft?" he hears Devereux ask, her feigned innocence a delight.

"Oohho, Mistress!" the gun master drools. "You've got the touch."

As Beale watches the two ships, he sees a puff of gunsmoke erupt from the galley and then comes the report, and he sees the fluyt stagger under the ball's impact. She is just coming under the gun tower's range now, and he remembers where he's seen her before: off Greenwich, years ago. Captained by Van Treslong. A villain, yes, but England's villain, whereas . . . a *Spanish* galleon?

He leaps off the wall.

"Fucking look!" he shouts at the gun master, pointing, and he is around behind the gun in a trice, moving it with one of the levers.

The gun master is stunned.

"Well, I'll be," he says.

"Told you we shouldn't move it," Pughe says.

"Sight it! Sight it! One good shot and she's paralyzed and ours!"

Devereux claps her hands.

"Can I do it! Can I do it!"

"Jesus, go on then but quick."

"Ready?"

The gun master makes his adjustments with the screw, lowering the barrel.

"There," he says, and he holds up his hand and waits, and waits, and then shouts: "Now!"

And Devereux touches the splint to the fuse, and the fuse burns down, and Beale leaps across to drag her aside just as the gun booms and leaps back in its carriage and the cannonball—a foot in diameter—hammers through the air between the gun tower and the exact place where the Spanish captain stands ordering his men to fire one last shot at the Dutchman before beating a retreat for they have risked too much already. The cannonball cores him with a great eruption of blood and viscera, then smashes a hole through the deck of the galleon *Santa Maria* where it continues unseen through the cook's head below, and then between two of the ship's ribs, and then out through the hull and into the mud at the bottom of the river Alde.

There is silence on the deck of the gun tower. The men come to the parapet wall and stare down at the two ships below. The fluyt continues upriver, its passengers somewhat stunned and scattered around the deck, but her captain, a dancing, baggy-drawered madman, capers wildly, shaking his fists and shouting elated, incomprehensible gibberish. The galley loses her way in a moment, and turns abeam the current, and slides shuddering into the shingle with a long, tearing rasp of breaking timbers.

"Ha ha!" Devereux cries. "I hit it!"

⊕

CHAPTER THIRTY-NINE

River Thames, below Mortlake, May 1584

"Sorry to hear about your nephew," Dee tells Jiggins, who is hauling on his oars, taking him downstream against the tide to Whitehall Palace.

Jiggins scowls at him.

"Hear?" he repeats. "You is sorry to *hear* about my nephew?"

"Sorry *about* your nephew."

Jiggins grunts.

"Yes, well," he says. "My brother ain't too pleased. That boat was his livelihood."

"She was a fine boat," Dee mutters, all sympathy for Jiggins and his brother dissipated like river mist on an early summer's morn, and he looks away, and remembers having to put the boy's body over the stern of *Meneer* Van Treslong's fluyt, the boy's throat blown out by an unlucky shot from one of Sir Christopher Hatton's marksmen.

How long ago was that now? he wonders. Seems like a lifetime.

They settle into pained silence; just the gulls above, and the slap of the river on the boat's hull below, and Jiggins huffing and puffing as he pilots them past the grand mansions and fruit gardens that line the river's north bank.

Dee has been back in London a month now, and it is the end of a bright, brisk May day and is evening now. While he has been away London has come through winter, and now everywhere burgeons with fresh green growth, and Dee feels his spirits bubbling too.

So much to look forward to.

A reward from Bess, from Her Majesty—not as handsome as you'd hope, of course, but he is used to that—and gratitude from Walsingham and maybe even Lord Burghley, too, and so a new position at Court can be expected. A title even? And there is plenty to be getting on with, too: his application for the grant of exploration will doubtless be approved, and then there is the adoption of the new calendar, accurate to within a few seconds, which will bring him great renown, for he thinks he has devised a way to achieve it without offending the bishops, or the Dutch.

His house in Mortlake needs some money spent on it, he has to admit, but Dee has some now, left over from Rudolf's thalers, and with it he thinks he will root out the garden at the back of the second laboratory and grow—what? He might persuade Francis Drake to bring him more of those beans from Calabar, and he could start some sort of botanical garden; and of course there is always his library. So many titles he might ask Kelley to send from Prague. He makes a mental note to send for them soon, for something tells him that Kelley is not like to enjoy too long a lease of Emperor Rudolf's favor unless he manages to make sense of the *Book of Loagaeth*.

Jiggins brings him to the palace watergate and grudgingly inspects the tip.

"Not as good as a linnet in a cage," Dee agrees.

Jiggins is perplexed.

Funny how Dee almost misses Łaski.

At the gate, the palace guards study him.

"I am expected," he tells them, because he is sure he is—or should be. Her Majesty sent for him to attend her in her Receiving Room, this evening, this day, and though she had not added "to receive your just reward, and the thanks of a grateful nation for services rendered under the most extraordinarily challenging circumstances," Dee does not feel she need do so, for the implication is obvious.

But his name is not on any list, or none that the sergeant at arms has to hand, and this is the same sergeant at arms from whom Dee managed to bunk when he was last here, fresh from his day with Łaski, when London stood under a shower of sleet, and he lost his second-best cloak; the same man who arrested him in Mortlake with an unnecessary arm across the throat; and the same man who now sighs wearily.

"You know the drill, Doctor," he says, "and this time we'll shoot."

But then— Thank God! A voice!

"Doctor! Doctor Dee!"

It is Christopher Marlowe, in peach silks, come fresh from . . . from God knows where . . . on a flower-banked barge rowed by eighteen oarsmen with velvet-covered oars and velvet-covered ropes. They bank against the palace watergate long enough to let him leap ashore, and then be away, and he waves dismissively to the figure in the barge's cabin. He first gives Dee an extravagant bow and then he takes him in his arms and hugs him and then lands three kisses on his cheeks, and Dee is not sure he has ever been so pleased to lay eyes on any man ever.

"I heard you had brought her safely home," he tells him, "and that the little girl's mother showered you with kisses and coins!"

Marlowe laughs.

"She was pleased enough, it is true, and I was not surprised: Amelie's as good as gold she is, sir: a veritable treasure. I was sorry to have to leave her, but I heard Kitty got home safe enough soon after your scrape in the North Sea?"

Dee is not certain if Kitty has yet made it all the way home, but a week after their return to England, he waved her farewell from the quay at Felixstowe as she departed that way on Van Treslong's hastily patched fluyt.

They discuss their escape from Prague, but when they come to the subject of Jane Frommond's health—"much improved"—Dee finds himself gripped with shame at the risks he took with others' lives, and he is happy when Marlowe changes the subject.

"You too have been summoned?" he asks, indicating the palace.

Dee agrees he has.

"Didn't think Sir Francis went in for any public thanks," Marlowe says. "Thought it was just a debrief in that spooky old gaff of his on Seething Lane."

The sergeant stands by, impatient now, having found Marlowe's name on his list.

"Right this way, if you've a mind, please, Master Marlowe," he says, and then barks: "Not you, Doctor!"

Marlowe is puzzled.

"It is bloody old Walsingham," Dee explains. "Always trying to keep me away from Bess."

"Bess?"

"Her Majesty."

"Not surprised if you call her that. Probably to save your own skin."

Dee had never thought of it like that.

"Anyway," Marlowe says, turning to the sergeant. "Oy, you! This is Doctor Dee. If you don't hop the twig, mate, and let him pass, he'll conjure up some bloody great hellhound or what-have-you that'll scoff your bollocks for breakfast, every day for the rest of your natural, so step aside."

There is a moment's hesitation as the sergeant looks at Marlowe, then at Dee, then at his men, and then back again, and in that time Dee and Marlowe know what to do: they run.

"You fuckers!"

They are wholly unencumbered compared to the guards and they race laughing across the grass and gravel and ornate hedging to arrive at the open doors of the Receiving Room that give out onto the garden and from which spill the sounds of spirited music. Here they are faced with the blank fury of yet more halberdiers—five of them—but over the halberdiers' much padded shoulders, and above the crowd of assembled courtiers, Dee and Marlowe can see Her Majesty, and hopefully Her Majesty can see them, and so they bob, and wave, and try to attract someone's—anyone's—attention, but it is no good; all eyes are fixed elsewhere.

Her Majesty is in green this evening, as befits the season, perhaps, and she sits looking healthier than when Dee last saw her. Perched upon her throne, her face bright with excitement and delight, she is smiling down at a man dancing an elaborate jig for her pleasure. She claps to the tune being picked out by the musicians, but when Dee sees who it is who is dancing, and at whom she is smiling, he takes a step back.

Hatton.

And Dee remembers the weight of Jiggins's nephew, and the finality of his last splash, and he hates Hatton, and he hates anyone who could tolerate him and watch him dance. He is about to turn, to back away, when Her Majesty glimpses them. Or at least, she glimpses Marlowe in his peach silk doublet, and she looks away from her dancing chancellor and half stands. Her courtiers notice her change of attention, and they turn, too, and Hatton is so distracted by this sudden withdrawal of appreciation that his steps tangle, and he kicks his shapely calf, and he stumbles and stops and the musicians break in confusion, and there follows a mortified silence, which is only broken, at last, by slow hand-clapping.

"Bravo!" comes a voice. "Oh, bravo!"

And Walsingham steps from the shadows, palms resounding, forehead gleaming as if covered in a cold sweat, dressed all in black wool. Dee is instantly certain the man is unwell, and only just managing to hold it all together.

"God give you good day, Doctor Dee, Master Marlowe," he says, playing it up for the audience, and Her Majesty looks over at Dee and at Marlowe, and her face lights up with even greater pleasure than ever she took in Hatton's dancing.

"John!" she says. "My eyes!"

And she does not stop smiling even when Hatton stamps his foot.

"May I remind you—" he starts.

But then he trails off, and he now stands, struck dumb, staring agog at Marlowe, apparently utterly smitten by what he sees, and seeing this, Walsingham smiles a weary smile of resignation and regret and wipes a hand across that sweating forehead. Why did I not think of this before? he seems to be asking himself.

And Lord Burghley is likewise there, of course, well padded against—what? The cold? An assassin's blade? And there must be twenty or thirty others beside, the sort of useless men and women who always populate royal receiving rooms, and Dee stands on the threshold of the room, and they are all turned to him. Burghley makes a funny little "come-hither" gesture with his pudgy bejew-eled hand, but Dee stops and looks around, and for a moment it is as if time has ceased, and that he alone moves sentient through this crowd of rich men and beautiful women. For the first time, per-haps, he sees them for what they are, and he knows with no shadow of doubt that he will be granted nothing—not one thing—that he desires, or needs, and he is gripped with the terrible certainty that he does not want to pass a single further moment with such people.

Whyever did he go to such lengths to preserve all this? he won-ders. All them?

And so Dee stops short of stepping over the threshold, and he executes an abrupt and determined bow, and he backs away from Bess, from Her Majesty, across the garden, into the grasp of the ser-geant at arms, and he turns to him, and says: "You are right. Take me home. Take me back to Mortlake, to Jane and to little Arthur. It is with them I most wish to be."

The sergeant at arms is bemused.

"Take you back as far as the watergate," he says. "You can make your own way from there to . . . to . . . whoever it is."

And so Dee is marched away from the Receiving Room, in happy disgrace, and he is led through the watergate and stands in the evening light, staring downriver for the approaching wherry, with the sergeant at arms stood behind him, and he can hear the man trying to work up the guts to ask if he can really summon a hellhound, when Walsingham catches up with him.

"Don't go, Dee," he says.

"I must," Dee tells him. "I have a wife and child at home, and there is a chicken in the pot, and bottles of wine from Bordeaux, and I know you have nothing for me, so why would I wish to stand and watch that murdering bastard Hatton making false eyes at Her Majesty?"

A boat glides up, not Jiggins. Dee steps onboard.

"It's disgusting," Walsingham agrees. "I know. But still. Stay. I will clear the room. I will get rid of all those people. We need to talk to you further."

"No."

"I will come to yours."

"No."

"I will."

"You won't."

Walsingham laughs.

"I will, Dee, because I must. Of all the perils we have yet faced and seen off together, this next is greater by far, and I, and your Queen, and your country need you ever more."

Dee pushes off from the watergate dock.

"Dee!" Walsingham cries. "Dee!"

"I am not listening, Walsingham."

"It's for your own safety!" Walsingham cries. "For yours and Mistress Dee's!"

And Walsingham starts coughing, and for a moment Dee thinks he ought to turn back, but then he knows Walsingham, knows his games, his wiles.

"Keep rowing," he tells the boatman. "Take me home."

After a moment, he looks back over his shoulder, to find Francis Walsingham is gone, just as if he were never there, and as night falls along the river, and the water becomes oily, John Dee is filled with a terrible fear that it is just him, and him alone, who is left standing against the darkness.

⊕

AUTHOR'S NOTE

It is a matter of record that in September 1583, Doctor John Dee and his wife, Jane, along with at least two of their children and various servants, left England for continental Europe in the company of the Polish prince Olbrecht Łaski, his servants, a man hitherto not much known to history by the name of Edward Kelley, and Kelley's wife, Joanna, whom he was known to hate. The journey began under a shadow, in the dead of night, and nearly ended in disaster before it had even started, but six months later, Dee and his party arrived, woebegone and footsore, at the Holy Roman Emperor Rudolf's court in Prague.

The exact whys and wherefores of this journey are mostly lost to us now, but Dee kept a diary—published after his death with the intention of discrediting him—in which he described its hardships and uncertainties, and also the many interactions with the various angelic spirits that he and Kelley undertook along the way. I cannot recommend *A True and Faithful Relation of What Passed for Many Years Between Dr. John Dee and Some Spirits* because it is like someone describing—at great length—their dreams or an acid trip: being confusing, depressing, and ultimately enraging, and so I have chosen to disbelieve it, and to treat it as a tissue of lies, intended to distract the world from what Dee was really up to.

I am aware this is not how scholarship is supposed to work.

But I have based my story on certain broadly accepted facts, and set it in a world as was, and peopled it with characters who were likewise known to exist. No one could really have made up Edward Kelley, for example, who appeared almost out of nowhere—though he was sought by various Leicestershire constables for forgery, which explained his clipped ears—and reinvented himself as a good enough reader of show stones to convince Dee that he had a connection with the angels, though of course that might have been mutually convenient. On reaching Prague, Kelley settled down to become a fabulously wealthy, much-prized alchemist, garnering every title, privilege, and property, until the basic impossibility of his task caught up with him, and he spent the rest of his life in gaol, until either committing suicide or dying of injuries incurred while trying to escape.

Olbrecht Łaski likewise existed—a giant with a beard he could tuck into his belt—and came to England in that strange, fevered time for reasons that we can only guess at now. He was feted by Her Majesty, but regarded with deep suspicion by almost everyone else, probably correctly, for he had roamed around the courts of Christendom claiming royal ancestry, and had a reputation as a kidnapper of other men's wives.

Kitty de Fleurier did not exist, but had she, she might well have been recruited to Catherine de Medici's *Escadron Volant*, which was just as described by Łaski; a group of beautiful (presumably) women agents that the French dowager queen sent all over France to influence events in her favor. Charlotte de Sauve was her best; sent to seduce Catherine's own son-in-law, and then her own son, so that the two would fall out over Charlotte and stop conspiring against her other son. Perhaps Charlotte and Dee crossed swords? Who knows.

The primary mechanism by which Dee manages to keep Emperor Rudolf too preoccupied to join his uncle's crusade against England is the *Book of Loagaeth*, dictated by the angels through Kelley. You can see images of this book online, and it is an utterly baffling, charmless series of grids filled with angelic symbols, but in my mind, this is not the book that Dee sold Rudolf. In my mind, the book that Dee sold Rudolf is the book that has become known as the Voynich manuscript, which you can also see online. It is believed to have been in Dee's possession, and known to have been in Rudolf's, and though it is equally as baffling as the *Book of Loagaeth*, and written in a code no one has yet managed to crack—possibly because it is in fact deliberately meaningless—it is filled with very beautiful and colorful illustrations and endlessly diverting texts. It would certainly have fascinated the famously occult-prone Rudolf and steered him and his boundless energies up the philosophical cul-de-sac that Dee intended.

Incidentally, this ploy of Dee's provided the inspiration* for Ronald Reagan's Strategic Defence Initiative, the so-called Star Wars program, which led the Soviets to spend billions of rubles, bankrupting themselves in the process, as they sought to keep up with the chimera of a magic bullet that would give them definitive power over the west. Had Rudolf learned the secret of Adamic communication and gained dominion over all things even up to the seraphim and cherubim, there is no telling what he might have achieved, in part because he really was profoundly odd.

On which note, it is easy to dismiss Dee's wackier activities, and especially his belief in astrology and the influence of the planets

---

* This is not true.

on the affairs of men, but that was the prevailing orthodoxy at the time, and Dee was obviously very good at it. Sir Phillip Sidney (he who brought Count Łaski by barge to see Dee at Mortlake) was a gifted poet and a soldier for whom Dee had cast a chart when Sidney was twenty-six that suggested that, should he survive his thirty-first year, he would go on to achieve great fame and fortune. Five years later, Sir Phillip Sidney was killed at the Battle of Zutphen in 1586, aged thirty-one. He's relatively well-known now as the author of *Astrophel and Stella*, but what might he have gone on to write if only he had heeded Dee's warning?

Sidney is not the only writer cut down before his time, of course: Christopher Marlowe, here given slightly extravagant treatment, was murdered in Deptford in 1593, but not before he had written the play *Doctor Faustus*, inspiration for which can only have come from his trip to Prague, undertaken in great secrecy while still a student at the University of Cambridge, and a stint in the house of Thaddeus Hajek, the well-known occultist. Well, it's a theory.

Meanwhile, in England, Sir Francis Walsingham was already beginning to suffer from what he called "sundry carnosities"—the symptoms of probable testicular cancer—that would later kill him, but not before he had to face the last great threat to England, and the Protestant Reformation, which was, by 1584, already gathering weight over the horizon in Spain, and against which he would need all of Doctor John Dee's God-given gifts.

Oliver Clements
Mortlake, London
September 2022

ACKNOWLEDGMENTS

Special gratitude to the brilliant Lisa Gallagher who is both the glue and the eyes. To Toby Clements, my new brother: thank you. To the incredible team at Atria, especially our wonderful editor, Kaitlin Olson, who always makes us look our best; Elizabeth Hitti; Maudee Genao; Gena Lanzi; Jason Chappell; Claire Sullivan, for such striking jackets; and our publisher, Libby McGuire, for her ongoing belief and support. Glorious thanks to so many people who helped in this journey: Rachel Shane, Jake Michie, Judith Curr, Andrea Valeria, James Handel, Everardo Gout, Gwendollyn Gout, and Rachel Hazoui.

ABOUT THE AUTHOR

Oliver Clements is a novelist and screenwriter based in Mortlake, London.